FOG AND MIST

Fog and Mist

A FAIRY TALE INSPIRED SERIES

THE CANENS CHRONICLES
BOOK ONE

KELSIE ENGEN

LITERA SCRIPTA MANET

Contents

PART 2
THE SLAVE

EPILOGUE

BONUS MATERIAL

Prologue

WINTERBERRY

I do not trust beautiful things. They always hold something ominous beneath the surface; something that ought to be as kind as it is beautiful is never so.

When I was young, I decided beauty, kindness, and queenliness could not mix. In order to be a queen, you must be a warrior. And in order to be a warrior, you must not be kind. A beautiful queen, therefore, would have her kindness destroyed.

I watched it happen. I know it to be true.

So many of the Queen's efforts go into suppressing me that I wonder at what she has left to give the people of Canens. What am I to her, after all? What is this country to her? It is the throne that calls to her, demanding every ounce of her, leaving nothing for anyone else. Answering its call, she has filled its seat with dark magic, polluted the land, and cursed us.

The throne has become nearly a living thing, as dangerous as the most dangerous enemy.

I do not want it. I have never wanted it. And yet I would protect it to the death.

I always knew the throne would be her downfall. I just had no idea it would also be mine.

Part 1

THE PRISONER

I

Arrested

WINTERBERRY

They come for me as I stand in my cold, impersonal, stone room, while my fireplace snaps in hunger and ravages my last, precious log.

When the Queen's guards enter, I whirl away from my window, furious at their invasion.

"What's going on?" I fear I already know the answer.

"Winterberry Scilla, you are under arrest for treason to the Crown," says one of the men as he grips my arm like a wolf's teeth grips its prey.

"Treason?" I scoff. "Impossible. I've not left this room in six months." I motion to the threadbare, velvet curtains which block out what little sun musters the strength to shine through the ice-crusted windows. It's all but been my prison since my father died. Am I now to exchange it for a true prison?

Another guard reaches for me, and I jerk away. The first digs his nails into my flesh like teeth.

"Let me go!" I demand. "I am your princess."

The first guard chokes out a laugh, as if he has had little to laugh about for too long.

I have never been so helpless as I am struggling against the unyielding grip on my arm. I try to rip myself free, but a second armed man lunges toward me, his sword sheathed on his hip. Two more men step forward, one drawing a knife from his belt, the other putting a hand to his sword's hilt.

They have come prepared for battle; I'll give them a battle.

From my loose sleeve, I pull out a short, *adamas*-tipped knife, lashing out at the men. Unsuspecting, the one gripping my wrist moves his fingers too slowly, and I slice the blade across the top of them.

He curses as he releases me, but the respite is short. Growling, he lunges in, wrenching my wrist upward and bending it back until I gasp and my fingers loosen. In a pitiful echo of my own cry, the knife clatters to the stone floor.

The injured guard leans close, his breath a hot cloud against my cheek. "That was foolish, girl. Very, very foolish." He spits the words, spraying me with venom I have never heard before from a guard.

But it's his disrespect which casts a long shadow on me. The other men tighten their grips.

"Hurry up," the captain of the guards, a cold, brutish man, snaps from the hallway.

His four best soldiers each grip one of my limbs, carrying me from the room as though I am a disobedient child.

"Where do we take her, Captain Plaga?" the soldier with his hand on his sword asks. Beside him, the one who drew his knife plays with it, letting it catch the light of my dying fire as he tilts it from side to side.

"Take her to the dungeon," he purrs, eyes narrowed on me. "Then inform me so I can inform the Queen when the job is completed."

My face drains of blood.

Catching sight of my panic, the captain grins, revealing a missing incisor and a chipped front tooth. His face is battle scarred, the ugliest I have ever seen. His eyes sweep over me, my frailness, my malnourished child's body, too thin by far for a woman my height.

The back of the captain's hand brushes against my cheek. I wish to recoil, but to do so would be to lean into the soldier holding me from behind, and I refuse to give either man that pleasure. As Captain Plaga leans in, he inhales deeply, taking in the scent of my grimy skin.

Repulsed, I turn away and his lips fall on my cheek.

Face to face with one of the other guards, I meet cold gray eyes. The hint of a snort reaches my ears, the soft rise and fall from the chest of the man who holds me betraying it as his.

Is he amused? Inwardly, I gape at the audacity of this soldier. But I have no time to react as the captain wrenches my chin back toward him with cold, bruising fingers.

I struggle, pulling at the vice grips that hold me. Kicking and shrieking, I make a last stand, desperate to avoid whatever they plan for me. I manage to jerk my legs free and twist in the grip of the two other soldiers.

"Stop it, girl!" one of the guards snaps. He sweeps at my legs with a trunk-like arm and whisks them out from under me so fast that only the two guards holding my arms keep me from falling to the ground.

A startled gasp works its way out of me, cutting off my current scream.

"Put her on the ground," a voice growls.

Fear trembles through me. I kick, catching something that grunts in irritation. A long, piercing scream leaves me, only to be cut off by a gloved hand slapping itself over my mouth and nose.

"You finished?" One of the guards is sprawled on the floor beside me, half on, half off me. His eyes, blue and pale, all but beg me to stop fighting. "Quiet down, stop fighting, and it will be easier."

For whom? I want to cry out at him, but unable to breathe, I give him my best glare.

The captain barks directions at his men, and when they lift me from the ground, I can do nothing but let them hold me above the ground.

The captain's hand goes around the back of my neck.

"Did you laugh at me?" Anger flushes his face except for the jagged scar rushing down from his ear to his chin. "Do you dare to scoff at me?"

I try to shake my head, but he holds me tight. "No," I manage through the pressure of his fingers against my cheeks. "No, I—"

His mouth slams into mine, crushing the tender insides of my lips against my teeth. It is hot and tastes of the beer he had for dinner, along with the sharpness of onion mingling with my own blood.

The soldiers are laughing. Someone's hand gropes my thigh, shocking me into action. With the upper hand of unexpected movement, I jerk my head back from the captain's lips and spit in his face before anyone can react.

The soldiers go silent. I hear the drip-drip of a melting icicle on the window frame, and absently I realize that my fire must have gone out.

The captain's hand lifts; he wipes his face with the back of it, but it only smears my blood across his skin.

My heart thumps in my chest, uneven, the frantic heartbeat of a captured animal. Then his hand slams across my cheek, and I slump to the floor.

II

Pursuit

RUS

A waft of warm air buffets my tunic hem around my hips as I crouch over a set of hoof-prints. It's been three miles since we found the gypsies' wagons, burned and abandoned, but no sight of Elaina or any other being—living or dead. Thank the Creator. Even with no evidence of her death, it's still as if a bear has pawed out my heart and left a gaping wound behind.

I stand and brush dirt from my knees. Cursed gypsies know we're after them. They won't get away with this.

"What do you see, Your Highness?" asks a guard mounted upon his horse behind me.

"They're continuing east." With my eyes, I follow their path along the mixture of hard dirt and crushed rock toward the border of Ostium ten miles distant.

"Why?" another guard asks. "Why east?"

Rubbing a tickle of dust from my nose, I shake my head and chew on the inside of my cheek.

"They're gypsies. They go where they think they'll be safe," Cito Fati's voice says from my left shoulder. "They know they have the future King of Heia after them. They made a mistake in taking Princess Elaina."

Glancing up, I find my advisor watching me while the guards stare eastward. We exchange a knowing look. They're gypsies. They steal whatever and whomever they want and do whatever they want whenever they want. That's the life of a gypsy—no respect for anyone but themselves.

Bitterness burns in my gut, and I shove myself to my feet. "We must follow."

"Sire?" the nearest guard, captain of my protection detail, says as if he hasn't heard me correctly. "We don't have the authority to enter Ostium."

Needing his agreement, I position a careful smile on my lips. "Then we must catch them before they enter."

There's a pregnant pause where Captain Praeter's men stare at us both.

"Of course, Sire," the captain finally agrees. He inventories his men, almost all of whom are already mounted. A quick glare at the two dismounted makes them swing into their saddles almost as quickly as I swing into mine. "Ride on," he tells them.

An hour of riding passes with frequent stops to confirm the gypsies' trail. They need my eyes, the best tracking eyes on this side of the Seven Kingdoms. Once again, I'm grateful for all my practice hunting and tracking game across the Heian lands. Though once we hit the border, I'll be painfully at a disadvantage. My last visit to the middle country was six years prior, before the plague that eradicated much of the Ostium population. I was a mere eighteen. A child under his father's tutelage. What I wouldn't give for those days again. Now the weight of the crown looms heavy before me.

Captain Praeter pulls up his broad-chested warhorse beside me. "Sire, we can't enter Ostium."

"So you've said," I mutter, inspecting the ground before us. The path through the trees is easy enough to follow, but the gypsies might have stepped off the path at any time, for the trees are sparse enough to allow single-file passage on light horses such as theirs.

"What are your plans at the border then?"

I turn my attention to my captain. "I will find her."

The captain's cheek twitches, but he must see something in my expression to hold his tongue from wagging needless advice.

Spurring my horse ahead, I crest the hill atop my stallion before any other man. Sprawling below is the border between Heia and Ostium. We've long had a peaceful history, but the Ostium plague put rifts between our two countries. My father had to turn away immigrants, close the borders to protect our people. He tried to make amends, risking his own goodwill tour to visit King Leve of Ostium and offer his belated help. His risks failed. Now, my father is dead from plague; although we've had no other reports of outbreaks, he played a dangerous game and lost. Dangerous for all of Heia, including my sister and me. Elaina, so inspired by our father's actions, decided to follow in his footsteps.

My chest still burns when I recall the letter I found when I went to find her.

"My dearest Rus, I know you'll hate me for what I'm doing, but I cannot sit by and allow people—any people—to suffer like Father suffered.

"So I go to Ostium in secret, with the help of my lady's maids. Please don't be angry with them—I swore them to secrecy. And don't be angry at Cito. He tried valiantly to talk me out of this, but it will not be done. I convinced him that he had convinced me. But I go now to help where I might help. If I am to be a queen one day, even queen of another country, I must help wherever and whenever I can.

"I know you agree with me but not with my methods. I am sorry to leave you like this. Remember, whatever happens, I love you and I will return to you. With all my love, Elaina."

My hands ache from how hard I hold the reins, and Umbra dances underneath me. Loosen your grip, idiot. You'll have Umbra bolting across the border before you can stop him, riding like you are.

I take a deep breath, loosen my fingers and my legs. The stallion calms under me, but his ears flick back, ready for my instructions as I squint at the landscape.

"There!" The cry breaks, not from my lips but from Cito's.

I follow his finger with my gaze, and my heart stills. "She got what she wanted," I murmur. "She's in Ostium."

The dozen guards shift almost as one in their saddles.

"Sire, she's across the border," the captain points out.

I bite back my retort, instead putting my thought into the path ahead. The trees are thin here, and the border station lies unmanned now, the guard's house at the bottom of the hill with its door and windows boarded up. I still. Then without another word to my guards, I spur Umbra down the hill.

His head up, haunches down, he skids halfway down the hill, kicking up a pile of dust at the bottom. I give him little chance to recover himself and slap the reins upon his shoulder, urging him toward the house. A dozen feet before it, I tug the reins and he slides to a halt, snorting as I tumble from the saddle and dive for the figure lying underneath the window.

It's not Elaina. Halfway there, my sword flies from its scabbard into my hand. It's a gypsy.

With anger making my hand steady and my jaw tight, I reach the slight man with his long, matted hair and yank him to his feet. His eyes open, crazed with fever and fear.

"Where is she?" I demand, voice emerging like a growling bear.

His eyelids flutter as his gaze tracks across my face. "I-I-I don't—"

"The girl you stole. Where is she?"

"Which one?" The gypsy's voice is harsh and ravaged from fever as he chokes out an answer in broken Heian.

He's Ostiite. The coward. I lift him higher, my hand at his collar, wanting to choke the life out of him and watch it fade from his eyes. His feet scrabble underneath him, too weak to hold his own weight; his hands claw at my wrist as my hand tightens the fabric around his neck.

"The young one. What have you done with her?"

"There were four—" He breaks off, coughing and gasping for air.

I loosen my hold enough for him to breathe.

"Four girls. They're all with the rest of my people."

"What have they done with them? Where are they going?"

He gives me a dirt-smudged smile. "I won't tell. You'll just kill me."

I shake him and growl. "I'll kill you anyway."

"Then do it. I won't talk."

Lip lifting in a sneer of disgust and fury, I watch with satisfaction as his eyes widen, his mouth parts, and he gives his death gasp. When the life fades from his eyes, I release my grip and he slumps to the ground, my sword emerging from his gut painted red.

"Sire!" Captain Praeter pulls at my shoulder, half turning me to him in his shock. "Sire, we could have interrogated him, we—"

"He wouldn't talk." I pull myself free from the captain and lean down, wiping my sword's double-edged blade upon the gypsy's green trousers.

"But—"

"He got less than he deserved." I glare at the fallen gypsy, half regretful, half furious. "I should have tied him here and left him for the vultures. Left him to die of thirst and hunger." I sheathe my sword. "Let's ride."

Murmurs ripple across the guards. The captain looks to me. I meet his annoyed expression with outrage of my own, knowing exactly what he will say.

"You cannot go after her, Sire."

This time, I don't care about his approval. The time for being a frightened child or outraged prince is over. "Captain, I will be crossing the border."

He puffs out his chest, sets his jaw, and says, "Then you will do so with me and my men."

Surprised, I blink at the burly man sitting astride his warhorse. He is heavily armed but not so much as to slow me down. It's traveling with a dozen men that has <u>already</u> slowed me down. A sigh escapes me as I regret the words I must say.

"In that case, I release you and your men from your current duties and request that you return to the palace and to my uncle." I raise my hand at his expression to halt his argument. "Tell my uncle that until I return, he is to rule Heia in my stead."

"But, Sire, I must urge you strongly to reconsider. You are not prepared to cross the border into Ostium and certainly not equipped to follow the gypsies into Canens." The captain spreads his hands before me, pleading with me, knowing that his argument falls on deaf ears. "I will not let you go alone."

"Return to Heia, captain." I settle in Umbra's saddle and nudge the animal forward. I shoot him a dark glare over my shoulder. "If you follow me, I will kill you myself."

He blinks, his lips parted. "Sire!" he calls a moment later. "The country will falter under your uncle Karl."

Two steps over the border, I rein Umbra to a halt and face him. "Then I trust you will advise him appropriately."

He rides forward to stop at the edge of the border and speaks in a low voice. "Sire, consider that you risk war by crossing these borders without permission of King Leve."

"I believe the King will understand when I explain the situation to him." I turn Umbra back to our path. <u>If</u> I explain the situation to him, which I have no intention of doing.

"Take this then." He sweeps his cape from his shoulders and his tunic from his body, thrusting them toward me in a ball of fabric. "Dispose of yours when you can. Do not reveal your identity."

Reluctantly, I take them and exchange my gilded tunic for the plain guard's fabric.

When I look up, he's holding his food sack out to me.

I hesitate, for he and his men have many miles ahead of them.

"Take it. Or I come with you."

Grunting, I accept the gift with a muttered thanks and toss my tunic at his chest. I tie the food sack to my saddle, then before he can delay me longer, I wheel Umbra around and kick him forward. The gypsies are dots on the road ahead, and I intend to reach them tonight. I will not let them reach Canens. I will not let Elaina slip through my grasp.

III

The Light

WINTERBERRY

All it takes is one day, and I know exactly what the guards will do and when they will do it.

And still, that one day has nearly killed me. If I thought the monotony in my room was infuriating, it is a hundred times worse in this black-as-Sheol cell. Not even a sliver of light breaks the blackness—except when the guard delivers my meals. One in the morning, one at night. Only then do shards of his lantern's light sneak into my cell, and like a distant friend, I pine for it.

The second day, I don't allow myself to hesitate. Upon hearing the keys, I scramble to the door and grasp at the hand reaching in.

"Help me, please!" The words burst out of me in a croak.

"Get off!" comes the gruff response, and the wrist jerks free from my clutching fingers.

"Wait!"

The flap slams shut; the darkness returns. Keys jingle then scratch, and then a lock clicks back into place.

"Wait, please, come back. Please. Speak with me."

The only answer are quieting footsteps thumping away.

"I am your princess—I command you to return and speak with me!"

A low chuckle echoes in the corridor, but the footsteps grow quieter.

I slam my hands against the solid wood door, detesting the thunk that does nothing to weaken the door but shudders down my hands like a shattering mirror.

Defeated, I sink down to the floor of my cell, clenching my fists, refusing to cry. Instead, my thoughts turn to a long-ago execution I witnessed here in the dungeons, when a traitor lost his head for treason.

I won't be next. I won't.

Even as I think it, hopelessness overtakes my determination. I have no window, no connection to the outside world except a guard who will not speak to me. There's nothing in here to pick the lock on the door and no way to dig through the rock.

The lock is my only reasonable hope.

Running my hands over the thick wood, I locate the metal of the lock. Only the tip of my smallest finger fits inside but fails to reach the locking mechanism.

A growl of frustration escapes me. What can I use to escape? A rock? A bone? With the meager contents of my bread and cheese meals, a bone is out. On hands and knees, I crawl across the cold, scratchy rock of my cell and run my hands over every inch of it. In the far corner, I find it: a long, slim shard of rock.

That night I spend picking the lock—and succeed in nothing but filling my time.

Just like that, my hope of escape slips away. For she will not let me languish in prison long. She won't be able to forget me, even locking me away as she has. The people will remind her, especially with my most important birthday arriving soon. Why did she arrest me now instead of waiting until I came of age and could officially abdicate to her?

The answer is simple, of course. If a man proposed on my birthday and I accepted, it would threaten her crown. Even if I died before we married, he might then have enough support from the commoners to overthrow Blanche. Not like I have any man to propose though.

If I married a man of inheritance age, I could ask him to seize the crown from her on my behalf, or will the throne to him as soon as we were engaged. I never would have done that, but now I wonder if I should have tried harder to find a fiancé.

Too bad. It's already too late.

I try one more time. "Hello? Guard?" It takes several more calls before a gruff voice answers.

"What?"

"I'm lonely," I say. "Will you speak with me?"

He scoffs. "Nay. I'm not 'ere for that."

"Please," I beg, fear clouding my voice. "I can't take it much longer. I'm going crazy."

He doesn't answer for a moment, but I can hear his shoes scratching at the rock floor in the hall. "We've been ordered not ta speak ta you."

Surprise freezes my veins. "Just me?"

"Just you." While there is caution in his voice, there is also compassion.

"At all?"

There is a pause before he answers. "At'tall."

I close my eyes and lean my forehead against the wooden door separating us. "She means to kill me slowly, doesn't she?"

The silence lasts so long that I think he has gone away or simply decided to follow his orders. But then he says, "P'haps not as slowly as yeh think."

"So you mean my time runs out? Do you know..." I almost don't want to ask, but I force the words off my tongue and into the air. "Do you know how long I have?"

His answer is long in coming. "A few days. P'haps."

A few days. That's all I have left. A few days in prison feels like eternity. And yet so short. But maybe—just maybe—he will help me?

Before I can ask, I hear his footsteps move away, and nothing I say or do can call him back to me.

"Please!" I beg, tears running down my cheeks. "Please don't let me die in here!"

There is no answer, none but my own ragged breaths.

For once, I give myself over to my rage, pounding my fists against the solid door until my hands go numb. Something trickles down my wrists, the only clue I have that my hands are being flayed open with my vehemence against my prison.

Finally, I sink to the ground, tipping my forehead against the door and exhaling a huff of defeat.

Through my closed eyes, a light illuminates me. I freeze, forgetting to breathe. For a moment, I think I've died and the angels are calling for me, leading me to the Great Beyond. Then I frown. I don't feel any different. My hands throb, and if I were dying, surely I'd be pain free.

I open my eyes. A dazzling light greets me, glimmering in the cell. After my eyes adjust, it reveals no window or grates, but simply an underground cave with no escape. Cell walls of wide, almost perfectly square bricks are smooth like marble, stronger than brick, stronger than stone.

My fingers lied to me. I could never tunnel through these lapis bricks. The only way these can be broken is by *adamas*-tipped tools —rare even in Canens and certainly unavailable to me.

If only I hadn't lost my knife.

The light grows brighter, gathering together in the middle of the cell until it forms into an orb of light that nearly blinds me. Tentatively, I reach out a hand then jerk away as it begins to move.

It floats toward the door, illuminating the metal of the lock from within, showing me how futile it is for me to try and break free when I know nothing of locks. It enters the hole of the lock and twinkles. A loud click fills the air. I straighten, alert, waiting for the guard.

The light winks at me and goes out. Silence descends. Then a thump, as though something—or someone—heavy has hit the ground.

I creep for the door, put a hand out, and hesitate, gnawing on my lower lip. Is this some trick? Is this magic? The idea terrifies me. If it's magic, I can't follow it. I can't allow it to corrupt me. I shake my head at my protest. It could be the Queen, trying to trap me. But...what if it's not? Others have magic. And if it is the Queen... But why would it be? I must escape however I can. This is my best—my only— chance. I won't just wait for death—I'd rather go seek it.

I make up my mind. Despite everything—despite what it costs, I want to live. Even if that means living outside this kingdom as an exile or a fugitive.

Could you so abandon your people? a little voice whispers in my ear.

I start and turn around. I am alone; it's only my thoughts.

"If it means my life," I whisper, wincing at the stab of self- betrayal.

Shoving aside regret, I reach for the door.

Under my touch, it slides open. A small breath of air escapes my lips into the silence.

How is this possible? Am I dreaming? I must be dreaming. The only magic in Canens this powerful is the Queen's, and she would not help me.

Except for the guard lying six feet away from my cell door, the hall is empty. And exactly as it was so many years ago. I shake away the memories that cling to me like sour milk.

Left or right?

I tiptoe left, away from the fallen guard and down a short hallway that curves right. The ground seems to slope up; I pause and glance behind me, struggling to remember the location of the sewers. I should be going down.

A few more steps forward and I reach the corner, holding my breath as I peek around it. The ground <u>had</u> been sloping up. This is the way I must have entered. And not the way I want to go, if I am to use the sewers to escape.

Gutters run down the side of one hallway, mostly empty up here but fed by stone pipes attached to the walls and connecting the floor above to the floor below. The contents run down the gutters to the end of the hall, where a larger stone pipe repeats the process of draining the contents from this floor to the one below it. At the bottom is my escape.

But I'm too high above. I expected to be imprisoned in the bowels, where the worst prisoners go, with least hope for escape. Slipping into the gutter with my bare foot, I wince, turn my back on the empty hallway and stairs, and head back toward my gaping cell. The guard hasn't moved, and for the first time, I realize that the bobbing orb of light hasn't either.

Tiptoeing past the fallen guard, I hesitate at the next cell. It feels wrong to leave the light behind, but as I chew on my now-tattered lip, it flickers and moves. Questions race through my mind as fast as my heart races behind my ribs; before I can think of answers, the orb rushes at me.

My mouth opens, and the orb enters. Too late, I snap my mouth shut, expecting a burn. Instead, the gentlest tingle goes through my tongue, and the light goes out as surely as if I have swallowed it. Hands clapped over my mouth, I barely stop myself from scraping my fingers over my tongue. I force myself to swallow and then look down, half expecting the light to glow in my chest, but it's dark.

Footsteps scrape down the hall. I suck in a breath and freeze. My gasp echoes around me, and the footsteps stop. Four heartbeats later, the footsteps resume, this time to my right. Turning my head, I stare through the dimness at a sewer pipe.

Sounds carry through the pipes. I must be quiet. Whatever happened to my guard, it hasn't happened to the guards above.

Heart galloping, I beg my feet to whisper across the cold stone as

I follow the sewer's contents to the end of the hall. At the end is a shadow that I mistook for another cell door. These are the stairs down to the lower levels. I glance up then down. Breath trapped in my lungs, I step forward as if stepping off a bridge and descend into many a person's Sheol.

Let's hope their Sheol will be my escape.

IV

The Queen

BLANCHE

I stand before my scrying mirror, staring intently upon my own reflection. My sun-colored hair is tightly drawn back; my pale skin and eyes the color of the frozen sea of Merise give the illusion of my being an ice carving.

The figure in the mirror wavers around the edges the longer I gaze, replaced by indiscernible shapes at the edges of my awareness. Try as I might, I cannot force them into focus. Sighing, I turn away, my silken dress rippling around me.

Upon the round table nearby is another scrying mirror, and beyond that lies a table littered with ingredients for my latest potion. Shelves line the wall beyond, each filled with jars of ingredients one would need for creating any sort of potion and for enhancing any sort of spell.

"Everything but what I need," I murmur. After all, what kind of magic will make an entire country forget the throne's true heir? And what tale could I spin that might convince them instead?

I've already told them the princess is unworthy to rule, and they believe me. Addled as a lamb. But not nearly so innocent as one.

"And they still love her," I murmur, trailing my fingers along the delicate, wooden frame of my prized hand mirror.

Must I now tell them of the princess's death? Is that what it will take? No, it will merely make her a martyr.

I rub a weary hand over weary eyes. What am I to do with this girl? The problem grows more and more troublesome as she nears her twenty-first birthday.

I face the curtain hanging down the wall that hides my most prized mirror from view. The mirror that reminded me of the Crown's Curse. The one that showed me my future should I kill my stepdaughter.

I slam my fist on the table.

It's wrong. And if it isn't, I will prove it wrong. I smirk. I <u>will</u> prove that mirror wrong.

But in the meantime... My smirk slips from my lips into a scowl. I hadn't quite thought it through, merely demanded that my guards arrest and imprison my most annoying stepdaughter.

Now I have a princess in prison—a princess who is far from the person I've told the peasants she is.

I stride thoughtfully across to my shelf of poisons and potion ingredients. I'm not willing to kill the little minx, difficult though she might be. Not if it kills me. And she has purpose enough, it's true. But the Crown's Curse suggests that anyone who kills a monarch— or heir—to Canens will die.

Sighing, I draw a long fingernail across the handwritten labels of the odd-sized jars, my admiration of the perfectly legible script and the stuffed jars filling my shelves marred by my thoughts.

As my finger trails along a jar full of bitter apple, I run over my options. Poison is too simple and sometimes too messy. Killing the princess is simply not possible at this time, and it would be risky even should I order someone else to do it on my behalf.

But I can't very well auction the girl off to the highest bidder.

I pause, my finger tapping a jar of elderberry.

Or could I?

My finger trails across a bottle of hemlock. Below it is the small, red rosary beads. The Abbatian-grown seeds give me an idea. The huntsman found them for me, at my request, while on one of his long hunts.

A decision forming in my mind, I leave my shelf of poisons and my potion chamber behind.

It will be the perfect solution. One that will not evoke the curse but will also rid me of the pesky princess. As I leave the room, I say to my waiting slave, "Summon my huntsman to me."

The man bows his head and floats away, leaving me to my guard as I traverse the halls. But before I can meet with my most trusted of men, I must arrange something else.

He is exactly where I expect him to be, the captain of my guard. With one glance at me as I appear in the vestibule, Captain Plaga jumps to attention, eager to inform. A tilt of my head is all it takes to encourage him to follow me to my private drawing room, where my dinner awaits.

Inside the room, I seat myself in a comfortable armchair beside the fire before examining Captain Plaga. The pale scars crisscrossing his face catch in the firelight, and for a moment, I wonder how he obtained them. "It is done?" I ask him.

A leering grin on his face, he dips his chin into several enthusiastic nods. His eyes alight with a lustful gleam. Either for money or women, perhaps both. "Yes, Your Majesty. To great success. She sits in the darkest dungeon cell as we speak. I saw to it myself."

"Perfect."

The captain swells at the one-word praise, his chest rising to press against the wool of his tunic, and the buckled leather of his scabbard at his waist strains.

"Then prepare her for auction."

His enthusiasm fades into confusion. "Auction, Your Majesty?"

"Yes, Captain Plaga. Auction. She goes to the blocks."

He nods, puffing his chest out again. "My men will see to it. Is there anything else, Majesty? Anything at all?"

"No. I will visit her. Very soon." I gaze into my fire, admiring the crackle of the flames. The scent of roast venison taunts my nose, along with the accompanying buttered vegetables. "But tell her nothing. And no one speaks to her."

He bows low. "Yes, Majesty."

I ignore his bow and wave a regal hand his way, dismissing him before I take up my drink. I will visit my stepdaughter as soon as I finish my meal. It has already been a long day.

V

Escape

WINTERBERRY

The deeper I go, the worse the stench.

I descend into the bowels of the palace prisons, never thinking I would ever go this far. Something protects me, surely, for I hear and see no one. It's the light. It seems to burn within me, keeping me warm and even calming my racing heart. But where does this light come from? I force the niggling thought into the back of my head. I may not be able to trust this light—magic is never trustworthy—but I am more desperate than I've ever been before.

My barefoot step murmurs against the stone, and a shiver runs up my legs to shake my body, although I'm not certain it's the cold that provokes it. With a jolt that starts in my foot and echoes in my heart, I reach the bottom of the stairs. Somehow it feels more dangerous to leave the narrow staircase and emerge into the hallway, but I must.

I pause to listen for any sound of movement and hear nothing, not even the scratching of a rat. Willing myself to move like a ghost, I step out into the hall.

Two guards stand at the end of the hallway, staring my direction.

I give a gasp then slap my hands over my mouth with a smack that cracks the air like a guard's whip.

Neither guard moves.

For several wrenching heartbeats, the three of us stare down the hall at each other. Every second, I expect them to shout and bolt at me, weapons drawn.

But...they don't.

Then I truly see them. They don't blink. They're unconscious. Or...incapacitated somehow.

On silent feet, with my breath captive, I creep forward. Their stares are glassy and unseeing, as if they are frozen. Short furs peek out from the cuffs of their heavy, gray uniforms. There is no fire down here, and their furs are practical bits of their clothing.

A chill runs its hand over my exposed skin. The halls are freezing, even inside, and shivers rack my body beneath my thin gown all the way to my bare feet. It's going to be even colder outside. The uniform for prisoners practically cements that I'll die before I get an hour away.

Although time is precious, and my heart thumps uncomfortably in my chest at every whisper in this prison, I need more clothes. Warmer clothes. The sewers exit near the frozen sea, which has little cover from trees or mountains, so I must equip myself before escaping. Or else walk into a certain death.

After a quick inspection of the floor, I find only cells, open and empty. Even if they weren't empty, I'm not here to save anyone else, I remind myself. But I have to find boots and stockings—and a cloak and hat and mittens.

Grimacing, I dart back up the stairs. One level above, I hold my breath and peek out, hoping to see an empty hallway leading to a guard's supply room. I should get some food, too. I don't know when I'll be able to catch anything, and I can't hunt without weapons.

My attention on my task wavers as I consider future survival, and my foot slips off the path, splashing into a gutter whose contents coat my shin under my long dress. My lips twist in disgust at the smell that rises with it.

The hall is empty; the second guard below must be the guard for this level. Or else he's hiding somewhere else. Awake? Asleep? I will my feet to be quieter and carefully avoid the edge toward the gutter and its slippery slope.

I tiptoe past the first cell door, wide open and vacant. It's even more barren than my own cell, with no straw or chamber pot. I hurry past as if it might sprout arms and drag me inside by itself.

A closed door at the end of the hall looks different from the others with a rectangular sign. The storeroom! It has to be. In my excitement, I surge forward, rushing toward it without thinking.

Once there, I reach for the door and tug the handle. Locked. Why is it locked? Despair tugs at me, dragging my shoulders down in defeat as I dip my head against the door and exhale. What do I do? A little voice answers me: *find the keys. A jailor has to have them.*

"Of course." My response carries in the stillness.

Without giving myself any time to argue with the little voice, I turn and start back the way I came, now looking for a guard.

"Who's there?" someone asks.

I skid to a halt, slipping to my knee in shock at the husky, deep, male voice. I stare at the closed door, all that protects me from whoever is behind it.

"Who is it?" a second voice asks from across the hall.

My gaze jerks to the next impenetrable door.

"We can't hurt you," says a third voice in a carrying whisper from two doors away.

I'm surrounded. By disembodied voices.

Hysteria rises in me, and I bite my lip to keep from bursting at it as I gape at the half a dozen doors hiding half a dozen mysteries.

"Are you a prisoner?" the voice from the door nearest me asks. He gives me a few seconds to answer, but when I do not, he adds, "If you are, let us out, please."

"We can help you," says a pragmatic voice, the second voice that spoke.

"We can help you," echoes down the hallway in too many voices to count.

Prisoners? How many are in here? I count seven closed doors.

"Let us help you," whispers a voice across the hallway.

"How can you help me?" I ask.

"We will protect you."

"We can distract the guards."

"There is safety in numbers."

Uncertainty eats at me. The disembodied voices are right. There must be a half dozen of them, men who could fight the guards for me. "I don't have the keys," I finally say.

"How did you get out then?" responds the pragmatic voice across the hall from me from the bottom of the door.

I look over and see an eye staring out from underneath the cell door. "I—" Attempting to explain about the orb of light seems impossible, so I don't bother continuing, closing my mouth instead. Why can't the light do it again?

Turning back to the storeroom door, I open my mouth and whisper, "Please unlock the doors."

As if waiting for my command, the orb erupts from my mouth, filling the hall with lightning. It blitzes first to the storeroom then, with a half shrug from me, down the hallway, touching each lock. Each emits a gentle, yet audible, click at the touch. At every door, the light dims a bit more, as if reflecting the sudden drain on my own energy. My flesh cools further as each lock opens until the hair on my arms rises and my body trembles.

The light flickers out. Seven doors creak open in the darkened dungeon.

"Princess?" a voice asks uncertainly.

Gaze turning slowly to the speaker, I weave where I stand. Seven men, their heads brushing the ceiling, stare at me. As I watch, first the speaker, then the rest, lower themselves to one knee, bending their heads to me as if I am the Queen.

In sudden weakness, I sink to the ground.

"Princess!" the one nearest me, a giant of a man with gold eyes and ginger hair, lurches to catch me before I can fall. His hands are firm yet gentle, at odds with his image. An iron spike slices each ear through the tragus and transverses the lobes. If his eyes were not the gentle glow of a rising sun, filled with much-needed warmth, I would shrivel and freeze under his touch. "Are you ill?"

"What are you doing down here, Your Highness?" Another of the men, equally as large and possibly as terrifying, approaches. Whereas the first is the red and gold of a sunrise, the second is the grays and shadows of a moonlit winter night.

I simply shake my head.

"We must carry her out." The first, who looks to be younger than the darker one, scoops me into his arms as though I am a pile of clothes.

"Yes," come murmurs of agreement.

"No," I protest, the weakness slowly leaving me. "No, get out. Put me down. I can escape through the sewers, I just came here to get supplies, but you—" I glance around at them. "You're too large; you can't fit."

The one carrying me shakes his head. "You are ill."

One man, a man who looks like a younger version of the shadowed one, strides purposefully toward us, but instead of stopping at us, he walks to the storeroom and throws open the door to disappear inside.

I turn my attention back to the one holding me. "No, I am not ill. I am well."

"I cannot leave you," he says, standing in place with his eyes on the others.

They act as a team of wolves might, one scouting out ahead and visually checking in with each other. They're too similar to simply know each other; they must be family—brothers or perhaps cousins. The one emerges from the storeroom with bundles in his hands, tying them around himself and passing something to the one holding me. Perhaps they are bandits. I push the thoughts aside.

"Please, I want you to—" I pause as images of them kneeling to me and naming me with respect filter before me. "I command you to leave me and escape for yourselves."

The men hesitate. The older, shadowed man clashes eyes with the man carrying me. Muscles bunch against my hip and shoulder, as though the younger giant longs to disobey. The moment stretches thin; his heart beats against my ribs. Then a breath leaves him.

"I cannot disobey my liege." The man carrying me turns to the older man. "Amos, take them out. I'll take her down."

The older giant nods and doesn't look back as he darts for the stairs. The other giants, silent and stoic, beat him there, pausing at the shadow where the stairs begin and listening before dashing onto the steps and taking them two at a time up. I hear them murmur something about releasing another prisoner.

"Who are you?" I ask the man carrying me.

"I am Caleb."

"Who are they?" I point at the stairs which we quickly approach.

"My brothers."

"What did you do? Why are you in prison?"

We are at the stairs, but instead of following his brothers up, he looks at me. "You can walk?"

"Of course."

A shout from above jolts us both. His fingers dig into my flesh, and I grab the stone wall of the doorway in surprise.

"The guards," I whisper. "They must have awoken."

Caleb frowns at the ceiling, sets me down, and gives me a small shove toward the stairs. "Go. Fast."

"I—"

He shoves a fur-lined guard's cape at me, the thing he must have taken from his brother. "Go!"

Mouth open to protest, I instead clutch the cape to my chest and turn away. Any guard that runs into him will be woefully unprepared.

I stumble down the stairs, falling to my knees at the bottom. Snatching the cape up from the ground and looking over my shoulder, I wrench myself upward and right into a pair of waiting arms.

VI

The Huntsman

BLANCHE

I remove my cloak as I enter my chambers and toss it into the waiting arms of a maid. The slave curtsies and backs up, as though there is nothing in the world more important than protecting her queen's cloak.

I turn to my desk, barely sparing a glance at the crackling fire warming the room.

A knock sounds upon the door, but I do not turn. I summoned him, and he has come.

The door opens; there are soft footsteps, two sets, and then the door closes, and there is only the sound of one other person in the room, breathing gently. I recognize my huntsman's breath, nearly inaudible but for the cadence of the way it falls over his bearded upper lip. That slight rustle sends shivers of pleasure down my spine.

I turn and find him with his gray eyes solemn and patient. His narrow face reminds me vaguely of the first wolf pelt he brought me: a huge, silvery blue beast that I had sewn into my favorite cape. Eyes upon him, I pull off my thin, black gloves and fold them in half before dropping them atop a side table.

"My queen," he murmurs as I approach. He casts his eyes reverently down.

I extend my hand and allow him to press his lips to the back of it. My lips twitch, but it would not be proper to show my pleasure at his touch, though if the warmth of his skin is anything to judge by, he well knows of it.

"What is your command?" His eyes flick up to my face and linger there.

I motion him to a chair before the fire. His cheeks are red, as if he has been summoned from outdoors and is chilled. A bottle of wine and two glasses sit beside the chair, awaiting us.

He moves to the chair but stands behind it, waiting for me to claim mine first. With an inward smile, I seat myself before the fire, finally taking the moment to admire its red-hot flames with a half-smile. I smooth my soft, Heian silk and reposition my *adamas* ring on my finger as he seats himself across from me. His white tunic and trousers suggest that he was preparing for a hunt when summoned. During his visits, I enjoy the choicest game Canens can offer. Giant deer, bear, venison, even seal and salmon, grace my table.

He pours two glasses of wine, the liquid startling red through the clear glass and against the pale white of his clothing. Even the fur peeking out from his wrists is white and soft as freshly fallen snow.

"How can I serve you, my queen?" He passes me a glass with a steady hand; there is no evidence of fear before his ruler, although one word from me would end his life.

I suppress a smug smile. This is why I use him. "I have a job for you."

He takes the other glass of wine and sips from it, waiting for me to elaborate.

"But first. Tell me all about your escapades."

He clears his throat with a half-formed smile.

"I hear there has been some trouble with the peasants from your cousin's lands?"

Shifting in his seat in an unusual display of discomfort, he dips his head into a thoughtful nod and sets his glass down on the table. "Yes, I'm afraid a small band of peasants rose up against my cousin, Count Celscus of Bellari. I assure you, it's through no fault of his own."

I purse my lips and give the slightest nod. In response, my huntsman presses his hands together in thanks.

"But the small uprising has been quashed, thanks to Lord Tueor's army."

"Tueor. That is your...brother, no?"

"Yes, Majesty."

"And he quashed the rebels with only the assistance of his men?"

"Yes, Majesty."

"I am pleased to hear it."

"There was no true danger to begin with. Simply a few peasants that believed they were owed more than they are in life." His lip curves to reveal a yellowing incisor.

"What fools." There is the slightest mocking lilt to my words.

"Aren't they?" His voice warms with amusement. "But rest assured that the rebels will not be rising again. None were left alive. And they were all killed with such miserable methods that no one will dare whisper of them again."

I chuckle low and slow in my appreciation. No one thinks like me but for my huntsman and perhaps his kin. "How that pleases me," I say. "What other news do you have to report?"

At this question, he picks up his wineglass and inspects the wine's surface before taking a swallow. "There is...displeasure at the upcoming birthday celebration."

I wrinkle my nose. "Of course. Today is my darling stepdaughter's twenty-first birthday, is it not?"

He bends his head in acknowledgment. "An important birthday, Your Majesty, as she enters her year of choosing a future king. One which the people have been preparing for."

"How so?"

Discomfort plays across his brow as he twitches his wrist, swirling the wine around in his glass. "I suspect some supporters of the princess are attempting a display at the yearly parade."

"I thought all the rebels were suppressed, according to your brother?" I arch an eyebrow.

"Those ones are. But there has been talk in the capital, even as I have been amongst them, of some sort of...surprise."

I sit back in my chair, mind turning over his words. "What sort of surprise?"

"That, I have not been able to discover." He throws back the last of his wine in a large gulp. "But I shall." He sets his glass upon the table. "Is there anything else Your Majesty desires of me?"

At this question, my gaze travels across his familiar face, the angular cheekbones, the long, blond hair with streaks of silver tied back with a leather thong, the neatly trimmed beard that fails to fully cover up the narrowness of his chin. And his eyes, ever the hunter's, watching, waiting, biding his time. They are the sole reason I both trust him with my life and do not trust him at all. His breathing does not change as he waits for my examination to cease, and he holds my gaze with his own, steady and patient. I collect my words on my tongue and position them deliberately, knowing he will see through them to the truth.

"There is a prisoner I need you to purchase."

His face remains implacable, and so I continue.

"She is young, perfectly trainable." I wave a hand in dismissal but carefully include a wave at the velvet pouch of coin I slip next to his empty wineglass. I don't miss the twitch of his gaze toward it. "And I want you to purchase her and train her at your manor. Treat her like any other slave."

"And what will I train her for?" His fingers flex on the arm of the chair.

I shrug delicately, lean forward, and refill our glasses with my favorite strawberry wine from a decanter this time. "Whatever you like."

His brows lift. "A Red?"

I sip my wine thoughtfully. "I'll leave that to your discretion."

"Of course."

"Train her. Keep an eye on her. Make her..." I trail off, a sneer pulling at my lips. "Make her into something worth buying."

A small wrinkle appearing on his forehead, he dips his head in a nod and reaches for his wine when my next words stay his hand.

"Break her."

His hand hesitates. "Break her, Majesty?"

A chill settles over the room.

"Whatever it takes. Break her."

A small smile twitches upon his lips, his beard jerking in something like cynical amusement. "As you wish, my queen."

VII

Humbled

WINTERBERRY

oes my stepmother expect me to die from starvation? If that were my punishment for trying to escape, I could believe it. Two hunks of bread and moldy cheese every day will either poison me or leave me a wraith.

Does she wish to destroy my image? If starvation hasn't worked over the past eight years, it can't very well work now. But if that's it, she can take it. I don't care. I never did. After all this time, surely she would know that?

The door to my cell clangs open, startling me into pressing myself against the wall where icy water drips.

Framed in the doorway, majesty dripping off her white gown, stands the Queen. Her shoulders glitter with gold-set jewels, their depth of color breathtaking even in this dismal setting, while along the bodice and skirt are gems of the clearest order, sparkling brighter, colder, and harder than diamonds.

"Rise," she commands when I do not.

For a moment, I consider refusing. She is so clearly in control, and I powerless. Even an animal would know and bend to the authority.

Her eyebrow arches, and a shiver ripples over my skin, followed by the irrepressible urge to rise and walk to her. My mind goes blank, my limbs numb, as I obey.

Her beauty is arresting, her skin as icy as the eternal winter our country endures, her hair yellow as the marigolds I had once glimpsed in her growing house, her eyes as blue as the clearest frozen lake or the sky on a clear day. When I stand in front of her, my eyes downcast upon her dainty toes in rabbit skin slippers, she whispers, "You dare to challenge me?"

"No, Your Majesty." The words come from me, distant, echoing. I cannot recall forming them in my mind and hardly know I speak them.

"Wise." She tilts her head back, looking down her narrow nose at me. "Hard to believe you are the one my mirror warns me of. The one who—" She murmurs her next words so quietly that I don't catch them. "You are no beauty to me." From her belt, she withdraws a long, jagged knife and raises her voice again. "Why should I fear you?"

I inhale a breath as sharp as the blade she wields. Her magic pushes at me, calling me to be obedient and respectful, but with all my inner strength, I push back at it, refusing its evocative call.

Something warbles in the air, a whisper echoes in my head, and her influence fades; I lift my chin and meet those impossibly calm, cold eyes. "You can't kill me, Stepmother. Not without bringing down the curse of the throne upon you."

She blinks, for once taken aback. I have never spoken to her with such derision, but after three days in prison, I finally know how little I have to lose. There is no one outside the prison who remembers their princess, no one to care that I am imprisoned, no one who loves me, no one to rescue me. I am utterly alone and powerless to change anything. And I know very well that the only thing staying my step-mother's hand is the long-standing rumor that any person who kills a blood heir to the Canens throne will immediately die. I have my suspicions that an early Canens king invented the rumor simply to protect the throne from usurpers, but for hundreds of years, it has kept the throne pure. Because another part of the rumor is that if the heir is unlawful or evil, he or she will be struck down and unable to inherit the throne.

"Kill you?" Blanche asks with warm syrup in her voice, a trap of sweetness. "What use would you be to me dead?"

"You don't—I'm your only threat." I blink at her. "Why won't you just kill me? You know the supposed prophecy is as good as a rumor."

"Only threat?" A slow smile pulls up her delicate lips. "Oh, no, my dear. You...you...are no threat. You are merely an annoyance." She puts the tip of her finger on the knife point, twirling the blade with her other hand in thought. "Besides, why kill an annoyance? They may one day be useful."

"Useful? I am so useful that you decide to keep me in a prison?" My words rise in anger.

Her smile is demure and collected as she beckons me forward. I have not taken her by surprise.

"I have no need of you dead and no need to risk my own life, for all I need is your signature." From her side, she produces a parchment and holds it before me. "One signature, and you can walk free."

I don't even glance at the paper to know that I can't believe her. She will never let me walk free. "No."

"No? You don't even know what it's for."

"I don't care. Anything you want from me, you won't get."

Her mouth flattens and slips into a thin grin. "Then I suppose I'll have to go forth with my other plans."

The edges around her smile tighten, her eyes sweeping over me in a glance that observes everything and yet seems casual.

While I stand before her, she raises the knife I have almost forgotten, almost forgotten to fear, and lifts it to my neck.

My breath stills, eyes widening as I attempt to detect her bluff.

With an icy smile, she lifts her other hand, sweeps back my ratted hair, and makes a slashing movement.

I inhale sharply, expecting pain, the wetness of blood gushing over my chest. But instead, I feel nothing. Raking a breath into my lungs, I look down. In her hand, she holds a clump of blackness.

Her smile turns smug as she grasps a second handful of my locks and draws the knife against them again. It's a testament to the sharpness of the blade that it doesn't snag on the thick clumps. She finishes her task, and I don't resist. If this is all she wants, I will gladly give it to her. What does it matter to me?

She steps away and motions with a finger for me to twirl. I put several feet between us before her magic forces me into a quick rotation. "Yes, I think that will do," she murmurs as I face her again. "Jailor?" she calls with her dulcet tone. "Lock her up."

As I am once again in the cold darkness of my cell, I realize her intention.

She thinks that all my power lies in the one thing I have: my beauty. Not my life, nor my lineage. Neither has ever mattered to her. It is only in my beauty that I hold power. And, day by day, she will strip it from me, until I am a wasted shell of what I once was.

The door to my cell bangs open, and the captain of the guards stands there, framed by torchlight beyond.

I instinctively shrink back. I have not seen him since he kissed me and deposited me in this dungeon.

He studies me, his nose wrinkled and lips curled in a mocking way. I am sure I look nothing like he saw before, where I had at least brushed my hair and put up the image of being halfway normal. Now, the Queen has taken my hair, and my dirty and damp dress sags on my frame. Feeling like an inadequate filly up for sale, I shiver under his impersonal inspection.

"Bring the bucket," he commands to a person in the hallway.

My eyes widen as my heart leaps into my throat. Bucket?

He stands and waits, eyes hard.

Warily, I watch him.

He grins.

When a guard holds a wooden bucket out to him, he motions me toward him.

I don't move.

"Don't make me come get you." With a scoff, he turns to the guard with the bucket and jabs a finger at me. "She stinks." He jerks his chin down the hallway as if instructing someone else to do something else.

"Wha—?" As he moves back, I move forward, and the jailor turns on me with a wicked leer.

He swings the bucket back then forward. Water arcs across the cell, almost lost in the darkness before it collides into me, directly in my face.

I gasp and sputter, losing my breath as shards of ice in the water break across my skin. Instant shivers ripple over me, sending my body into a shudder that seems like it will never end. Before I can catch air in my lungs, a second clump of water hits me in the neck, sending ice through my skin and into the depths of my body.

"Strip her," he commands through my agony.

My rasping gasp echoes in the confined air of the cell.

"Scrub her down."

Stomach knotted, I stumble back against the wall, into the waterfall that leeches through the cell blocks wraps me in its icicle embrace.

"Bring her out," the captain demands impatiently.

A guard lunges across the cell. He grabs my wrist and yanks me out into the hallway, where torchlight illuminates us all but brings no warmth. My ragged breaths barely create a cloud of perspiration in the air, next to the guards' large breaths misting between us.

"Make her presentable," the captain instructs through a cloud of his own. "Then get her to the square by noon." He throws a rumpled white dress at me, and a guard immediately takes it away.

Then there in the hall of the dungeons, they strip me, scrub me, and shave my head.

VIII

Gypsies

RUS

Under cover of darkness, Umbra and I ride after the gypsies. Three hours ago, I lost sight of them in this cloudless night; now I watch their campfire from two miles away. Fools. They must believe they lost me at the border, convinced we would not follow. Within twenty minutes, I am a quarter mile from their camp.

"Stay here," I murmur to Umbra. I don't bother tying him, as he'll simply tug free, but he won't wander far. Instead, when he is free, I can whistle and he will come.

The stallion snorts and blinks his warm brown eyes at me. I check my sword and dagger and turn to walk away when a snapping branch pricks both Umbra's ears and mine.

Whisper-quiet, I unsheathe my sword and hold it at the ready.

A horse snuffles; Umbra snorts in answer then tosses his head as if he wants to roll his eyes. The outline of a horse and rider appears a dozen feet away, walking slowly forward in the black night.

"Sire?" comes a whisper. "Are you there?"

Seriously? I bite back a reprimand and remain quiet.

"It's me, Cito. Cito Fati."

I spare a roll of my eyes at the obvious statement and shift my gaze to our surroundings. Perhaps he's not alone, perhaps he's been sighted and is leading the enemy to me now. I keep my sword at the ready and silently draw my dagger.

"I'm alone. I followed you, I—" Cito's mount comes upon Umbra, and both horses snort at the other then touch noses. Cito's horse, a speedy but easygoing gelding, sways to a halt as Cito draws on the reins.

"Clearly you followed, Cito," I finally murmur and step out from the other side of Umbra's neck. "The question is why?" While he jumps and catches his breath, I peer around him and see whether he truly is alone. And how did I not see you? I add to myself.

Cito's expression is difficult to read in the darkness, but his eyes glint earnestly. "I could not let the future King of Heia go off alone on such a foolish journey."

I propel a sigh through my nostrils. "Out of all the men to accompany me—"

"I know I'm your last choice. And believe me, the others wanted to come, but I figured I would be your best ally."

"Shh." I sheathe my sword but keep the dagger out. "And how do you figure that?"

"Because I won't talk you out of whatever you're about to do."

I meet his gaze before dropping my chin in a nod. "Fine. But that's the agreement. No matter what happens, no matter where I go, you support my decisions and back me up."

Cito hesitates only a moment before dipping his chin. "Yes, Sire."

"And no 'Sire' or 'Your Majesty' or 'Your Highness.'"

"But—"

"From now on, I'm just a brother searching for his sister."

Cito nods again and dismounts, all but crumpling to the ground in his lack of elegance. He ties the reins to the saddle horn and pulls a crossbow and quiver from his saddle. "Then what is our next step, sir?"

I narrow my eyes. "I said no—"

"You did not say anything about 'sir.' I will not call you by your given name, sir. So accept my support under this rule."

With another roll of my eyes, I grunt. "Fine." From my saddle, I retrieve my own bow and arrows. "I go to talk with the gypsies. They're camped less than a half mile from here."

"Talk?" Cito eyes my weapons.

Allowing myself a wicked grin, I say, "It might come to more than talking."

"Be cautious, sir."

"I thought you weren't going to talk me out of anything." I adjust my tunic and belt, testing my scabbard's position and then the strength of the bow.

"I'm not. I'm merely reminding you that a country could fall if you do." Cito's voice is dark with worry but also with unusual bravery for the palace advisor.

He's not a warrior, although he is well trained. He's far from my first choice, perhaps even the last. I bite back a sigh and turn in the direction of the gypsy camp. It might be useful to have someone watching my back after all.

I face him again. "Here's the plan. I will enter the camp," I say, not giving him time to argue. "And you will stay in the darkness at the edge with your crossbow. If you must shoot, do not reload from the same location. These gypsies have excellent bowmen. If Elaina is with them, we will take her by force if we must. So be prepared to kill."

Cito dips his chin then looks skyward. "A bit of moon would help us."

I shrug. "It would also help them. Perhaps help them more. They are illuminated by their foolish fire. You will be hidden in the shadows. Use them."

"Of course, sir." Cito readjusts the strap of his crossbow then pats his scabbard. He's not as skilled with the sword as I, but he can hold for a few minutes against a skilled swordsman. Usually.

"Let's go," I mutter. "Keep your bow ready."

Cito falls in behind me, his steps loud against the near-silence of my own. I bite back an admonition. He has only come on one of my hunts for this very reason—he scares away the game with his clomping steps. Still, having another set of eyes I can trust and another set of weapons to defend me is invaluable.

Soon we're at the edge of the camp, crouching behind a conveniently wide tree trunk with low, bushy branches.

After a few minutes' study, it's clear that only one man keeps watch, and he's leaning against a rock near the fire. The rest have bedded down for the night, covered in light blankets, their weapons undoubtedly at their sides. Having lost their wagons, they sleep under the constellations in the cloudless night.

"Keep watch," I murmur to Cito. I wind through the shadows along the edge of the camp and emerge from the trees fifty feet away from Cito.

Creeping through the camp, I inspect the faces of every single person under the blankets. I'm at the edge of the fire before I pause and say in Ostiite, "Excuse me."

The watchman's entire body jerks, then he bolts to his feet, pulling his dagger in a smooth but belated fashion.

I raise my hands as two other men emerge from under their blankets, weapons lifted. "Please, I come asking for help."

The watchman motions to the other men to lower their weapons.

"Are you alone?" he asks in heavily accented Ostiite.

"Yes, of course. Are you expecting someone else?"

"What do you want?" one of the men who woke says. His pale brown beard extends to his belly, and his matted hair falls over his shoulder in thin ropes.

"Shelter," I say simply, lowering my hands. "I saw your fire, and—"

The second one steps forward, his dagger held between us. He's younger, with a mustache that trails down the sides of his mouth and a clean-shaven chin. I would easily be able to wrest the weapon from him if it should come to that, and I hope Cito realizes that. Don't waste an arrow on the one I can take.

"Where do you come from?" the watchman demands. "How did you find us?"

"I said, I saw your fire and—" I break off and glance around. There are a dozen other gypsies, each various shades of gray in the muted firelight. Eyes stare at me, arms slowly moving under blankets as the firelight illuminates faces full of mistrust and fear.

But no Elaina. My gaze shifts to the last clump across the fire. A small face peers out, about the same age as Elaina, but dark haired. Not her. She's not here.

My hands clench into fists. "What have you done with the girls?"

A slow smile spreads over the watchman's face. "Ah. I knew you would come."

The two men beside me close rank.

"My men thought the border would stop you. But I knew."

I narrow my eyes. "It takes more than that to stop a brother from finding his sister. Others might abandon me and my search, but I won't give up."

Surprise ripples across the man's face. "Brother?"

I don't spare him a nod. "You're the fools that kidnapped a princess. Now, where is she?"

Instead of answering, he searches my face with a frozen smile on his lips, and a slow, deep chuckle creeps out from his mouth.

The man with the matted hair shifts his weight, his fingers tightening on the hilt of his thin sword, the firelight glancing off his white knuckles as much as the metal. "A princess?" he says, voice hoarse, and glances at the watchman. "We sold—"

My gaze locks with his then flies to the watchman and back to him. "Where did you sell her? To whom?"

"Silence," the watchman says. "We tell him nothing."

I glare lightning bolts at him, but he remains impervious with his stone pride. He's no watchman. He's whom all the others obey. He's their leader.

My fingers flood with heat. Before the two men flanking me know what's happened, I've drawn both my sword and dagger. The sword flashes in the direction of the long-haired man, while I swipe away the dagger of the mustache man and dig my knife into his ribs. He clutches his side and falls, a whistle of air slipping from his chest as I withdraw my weapon.

My sword stabs toward the long-haired man as a half dozen men scramble up from their sleeping pallets.

Cito, I hope you have my back.

Thanks to my flashing blade, the long-haired man falls to his knees, but there's no time to celebrate. The rest of the gypsies attack. As I slice my sword through the air at one and jab my dagger in the direction of another, a third cries out, dropping his blade and twisting. When he turns, it reveals an arrow buried in his back, near his spine.

Thank you, my friend.

I waste no time in dispatching two more gypsies, and Cito finishes the third. Then, with eight bodies either still or moaning at my feet, I face the gypsy leader. "I'll give you one more chance to tell me where my sister is. Or you meet the same fate as your men."

A blank look has settled on his features as he sweeps his gaze over the bodies on the ground. I spare a quick glance for the remaining gypsies, all women and older children. An older woman has crept forward, cradling the head of one of the gypsies bleeding on the ground. A youth, perhaps sixteen, just enough man to be killed without regret. Much regret, at least.

Tears leak out from her hardened face, her jaw set against the unstoppable pain I've inflicted upon her with my sword.

The leader lifts his hands. "I have no desire to die today. Though you take my sons from me."

Hand steady and outstretched with my sword, I advance on him, my dagger closer to me and at the ready. "Then tell me what I need to know."

Pulling his gaze from the bodies strewn around us, he spreads his weaponless hands before me. "I won't stop you."

"Just tell me," I say, forcing my voice to be hard and unforgiving. "If I have to kill you, I will. Someone here knows where my sister is. She's thirteen."

The gypsy leader's gaze hovers upon the young man's body, now still under his grandmother's hold.

I must get out of here before the rest of them tear my limbs from my body.

"We sold her," comes the woman's voice, broken with unshared sobs.

Keeping my sword stretched toward the gypsy leader, I point my dagger at her. "Where is she going? To whom did you sell her? How do I find her?"

"She goes to Canens," the woman answers.

"She went to the slave traders," the man adds, his voice heavy.

Fury burns within me. I must leave before I lose control.

"She goes to Merise—"

Before the woman has completed her words, the gypsy leader and two standing women attack.

My sword and dagger flash through the air, landing wounds here and there. A knife cuts into my arm, and with a grunt, I stab with my dagger. It hits something hard, and a feminine shriek rises into the air. The man renews his attack, but as he lunges toward me, I step aside, and he falls past. With a shove from me, he tumbles to the ground and rolls over, ready to rise.

He freezes with a grunt.

"Do not test me." My sword point is at his throat.

His chest rises and falls rapidly in his exertion. "You cheated."

"Cheated?" I scoff. "You cannot accuse me of cheating when you kidnap young girls and sell them into slavery."

"You are a fool for allowing your sister to travel the country with a few maidservants."

I grip my sword tighter. "Perhaps I am. But you should not have tried to teach me of my foolishness." I wave my dagger hand at the bodies littering the ground. "Your mistake was deadly."

A shadow crosses over his features, distance growing in his eyes. "Yes. I can see that now." He lifts his gaze to mine. "Perhaps yours has been as well."

A rustle sounds behind me. I whirl. The woman holds a knife above my head. Dropping my sword, I grab her wrist, halting her arm from driving the blade into my chest.

Something collides with the middle of my back, driving me into the woman so that she falls back. My dagger flies from my grasp. Grunting, I struggle, wrenching myself around. I scrabble for my knife and shove against the body. Then I realize something. He's not fighting back.

Behind me, a gasp slips out of the woman's lips. She clutches her chest and sinks to the ground, an arrow sticking out from between her fingers.

About time, Cito.

Shoving the man's body off me, I wriggle out from underneath. The guard's tunic and my sand-colored trousers are coated in blood. I frown down at the gypsy leader's corpse, expecting an arrow to stick out from his back. Instead, a blade peeks out from his shoulder blades. I drag him over, his sightless eyes staring at the dark heavens. In the glint of the fire, the hilt of my dagger protrudes from his chest.

At another rustle, this one from my right, I rip the dagger from the gypsy's chest and lunge for my sword, rolling over my shoulder and coming up covered in leaves and bruised, but well-armed.

"It's me," says a voice I vaguely recognize through my battle haze.

I release a slow, tense breath and rise out of my defensive stance. "Is there anyone else—?" I break off. Around the fire is a trail of my destruction.

They brought this on themselves. It was an act of war to kidnap a princess. Still, the idea of so much bloodshed unnerves me. But I answered that act of war with violence I'd never before contemplated.

Cito steps up beside me. "What do you propose we do with the youths?"

I turn to him. "With the what?"

With a bemused expression, Cito raises a hand and points toward the gypsy's horses. A dozen animals are tied at the edge of camp, and from amongst their legs peek several children.

Gypsy children. My heart twists in my chest. Is there any salvation for them?

Cito wanders through the camp, peering down at the faces of men and women we've killed. I follow, half expecting to see Elaina's face, terrified that I might find her in disguise. It would be like the gypsies to trick me, to hide her from me. At the thought, I fall to the nearest body and pull at the woman's hair, stretching her head back in my efforts to rip her scalp off.

"Sir! Sir! Your Highness!"

It's not until the royal address that I look up into Cito's shocked gaze.

"What are you doing?"

With limp hands, I motion at the corpse. "It could have been Elaina. They could have disguised her, they—" My voice cracks, and a sob breaks free, horrifying me. I bend my head, desperate to regain control before trying again.

Cito's hand falls on my shoulder. "We'll find her, sir," he says calmly, his voice sounding more mature than his age. He's only seven years older than me; we practically grew up friends, and it was that which made me choose him as my personal advisor over many other gray-haired men. "Don't fret. We shall find her. And we shall bring her home."

Taking a deep breath, I shove the emotions roiling in my stomach away, back down to where they belong in a warrior. "Yes. You're right, Cito. We will." I scan the corpses. At least ten men and women have fallen. "But we've made orphans out of these children. We must help them first."

IX

Sold

WINTERBERRY

When the outside air hits me, it's as forceful as if the guard took his whip and slashed me across the front with it. I choke at the assault and try to catch my breath as the guards drag me down the slippery stone steps.

The men don't seem bothered by the cold; it's only I who shivers uncontrollably as they push me out of the dungeon and into a waiting sleigh. Three guards climb into the back with me, one at my side, two across. They wear thick, dusty gray cloaks over their charcoal guard apparel, which flutters in the breeze as we slide down the road away from the only home I've ever known.

At the base of the hill, I turn and look back. The castle, a black, turreted, spired thing, rises thousands of feet into the air above us.

Gargoyles with dragon wings peer down at us from the corners of the castle, their mouths agape, teeth bared. They have failed at their job, I want to tell them. The demon is already inside.

A large set of windows off to the left, above the main castle entrance, is the throne room. That is where she will be, if she's not in her rooms. That is where she terrifies my people. Until I can find some way to defeat her.

Sorrow rises in my throat, choking me. I part my mouth to take a breath, and my teeth chatter loudly in the stillness.

The guard beside me shifts, and I flinch away. He sweeps his cloak off his back and motions to me. "Lean forward." His voice is soft and invites my trust. Still, I hesitate before obeying.

He swings the cloak over me, and the fur inside, warmed by his body, immediately begins to warm mine. Before I lean back, the guard tugs the hood up over my bald head; a tingle runs down my spine.

The guard across from me scoffs and rolls his eyes. "Why would you bother with such a thing?"

"If we deliver her frozen, you think we'll be paid?" he snaps at the other guard as he sits back down.

The other guard frowns then shrugs and mutters something to the man beside him.

The kind guard, the one with the blue eyes who helped me up the stairs and now has wrapped me in his cloak, falls silent, his challenge won. The horses crunch down the snow-covered street, leading us farther from the castle and into the center of town. I cannot help it, but with every foot we travel from the castle, my heart lightens. Could I be going to someplace worse? It's possible. Hard to imagine, but possible.

I glance at the kind guard, who looks smaller and more vulnerable without his cloak. He stares resolutely ahead, ignoring me once again. Probably safer that way—for both of us.

I still shudder under my muslin dress, but the fur is warming me. I long for something hot to drink—even just water—something that might begin thawing my innards.

Twisted trees in perpetual winter arc over the snow-packed road we follow, dripping with fresh snow we must have gotten over the past few days while I was imprisoned. Always gaining snow that never melts and never seems to increase. A strange curse for the country. A deadly one.

We have several miles to travel to reach the town square, and with a quick glance at the guard beside me, I wonder if he will grow cold. He relaxes with his feet outstretched though, his gloved fingers twisted together in his lap, apparently unbothered.

As a breeze swirls around us, blowing snow off the trees and around our heads and shoulders, I tug the edges of the cloak tighter around my throat with shaking fingers. The minutes tick by, the two guards across from me chatting and laughing about something in low voices. My thoughts batter me in the oppressive almost-silence.

"Where am I going?" I finally whisper to the kind guard.

His eyelashes twitch; otherwise, he shows no indication of having heard me. "The sales block," he mutters out of the side of his mouth.

My eyes widen. "For slaves?"

His chin dips toward his chest while I sink back against the wood of the sleigh in shock.

She's selling me into slavery.

That realization does what the cold has been unable to do: make me numb.

The remaining miles pass in a blur of ice, wind, cottages, frostbitten children, stoic peasants, snow, and silence. Something in me burns, a dim memory of anger or maybe power. There is a spot in my chest that pounds like a heartbeat, only it's not my heart. It's something else, something that burns and thumps with a life of its own.

When we arrive at the square, a crowd has already gathered. Dozens of other sleighs creak as their occupants step down, mostly young women and men around my age. Some look sickly, others strong, but all are clad in simple, straight garments as they huddle underneath fur or wool blankets. Most huddled clumps of people are clad as I am, in thin, white gowns that peek out in flashes from underneath their blankets as one person shifts for a better position.

There is a group of females, some younger than I, huddled under the same dark gray blankets but with flashes of red peeking out from amongst their legs. These are the Reds, the women being sold as whores.

A young, blond girl dressed in crimson gazes vacantly at our arriving sleigh. She looks no older than twelve. I cannot contain my shudder, and I praise the gods that I am dressed in white underneath this cloak. It should save me from the abuses those girls are about to suffer. Abuses I cannot begin to imagine. She is one of the few Reds that looks like a Canensian. Most of them have darker hair and darker eyes, their appearance slightly more exotic than the rest of us. Some of the Reds are draped in a white sash across their hips, and by the lustful looks they receive, and the fear upon the girls' faces, I gather they are the undefiled. My stomach dips, sending bile up my throat.

I've never given much thought to slavery. When I saw slaves before, I had been young and it had been the way the world was. And when I got older, Blanche made sure I didn't have much contact with anyone else. I hadn't known how young slaves could be. How young the Reds could be. I hadn't known.

Our sleigh stutters to a stop with snorts of the horses pulling it, jerking me back to the moment.

The two guards across from me jump up and out of the sleigh before I can move, and the kind guard follows slower. As the kind guard jumps down onto the icy square, the other guard fingers his whip as if he wishes to use it on either his compatriot or me. Perhaps both. Their hatred for the kind guard is barely concealed.

As the kind guard offers me his hand to help me down, the whip guard glares icicles at me. I hesitate before I take it, but in the end, I do. When my bare feet touch the ground, I slip, falling into his chest. I blink down at my feet in confusion. Was I not given shoes? How strange that I did not notice until now. And yet now it sets me apart from the rest of the slaves, who all wear practical, sturdy, fur-lined leather boots.

"I'm sorry. I have to take the cloak now," the kind, blue-eyed guard says.

Without a murmur of protest, I unclasp the cloak from my throat and slip it off.

"Here." He glances around, then snatches a pair of boots from a nearby sleigh and sets them at my feet. Once I step my feet into them, he gives an approving nod then says, "This way." He has already swept his cloak back around his shoulders, and he points to a path between people into the midst of the square, which the captain shoves a route through. I follow, tripping every other step as the guards flank me up to the raised, wooden platform, where I join the other slaves waiting with their current owners.

Those in white are labeled as basic servants, while those in purple are sold as trained housemaids or chefs, and a few even wear green to demonstrate their skill as gardeners—those are for the elite who can afford to keep their own growing house. Another group of worn-down men and a few women—all no older than their mid-twenties—are dressed in charcoal, some with chains looped around their ankles so they can't run. Prisoners. Intended most likely for manual labor, unlikely to endure their slavery long.

But it's those in red that make me shudder. I watch a particularly defiant-looking girl who looks about sixteen be auctioned off to a tall, blond man dressed in fur-lined silk, who pays a decent sum for her. Across her thighs, where her arms hang, the white fabric bears several blackish marks. I recognize them as coming from dirty chains. She won't be an easy conquest. I transfer my gaze to her face, and a smile tugs at my lips. Anger glints like the brightest stars in the night sky in her dark eyes, confirming my suspicion. Despite her expression, her pretty face draws in a dozen different glares, and she meets every gaze upon her with unadulterated hatred. I can only pray to the gods that she finds her escape. One way or another.

Hopelessness rising in me, I tear my gaze away from her youth and beauty. How can the Crown allow this to happen? The history of Canens slavery goes back seventy-five years, to my great-great-grandfather's rule. And yet, I cannot agree with it, not when I look at such hopelessness before me. Not when I, myself, am being sold into this life. My stomach clenches, and I have to swallow back bile.

A handful of bedraggled children dash through us as we wait to be auctioned, dodging in and out of the crowd, probably picking pockets. If I had the freedom to live in the town and not the means to survive, I would do the same.

The bidders in the square are mostly peasants clad practically in wool, here to buy help on their homes or in their growing houses. Perhaps searching for a relative to rescue.

Unable to keep watching innocent people being sold like animals, I turn to the crowd. A dirty child that dodged past us a minute ago lingers too long at a nobleman's pocket, ending without any reward except that of his wrist being captured by a jeweled hand. A shiver races down my spine in cold fear for the child. I step toward him.

"Don't even think it, girl," the whip guard says, bending down so that his lips nearly brush my cheek.

I stiffen, refusing to give an inch, and meet his cold black eyes. The child manages to yank himself free and dashes off into the crowd, ignoring the nobleman yelling behind him.

"Give me any trouble, and *that*—" the guard jerks his chin at a couple of young girls dressed in red muslin dresses with white sashes, "—could be you," he finishes with a leer.

Like my white dress, their red ones fail to deliver any sense of modesty. Rather, these girls seem draped in shame. By the way the men in the audience can't stop staring, it's no wonder.

Although I don't believe his bluff, my stomach still churns so that I think I'm going to be sick.

The whip guard laughs and turns to his comrade.

Alongside the street, shopkeepers have set up tables to peddle their goods, but it seems the main event is almost at hand, and attention is diverted to the stage, where a group of five chained men in black wait with several guards nearby. The brothers I tried to rescue. My heart clenches.

The kind guard sees me watching them.

"Who will buy them?" I whisper.

He shrugs. "Stables, blacksmiths, whoever has coin. Don't worry. They're strong. They'll survive. Perhaps even work off their debts to the Crown."

I give a scoff to prevent my tears from falling, unable to stop staring at them from across the plaza. Only one of them, Caleb, finds my gaze. His eyes crinkle around the edges, but there is no other hint of recognition. Even my attempt to help someone else has failed. I cast my eyes to the floor and resign myself to waiting for the auction to begin.

In only a few minutes, my waiting is over.

One by one, the slaves for sale are paraded across the platform, their muslin tunics and gowns depicting their future place, the brands or tattoos on their necks labeling them as either indebted temporarily or forever.

"Why am I not dressed in black?" I ask the kind-eyed guard as I await my turn on the platform.

The whip guard overhears my question and again leans over to me, this time raising a gloved hand to brush a finger against my cheek. "Because you're worth more in white." His gaze rakes over me, more offensive than his touch as it takes in the thin, muslin gown and every bony prominence underneath it. "Too bad your hair is gone—it probably would fetch you an even higher price." His gaze shifts down my body again.

Struggling to suppress a shiver, I raise my chin again. "Is that why you've refrained from whipping me?"

He blinks in surprise at my challenge, but his eyes quickly narrow, and he grabs my elbow and clenches it. "Think you're smart, eh? Yeah, all right. We got orders not to mar your pretty face." A number is called, and he jerks his chin at the platform. "That's you, sweetheart."

My knees tremble under me, but I wrench my arm free and march up to the stairs by myself. I don't know what she thinks to gain by selling me, but I intend to meet it with all the grace and pride I have left.

Which, I admit as the auctioneer pushes me to the center of the stage and begins the bidding at the lowest price yet, is surprisingly little.

Part 2

THE SLAVE

I

Seen

RUS

As we travel toward the snowy north, my thoughts travel back to the scene we left. I can't help but feel a bit like I've abandoned the gypsy children, leaving them to their own devices. But we had no other choice.

It had taken several minutes to coax the children out from their hiding places, but we finally convinced them we meant no harm. By the time we resumed our journey, we had spent two precious hours attempting to help them.

It wasn't until I helped find rocks to cover their dead that they realized I meant what I said.

"If you return to Heia on the path you took, the palace will give you sanctuary," I told the eldest child, a boy of only twelve. His face, peering at me with mistrust, dry tracks of tears on his cheeks, reminded me so much of the grief Elaina must be feeling that I had to steel myself against despair. "Give them this." I passed him a ring from my small finger. Ornate and made of gold, it appeared expensive but really wasn't worth much to me—either sentimentally or financially. But to this boy, now trying to provide for five other children younger than him, it would be life. "Or, if you must sell it on the way there, then do not accept less than ten gold florins. It is equal to that in weight. Let no man tell you differently."

His eyes wide and locked on the ring in my outstretched hand, he nodded, his chin trembling.

I took his hand and fit the ring on his thumb. It just fit, barely being kept on by the joint. "Now, if you travel back on this road and see a retinue of guards, ask for Captain Praeter. Tell him that I sent you and show him this ring. He will take care of you and take you to the palace, where you will receive sanctuary."

The boy met my eyes with narrowed ones of his own, then they flicked over my shoulder to the mounds of rocks. The sun was breaking over the distant hills, and it illuminated the growing hatred on his face.

I sighed and gripped his shoulder. "I am sorry. Please understand, this is an act of mercy for you."

He snorted.

"It will not be an easy life for you, no matter which direction you choose. You may stay in Heia as long as you wish under sanctuary. We will not hold you there, should you choose to go."

His smooth jaw flexed.

"We'll go, sir," piped up a young girl about six years old. "We have nowhere else to go."

"Shh," an older girl, about eight, said. "Don't talk to him."

My gaze lingered on them. As I had spoken with the children, Cito had gone through and taken anything of value from the bodies. Now, he approached and said, "We're ready, sir."

I nodded heavily. "I wish you good luck, children."

"Annabelle," said the six-year-old stubbornly. "My name is Annabelle."

Her words drew a smile to my lips. I crouched down, staying still when the older girl drew the younger back. But the younger ripped free and stepped forward to stand before me, a mere six inches from my grasp.

She peered into my face, seeming to read the weariness that went bone-deep inside me. Then something like a cloud came over her face, and her breathing shallowed. Her eyes half closed; she looked as though she might faint. Before I could reach for her, the older girl gripped her from behind, holding her up but not taking her away. The six-year-old spoke, her voice dreamy. "You will find what you seek. It will not be easy; it will not be simple. But find them, you shall. You will save the kingdoms, you will be thanked for generations and rewarded handsomely. You will bring peace to the Seven King-doms, peace that has not been seen since the division."

My breathing hitched in my chest.

The little girl blinked and shook her head. "I'm sorry." Her voice had returned to normal, and a tired smile lifted her lips. "I am sorry. That doesn't often happen."

The older girl stared at the younger girl with her mouth shut tight.

"What just happened?" Cito asked.

This time, the eight-year-old answered. "Annabelle is a Seer." She looked to me with stiff admiration. "And she's Seen your future."

Frowning, I rocked back onto my heels. "My future?"

"You are a king," Annabelle said, smiling happily.

"Well, sort of. Yes." I ran a hand through my curls. "I haven't been officially crowned, but yes, I'll be a king."

She nodded. "You are a good king. Your people love you." Her face grew distant again. "But do not take too long to return to your people. Your throne will not wait forever."

I laughed at that. "My throne is my inheritance, little Annabelle. Its duty is to wait upon me."

With a sad little smile, she shook her head. "Already, plots move against you."

I stood, trying to ignore the staring children. "Well, there are always those who envy a king. But few have the means to become a threat." I cleared my throat. "Children, my advisor and I must go. But heed my instructions, and you shall find safety."

Cito and I packed our horses up, taking as much of the food as we could from the gypsies' stock, leaving the children with as much as they would need, and took one of their extra horses with us as a packhorse. The horses we didn't need, we left with the children, instructing them to sell them if necessary. And then we backtracked to find the path of the slave buyers, the path we now follow.

"Sir," says Cito softly. When I turn, he nods his chin in front of us.

Looming ahead, just past the forested path we follow, are the white mountains of Canens.

II

Desire

WINTERBERRY

I n the end, I am purchased for a modest price by the same narrow, wolfish-looking man who bought Caleb. He also bought a group of men in white and one of the red-clad girls, the young one I'd seen earlier with the vacant expression. We are the only two females in a dozen men.

"Get up there," someone barks at us from behind, shoving us away from the auction blocks.

I glance across the square behind me, but the sleigh that carried me here is already gliding up back to the castle. My gaze lingers on them, and as it does, the kind guard turns to me. Something in his gaze calls to me, makes me watch until my new owner's guard pushes me in the back, hurrying me along toward my new cage. All I have done is exchange one cage for another.

In my distraction, I hardly feel the bite of metal shackles as they encircle one of my legs and one of my arms to the petite girl beside me, making it impossible to run.

When I look for the sleigh again, it's gone.

My gaze shifts back to the wolfish owner as he surveys his new belongings. What kind of man needs so many different kinds of slaves?

As I muse, I follow the others blindly. At the iron door, the giant brother turns back, holds out an arm, and motions the females in first, silencing any protests with his implacable calm. When I open my mouth to speak, he shakes his head urgently but discreetly and glances at the wolfish man as if to say, "Don't let on that we know each other." I dip my head in a silent, subtle nod.

The guard hurries us into our prison, and the young girl claims the seat farthest from the door. Before one of the men who ogle her can push past me, I take the seat next to her. The least I can offer her is some physical distance from the men; she will be abused soon enough.

Before we leave, one of the new guards throws a pile of blankets and an assortment of hats, mittens, coats, and stockings in at us.

The men tear at the pile for blankets. I grab for a couple cloaks, but a tall man in black jerks them from my hands. Grunting, I snatch for a thick one with fur, but a second man already has it in his fists, and I don't bother to continue the fight. In the end, all I'm left with are three rolls of socks and one hat. My ears are already burning with the cold, my body shivering uncontrollably.

The warm glow inside me, the anger that kept me warm, has faded into a chill I cannot control. And now, I have nothing to trade with these men for warmth. Nothing but my body itself. Shattering that thought so that it can never return, I instead unroll the socks and offer a pair to the girl.

She doesn't react.

I frown. "Don't you want these? Aren't you cold?"

Still, the girl doesn't act as if she's heard or even sees me.

Without waiting any longer for an answer, I kneel and pull off her boots then pull the socks onto her feet as if she's a child. I thread them between the shackle and her flesh and tug them as high up as I can manage, while trying to avoid giving any of the men a glimpse of her legs in order to save her whatever dignity possible. I replace her boots and, with frozen fingers, tie them snugly, glancing up at her immobile face as I do.

Her red robes mark her as one to take advantage of, especially in this comatose state. It doesn't matter that we're all slaves here; I know there will be a hierarchy within our group, and neither of us can afford to be on the bottom.

On her hands and arms, I repeat the process, putting on another pair of the stockings, drawing them up to her elbows, over the thin muslin. Our breaths mingle in the air, hers thin and transparent, mine heavy and opaque, as I draw our only hat, made from what looks like a black wolf hide, over her head and down over her ears. My own ears tingle in something like regret.

Debating for a moment, ignoring the half dozen stares on me as I reclaim my seat beside the girl, I pull the last pair of socks over my hands and arms, tuck my legs up under my gown, and tighten it around myself, hugging my legs to my chest and shivering. I may not make it to our destination. Wherever that is. Not unless it's blessedly near.

From across the cell, the giant brother thrusts a bundle of material at us. "Here," he says gruffly.

For a moment, I gape at him in disbelief. Then, with a slight nod he doesn't acknowledge, I accept the bundle. It's a large, wool blanket with another hat and pair of fur-lined stockings tucked inside. My heart squeezes in relief. Thank the gods.

Without hesitating, I pull the stockings on my feet, not even caring that I flash the men more skin than is decent, and throw the blanket over the girl's legs, tucking the other side between her and the slats. I slide close enough so our legs and sides touch and wrap the blanket tight around us both. Perhaps with our combined body heat, we can make it through whatever faces us. Caleb watches me do all of this but neither offers to help nor speaks. I grit my teeth, frustrated by his observational indifference.

The girl stares blankly ahead as though she is moving through a private world of fog and mist. I want join her, I want to ignore the dangers and pretend they don't exist, although if I do, who will protect either of us in this barren land of ice?

The slaves and I settle into an uneasy rest as we sit in our prison and watch the streets of Merise travel by. The occasional child or peasant stares at us, but most avert their eyes, as if simply looking our way might cause them to be enslaved too. Most of the people we pass on the outskirts of town are not that far from slaves themselves. Half appear starving, their clothes little more than rags hanging off their thin, frozen frames. The other half keep their heads down and trudge along with the results of their hunts, purchases from the shops, or bundles of wood pulled in a sled behind them, hoping to stay alive by staying warm.

But they all have one thing in common: each one of them wears the cloak of defeat. The bundles of sticks are too small to heat their homes for long, the food too little to feed their families past tonight, the purchases too expensive to buy what they truly need.

I am half relieved to exit through the main city gate, leaving the tortured existence of the Merise poor behind. A gust of wind sweeps along the stone walls, and I anchor myself against the girl's cold body and long for the trip to pass quickly.

From my vantage point, I glance ahead at the driver and glimpse fog between him and my new owner. It brings gall to my throat to even think the word. Owner. I am property. My blood boils but fails to warm me.

As we travel, thick fog settles around the sleigh and the reindeer pulling it, concealing us, slowing our progress, and keeping us on edge. Nearby, but almost invisible in the mist, the guards ride thick-boned, hairy horses that are covered in frost and icicles before long. The other slaves rustle around me, frequently popping up to jog in place so they might stay warm. In unspoken agreement, some of them have shared blankets as I do with the girl, desperation bringing them closer than they might otherwise do.

We slip through the fog in an uneasy whisper, only the guard's horses giving occasional snorts, the men muttering, and the girl unmoving beside me. Even when someone speaks, it's in a whisper, and I cannot focus on it. All I can think is: I cannot stay in this life. What power will I have as a slave? As a slave, I must watch this girl become a whore, as I become whatever my new owner wants for me. How can I save her? I won't even be able to save myself.

Under the blanket, I reach for her stocking-covered hands, bundled together in her lap. She flinches at the touch but doesn't pull back or otherwise look at me. I take them in mine and check their warmth. She is still ice.

"What's your name?" I ask her softly.

At first, she doesn't respond. Then a small wrinkle appears on her forehead, as if her thoughts move at the pace of a glacier. She blinks even more slowly, eyes fixed in the center of the sleigh for a long moment after I speak. Then her mouth moves.

"What?" I lean over, putting my ear almost to her mouth.

"Desire," she says in the barest breath.

I lean back, certain I heard her wrong. "Désirée?"

Her pale gaze latches onto mine, as icy as the fog that wraps its tentacles around us. Slowly, she shakes her head. "My owner named me Desire."

My mouth parts. So many things run through my head at her words, but what comes out is "I'll call you Désirée." I smile broadly at her. "Or Des. Which would you like?"

The corners of her mouth flicker faintly, and her brow furrows in consideration before she answers. "Des. It's short. Like me." Her voice is smooth, melodic, almost like that of a bird's, and her accent is strange, one I've not heard before.

"Don't worry. You'll grow up." I try to inject as much confidence for something I cannot control as I can into my voice in the hopes that she'll feel as secure as I can make her. Which, I admit to myself only, is little. "How old are you, Des?"

"Thirteen."

I wince at her answer. Thirteen? How can someone sell such a beautiful, *little* girl into whoredom? Opening my mouth to reply, her breathy, melodic voice sounds again.

"Wait...you didn't tell me your name." As if just this talking has exhausted her, she sits back against the railing.

I was hoping she wouldn't notice. For I have yet to come up with a name for myself. We were all sold without one, just a number corresponding to our tattoos or brands for record keeping. I doubt the owner will care how we introduce ourselves, as there is no way to prove my name true, but I have no wish for him to discover it either. From across the jail, I feel the weight of Caleb's stare upon me.

Speaking the first name that comes into my mind, I say my mother's name: "Helena."

I find Caleb in the dimming light, but his expression is inscrutable. If I had not seen him in prison with his brothers, I would be made uneasy by his attentiveness. I'm not sure why I'm not now, except he must care something for me to give me such a chance at escape while sacrificing his own chance. I chew on my lip, uneasy with his reminder of my failed escape. How did I even get out of the cell? What was that light? Magic? A faery? Did I dream the entire thing?

"Would you tell me a story, Helena?" Des whispers. "About Canens?"

"A story?" My thoughts go blank, but at the hopeful glint in her eyes, I can't deny her. "I—I don't know—"

"Yes," says Caleb in his gravelly, deep voice. "We could all use a story, couldn't we, men?"

A chorus of nods and "yeses" echo around me, and a dozen sets of eyes now focus on me as I try to determine which tale I might tell. And so I settle on the most familiar to me, the one that I, being the princess of Canens, grew up listening to nearly every night before bed.

"Many moons ago," I begin.

III

A Faery Tale

THE ORIGINS OF CANENS

Many moons ago, when the land lay lush and untouched, and the sun was carried across the sky by the sibling gods, a family of explorers made their way north to what would become Canens. It was an arduous trek from their home, and many died along the way, but those that persisted were rewarded with the green grass foretold in fables and mountains that made the rest of the country look like hills.

The travelers found a peaceful glen to settle upon and soon began building a home. Before the next generation of children were grown, others had followed them, and a village grew up around them.

One of the children of the founding family was a girl, who grew up healthy and strong from grains and fruits grown by her own family's hands. And yet despite having everything she needed, she longed for adventure and riches. So one day, she went out exploring and began to climb the nearby mountain. It was hot and miserable, and the little girl had never enjoyed hot weather.

Only a little ways up, she came upon a hole in the mountain that breathed chilled air. And, being the curious little girl that she was, she decided to go in. It was very dark, but she had brought a torch with her, and it lit the way.

The cave snaked around, going deep into the side of the mountain. She considered going back, but she was too curious, and so she went on and on and soon became hopelessly lost. But deep in the cave, lights began to glint all around her. To her great surprise, jewels caught the light and threw it back at her.

This discovery could not make her feel better, for even with all the jewels in the world, she could not find her way out of the mountain cave. And finally, she sat down and began to cry. Tears shimmering like those jewels wound their way down her cheeks, and she could not stop them.

She sat there for quite some time, until her torch began to burn out. The thought of being trapped in this cave until she died was so awful that she couldn't stop crying, and soon she was in complete darkness.

It was then that a light illuminated the cave. The little girl looked at her torch, expecting it to be relit. Instead she found a ball of bright light hovering in the air a few feet away from her. At first, she was frightened, but then she heard a voice.

"Don't be afraid, little one," said the voice. "I come to rescue you."

"Rescue? But who are you?" she asked.

Then the light spun through the air and turned into a beautiful woman in a silver dress.

"I am a faery," the beautiful woman said.

The little girl gaped at the woman, amazed at her presence at this, the darkest moment in her life. "A faery? What is that?"

The woman laughed. "I am a magical person."

At this, the little girl recoiled. "A witch?"

"No." The woman smiled. "A faery is different from a witch. Faeries are born with magic, but witches must sell a part of themselves in order to gain their magic." She frowned gravely. "Faeries, some of the dark ones, will sometimes sell their magic for a price. A heavy price, for they will always ask for that which they value most."

"How do I know all this is true? My mother told me not to trust strangers."

"And she is right." The faery smiled kindly. Then she waved a delicate stick in her hand over her palm, and a beautiful orchid made from ice blossomed where there had been nothing. The girl gasped and reached for the flower.

"Careful!" The orchid disappeared with a flutter of the faery's fingers. "When you touch magic without permission, horrible things can happen."

The little girl recoiled. "I don't want magic. I only want to go home." She wrung her hands and glanced around them. "You said you came to rescue me?"

"Yes, I have."

"Which way do I go then? To go home?"

"Just a moment, my dear. You must do something for me first."

Sudden memories of stories the little girl had been told by her grandfather returned to her, about how magical beings never gave away their help, for it often required magic, and magic always cost someone something.

The little girl became very afraid. Because in those tales, the hero or heroine always had to accomplish impossible tasks. And so she again began to cry, convinced that she would never get home.

She thought of her mother and father and her sisters and brothers, for she came from a very big family. And she felt certain she would never see them again. But the only way to get back home would be to try to do what the faery asked.

"What must I do?" the little girl finally asked.

"Deep in the heart of the mountain lives a dragon. He controls the clouds and the sun, and he keeps winter at bay."

The little girl frowned, for she was intelligent as well as curious. "And if I defeat him, it will become winter all the time then?"

The faery frowns. "Well, yes, my dear, should you defeat him, the land will become cursed, for he is a protector of this land."

"So what must I do?"

"If you bring him a golden gift, winter will come when it is supposed to. Every season has its proper time, but when the dragon has been neglected, he keeps winter from arriving in his wrath and will turn this lush land into a desert."

At this, the little girl nodded, but something else occurred to her. "But what if he should eat me? I have nothing to bring him."

The faery smiled at her childish question and said, "Do not fear, for I shall equip you." The faery took her wand and produced an intricately engraved golden ring.

The little girl's eyes went wide at this, for she loved gold and envied riches.

"Dragons love wealth, and this will help you to defeat him. When all else fails, give this ring to the dragon, and you will accomplish your task. But take care that you do not remove any of his treasures from this cave, or else you and this land shall be cursed."

Properly warned, the little girl took the ring and went on her way. No longer was the tunnel chilled, but instead it began to grow hot, and soon she took off her cloak as sweat poured down her body. She knew she was close to the dragon now, and so she walked carefully.

A rumble filled the cave, like a giant sniffing the air. Then a voice growled, "Who disturbs my peace?"

The little girl froze, but, thinking about the gold ring the faery had given her, she gathered her courage and advanced into a large cave. In the middle, the bronze-colored dragon stood on four clawed feet larger than her head, and his long tail curled out of sight around a pile of multi-colored riches.

"Who are ye that disturbs my peace?" the dragon growled at her in a voice like the very fire he breathed. "Ye are a mere snack for me to break my fast upon."

The little girl quivered in fear but stood her ground. "Please don't hurt me. I'm just trying to find my way home."

The dragon roared in answer, filling the cave with acrid smoke. "What is it ye seek?"

She coughed at the smoke. "I told you, I want to go home. Will you tell me the way home?"

"Such information carries a price. What can ye pay?"

The little girl thought of the ring in her pocket, which the faery had given her to save her. But at the thought of the golden band, she became reluctant to part with it. She had never seen anything so beautiful as that engraved golden band, and she couldn't bear to give it to a dragon with so many riches around him.

"Nothing. I have nothing for you."

"Then what cause have I to let ye go?"

"I—"

Try as she might, she could not invent a reason for him to do so. And so he opened his mouth to scorch her with his flames.

"Wait! I have a present for you!" The words ripped from her mouth, desperate and pleading.

Her words stilled his fire, and she pulled the ring from her pocket where she had placed it, keeping it hidden within curled fingers.

"Gold?" the dragon asked, intrigued.

"Yes. Finest faery gold," she invented.

"Faery gold?" His black eyes alit with pleasure and desire before he could snuff it out and ask, "And what must I give for this gold?"

"Just... We want winter to return to this country."

He laughed, fire curling at his lips and smoke twisting from his nose. "Ye speak like a fool. Cold, wet, ugly...winter is not for the faint of heart."

The little girl shuddered, for she did not know that winter could also be beautiful, crisp, and refreshing. Yet, she knew that all the land wanted winter's return and that the faery had told her to do this, and so she pressed forward. "It is what all the people want—people who have experienced winter before want it too."

"Nay. They know not what they want." But the dragon did not seem interested in keeping her decision pure; instead, he was craning his neck around to see the gold that the little girl still hid from his prying eyes. "Show the gold to me."

"Do we have an agreement?" she asked. "You will leave and find another cave if you approve of this golden gift?"

He sighed, a little puff of smoke shooting out from his nostrils and rising into the air between them. "An agreement will be made when I hold the gold."

She frowned and clenched the ring tighter, for that was not the proper agreement.

"Reveal the gold or be scorched," he growled.

Quivering, the girl uncurled her fingers and held out the ring between them. "You can look—but do not touch."

At the sight, his eyes narrowed at the item then grew wide in greed and desire before he could feign disinterest. She could see that he longed for the little golden ring to call his own, to add to his hoard.

"I shall not bring back winter for that small, golden ring, but I shall spare your life."

"No," she protested, closing her fist around the precious gold. That was not enough. She could not return to her people with only her life.

"Deliver it to me." Each step the dragon took made the cave and its contents tremble in fear.

The girl stumbled backward as he advanced, and as she did, she tripped over a golden crown. The ring flew from her fingers.

Before it could fall to the ground, the dragon swooped it up with an arched, brown talon. His mouth gaping in something like a smoky dragon smile, he fitted the ring securely onto his finger.

At the same time the little girl realized her mission had failed, the dragon's expression began to change. Whereas it had been elated, now his eyes began to narrow. He peered at the ring with one eye and gave a hiss of displeasure. A panicked cry left his mouth as he and the little girl watched frost begin to creep out from the point where the magical ring touched him. It encompassed his claws, then forearm, then shoulder, and spread throughout his body until he stood as if a statue, his features frozen in fury.

And the words the faery had spoken to her came back now: "When you touch magic without permission, horrible things can happen."

With the dragon defeated, the little girl rose and brushed herself off. She walked around him, but he showed no sign of moving. She did not know the way out, although she thought it was past the dragon's hoard and out through the opposing tunnel. Yet the piles of jewels were too much for her to leave in place. Although she knew the location and could return here, she lined her pockets with the gems and jewels and treasures the dragon had collected over the centuries.

Long before she found the exit to the tunnel, the little girl felt the chilled air greet her. Thinking she had completed her task successfully, and now with riches to her name, the little girl emerged from the tunnel, having forgotten the faery's warning to not remove any of the dragon's riches from the tunnel. As soon as she emerged, the air swirled around her and the sun hid behind the mountain. Then a smoky light burned before her.

The faery appeared, dripping with majesty, before the little girl. "How dare you? You have stolen from the Fae."

"Stolen? No, I—"

"Because of your thievery, you have thrown your country into despair. You have destroyed the dragon keeping winter at bay, and so winter will never leave you now."

The faery swept her wand through the air, and the tunnel closed behind the little girl, never again to reopen. And so the little girl returned to her people in shame, for she had brought the curse of eternal winter down upon them.

IV

Prophecies

BLANCHE

Sweeping my cloak off my shoulders, I enter the stuffy air of the tunnel leading to the underground scholar's library, all the while fighting to ignore the headache pressing at my temples and threatening to cave in my skull. I overtaxed myself two days prior while secretly recasting the spells upon the growing houses in Merise, and despite an entire day's rest in bed, my head still pounds.

A light glints at the end of the tunnel, and I wince in growing irritation at even that pinprick.

The scholar caves are dark. Why does it already seem too bright?

Gritting my teeth, I press onward and round a curve in the short tunnel leading to the cavernous library the scholars created underneath the palace three hundred years before—before the Curse and its eternal chill made this little more than an icebox.

Pausing at the entrance, I try to hide my discomfort at the light after the tunnel's black relief.

The scholar's cave is lit by a dozen lamps on a dozen tables as well as sconces on the wall, each carefully spaced away from the shelves of books and parchment lining the walls and standing in the midst of

CHAPTER IV

the room. Bent over each desk is a man, some young and some old, each looking as pasty as the pages they study.

I survey them, my mind still half focused on the inspection of the growing houses. I am quite happy with the crops this year. The four houses are filled with a mixture of highly productive fruits, vegetables, and grains. This year, all of Merise will feast at harvest time, with some excess left over for the storage houses.

For once, we won't have to try and finagle food trades with Ostium. We can be self-sufficient, something the Canens people can be proud of. It's only too bad that it requires such magical effort from me. If only there were another way to increase the length of the spells or make it so I only had to cast it once. Or perhaps I could appoint a sorcerer or sorceress to cast the spells for me—in secret, of course.

It was only my husband's father's final edict that had sent the magic wielders into hiding, increasing the people's fear of magic and making those who embraced it outcasts. He had blamed them for the Canens Curse and thus further committed them to the cursed path they were on. The ignorant fools, thinking magic is to be feared and not embraced! Thinking that we should not fight magic with magic. My husband never listened...fearing it just like his father did.

Stepping forward, I straighten my shoulders, allowing the thoughts to roll off my back like arrows off a shield.

At the sound of my heels on the stone floor, one of the men looks up. He sucks in a sharp breath, the studious stupor sliding from his frame as he bolts to his feet only to stumble to the ground in a kneeling bow.

Several of the other scholars gawk at him until they lift their gazes to me, then they follow suit in hasty bows and murmurs of "Your Majesty" and "My Queen" until each of the men kneels beside their desks.

"You may rise," I say graciously, eyeing the eldest of the scholars who took a full minute to bend his joints into a suitable bow. I wait until even he has risen to his feet, so slowly and with such popping of joints that even the other men glance surreptitiously at him.

"How can we help you, Your Majesty?" a scholar with a gray beard down to his belly asks as he steps forward from the crowd of desks.

"I come to see how you progress with your tasks."

"Ah. Yes. Perhaps we can speak over here so as to not interrupt the others' work?" The man, perhaps in his forties, has a stoic confidence that reminds me of a temple priest. He neither shies from me nor cowers to me, and yet he shows the proper amount of deference.

I hesitate only slightly before nodding and following him over to an area surrounded on three sides by wooden shelves of books and rolled parchments that reach to the ceiling. Upon the table lies a parchment with notes upon it and a quill sitting next to a closed bottle of ink.

"If Your Majesty would like to sit," he says, motioning to a wooden chair.

I straighten. "No. I would not. I want to hear how the tasks are progressing, scholar."

His voluminous eyebrow twitches. "It's Nosco, Your Majesty." He clears his throat at my disdainfully answering look. "And it progresses slowly."

"So you have nothing?" I demand icily.

"I believe we have made advancements in where to begin with one of the important prophecies, Your Majesty."

"And which one is that?"

"The prophecy first given concerning this matter. As you know, that has governed our country for many years, made our prior great king suggest that whoever killed a Canens heir will die—"

I tap my toes upon the ground.

He clears his throat at my impatience. "I speak of course of the prophecy that states 'Out of the wilderness comes double the heirs, sister against sister, brother against brother. A curse of their own will be light to the dark and mercy to the merciless. Winter will bring its own end; she cannot be stopped. The sword that fells winter brings—'"

"'Death.' I <u>know</u> what it says," I interrupt him before he can build into a history lesson. With great effort, I try to inject patience into my words but find it difficult with the pounding of my head and the incompetence of my own scholars. "But what have you discovered about it? Is it accurate? Or is it rumor?"

He clears his throat and begins anew. "If you'll excuse me, Majesty, this is a prophecy that we scholars have concerned ourselves with for several generations. My own great-grandfather—"

"Yes, well, I'm not concerned with the past except how it relates to the present," I snap. "Get to the point."

His lips twist in disapproval, but he doesn't cower before me like the others would. I cannot decide if I admire or detest him for it.

"We believe it to be a true prophecy. We have found another manuscript that reads: 'When the country turns to ice, unrest will grow within the northern country, and the sword which fells the winter's curse fells also the sword-bearer. Only through a queen's death will the curse fall. Yet the throne shall endure through the ages, replacing a king for a queen. When two queens vie for the throne, death will come to whoever kills the true queen; a country will be left without a ruler. A fae gift, given in secret, will manifest, and the bearer of the gift will challenge the queen. Then shall the throne endure rest and the country prosperity.'" At the end of his recitation, he releases a long breath in a cloud of foul-smelling air.

I blink at him. "Why have I never heard that before?"

Clearing his throat, he steps over to a book lying upon the table. "This passage is from the holy texts, Your Majesty. You have—" He breaks off and glances at me. "It has not been a book approved for this study until your recent orders."

I scoff. "The holy texts? I didn't authorize that."

"Yes, Majesty. You said to consider any source we had concerning the prophecies." His lips turn down at the edges, wrinkles forming on his forehead as his face scrunches together in his disapproval.

I nearly chuckle. This man would never survive in my court; he'd be assassinated within a fortnight.

"The holy texts, as you know, are a wealth of history of Canens. Our origins, our people, even our history with the Fae are all presented in them—"

"Yes," I interrupt coolly. "As you said, I know."

He coughs lightly. "Of course, Majesty. Forgive a scholar his scholarliness. I had thought you were unacquainted with them, given your surprise at my quotation of the full prophecy."

At my inclined head and narrowed eyes, he clears his throat and continues. "But there is a mention of the prophetess, Hiemo, in them as well. And how important she is to Canens and what her prophecies—"

"Just out with it."

He bites his lip with rotting teeth. "We are convinced that Hiemo intended to say that if anyone were to kill the blood heir to the throne, that person would die. Immediately."

"So the rumors are true." I say this with finality.

"Yes, we believe so."

"Next time, just say that."

He bows his head. "Apologies, Majesty, I thought you would want the reasoning behind our thoughts."

I barely refrain from rolling my eyes. "Well, I have a new job for you, for which you can extend your researching abilities."

"Yes, Majesty?" He sounds almost eager.

"Examine the rest of that prophecy—especially the final part about the fae gift."

"The fae gift?"

"Yes. How are fae gifts received, when do they manifest, how can they be hidden, all of that sort of thing."

He frowns. "Majesty, I am a holy scholar, not a magic scholar."

"A scholar is a scholar. You know how to read, don't you?"

"Yes, but for this, I would need to find scholars familiar with magical texts and—"

"Then find them. And find out about that fae gift. The future of Canens could depend upon it—you read me the prophecy."

"I— Yes, Majesty. You are absolutely correct."

"Then find me some answers."

He dips his chin.

"You have one month to find me all the answers I seek. I want every cranny of that prophecy explained. What I plan must not be foiled by some lack of research by an inept scholar."

His eyes widen. "One month? Majesty, I have spent a lifetime—"

"I sincerely hope you do not intend to inform me that thirty days is not enough time to meet my demands?" My arched eyebrow pins him to the stone floor.

He stares at me. "Majesty, I have spent a lifetime studying these texts."

"Then you should be well versed."

"While I can promise to devote all my time and all the resources we have to finding the information you desire, I cannot guarantee an answer to all your questions in one month's time. There is too much to know."

"I expect you to find out all that is relevant. The prophecy has been made to protect the country, hasn't it?"

Stiffly, he bends his head in concession. "Yes, Majesty."

"Then the wisest men in the land should be able to interpret them for the safety of our country."

"Yes, that would seem true."

"One month. Or you pay with your life."

A stricken expression crosses his face, as though I have suggested murdering puppies and kittens to achieve what I want. "Yes, Majesty."

Despite my lazy reminder of my power, the effect is jarring upon the scholar. His muscles spasm as he folds into a bow before me. Without acknowledging him, I turn and sweep out of the cavernous library.

V

The Orb

RUS

"How do we get across the border?" Cito asks.

I shrug. "The same way we get across any, I suppose."

"You don't think the Curse will—" Cito breaks off, glancing around at the lush greenery, the blooming flowers, and the vibrant life on the Ostium landscape, then back toward the barren white mountains. "Can people cross the border and not die?"

"They must. Canensians have done so...although Ostiites don't welcome their enemies—just like Heians."

As a child, I had often heard of Canensians who had crossed the borders who were either publicly executed in the most gruesome way or torn apart by rabid crowds. Although Heia shared no border with the frozen land, a mangled body dressed in barbaric furs occasionally washed up in the river. Their entire land is shrouded in secrecy and mystery almost as thick as that of the walled Abbatian country bordering Heia to the north. With only Ostium as a trade neighbor, my father had worked tirelessly to maintain our relationship with the king. But the plague had set that relationship on edge; we couldn't invite the Ostiite people across the border until the outbreak ended. Just recently had the guard shacks been abandoned. But tensions were still high. Some Ostiites had even become thieves who preyed on Heians, leading to discussion of returning the guards to the border.

Like many, I'd been fascinated with all of the outlier countries as a child, but over time, my interest waned to be replaced with anger and mistrust. Abbatia was rumored to have enough wealth to boost all the Seven Kingdoms' economies, while Canens had once been full of gems and minerals that the other countries severely lacked, and Edormisco was a paradise filled with mortal danger. But it was Canens's supposed curse that had left Heia the most crippled, as Heia's adamas stores had long since been depleted. The closed borders had forced Heians to use lesser gems for tipping their tools or else steal adamas from priceless sets of jewelry to do so. There had even been theft attempts on the Heian crown jewels, resulting in a dozen men, including one of my father's personal guards, being arrested.

"But is the border patrolled?" Cito asks, tugging me from my thoughts of our neighbors.

"You're the expert, Cito, you tell me."

He opens his mouth to answer when his horse halts abruptly and throws Cito forward into his neck. As Cito spits out a mouthful of mane, the horse absently scratches his cheek on his foreleg.

Smothering a grin, I turn away. He's got to be the most unskilled horseman in all of Heia. How did he ever find me? And why is he the one I'm stuck with?

Umbra snorts as if to agree with my thoughts. I absently pat his well-muscled neck. "First we have to get some supplies."

"Supplies?" Cito's voice wavers as he kicks his horse to catch up.

"Yes. We can't enter Canens without some decent winter clothes."

"Where are we supposed to find that? It's the height of summer here."

"Then some peasants might be willing to give us a good deal."

Half a day later, we come upon a small Ostium village nestled in a green valley. The Canens border is fifty miles away, and I hold little hope that, with all our delays, we'll find Elaina before we reach the border. Our arrival in the village is met with mistrust until I reveal a pouch of gold coins and ask to buy their winter clothing.

"You go to Canens?" an elderly man asks.

The crowds have thinned, and we are now the owners of fur-lined capes and trousers, thick wool tunics, and leather boots a size too large supplied with extra thick wool socks.

I consider him a moment before replying. "Yes."

He fingers the earflap of a beaver pelt hat. "These won't be enough."

"No?" I chuckle. "It's hard to imagine that."

He shakes his head. "You'll need blankets for your horses and blankets for you while you're riding. You'll need waterproof outer trousers, waterproof outer mittens, extra inner mittens for when yours get damp, and you'll need food that won't freeze. You'll need a lantern that can't freeze, and wood will be scarce. Predators are plenty—human and beast."

I blink.

"You have sleeping sacks? A tepik?" the old man asks, his whiskery brows arching as he looks up at me from under a flop of unruly white hair.

"A what? I—"

"You'll need at least two sacks, preferably a spare for each of you if you can manage it. They won't have time to dry out except overnight by the fire when you want them. And a tepik to sleep in. You have flints?"

"Yes," I say, thankful to at least have something we'll need.

"Axe? Pots? Snow boots? At least two weeks' supply of food?" He rattles off another dozen things we'll need, less than half of which we have. He motions us toward his shed, where he shows us a heap of slightly mouse-nibbled and cat-clawed equipment.

Cito wrinkles his nose in the direction of the shed, but as a calico winds her way around his legs, he glances down. His lips twitch and soften.

"These aren't meant for Canens's winters, but they'll keep you alive until you can make it to a village and trade for better ones. You're hard-pressed to find something better near here, the weather never turns bad enough."

I nod and run my hands over the thick wool. We'll need more than this? That's not encouraging.

We spend another fifteen minutes haggling over the prices of the items he says we'll need—something that I would spend more time on if every second we waste is not another foot Elaina could travel away from us.

I pull the straps on the packhorse tight. We should have brought another of the gypsy's horses. Ours is well laden now, but it reassures me to have protection from the elements for all five of us, man and beast. And enough for Elaina too—if we find her. When, not if. When.

"One more thing," the old man says.

I bite back a groan and face him. My moneybag is nearly empty, and there's no guarantee Elaina has even gone over the border yet.

"You'll like this. It could very well save your life." He pats me on the bicep and motions toward his house with his other arm. It's a crude shelter of brick, mud, and thatch, and we've spent most of our time with him out in his shed, where he stores his winter supplies.

"We really must be going," I say. What on earth does he have for us now?

Ignoring my protest, he shuffles toward the door. "Humor an old man."

"Sir," Cito says quietly, glancing at the sun slipping from the sky.

I nod at his reminder of our limited time. "What is it you have, sir?"

Without answering, he leads us into his house. It's a one-room building with his bed in the far corner of the dim interior. He goes directly there and pulls a small, dusty box out from underneath the frame.

"I grow old, and I won't likely make it through another winter. I have no children or grandchildren left to me; the plague took them all years back." A distant expression clouds his face. "But this, this I would hate to have wasted or thrown away."

Despite myself, I'm intrigued. "What is it?"

He opens the box, but from where I stand, I cannot see the contents. Seeing my interest, he brings it to the rickety table in the middle of his home. He bends and blows into the box. When the dust settles, I examine the teardrop-shaped, opaque glass orb nestled in the middle of a soft bed of silk.

"What is it?" Cito echoes from the man's other side.

"This, my friends, is a *lacteus orbis*." He cups it and lifts it from the box with gentle, wrinkled hands.

Cito and I exchange a frown. "A what?"

"A *lacteus orbis*."

I shake my head.

"No?" The man chuckles. "I thought all Heians knew their magical talismen, being neighbors with Edormisco."

I shift uncomfortably. "It's not a history we're comfortable with. Heians don't trust magic, as a general rule. I'm not certain I'm willing to embrace magic."

"Well, this magic could save your life." The man lets the glass talisman dangle from a thin chain he holds between his arthritic thumb and index fingers. "A *lacteus orbis* is a magical orb, or *magicus orbis*, that produces warmth and promotes healing without fire."

"Warmth?" Cito asks.

"Promotes healing?" I say at the same time. That would be useful.

"Yes. I was gifted this as a youth and have used it to my advantage many times while hunting and," he pauses to eye us, "even while traveling in Canens."

"You've been across the border?" I lean forward, eager for information that might save our lives, the orb forgotten for a moment.

"Yes. Twice." A shadow clouds his face again, and he lowers the orb into the box, his fingers shaking. "Once to save a young girl from our village, and the second time to carry out a punishment against the man who later killed her."

Cito glances my way as if to ask whether we should trust such a man. I lift my shoulder. All I know is there is a lifetime of knowledge in him I would like to explore but have no time to do so.

"So how does the *lac...lacte...* How does the orb work?" I ask, still undecided about its usefulness or my willingness to use it.

"The *lacteus orbis* needs a simple word to be illuminated." He removes the glass orb from its bed again and hands it to me. "Hold this."

I put out my hand, and he places it in my palm. It's heavier than I thought, as heavy as a rock of similar size, but it's no longer than the length of my hand and no wider than my wrist. As the elderly man does something with the silk in the box, I bend close to the orb, examining the diamond-clear glass, half expecting it to sparkle or warm or do something instead of lying innocently upon my flesh.

"Thank you," the man says in his gravelly voice, turning to me. "Now go ahead and balance it upon the apex."

Turning to the box, I find it transformed into a stand with the silk raised above the wooden frame.

"*Incende,*" the elderly man says.

Before the word falls off his lips, the orb bursts into light so bright that I raise my hand and shield my eyes. A moment later, its warmth envelops me, relaxing the knots from my muscles and filling me with peace.

"Amazing," Cito breathes. "But...is it safe? Magic is not always safe, is it?"

The elderly man considers Cito with his steady, pale brown gaze. "It is wise of you to ask, young man."

Cito leans closer to the orb.

"While illuminated, touching it can lead to burns, similar to that of a fire." The old man takes Cito's hand in his and turns it palm up. "But while unlit—*orbis finite*—" He barely lets the light die before picking up the glass and depositing it into Cito's open palm. "It is safe to handle."

"And anyone can command it? You have no need of magical ability?" Wonder brightens Cito's face.

I eye my advisor. Cito has always shown more interest in magic than considered healthy for a Heian. Because of our close connection to the most magical of the Seven Kingdoms—and also the most cursed—Heia was built on a deliberate absence of magic. Even our succession laws require our king and queen to be absent of magical ability, or else they are forced to abdicate. It's been five generations since that happened though, and perhaps because of that, some people consider magic mythical and far more interesting than most Heians consider healthy.

"Anyone can command it, if they know the words. Otherwise, it is just a glass ornament." The old man takes the silk stand and lowers it back into the box.

Cito nods and gently nestles the orb back into its case. "And what is the cost of this item?"

The old man sighs. "It has very little value to anyone but me."

I frown. Surely that's not true. If he told others how to operate it—

"But I will not allow it to pass to one unworthy of its aid." He closes the box and latches it. "I will give it to you, if you but tell me who you are."

Warily, I step back and meet Cito's eye. His expression has become guarded, his unease growing on his face.

I take a breath and make a decision. "Sir, we are from Heia. And we seek my sister, stolen from me."

He all but rolls his eyes at me. "I know very well you are from Heia, young man. You practically bleed Heian arrogance."

I blink. "Excuse me?"

"Your clothes, your health, your riches." He shakes his head and tuts. "You hardly haggled prices, so you're very desperate and very rich. Not many men dare to cross into Canens. So prove yourself worthy."

I press a smile to my lips. "I seek my sister, who has been stolen from me. She came here on a journey to help the plagued, a journey of goodwill, and she was attacked and taken captive."

The old man keeps my gaze steadily, waiting for me to continue.

I bite back my sigh. "She is the princess of Heia."

His face remains a statue of patience.

I release the sigh. "I am Crown Prince Bonifaas Ruslan Solem of Heia. This is my advisor, Cito Fati."

At that, the man's eyes gleam. "So I hold the two most important men in Heia here in my cottage at the moment?"

I spread my hands. "We are at your mercy."

A long silence ensues where he glances between the two of us, then a slow chuckle rumbles over his lips that shakes his body like the Ardor earth so often quakes.

"If that's the case, then you'd best take this." He lifts the box and presses it at me. "You will need it on your quest. And, for the sake of all of the Seven Kingdoms, I lift you up to the gods in prayer."

Squirming, I cover my motions by accepting the box with a murmured thank you.

"Do not forget the words to power the orb." He taps the top of the box with an index finger. "And take caution in the frozen lands. No one there is your ally."

"Thank you." I tuck the box under my arm and take his hand in mine. "Sir, you have given us much aid, and we will not forget it. What is your name so I might find you after our journey ends?"

He pats my hand but shakes his head. "You have given me enough. I have nothing left before me anymore, young man. But you...you can change our worlds."

VI

Together

WINTERBERRY

After I finish my tale, we sit in silence, the sleigh lurching along underneath us, our breaths trailing behind in huddled clouds. Unlike me, the other slaves haven't received a bath prior to their sales, and the scent of unwashed people along with the heady aroma of horse mingles with the sharp crispness of the winter air.

As we travel north, the days will get shorter and the air even colder. Even the fog freezes midair, so dense that, in time, I cannot see Caleb sitting across from me. Here, now, perhaps I could attempt another escape? Perhaps with the fog for cover, and the clothing and blankets which we were given, I could survive?

But if I were to escape, where would I go? I would die, even with the extra clothing, for I have no shoes and nothing but socks for mittens. It was no doubt my owner's plan to keep us disadvantaged. Yet it is not in me to sit and wait for a rescue that will never come.

I have to be matter-of-fact about this; I cannot simply run into the forest and expect to survive. Survival is key. Something in me screams that I must not surrender. I have no weapons, no way to hunt, and...

Des shivers beside me. And a companion, I realize. Des leans into me now, away from the cold, slated metal sides. I cannot escape alone. Somehow, I must take her with me.

VII

Crossing

RUS

We will bring peace. And we can change worlds.

As I stand at the edge of the frozen land, the old man's words echo in my head, warring with the little girl's words the day before.

Except I don't want either thing—not unless I can find Elaina.

I peer down past Umbra's shoulder. He stands on green grass, but inches in front of his nose, the ground is as snow white as clouds. A breeze blows out of the land that chills my face but leaves my back warm. Its power doesn't extend far beyond the snow. But across the border, I can see nothing except a swirl of white. No trees, no mountains, no path. It's like staring into a void, a cloudy mirror filled with fog and mist.

"We spent too much time tracking her," Cito mutters from beside me. "Now we have to go in."

"Are you having doubts?" I don't bother to look at him, hearing the doubt in his voice and swallowing my thoughts of the deaths awaiting us on the other side.

"Of course I am. We go into Canens, and we might not come

back. Heia will have no heir—none but Karl." His words drip with disdain. "And you know what a tragedy that is."

"It's too late to go back." My answer is firm, but my thoughts eat at me. What did that little girl mean? Do I make peace by finding Elaina? Or by failing?

Cito makes a noise in his throat.

"We don't have time to return and gather soldiers to send across the border after her; they'd be too late," I say. "We're already far behind. And it took us an hour to find this spot on the border, you know."

"I know." He glances around us, probably checking for Ostiite soldiers or anyone to watch our attempt across the border.

"Then let's go." I dismount and turn to the packhorse I've dubbed Swallow in my head. For all his strength and thickness, he's fast as can be. It's no wonder the gypsies outran us as long as they did.

"Should we throw all our gear on now or wait until we get across?"

I peer down the line at the border. Snow heaps on one side, meeting grass on the Ostium side without so much as a puddle. I look away from the eerie sight and find Cito's gaze lingering on it also, fear frozen on his face.

"It's odd, isn't it?" I ask, more to distract him than anything. "How it doesn't melt? It just disappears. I wonder why people don't come to the border more often. Try to get in..."

"Why would they seek out a curse?" Cito shudders and takes the blanket I offer him. "What is this?"

"That's a blanket for your horse. He doesn't have a thick enough coat yet to go without it. Here's your hat."

"Oh, right." Cito tosses it over the saddle and turns back to grab the cap.

I lay out the rest of the heavy fur clothes, two sets in the same size. At least we're both about the same thickness, but Cito, standing a few inches shorter than me, will be suffering with trousers and sleeves a few inches too long. Staring at all of it, including a thick hat and mittens, wool socks and undergarments, I cough. "I'm going to lighten my load first."

Cito looks at me then at the piles of clothing and nods. "I'll stay here."

It takes half an hour to gear up and another five minutes to figure out how to mount our horses while dressed like snow warriors. Sweat begins to form on my skin, which the wool wicks away but still leaves me hot and itchy. I pull down the scarf around my neck. "I rather hope we need all this."

"I hope we don't," Cito answers darkly, his voice muffled from behind his wool scarf.

I snort. "Let's go then. Before we're discovered."

"Not like any sane person would follow us," he mutters.

Grinning, my usual thirst for adventure flaring inside me, I nudge Umbra forward. The stallion requires a bit more prodding than normal, as if sensing something different about the expanse of snow before us, but finally jumps forward as though over a fence.

A shock of bitterly cold air and sharp winds collide with my exposed face. Umbra lands with a crunch atop the snow and sinks nearly a foot down, jarring me in the saddle.

Behind us, Swallow snorts his distaste at the change. I glance back, catching Cito's widening eyes as he crosses the border.

A visible shudder works its way down Cito's body from head to toe. "How do people endure this?" He already speaks like his teeth are chattering. He tugs his scarf up around his face so only his eyes peek out from the layers of cloth and furs before I face forward again and let Umbra pick his own path through the snow.

"Perhaps we'll grow accustomed to it." I glance at the sky. A few feet ago, the sky was clear and warm with few clouds. Now, it's white and sleety, holding the promise of worsening weather. Perhaps. Maybe this is all Canens does...maybe it doesn't snow or melt or change at all.

After Cito's answering snort of disagreement, we fall into silence and let Umbra lead. Every so often, I pull out my compass, checking our path. As best as I can tell, we follow the path the Canens slave traders took after meeting with the gypsies. The narrow path in the Canens wilderness is bordered by skinny trees laden with snow and ice, a clump of black and dark green here and a clump of ice-blue and gray there. Snow seems to climb six feet up the trunks, turning my mind to the mechanics of this curse.

"How do you think the curse works?" I ask aloud.

"What?" Cito grunts from behind. "What about the curse?"

I twist around and repeat my question louder, pointing to the trees. We've found the narrow path, and it's packed down as if many have ridden on it. It's no wider than one horse's width; the packhorse stays behind me, and Cito rides behind him. At his look askance, I add, "Do you think it snows and storms here? Does the snow continue to build up, or does the curse make it stay at one level?"

"And one temperature—freezing," Cito growls, pulling his shoulders up so that his neck appears only an inch long.

Amused, I turn my back to him and contemplate the trees again. Despite the trail through them, they seem untouched by human hands. "What do they burn here? Wood? Coal?"

"What?"

Instead of repeating myself, I resume my internal line of questioning. Perhaps if the path widens, we'll chat more. Or when we camp.

We travel for hours with only the crunch of snow under hoof, the odd chirrup of ravens from the trees, and the rustle of wind through the branches. The land feels expansive, though we can't see more than a mile in any direction thanks to the low clouds.

Even on high alert, it takes Umbra's unease and several gray flashes out of the corners of my eyes for me to realize that we're being stalked, by not one but several wolves.

They are hunting us.

"What is it?" Cito's voice breaks through the creaking of the snow and the call of the wind sweeping through the trees.

I grimace at the question and raise a hand, pointing to where I see a blur of gray fur. "Wolves."

His answer is to suck in a sharp breath and ready his crossbow, holding it in the opposite direction than I hold mine. Without any other options, we continue following the path.

I chew on my lip, willing Umbra not to catch onto my nerves. There are at least three: a silver, a gray, and a gray-blue. Each looks as though they are as large or larger than me. I keep one eye on them and alternate my other between the compass, the path, and the sun. My hands I keep atop my crossbow and my knotted reins. At any moment, I'm ready to drop the reins around the saddle horn and draw my sword.

We're running out of daylight. What happens when it's too dark to travel? We'll have to set up camp soon, feed the horses, and sleep.

As if he's heard my thoughts, Cito calls out, "Should we start looking for a place to camp?"

I glance around. Fog is settling in around us, reducing visibility to a hundred yards. I haven't seen one of the wolves in a half hour, but I doubt they've abandoned what they might consider an easy target. In less than two hours, it will be dangerous to travel; we won't know if we stick to the path or stray. The stars will only help if we can see them, so unless the clouds lift, we'll be stuck until sunrise.

"I suppose we should," I answer reluctantly.

"Should we look for a copse?"

I grimace. Trees will give the wolves a spot to attack from, but it gives needed shelter to the horses. We only have one tent and one <u>orbis</u>, and we'll only have one chance to live through this night.

Not for the first time, I wish for a map of Canens, which would show us how far we have to travel before we find a town. This is uncharted territory; we're completely at the mercy of the Creator.

"Let's keep an eye out for something not too close to some trees." I nod ahead. "Let's go another mile or two."

It takes three more miles, until the sun is dangerously low in the sky, before we find a group of trees that will offer roughly what I'm looking for. As we set up camp, I keep an eye out for the wolves but again see nothing. Perhaps they have given up.

"You might as well get some sleep." I pull out the tepik from Swallow's pack and begin to lay it out. "There's not much point in both of us staying up."

Cito nods, but a crease of his forehead suggests he's not convinced. In a few minutes, we've erected the tepik and spread out our sleeping sacks. "You're sure one of us can watch well enough?"

I lift a shoulder. "No, but I haven't seen them in hours now. I think they've given up."

"I hope you're right." Cito stares into the darkness for a moment then turns to me. "Do you want first watch or second?"

"I'll take first. I'm not that tired."

Cito's eyes narrow slightly, but he nods. "Wake me when it's my turn." He climbs into the tepik, and within minutes, gentle snores fill the air.

I cover my yawn with a mittened hand. My eyelashes have frozen over the course of the day, but the fire we've built from scavenged wood has begun to melt them, and I pinch off the remaining chunks of ice. Vision blurring, I blink at the gleaming fire. The hours pass by with little more than the crackling of the fire and the occasional creaking of trees as wind runs through them. To keep from falling asleep, I walk around the tepik and the fire, checking the horses as they slumber and peering into the shifting shadows behind the light of our fire. Nothing. I return to my seat by the fire and drop my head into my hands. It's warm enough right here that I could fall asleep, nod off.

A howl slices the air. I jolt to my feet as several howls answer. The horses shuffle and whinny nervously. I dart toward them, drawing my sword as I go. As they huddle together beside the trees, Umbra's ears tilt toward the woods. A rustle from the tepik and Cito's head appears through the flaps.

"Wolves?" His crossbow pushes the flaps aside underneath his chin.

Pairs of glowing pinpricks peek out from amongst the tree branches.

"Yes. Cito, we must stay together."

Cito creeps over, his feet crunching on the partially packed down snow. "Shall I shoot it?"

I hold up my hand as two more pairs of glinting eyes appear nearby. "It'd be best if we take out the alpha."

"And how do we tell which one that is?" Cito answers, turning his back to me and peering into the darkness, pointing his crossbow out at it.

I search the trees in front of me, but it's too dark to tell if a shadow is a wolf or a tree until it dashes from one shadow to the next. Lifting my sword, I find the wolf already gone. "The alpha will be the biggest. But without seeing the entire pack, we can't know. Staying near the fire should keep us safe tonight. Get the horses and bring them in as close to the fire as they'll stay." I hold out a hand for his crossbow. "I'll shoot him if I see him."

Reluctantly, Cito hands over his crossbow and the quiver. "I only have a dozen arrows. Where's yours?"

"Next to the fire." I don't take my eyes off the pack as Cito wrangles with the horses' leads and drags his gelding and Swallow toward the fire. Umbra snorts with displeasure at being left behind. "Shh, shh," I reassure him. "We aren't going to die tonight."

I slowly untie Umbra's lead and work him backward, toward the fire, keeping the crossbow aimed at the trees. A low growl from my right makes Umbra shy left. I swing the bow toward the wolf, even as I realize it's a distraction.

Cito mutters behind me, saying something I can't understand. Then there's a frantic neigh, and Cito shouts.

Though instinct screams at me not to turn my back to the pack, I wrench my head around in time to see two wolves darting toward Cito and the horses. I whirl and let loose with an arrow. It zings through the air and lodges in a log near the fire, missing the silvery wolf by inches. Cito shouts as the wolves snap at them, but when the gelding kicks out, they scatter.

With a frightened whinny, Umbra rears low and paws the air. I whirl back toward the woods and realize the wolves have done exactly what I should have known they would—separate us. Yet Umbra is far from the weakest, and so am I. So...who is their target? With a grunt, I swing the crossbow around and, Umbra's lead looped around my arm, struggle to reload with one eye on the wolves.

One lunges in, snapping at my ankle. I swing the crossbow and hit him across the face. He answers with a snarl before dashing away. Umbra aims a back leg out in a kick, and a sharp yelp fills the air. The wolves snarl and, the air resounding with howls, they disappear into the trees. I hurry Umbra to the other horses, Cito, and the fire.

"We can't let them separate us," I tell Cito. "Umbra and I will face this way and watch the woods. You watch the other direction."

I position Umbra nearest the fire and nudge Cito into doing the same with his two. He struggles to keep the nervous packhorse from falling into the fire or dashing out into the wolves.

"Here, trade." I hand him his crossbow and take the gelding's lead. The animal rolls his eyes and whinnies nervously. I put a hand to his shuddering neck, whispering to him as I sidle him up next to Umbra. The larger stallion snorts, his eyes on the woods. "You'll help me protect the herd, right, Umbra?" I murmur.

He doesn't answer, but his nostrils flare as he stares at the wood, ears pricked.

We hold our ground throughout the night, depending on the horses' senses to alert us to the wolves' movements. They don't near the fire, but we cannot move, not with the misty darkness. As the night goes on, the clouds descend so that we cannot see farther than fifty feet beyond the fire.

When the sun rises, I look at Cito with a mixture of exhaustion and disbelief that we've made it through alive.

Cito rubs a hand across his face. "They're still here. What are we supposed to do?"

"We hold until the weather lifts." My stomach squirms. "It's only the fire keeping them back."

Cito points to the flames. "That's all the wood that's left. I'm surprised we have any at all."

I grimace at the trees. "We'll have to get more."

"What about the orb?"

"The orb? It's—" I shrug. "I don't think it's meant to protect against wolf attacks."

"Perhaps they'll fear it?"

"Even if they do, what do we do, run around with it burning all the time? That'd be like riding a horse with a burning candle."

Cito gives a dark laugh. "Only as long as we need to—if it keeps the pack at bay."

I shake my head. "It's an option, I suppose."

"We can't stay here forever anyway. We'll run out of food within a couple weeks."

"The wolves won't wait that long to attack. They'll wait until one of us goes for more firewood."

"True." Biting his lip, Cito glances at the edges of our camp.

The trees are hardly visible, mere fingers reaching through the fog, and so with deep misgivings whatever we choose, we resolve to wait.

VIII

Hunted

RUS

The fog remains for two tense days, and the wolves remain within it. Cito and I take turns dozing for a few hours at a time, all along wondering which will break first: the fog or the pack. Traveling to the trees for firewood becomes trickier as less wood is easily available. We cannot leave the horses to themselves beside the fire, nor can we gather wood alone.

But with the fire dying, and Cito awake to guard the horses, I take a chance.

"Keep your crossbow ready," I tell him and, taking our axe, head to the tree line. Working quickly, I fell a young tree, and I have an armful of thick branches when the attack happens. A small wolf darts in so quickly that I can't pull back before he's snapped at my arm. His teeth descend through the leather of my mitten and scrape at my skin.

Cursing, I drop all but the largest of the sticks and swing it at his head. He lets go and disappears before I connect, and I readjust, swinging it at the one attacking my heels. She yelps when it connects with her skull and darts away. Abandoning the wood, I draw my sword, ready for the next attack, but it doesn't come.

With a quick glance around, I drag a few pieces of wood into one arm and hurry back to the fire, sword still at the ready.

"Are you injured?" Cito asks over his shoulder, trying to keep the three horses calm.

I dump the few precious pieces of wood down beside the fire and help Cito calm the horses. "Just a scratch."

He nods and glances at my torn mitten. It feels damp, and I'm sure it's blood. Hades. That could make them more eager to attack.

Hurriedly, we tend to my wound and settle around the fire, on edge.

"They're wearing us down," Cito says. "Biding their time." He glances at the trees where a dozen eyes stare at us. "I hate this."

"We'll have to break for it eventually. Whether or not they give up, we'll have to fight. Take them out before they take us."

"How?" Cito's one word is full of fear and dismay.

Briefly, I meet his gaze. "Tomorrow morning, as soon as it's light, we go. Fog or not."

Burrowing his face down into his scarf, he nods, but the fear has never been more evident in his eyes than it is now.

Neither of us sleep that night. We pack up the tepik and other supplies before it goes fully dark. The fire goes out before midnight, and I pull the orb from its case, praying to the Creator of All that it keeps the animals away.

He must hear my prayers, for the orb lights up the clearing like a lighthouse in the night of the darkest sea, even stretching into the trees.

Cito gasps, and the horses start. The dying fire had slowly closed the darkness in upon us, and under its cover, the wolves had been creeping in, unnoticed by us. At the abruptness of the light, they whine and dart off, disappearing into the shadows a hundred yards away.

Too stunned to reach for our weapons, Cito and I exchange a glance.

"Maybe we will be traveling with the orb," I murmur as its heat washes over me.

Letting out a little huff of awed breath, Cito nods.

A moment later, my injured hand begins to sting. I rip off my mitten and peel off the cloth I've wrapped over the cuts.

Another gasp breaks the silence as, entranced, Cito and I watch the edges of the scrapes knit themselves together, leaving nothing in their wake, not even the faintest scar.

"He did say it had a healing effect," Cito murmurs when I've pulled my mitten back on.

I peer around us. The camp is broken down, the fire extinguished. We have nothing to do but saddle the horses and mount up. "Let's go."

"Now?"

I lift a shoulder. "Why not?"

"Because it's dark—how are we supposed to hold the orb so that we don't get burned?"

I spread a palm upward. "I'll find a way. Let's go while the wolves are frightened. Before they regain their courage."

Hesitating a long while, Cito finally nods.

We saddle up and ride out, with me holding the orb above Umbra's neck as it nestles in its box, praying all the while that the wolves abandon their hunt and I don't drop the orb.

We travel in roughly the same awkward fashion for three days. We're no longer following Elaina's path—I don't know where her path is anymore. Instead, we're simply searching for civilization.

Following the broken path in the snow is easy enough, thanks to the lack of fresh snow. It's clear that someone has been here since the last snowfall, and they're familiar with the land, so we follow it, praying that there won't be a snow to cover the only path we have. Occasionally we find bodies. Some with their loyal horses next to them, half buried in snow. An injured horse is a death toll in this land, leaving a person without transportation or another's warmth. Sometimes there is a horse corpse, picked at by the wolves, sometimes frozen solid, and a few miles later, a human corpse, eyes pecked out by the ravens, face nothing but sinews and bone, and sometimes the human comes first, the horse second.

Even as an experienced soldier, I've never come across bodies as ravaged and hopeless as this. But at least we haven't found Elaina like this. Please, Creator, do not let that be her end.

It takes only a few hours before holding out the orb becomes dangerous and tiresome. Our exhaustion leads us into treacherous situations. My head nods, the sleeplessness of the past two nights catching up with me, and my hand dips over Umbra's neck. The orb teeters then slips forward, resting precariously upon Umbra's neck. I jerk awake, and Umbra jerks under me, slipping from the path. Gasping, I drop the reins and fumble for the orb with my mittened hands, but it flies from my grasp into the depths of the snow as Umbra's feet skitter under me.

I put a hand on his shoulder and murmur a calming word in my mount's ear. When he freezes in place, I slide off his back into the deep snow and dig out the orb. It shines through the snow, and I dig it out easily, thankful to find it fully intact. But no longer do I ride with it lit; it is safely stowed now instead.

Within hours, the wolves pick up our trail. We race for a village we don't know exists, and when the ice walls appear in the distance, I think it's a mirage.

"Does that village really exist?" I ask, breathless, as Cito and I race toward the image.

He shoots me a glance with all the spare attention he can muster; he requires almost everything he has to stay on his horse over the bumpy, slick snow. "I hope so."

As we near, we race through a small clump of spindly trees then up a dirty gray path of packed snow. The wolves advance, growling and snapping at our heels, knowing their time runs short.

"Close the gates!" comes a cry ahead of us.

"Wait!" I call out. "Please wait!" With my sword, I swipe at the nearest wolf when he attacks; he yelps and falls back, the pack retreating with him to regroup. I kick Umbra forward, and the three horses slide through the gate before it closes.

Breathing heavily, we stand in a snow-covered square as an entire small village stares at us.

"Do you think they'll let us warm up at one of their fires?" Cito asks. "My ass is numb."

I gape at him, then a slow chuckle rumbles my chest, shaking loose my disbelief at his nerve. At least he spoke in Canensian. The last thing we need is for this village to believe we're Heian. "Let's hope so," I mutter to him.

The villagers call to each other, peering through the iron gates in the midst of an ice wall. They murmur amongst themselves, some holding swords and sticks at the ready or pointing out the gate with their weapons.

One man approaches. "Any injuries?" he asks in a clipped accent.

"No," I reply in Canensian, my mind turning to my hand. "No injuries."

"You're lucky. That's a vicious pack out there."

I nod, and Cito snorts his agreement. His gelding is spooked still, dancing underneath him, threatening to throw him at every surge until a man grabs the horse's reins under his whisker-frozen chin to protect us all.

"Are you in need of warmth? Any frostbite? There's an inn with a healthy fire and warm food and ale."

"No," I answer, remembering the warmth and healing of the orb. How different would my answers be if not for its power? But I can't reveal it to this man or anyone in this village. I don't know how the Canens people even perceive magic. "Though we might stop in before leaving. They have rooms?"

"Aye, plenty of rooms. What were you doing out there?" the man asks, his eyes narrowing over the furry muff that covers his face.

Judging by the wrinkles around his eyes, I imagine that he's less than two decades older than me.

"Traveling to Merise," I answer. "We're looking for some slaves." I feel, rather than see, Cito's glance my way as he finally relaxes atop his horse.

The man doesn't seem surprised but shifts an ornately carved stick made out of ebony wood from his left to his right hand. "You might talk to Lord Tillmore. He took some off the hands of some traveling slave traders the other day."

"Lord Tillmore?" I ask. "Is that who runs this village?"

The man nods, his expression neutral, giving no indication of what we might find.

I glance up the hill of the small village, where a large manor house perches, overlooking the village. "He lives there?"

"Aye." The man leans against his stick and surveys us. It's such a work of art that I can't wonder if he means to draw attention to it or if it marks him as a sort of elder amongst the others.

"Shall we, Cito?" I ask, jerking my chin at the manor house.

"Of course."

The man straightens and points at the path with his stick. "Follow this road past the—" he says a word I don't recognize, but his pointing tells me which direction to go "—and knock on the front door. They'll take care of your horses."

"Thank you." I readjust the packhorse's lead on Umbra's saddle horn and nudge him up the hill, where a cloud has begun to descend. Does the sky ever stay clear in this gods-forsaken country?

We pass over the road, hooves crunching on the packed, dirty snow, the great house towering over us. The village has, at most, two dozen homes of modest size, a handful of shops, and two inns with pubs. From the looks of it, nearly everyone emerged from their homes to watch our entry.

The manor house towers up two stories in the returning mist. A half dozen windows watch our approach with their dark eyes as the villagers return to their homes in order to watch us from warmth. A few armed men remain at the gates, guarding against the pack howling its disappointment outside.

"What's that building?" Cito asks.

I glance over to a strange-looking building made mostly of glass windows. It's heavily frosted over, but smoke emerges from the top of it, just like every other building in the village. Except it has a greenish hue to the walls, as though whatever is inside is green. "I don't know. Some sort of drying house?" I remember the word I hadn't understood and gather the man must have been referring to this building.

We continue up the hill until we reach the front door of the manor. With a glance back at Cito, I dismount, climb the three steps to the front door, and knock.

IX

Fevered

WINTERBERRY

As we ride through the Canens wilderness, the fog lifts enough to see a few hundred yards away then begins to thicken again. The guards light a dozen torches, but they prove ineffective, only leading to murmurs of stopping early for the night. Losing the path here in Canens would mean death. Death by wolves, bears, or exposure.

I shudder and pull Des and her warmth closer to me. She shivers in her sleep, her teeth chattering, although her cheek feels hot against mine. She's burning with fever. I need to keep her warm. As soon as we stop for the night, we'll have to light a fire, and I'll get Des as close to it as possible. Our owner has to want her healthy. I glance up at the front but can't see the Wolf Man as he rides ahead of the slave's sleigh in the fog.

Not thirty minutes later, a couple of cries go up. At them, I straighten, on edge, but after a moment, it's clear that we've simply found our campsite for the night. The men around me shift. Two or three of them exchange significant glances that I can't interpret.

For several minutes, there is jingling and creaking of men, horses, and reindeer around us. Low voices murmur through the darkness, and distant torches bob in the skies. A guard comes to stand beside the sleigh, peering in at us as though we are animals. To him, we probably are. Anger burns in me, but I stuff it down, turning my gaze back to Des. She's woken and blinks at her surroundings in silence. I whisper that we've stopped and are going to camp for the night. Before she can answer, keys jingle at the door to our jail.

The guard slams on the door to gain our attention, although we've already given it. By now, a second guard has joined him, looking bored and cold.

"Listen up!" the first barks. "Before I open this door, there are going to be some rules. You've each been chained to another slave in case any one of you gets an idea of escape. And if any one of you attempts to escape, regardless, you'll all pay the price. I'll explain more of what that might mean when you come out. Maybe." He grins through the slats at us. "When you come out, show your tattoos and brands to us. After you're recorded, you'll each help set up camp."

He glances at the other guard, who gives a nod and inserts the key into the lock.

With a grunt, the second guard motions us out one chained pair at a time. The first guard inspects our tattoos and brands, jots a note in a notebook, and motions us along the path.

"Follow the path," the first one says, nudging at one of the slaves.

Still clutching the wool blanket around Des's and my shoulders, I fall into line with Des as the slaves ahead of us disappear into the fog.

A few more steps, and a large dome looms out of the fog. My muscles tense before I realize it's just a building. We must be on a well-traveled route if there's a permanent building for us to sleep in tonight.

Inside the wooden house is no warmer than out, although there is a cold fireplace in the center with dry firewood waiting beside it and a hole through the ceiling for smoke to escape through. Judging by the large, snowy pelt and the long stick near the corner, the hole is covered when the house is not being used in order to prevent the snow taking over the room.

"Build a fire," one of the guards instructs the first pair of slaves into the building. The two men, a thickly built man and a lanky, bearded man, glance at each other and move to obey. The guard puts out a hand to the next pair of men, Caleb and a white-blond man. "You two, go find some firewood." He glances over their shoulder at the darkness in the doorframe. "Take a torch and a sled. And be careful. Or else we'll be picking up tufts of your hair after the wolves have done with you."

Caleb's expression, always stoic, flattens, if possible. The blond beside him narrows his eyes, surprising me with the hatred I see in them.

Ignoring them, the guard continues handing out jobs, taking one glance at me and Des and saying, "Roll out the bedrolls," and pointing to another corner where heaps of pelts and pads rest.

I move to obey, although my will resists it. There's no point in disobeying. I can't escape now. Like the guard said, there are wolves around here. I wouldn't be able to steal a horse, and even if I did, that horse would just be a meal for the wolves. Unless they got me first.

Suppressing a shudder, I tug Des along with me, and we begin rolling out bedrolls as the guards look on. A couple of the slaves have been tasked with handing out dried food from the stores, and it's no time before Des and I finish our task and take our share. I pull her toward the fire, which is still young, but I don't care. The weak flames are snapping over the dry logs and sticks as I push Des down onto the floor beside the fire and pull a spare wool blanket over her. As I crouch beside her, thawing my own hands at the fire, Caleb and his companion enter, each carrying an armful of logs.

Des shudders beside me, leaning precariously to one side before I steady her.

"Excuse me," I say to a guard.

He ignores me and continues talking to another guard.

"Excuse me!" I snap with iron in my voice.

His eyes widen slightly as his mouth slackens then sets into a firm line. His gaze turns to me, and I realize that my actions have gained me the attention of the entire room.

He advances on me, but I refuse to shrink back. "How dare you?" he begins.

"I dare because I need—"

He holds up a hand, and despite myself, I flinch away. He grins. "You don't need anything but a good whipping to put you in your place."

I lift my chin and narrow my eyes in defiance. "You're right. I don't need anything. But my companion here needs medicine."

Confused, the guard snaps a glance over Des. "What's wrong with her?"

"I don't know," I say crisply. "But arguing with me about my behavior isn't going to change her needs. She needs medicine," I go on before he can argue again. "She has a fever."

He shrugs. "What's that to me?"

"As your...employer purchased her, he must have thought her worth some money and investment. Therefore, I would suggest keeping her alive." I glare at him. "Or maybe I should just ask him. Where'd he go anyway?"

The second guard comes up behind the first, ignoring me and inspecting Des instead, waving away my protective jolt toward her. He touches her forehead in an impersonal touch, like a healer might, pries open her eyes to look at them, then steps back. "We can do little for her in this state. Her best hope is to stay warm until we reach the Manor."

I bite my bottom lip. "She won't die," I say stubbornly.

The guard meets my gaze with an unreadable expression. "I hope you're right. She's the only new Red we've had in a while. Some were quite excited about that."

My breath catches over my lips, but he turns and walks away without another word.

The other guard leans close to me, his breath washing over my cheeks. "And you'd do best to keep your mouth shut next time." With a motion so sudden I have no time to react, he strikes me across the cheek with the back of his hand.

I fall to the wood floor with a gasp, my cheek burning in both humiliation and pain. Starting up, I scramble after him before a firm hand grips my upper arm and stops me. The guard glances over his shoulder at me, a taunting grin on his lips.

"I wouldn't, princess," comes a soft voice in my ear.

The words take several slow seconds to sink in before I focus on the speaker. Caleb crouches beside me, having deposited a pile of logs near the fire, which his companion sees to while ignoring me completely. As soon as I stop fighting, Caleb releases me, returning to his task as if he has always been a slave and has no thoughts of escape or another life.

"I'm just supposed to let them—" I bite my words off and glance at Des.

Caleb considers me, darts a look at the guards, and shakes his head. "Now is not the time."

"But there are fewer of them—" I begin.

He shakes his head firmly. "We are not yet balanced in power."

"But—"

"Here. It will help the girl." He passes me a stick I recognize as from a willow tree.

I take it begrudgingly. "So you won't help me?"

"No."

At his simple and flat refusal, I open my mouth, but booted foot-steps clomp up behind me and silence me. Without any other choice, I settle in for the night, defeated.

Despite my plans for eventual escape and the additional sleep Des and I both got while traveling, we fall into a restless sleep. Her fitful-ness wakes me several times, and I soothe her, either pulling off her covers or piling them on, depending on her needs.

It's difficult to keep my eyes open in the dim house, so I rest my head on my crooked arm. Eyes drifting shut, I feel my body giving in to the lull of sleep when a bellow outside issues over the crackle of the fire. Eyes flying open, I stay perfectly still but tense. A rustle around me tells me that others have awoken as well. A few seconds later, yipping and howling fills the air as wolves descend upon their prey.

Long after the frantic cries and bellows stop, I lie awake on my pad and under my pelts while Des tosses in her sleep. Eventually lulled by the crackle of the fire, I drift into an uneasy slumber.

I jolt awake at the sound of a dry log hitting a fire-ravaged one. Rolling over, I find Caleb bending over the flames, his back to me. He's still attached at the ankle to the pale blond, who remains stretched out under his blankets but whose eyes are open and staring at me without emotion.

I roll out of bed, bending over Des to check her fever. She's hot but wakes at my touch and gives me a small smile. "Is it time to go?"

Before I can answer, a guard claps his hands together and gives the blond shackled to Caleb a sharp nudge with his boot. "Wake up. Time to get going. Everyone, break down camp. Put out the fire, pick up the blankets."

In unspoken agreement, all of us take on the same duties we had the night before. As Des and I roll the blankets and place them back as we found them, a guard enters from outside, shaking off snow and advancing inside.

"The wolf pack brought down a giant deer last night," he says to another guard as he pulls off his gloves. "We should be safe to travel if we avoid that area."

The other guard nods. "Perfect. They'll not be hunting. Couldn't ask for anything better."

I steal a glance at Caleb as he bends over the fire, pouring a bucket of snow atop it.

If the wolves are distracted, now would be the perfect time to escape. Steal a horse, race back to Merise... As if he can read my thoughts, Caleb turns to me and gives me a sharp shake of his head.

But if we go all the way to the Manor, then... I chew on my lip and stack another bedroll. Leaving from the Manor, however many days away from it we are now, we'll be too far from Merise for me to get back safely. It will be easier now.

By the time we're dressed and lining up in the cold to reenter our jail—this time in more appropriate clothes supplied by the guards— I've almost convinced myself to steal a horse, throw Des on it in front of me, and make a mad dash for the capital. A short distance away, a packhorse startles at something only it sees, rearing up and giving a muted neigh of fright.

This could be my chance. I aim my feet in the opposite direction, where a docile horse stands, ears pricked toward the spooking horse but looking easily controlled. Having spent much of my recent years trapped in a palace, I am not the best rider, although I can stay on a decently trained horse. Still, I hesitate. There are eight guards with us, not counting the owner. We slaves may outnumber them, but they probably won't help me escape.

While I pause, another guard dashes over to the spooking horse to help. I take Des's elbow in my hand. She frowns at me.

A hand falls onto my shoulder. I jump.

Close behind me, Caleb leans down. "I wouldn't do what you are thinking."

My gaze darts to the guards around us, but no one is paying any attention to us. "And what am I thinking?" I murmur, shifting my cape around my shoulders and clutching a folded blanket to my chest.

He shrugs one shoulder at my suspicious glare.

I grit my teeth but don't move. "Why not?"

"You won't make it."

"It's better to try than to sit here and endure slavery," I grumble.

Des glances between us with glazed eyes.

"I thought it was better to live than to die," Caleb responds calmly.

"Not if living is this."

The spooking horse settles with a snort and is quickly laden with his pack and led to the other packhorses.

As the guard returns to our line, I shuffle along toward our prison.

"The time will come," Caleb says. "But not now."

A guard with bushy blond hair sticking out of his fur hat leads the packhorse up to the side of the sleigh and ties his lead to it tightly.

Regardless of whether I agree with Caleb, this chance for escape has slipped me by. This time.

X

The Canens Witch

BLANCHE

Even as I watched my stepdaughter ride away from Merise with the utmost satisfaction, it wasn't enough.

I must destroy the people's *memories* of the girl. No more men requesting her hand, no more celebrations of her birth, no more mention of her in the streets. Like I had with the previous queen, I would wipe her name from the land of Canens and destroy the monuments, exactly as it is foretold. But not yet. Not until it best serves the country. One more birthday celebration...but she will never come of age. I snicker.

To keep up appearances, I tug my heavy cloak around my shoulders, despite the interior of my sleigh being as warm as if a fire were my companion in the seat across from me.

The sleigh slips to a halt, and I peer out the window.

There's low murmuring around the sleigh, without any undercurrent of alarm, and so I settle back into the royal purple velvet seat, closing my eyes.

Answers. I just need answers.

A knock on the door interrupts my thoughts, and I open my eyes.

"Excuse me, Your Majesty, but it appears the path becomes too narrow and unstable for the sleigh from here on."

I raise my brows at my coachman.

"If you wish to continue, you shall take one of the soldier's horses, and I will remain with the sleigh with the footed soldier."

I consider a moment. "Yes. Yes, that shall suffice."

The coachman dips his head into a nod. "Do you require a moment to get your things in order?"

"Yes."

With another nod, the coachman steps back and closes the door, leaving me with a lingering chill in the air.

I sigh. Traveling by open air. Too bad it will cost too much magic to cast a spell keeping me warm. I need all my magic for whatever greeting I receive at the end of this journey.

Gathering my gloves and pulling them on, I find my fingers trembling. Pausing, I stretch them out over my thighs, gripping my knees with my fingertips to still them. Nothing to fear.

With now-calm hands, I place on my ruffed rabbit fur hat and check the clasp to my cloak. I wear my thick boots in case of a situation such as this; one can never be too prepared.

Through the window, my coachman stands immobile, not glancing back at me but guarding the door. He wears a Canens crossbow slung across his back, suggesting that no danger is sighted but that danger is always possible.

Steeling myself for the chill, I rap a knuckle on the door.

He jumps to swing open the door, shouting to someone nearby to bring the horse.

I emerge into a world of fog and ice. The air cuts into my lungs with a thousand knives, and I resist the urge to tuck my chin into my scarf and huddle inside my cloak. I hate the cold.

In a minute, I have mounted a docile beast laden with soldier regalia and ride with my twenty soldiers. The grounded soldier does not look nearly as disappointed at being left behind as I expect for one so young, but then, they do ride into what many have called the White Bear's den.

The ice-coated tree branches hang heavy over our heads on the path we cut through the quiet trees; not even a bird breaks the silence.

It makes the men antsy, and the horses have picked up on it. They have hardly accepted the idea of their queen's magic yet, and now I ask them to visit the Canens Witch.

Now I push my horse ahead of the men, determined to reach the house before midday. I've known of the Witch's whereabouts for years and let her live because the woman did no harm to the Crown. I've always wondered if I would need this woman for something, and now...I do. Perhaps she will earn her keep today.

The cottage materializes out of the darkened mist; a thin coil of smoke rises from the stone chimney. Two feet of snow rest atop the roof, a roof which has probably never seen summer.

I pull up my mount at the vision before me. A squiggle of unease wakes in my stomach. Not fear of the Witch, and certainly not of magic, which the men and horses who shift in the creaking snow around me innately fear, but fear that I will not find any answers inside the cottage.

Before the fear can turn into something greater, I nudge the horse forward. The animal tosses his head and tries to back up, but I refuse him the opportunity.

The lines of the cottage sharpen as I ride up, the lone window in the front dark as night, the door a gateway to answers.

A fence marks the edge of the Witch's property, with a narrow gate breaking up the line of snow-topped hedges. Magic emanates from the land, and curiosity begins to replace my fear.

At the gate, I dismount and hand the reins to the nearest soldier, who is still mounted. Magic hums in the wooden gate underneath my hand, and I hesitate only a moment before pushing it open.

I step across the threshold, and my breath halts before my lips. This woman is a powerful witch indeed.

Around me, the snow has gone. The cottage is transformed. A garden, greener than I've ever seen, grows within the fence and gate. Flowers trail along the ground, scatter the hedges, and line the cottage door and window. All colors of the rainbow intersperse the luscious greenery. Roses, amaryllis, crocuses, dahlias, and plants even I cannot name create a bouquet of scents that has never been found in Canens before.

I linger by a thick rosebush with roses the blackest I've ever seen. Could this be the mythical black rose? There is a potion that calls for its petals, petals I've never been able to find in all my searching.

I'm tempted to take one, but I will wait. Perhaps the Witch will offer one in lieu of knowledge. Or in addition to.

I move to the front door, lift my hand, and knock. No answer comes, so I knock again. This time, there is a rustle inside.

The heat of the garden makes me swelter in my cape. I swipe off my hat and raise my fist again.

At the final thump, the door swings open, and I blink. An elderly woman in a tartan dress stands before me, looking both amused and tired at once. "Ah. The day of the Queen's visit has at last arrived." She cocks a hip out to the side and surveys me. "I knew something would happen today, but I knew not it was ye."

I straighten under the woman's stare. "Are you the Canens Witch?" I keep my voice as icy as the winter outside the woman's cottage, refusing to bend to whatever insincerity or amusement the Witch offers.

The Witch snorts. "If I were not, would ye be here?"

My lips thin. "Perhaps I have found a lesser witch."

The Witch grins a grin that displays blackened, broken teeth and motions with her head to the garden behind me. "Should that not have set yer doubts aside?"

"Of course." I raise my chin. "I come with a question."

The Witch tilts her head, considering me as if she is debating whether to allow me inside or to force me to stand outside and speak my question before entry will be allowed.

"May I come in?" I finally ask. "I have men—" I half turn and motion behind me, then break off. My soldiers must stand just outside the hedges and gate, yet they are invisible to me now.

"Ye had men," the Witch corrects and, stepping back, widens the opening to her cottage. "Don't worry," she calls as she disappears into the cottage, leaving the door open behind her, "they'll be near when ye leave. Although they won't have seen what ye've seen, and they won't believe ye if ye tell them."

Unease rises in me, but I push it aside. I know nothing but rumors of this Witch. Rumors that suggest she's more powerful than me. I straighten only to stoop and step over the threshold into the low cottage.

The door closes behind me as if caught in a sharp breeze.

Darkness descends, and I hesitate, my sight failing me.

"Come in, don't linger," the amused voice of the Witch calls from a few feet away. "I'll serve ye some tea."

Hesitating again, I shake myself and stride toward the voice. "Can't you light a lamp?" I hate myself for asking, as I could easily cast a light spell to solve the problem, but I detest the idea of revealing myself in such a crude way.

My answer is a chuckle that sounds almost childlike, and then a spurt of light flashes a short distance away. "What, can ye not see?"

Flames crackle in a fireplace and illuminate a rugged wooden table and chairs not two feet from me. The space is clean and organized, with books resting on shelves against the walls and potion ingredients lined on shelves alongside them. A white bear rug covers half the floor before the fire, worn thin from years of use.

"Sit. I'll brew tea, and ye'll tell me why ye've come."

I find myself obeying, moving to the table and sinking down into the chair. As I do, I shake my head, shaking away the touch of magic from my skin like water. The Witch's touch is light indeed.

In a moment, a mug of tea sits before me, warm and inviting.

"Drink." The word is not a request, and I have the cup in my hands before I stop to think. Pausing, I smell the liquid and find it an unfamiliar brew with a familiar essence. There is a potion in it.

I set it down.

"Drink, drink," the Witch says, nudging the mug toward me.

"I'd rather not," I say firmly. "I would rather discuss things with you without a spell or potion clouding my mind."

In the light of the fire, the Witch's face crinkles. "What's that?"

"You've been using both since I knocked on the door."

The Witch leans back in her chair, her lips thinning in her first display of discomfort.

I press my advantage. "I've heard you have knowledge of old tales and prophecies."

Piercing eyes shine like fire out of the darkness between us. "Aye. I have some knowledge. What is it ye seek?"

"Information," I say.

"What information?"

"There is a rumor," I begin, "a rumor concerning the end of the Canens winter."

A twitch of the Witch's lips is all that betrays her amusement. "There are always rumors."

"Prophecies."

"Prophecies." The Witch lifts a withered shoulder in painful skepticism. "What are they but stories told by old women to amuse themselves?"

I dart a glance at the Witch's front door. "There's a rumor that you know how to end the Winter Curse. And from the state of your garden, I'd say there's truth to that rumor." I inject warning into my tone.

"Hmm. Why don't ye say what ye mean then?"

I pull a small, leather-bound book from under my cloak. "In this book are prophecies made over the years."

"By whom?" The Witch scoffs. "Not every statement made is a prophecy."

I blink slowly. "By legitimate prophets and prophetesses of the Seven Kingdoms."

"Such as?" The Witch's lips thin again, but her eyes dance in the firelight.

Narrowing my eyes, I push the book across the table toward the Witch with one hand. "Inside is a prophecy that my best scholars cannot decipher."

The Witch does not move, her gaze not shifting from my face.

"And I want you to interpret it for me."

At this, the Witch's thin lips crinkle into a small smile. "And what do I get in exchange for this benevolent act?"

I tighten my jaw. "My gratitude, coin, adamas, undisturbed life? Take your pick."

The old woman's gaze remains steady upon me. "This must be an important prophecy then, that ye would offer me whatever I want as reward." She taps her bent fingers upon the table. "Perhaps I need nothing."

My teeth grind. I have never been good at bartering and gaining people's trust without the aid of magic or threats of violence. This is different. I cannot use magic against this woman if I want her help, but I have nothing to threaten her with. Nothing but her life, and she seems to care naught for it. A scream of frustration builds in my throat. All of Canens depends on this information—and what does this woman care? She has sequestered herself away a hundred miles from Merise and created her own Garden of the Gods for her own use. But for me—only through understanding this prophecy can I restore Canens to its former glory. If only we were returned to that glory, the worlds would be different. The familiar ache of longing awakes in my chest, hurting so much that needles jab at the backs of my eyes.

"I must rid myself of this threat to Canens. To the throne," I whisper. "I need your help to do so."

Having been watching me and, I fear, seeing too many of my

thoughts upon my face, the Witch finally leans forward, a strange light in her eyes. "I will read yer prophecy. But I will defer payment."

Joy and relief surge through me only to crash down at the Witch's latter words. I catch my breath. "No. You choose your payment today."

The Witch smirks and pushes the unopened book back across the table. "Then I refuse."

"You refuse, and you die." My voice is ice again. I no longer desire to gain trust. I will make her do what I wish.

The Witch raises one hand palm up. "So I choose death."

"You would choose death over a simple interpretation? An interpretation that helps your country?"

"My country?" The Witch tilts her head to the side. "If that were all it was." The Witch's pale eyes study me with the utmost care, as though she is examining a sculpture and looking for flaws. "But we both know ye look for more than that."

I force my gaze not to waver. There is too much at stake here. I must convince the Witch. "If I can find a cure, it will benefit the entire country. I do not do this for my own sake."

A twitch lifts one corner of the Witch's mouth. "The threat is not what you think it is, Queen."

"Then what is it?" I shake my head in confusion. "All the people suffer under this Winter Curse. I am only here to help them."

The Witch scoffs. "And how am I to believe that? Why would ye want to relieve the curse when ye have spent years cultivating inside gardens that ye control? Ye are profiting from the people's plight, not suff'ring."

"I do it for the people. It is only for the curse that I must do so. Do you think I want—" I break off and shake my head. "If there is a way to break it, I must know. There must be a way, and I believe at least one of the prophecies in this book can show me how."

"Prophecies yer wisest scholars cannot interpret." The Witch smirks.

"No scholar knows everything." I clench my fists at what I say next. "I was, of course, hoping you had some other knowledge to share."

"Of course ye were." The Witch's amusement returns, and her gaze travels to the small book of prophecies sitting on the table between us. "Perhaps I will deign to take a look. Although I cannot promise ye an answer."

A surge of hope blossoms inside me, although I hasten to hide it. Without a word, I slide the book across the table again.

This time, the Witch reaches out and takes it into her hands. She studies the cover, her pale gaze as unfathomable as the prophecies which the pages hold.

"I have seen this book before, long ago." She turns the leather-bound volume over in her hands before cracking it open and flipping through the aged pages.

I pull my tea close before recalling the potion it's laced with and push it away.

The Witch's lips twitch. "There is more water in the kettle, should ye wish," she says without looking up.

I wave a hand without speaking my refusal. But after another ten minutes of silence, I rise and help myself to a new cup, fresh tea leaves, and boiling water. I reclaim my seat and watch the Witch page through the book, half unaware that my heart is in my throat with every twitch of the woman's eye and every flick of her fingers.

Finally, the Witch sits back against her chair, pushes the book away, and shakes her head. "This will not help ye."

"What? Why?"

"It is incomplete."

"Incomplete?" Leaning forward in desperation, I blink at her. "What do you mean? That's the most complete copy of prophecies that we have."

The Witch smirks. "Yes? Sad it was not written down in full then."

"And how do you know?" I challenge.

"Because I gave half the prophecies in that book." She fixes me with a cold stare. "But if ye care for me to interpret simply this portion of the prophecy, by all means, I shall."

She gave the prophecies? Then this is the legendary Vatia? I sit back, stunned. "No. Of course I want the full prophecy. <u>Need</u> the full prophecy. I must know the full truth. What—what is it? Do you recall?"

The Witch rises from her seat and walks to the small shelf along one wall, running a finger along the dusty edge until it comes to a pamphlet. She takes it from the shelf and opens it, pulling out a sheet of parchment. She returns the book to the shelf and returns to the table, pressing the parchment into the middle of it without explanation.

Curiosity overpowering all else, I reach for it and slide it in front of me. Bending over, I squint in the poor light at the narrow, slanted handwriting.

> In ages to come from future to present, the world will break into seven.
> The seventh will fracture to the eighth.
>
> Out of the wilderness comes double the heirs, sister against sister, brother against brother.
> A curse of their own will be light to the dark and mercy to the merciless.
> Winter will bring its own end; she cannot be stopped.
>
> An heir goes missing, a country is banished;
> An heir is banished, a country is cursed;
> An heir is cursed, a country revolts;
> An heir revolts, a country dies;
> A king dies, a queen in mourning;

A queen in mourning, a country too pious;
A country too pious, a country too poor;
A ruler too poor, a country goes missing.

Through the sacrifice of one, many will live.
Through the sacrifice of many, one will rule.
The sword that fells Winter brings death,
But death will bring life, and life will renew.

I gape at the parchment then reread the entire prophecy. How did I not know there was this much more to it? All we had was a mere fragment to work from. And here, to have the entire thing! What might my scholars do with it...?

I look at the Witch with hunger. "What is the counter curse?" I demand, my voice emerging low and eager, even to my own ears. "How do we fell Winter?"

The Witch frowns and motions to the parchment I hold. "I know not what that means."

"You must." I refuse the Witch's answer, forcing magic out from my own aura into the room, despite the cost. "You know. You will tell me."

The Witch is pushed back a half step by the force of my spell. "Do not use magic upon me; it will not gain ye the result ye want." Her eyes darken and swirl as she pushes back with her own spell.

The air chills around us, a swirl of spells clashing. The window darkens outside as clouds roll in.

Amusement flickers in the Witch's eyes. "Ye kill me, and ye lose all the information I know."

My fury grows. I need this information, cannot go home without it. It is not amusement in her eyes—it's fear, I realize with satisfaction. She has not been challenged in years, not magically at least.

The sky goes dark as I draw the cottage under my realm. Something rumbles outside, and it is several seconds before I recognize thunder. I have heard it only once before, when I crossed into Ostium's borders. Thunder preceded lightning and rain. I falter. I cannot call thunder and lightning, nor rain.

The Witch smiles. "You are far from my match, Queen."

I rise from my seat, squeezing my hand together in front of me.

The smile freezes on the Witch's face in a grotesque manner as her breath is cut off from her. She struggles against the act, her hands going to her throat.

"It will not take much longer to kill you," I say.

The Witch gags, her eyes bugging out as she holds her throat.

Satisfaction rises in me as the Witch chokes.

Just when the Witch begins to sag, I release her. The Witch falls to the ground of her humble cabin, and I watch her gasp air back into her lungs. Her tartan skirt reveals black stockings up to her knees, the only hint that perhaps she does not always live within the realm of her own magic. Perhaps she does venture out of doors.

"Tell me what I need to know. Tell me what you know."

"I told ye," the Witch gasps, "I do not know." She pushes herself up from the floor to fasten me with a glare. "A prophetess does not give solutions to the prophecy, nor interpretations, she merely makes them." She stands on trembling legs, gripping the back of a nearby chair. "I do not know."

"Then you are no more use to me."

I clench my fist again, and the Witch clutches her throat. I was mistaken; this is no great sorceress—she is just a witch, and a poor one at that. I watch the woman's life ebb from her eyes. Then I loosen my hand and let the corpse thump to the floor, eyes wide and staring, but unseeing.

I feel no pity, no regret. I will get my answers elsewhere. There are high costs to protecting a country after all.

I search the cottage, swiping up the piece of parchment along with an interesting spell book the Witch had lying open on the table. Then I inspect the meager cupboards, taking a few of the rarer potion ingredients I find there, before leaving.

As I step outside, the chill in the air rushes at my face. I scan the garden. Snow will soon invade this witch's private sanctuary. As the corpse decays, the spell will die. Depending on its strength, it may be minutes, perhaps days, perhaps even years. But on my way out of the garden, I waste no time in cutting myself a bouquet of the black roses I so envied.

XI

Lord Tillmore's

RUS

Dressed in black robes, a young girl with pale hair and pale skin opens the door, her gray eyes narrowed with distrust above a scowl. "Can I help you?" she asks in a voice like a chirping bird, both high and delicate despite the suspicion it houses.

I open my mouth, taking her in. She speaks boldly, despite her obvious slave status. A three-inch scar trails down her cheek and joins several other smaller scars, suggesting that she's far from compliant in her slave status. It's the darkness of her appearance that startles me most of all. She's harsh looking at best, all angles and planes, knife blades like furious slashes thinly veiled, if at all. Even her eyes are piercing and ready to spear anything she directs them at.

"What do you want?" she demands when neither of us answer.

Expecting the sweetness of her tone this time, I offer an apologetic, pacifying smile. "I'm sorry. We were expecting someone else."

She snorts. "Who?"

"Is the master at home?" I ask.

She cocks a hip out and crosses her arms. "Are you expected?"

I press my smile out farther along the edges. "No..."

Cito casts me a glance. "We're interested in discussing business with Lord Tillmore."

The girl rocks back on her heels while I debate my next words. How does one treat a slave? Like a servant? Or with less respect? Before I can decide how to respond, the girl shakes her head.

"I'll get Tillmore. Come in out of the cold." The invite she issues is not kind but seems the least of what might be expected in this country. Included in it is a condescending scrutiny of our appearance.

"Thank you." I precede Cito into the house, and the girl shuts the door behind us with a sharp snap. I pause inside, stunned by the blazing colors on the walls.

"There's a fire in there. You can wait there." The slave girl points to a room off to the right of the small room we've entered.

"Thank you," I say as the girl steps off toward a set of stairs in front of us, wide as a man's height and made from black stone with blue shards glinting within.

The girl takes her time ascending the stairs while the heat of the fire from the room behind tugs at me. For all the chill of Canens, there is some warmth after all.

Still, I spare a moment for a quick inspection of the great house as I remove my hat and mittens. The walls are coated with bright blue paints and yellow wainscoting. Elaborate statues stand alongside the front door as if keeping guard, not quite life-size. One is of a woman in armor looking as though she's from an earlier era, the other of a man in a Canens tunic and cloak, his gaze authoritative and condemning. That must be Tillmore.

I turn away from it and follow Cito into a smaller room that exudes heat, along with the crackling of healthy flames. Inside a generously sized room are leather chairs draped with furs. I run a hand over a black pelt that looks like bear fur and a silvery pelt like a wolf, which is almost as large as the bear. I shudder. The wolves here are frighteningly large.

"What do you think of that girl?" I ask.

Already warming his hands in front of the fire, Cito shoots me a curious glance over his shoulder. He's pulled down his scarf so I can finally see my companion's lips curve down into a frown. "She's not what I expected for a slave."

"But the robes...they must indicate some sort of slave status."

"Right." He faces the fire and shuffles closer, holding his face out toward the warmth. "But perhaps she can tell us what we really want to hear. I think we could turn her around." Cito gives me a tiny glance. "For a price."

"We have gold."

"It's disappearing rapidly, with all the supplies we bought. We need enough to get out of this gods-forsaken country."

Eyes down, I dig my fingers into the bear pelt. I don't know if we're ever getting out of this country. But that's the goal. With Elaina. I bite my lip and move toward the fire, dropping my hat and mittens atop a fur-draped chair on the way, where they stand out as pale gray on black. A pair of mittens that must belong to Lord Tillmore or someone in the manor rest on a nearby table. In comparison, my mittens appear shabby and crudely stitched. No wonder the slave girl gave us such looks when we entered. Strange that I hadn't noticed when we entered the village, but the wolves had been a great distraction.

"Well," I say as I hold my hands in front of the heat, "I think if we get the chance, we need to ask her. If Tillmore won't speak to us, perhaps that's a good thing."

The seconds tick by, with the silence broken only by the crackling fire. Finally, footsteps tapping against the stairs filter through the cracked door, followed by muffled steps on the rug covering the entry room. The door creaks open.

"He's on his way," the girl says, stepping inside. "I had to send the new girl out for him."

"The new girl?" I ask instead, trying to prevent any eagerness from leaking into my voice.

She shrugs, crosses her arms, and leans against the doorframe.

"One of 'em. He's always snatching up one girl or another, sending 'em out to the growing houses."

Growing houses? I frown at the unfamiliar Canensian words. But not wanting to ask about them, I instead wait for her to continue.

"For one reason or another," she adds as if there's an obvious double meaning to her words.

"And that reason might be?" Cito prompts.

She scowls at him. "Come on."

"What girl?" I ask. "We heard Lord Tillmore purchased some new slaves."

"What?" Her brows furrow with quick intelligence. "You want the girl he bought? He won't sell." Her lips curve into a sneer. "He has reasons for his purchases."

I tilt my head to one side. "Do you know her name...the new girl?"

"Nah. Don't know, don't care. Besides, slaves like us change names whenever our owners want us to."

"They do?" Cito asks then winces when I shoot him a glare at the naiveté of his words.

"You really ain't from here." The girl smirks, but there's an edge of fear sharpening her expression. "As if that weren't obvious from your clothes."

"What's wrong with them?" I ask.

She snorts. "You either hermits whose mama died and left you orphans or you strangers who never sewed winter clothes before."

"No." I hesitate. "We're from Ostium."

Her eyebrows fly up toward her hairline. "Ostium? You admittin' you're from there?" She laughs, eyes alight with cynical amusement. "You two are either fools or bold as asses."

I glance at Cito and shrug, but offer the girl a sly smile. "I suppose we're foolishly bold. But we were thinking about investing in the slave market."

Her eyebrows climb, if possible, farther up her forehead.

"Investin'? Like, takin' people outta here? To Ostium? Don't you have the plague?" As she speaks, her eyebrows descend, but hope flares in her eyes, slow and reluctant, as though she's had too many disappointments in her short life.

"No. Not anymore." Examining her, I hesitate in my next words. Is she a slave that would be loyal to her master or loyal to herself? With a quick breath, I plunge in. "Perhaps we could take some out of Canens. If that would be possible."

She's trying to read me, her eyes flashing across my face then turning to Cito as if to confirm her thoughts and back to me. "It's none of my business, but you thinkin' of asking Tillmore to be a partner?"

I hesitate. Have we stumbled onto something bigger with this slave market comment? "We're simply here investigating the market at this point," I say instead of answering. "We thought Lord Tillmore would have some information to benefit us."

"What've you been told about him?" The girl readjusts and tightens her arms.

I glance at the door, wondering how much longer we have before Tillmore shows up.

"He won't be here for a while. He's not in the growing houses. I don't know where he is." She smirks.

I bite back a smile in response. "How did you come to be a slave in this house?"

Her lips curve into a sneer. "You mean, why did he buy me?" She motions down to her charcoal robes. "I'm a thief, ain't I?"

"I don't know." I shrug. "I just know you're a slave."

A wicked grin darkens her face. "I'm a slave because I'm a thief. And I'm here because Tillmore likes young girls."

My stomach clenches as if she's put her fist into it. "Oh? Is there any...particular type of young girl he likes?"

"Whatdya mean?" The girl frowns.

"Any particular age? Take the new girl, for example? Tell me about her."

"The new girl?" She scowls dismissively. "She's thirteen. A small little thing." She curls her lip. "He likes 'em small too."

A chill of dread runs down my spine. "And her coloring? Is it like yours?"

Her frown deepens. "Why do you ask so much about this girl?"

"I'm simply trying to get a feel for what types of slaves Lord Tillmore might purchase."

"Why?" she presses.

"So that I know what sort of slaves we might expect from him. It's a business," I tell her, surprised by how easily the lies come.

"Miss—" Cito begins.

She snorts a laugh. "You can't call a slave 'miss.' We're dirt." She grins, and the act turns her scarred face into one of the criminal she professes to be. "Dirt. Buried under a half dozen feet of snow. Yes. We're that low."

"And yet the slaves seem to maintain a great deal of respect here..." Cito says.

"Where did you get that idea from?" she snaps. "We sleep on the floor with barely a fire and blankets to keep warm. We're far from pampered servants. We're not even indentured servants."

"You can't work out your freedom? None of you? What is your crime?"

"My crime?" Venom laces her voice. "My crime is stealing to feed my cripple mother and siblings. Stealing a loaf of bread and a cut of meat. And for that, I face a life of slavery."

"Surely not for a simple loaf of bread and—" Cito begins.

She quells his argument with a look. "Yes. For a simple loaf of bread and hunk of meat. Something that my family would make last for a week. I don't even know if they're alive now." Tears glisten in her eyes, but her jaw sets as she stares past us into the fire.

I glance at Cito. Even if Elaina isn't here, how can we leave a girl like this here?

Cito's eyes harden as if he's heard my thoughts. He gives me a look that says, "We can't save them all."

"Listen," the girl says before either of us can speak. "I don't know what your motives are, but I'll help you if you help me."

Cito opens his mouth to protest—I can see it in his eyes—but I speak first. "We'll do what we can for you."

"Promise?" she pushes.

"Yes," I say without hesitation, ignoring Cito's glare.

She chews on her lip and searches my face. She must like what's there, for she closes her eyes and lets out a sigh of surrender. "If you wanna convince Tillmore you're really from Ostium, you have to ask him about his growing houses."

"What are growing houses?" I mutter impatiently.

She shoots me an equally impatient look in return. "They're where we grow a lot of our food here. So we don't have to buy from other countries. It ain't enough, and food is scarce still, but Tillmore's are gaining popularity. His are most efficient. You heard about 'em? About his?"

I shake my head.

"Well, he's insanely proud of them. Thinks they rival the Queen's. He wants to grow his bigger and better, become a food supplier—there's more money in that than in slaves these days." She snorts. "Slaves are far too plentiful."

"So he won't be interested in slave business?"

She juts out her scarred chin in consideration. "He might. But you have to do it the right way. He buys lots of slaves. But he'll only tell you what you want to hear if you give him something in return."

"All we want—" Cito begins.

"All I want is to find a certain slave," I interrupt. "But I promise to do what I can to help you in the process."

The girl's lips purse and press out to the side. "Who are you finding?"

"My sister. Elaina is her name."

"She Ostium?"

I hesitate. "She could pass for Canensian. She has your coloring."

"Any distinguishing marks?"

"I—she is thirteen. She's petite, and her eyes are pale brown with green in them, hazel, we call them. Her hair is dark blond."

The girl appears to consider. "That's too vague. There are five slaves here that might be her."

"All that arrived recently? She would have been sold recently, probably by the slave traders that passed through."

"Oh, well—" The girl stops and considers. Then shakes her head. "No. She ain't here. We only got two new ones yesterday. They're for the growing houses."

Annoyed, I clench my jaw in frustration. "You're sure? That you only got two new ones?"

The girl turns to me. "Absolutely. I was there myself."

"She might have come in with three other young women?" I press. "All about fifteen or sixteen?"

"You aren't just saying that so we'll help you?" Cito asks at the same time. "To keep us from putting our efforts into gaining whom we seek? I mean—"

The grin that twists the girl's face is nothing short of cruel. She's caught Cito's words for their true meaning: we don't want her. The darkness in her grin makes something else evident to me: this is something she's heard a lot in her life.

"Maybe?" she suggests with a laugh. It's not a happy sound but a mocking and derisive one. "I have to look out for myself." Then she sobers. "But no thirteen-year-old needs to be here." She glances behind her at the foyer. "This is the worst place to be."

"How do we convince Lord Tillmore we're looking into the slave market then?" I press. "And you didn't see two fifteen- or sixteen-year-olds?" I try to remember Elaina's lady's maids and what they look like. There was the one Elaina's age that always giggled, then the quiet, older one, and another who gossiped all the time. "There would have been a tall brunette with dark brown eyes, a shorter, dark-skinned girl blond with dark green eyes, and another that always wears her brown hair in a long braid. Then of course a younger girl, my sister, whom I've already described to you." I glance to Cito, but he shrugs.

With an expression of something like recognition, the girl opens her mouth just as a door slams open in the foyer. All of us flinch, caught in a guilty discussion.

I hesitate too long to ask the girl another question though, and a commandeering man strides through the door. He doesn't acknowledge the girl standing beside us; stepping back from the conversation, she passes him a sneer behind his back.

"Gentlemen," Lord Tillmore says in an arrogant, oily voice. "To what do I owe this visit?"

"Lord Tillmore, I am Rus Solem, and this is my companion, Cito Fati. We are visitors from Ostium."

"Ostium?" Lord Tillmore sinks down into the cushiest leather armchair near the fire and slaps his hands down on the arms, taking up as much space as he can. His angular face is like most of the Canens' men's we've seen: a large, hooked nose, pale eyes, pale hair peeking out from his fur cap, and pale skin, as if he has spent most of his time inside and far from the sun. His thin frame is gangly but wiry.

I take a steadying breath. I should not underestimate this man.

"Yes, sir," Cito says. "We're looking into the specifics of opening a slave trade discussion between our two countries."

Lord Tillmore looks at Cito then me. In a strong, clear voice, he gives a traditional Ostiite greeting in a flawless accent. "May your day be most blessed."

A flicker of panic rises in my gut. He speaks Ostiite?

Cito's response, however, is immediate and natural. He smiles and, in an accent as flawless as Lord Tillmore's, gives the traditional response. "And may your day be beyond all blessing."

I lift my hands to the fire as if to warm them but really to let my pounding heart still. We have to get through this meeting to find out about Elaina. About the slaves he purchased. And to help this slave girl.

After warming my hands, I face the others again. Cito has taken a seat in another armchair near the fire, and I meet the pale, slightly suspicious eyes of Lord Tillmore.

"Lord Tillmore," I begin in Canensian, "we've heard great things about your compound."

"Oh?" Tillmore's eyebrow lifts with an air of skepticism.

From the doorway, the slave girl's gaze flashes with concern.

"Yes," I say, injecting confidence I don't feel into my voice. "All throughout Merise, we were told of nothing but how much your village has advanced in recent years."

That's true, right? I barely resist the urge to shoot the slave girl another questioning glance.

"I see." Tillmore's expression is inscrutable.

I seat myself casually in between Cito and Tillmore. "To be honest, sir, the things we heard made us quite curious about your village. It's unique, isn't it?"

Tillmore frowns at this. "Is that what they're saying in Merise?"

"Well..." I give a little laugh as if I might have embellished a little to be more flattering. "We've not been to Merise yet, but we've heard some...mixed comments."

At this, Tillmore grins, and his face transforms from something distant and tolerant to one of amusement. "Now that I believe."

I relax a modicum. This is just another political meeting. Play the charm card, Rus, but do it carefully. I lean toward him conspiratorially. "How did you build this village from nothing but snow and ice?"

A wrinkle appears on his forehead, and his fingers tighten slightly on his armchair. "It seems you've been misinformed, sir."

"Misinformed?" I resist the urge to glance at the slave girl again. "About what?"

"This village. It was my father's village before me and almost died out."

"Oh?" I school my face into one of deep interest.

"It used to be twice this size, but after the last great snowstorm, half the population was buried and killed." He makes a motion with his hand as if to add something then stills it and stares into the fire in thought. After a moment, he turns to me and says, "But this isn't why you're here."

"No?" I lean back.

"No. I want the real purpose."

I chuckle, allowing my discomfort onto my face. "We want to start an illegal slave business between Ostium and Canens."

Cito shoots me a shocked look. I meet it and shrug as if abandoning all secrecy.

Amusement on his face, Tillmore tilts his head back and laughs.

"We heard you purchase slaves on a regular basis from traveling traders. We'd like to be one of those traveling traders—but we'd like to buy from you and sell in Ostium."

Tillmore's mouth quirks under his pale beard. "How does that work? When you cannot legally cross the borders?"

I grin. "Anything is possible. You leave that part of the deal to us, and we leave the slave purchases to you."

He frowns slightly. "I only have to assume that you have a bribe in place to ensure your departure goes as smoothly as your entrance."

Chuckling again, I feign discomfort. "Well, sir, I can see you know the business as well as we hoped."

Tillmore allows a smile to part his thin lips. "What do you want from me then, gentlemen? Simply the bodies?"

"We were hoping you had an excess of slaves, quite honestly," I say simply. "And that we could trial our slave trade business with a few of them."

Tillmore's eyes widen, betraying his shock at this perceived honesty. He searches my face then Cito's, and a slow smile dawns on his lips. "Drinks for my guests," he announces.

It takes me a moment to realize that our host is speaking to the slave girl. Only when she moves silently across the wall toward a wooden bar in the back of the room does understanding come.

Tillmore has continued speaking, as if confident in her obedience. "How do you know I am one to trust?"

"An educated guess." I smile, deliberately vague. He needs to know only what I want him to know or to think. Not everything.

Tillmore's chuckle is low and deep with amusement. "Quite the risk."

"Yes, well, all businesses are a risk. Some more than others." I shrug.

"And with greater risk comes greater reward, no?" Tillmore agrees.

The slave girl slides a drink into her master's hand, which he accepts without a blink. Her approach to Cito and me is equally unobtrusive. With her plain looks and silent footsteps, her thief's training no doubt, it's as if the girl has been groomed to be a silent slave in the presence of her master. Too bad her master couldn't tame her spirit.

"And why do you think that I might be willing to partake in this risk? The risk for me might be greater than the risk for you," Tillmore continues after a sip from his drink.

"Ah, well, you seem like a man full of calculated risks." I swirl the honey-colored liquid around in the glass, ignoring the unease that emanates from Cito in his chair.

"Yes, and what do you offer me for my risks?" Tillmore continues.

"Obviously, a part of our profits."

Tillmore begins to raise a hand, as if to brush away the thought of money, when Cito speaks up.

"Or if money is not to your preference, we might be able to supplement your growing houses with seeds and plants difficult to find."

At this, Tillmore's hand stills.

I suck in a silent breath and turn wide eyes to Cito.

Tillmore lifts his drink to his lips then says, "Go on."

"Well, Canens doesn't have any naturally occurring produce here now, does it? So we can find you seeds you might want from other countries. Outside of Canens, as Ostiite citizens, we can travel more freely than you or your men."

Tillmore nods, following Cito's thinking. "Yes, that is true."

You're a genius, Cito.

"And if you give us a list, we'll take the cost out of your profits," Cito continues.

This is almost going to happen—and I don't even want it to. What do we do if Tillmore agrees to this plan? Do we buy some slaves and take them to Ostium? He'll expect us to come back...

"Gentlemen, this idea is intriguing, I admit. I don't know how you discovered that my ultimate desire is to become a produce supplier for Canens. Slaves, eh, they don't interest me except as a means to my ends."

"And yet they interest us," I remark.

"Yes."

"Don't you want to know why?" Cito asks.

Tillmore waves away the question. "No. Canens has more mouths than it can feed—even with our growing houses and exporting the slaves we already have. I think exporting some of those mouths is an excellent idea. And Ostium had that plague recently enough, I think the reasons for exporting the excess slaves is obvious."

A little breath I hadn't realized I was holding escapes my lips. "Excellent then."

"But I'm not quite ready to agree to a business venture."

My hope nosedives. "No? What about a trial?" I suggest. "We purchase a couple of slaves from you now, transport and sell them in Ostium, and then return to you with either a cut of the profits or else the goods you ask for."

Tillmore taps his glass with his hand, and a clinking sound rises into the air as his thick gold ring around his middle finger knocks against the glass. "It's an enticing possibility. I assume you have gold to purchase those slaves now?"

"Yes, of course," I say.

Cito shifts in his chair.

Tillmore's gaze glances between us. "One or two?"

Hope warring with caution within me, I dip my head in a nod. "Yes, I think that should be sufficient to prove ourselves to you."

"And a bill of sale." Tillmore drains his glass.

I do the same. "Of course."

"I think I'm willing to agree to such circumstances."

My heart leaps. Despite my caution, my gaze slides to the slave girl in the room. Her expression is frozen, not quite one of fear and not quite relief. In fact, I can't determine what emotions battle there. Only that they are not joy.

"So I think we have a few details to arrange."

I tear my gaze away. "Yes. Quite a few."

"Then I think, perhaps, it would be best if you stayed the night."

"Considering the wolves we left outside the gates, as well as our business, I think that might be the best option," I say.

"Prepare them rooms," Tillmore says as he rises. He drains the last few drops of his glass and sets it on the table beside his chair. "In the meantime, can I show you my houses? Perhaps you will spot an agricultural gap of mine."

"Of course. We'd be delighted." Exchanging a glance with Cito, I barely hold back a shiver. We're going to become exactly like the people that took Elaina—whether we like it or not.

XII

Smoke

BLANCHE

"Due to Princess Winterberry's illness, the princess will not be participating in the festivities this year. Her Royal Highness implores the people of Canens to eat and be merry at her birthday celebration."

I already read the proclamation and signed off on its being delivered to the people that morning. They would be disappointed, surely, but would anyone truly care? The girl hadn't made it to any of the parades for years, not after I gave them that story of her unfortunate accident. After that, I'd forced her to wave from her rooms like an invalid...

Still, doubt niggles at me as I stand at the window of my private rooms, staring out at the city sprawling below. The people have an odd affinity for their princess. If it hadn't been for the princess, the winter wouldn't be as severe, I am sure of it. My study of prophecies had all but proved it. Every day of cold takes its toll on Canens, a toll that has been worsening with each year and adding to the divide between the countries.

Then I introduced the growing houses. And at least we had our own food. But when I shut down the borders... We weren't ready. I direct my anger inward this time. But what else was I to do? We must become independent again, and this is the way. That and breaking the curse. The people must see that. They do. That's why they still love me. That's why I deserve the throne, and if they knew what I knew, they'd know it too. They wouldn't keep trying to put that cursed little girl on the throne.

"Majesty?"

I tense at the familiar voice of my lady's maid. "What is it?"

"The sleigh is prepared."

I dip my head in acknowledgment but don't turn from my position at the window. Far below, outside the palace gates, people mill over the snow-packed streets. Some have taken the opportunity to wear their best cloaks, and splotches of color lighten the otherwise dull Canens landscape, providing a refreshing brush of color amidst the grays and blues and whites of the cursed land. Beyond the city, just within the city walls, are the storage houses and the growing houses. Their stores are decent now, kept in case of siege, and at least here in the capital, the growing houses can grow enough to feed everyone. If not to fullness, at least to keep them alive. Starvation is not as common now; houses are not being newly abandoned every day. That happened years ago, back when the growing houses were still being developed. When I made a few mistakes—like closing the borders prematurely.

With a sigh, I take another minute to observe the crowds—still a wonderful turnout, despite the town criers announcing the princess's anticipated absence.

Surely due to the significance of this birthday. I brace myself. I am queen, not Winterberry. They are here to see me today. My thoughts don't quite suppress the sliver of doubt that festers within me. There's a feeling I can't quite shake this morning, as if something terrible is going to happen, and my huntsman's warning of a surprise on Winterberry's birthday comes back to me. I forgot to ask if he discovered anything more of it. But it's too late now. I'd best hope the surprise is innocuous and not deadly.

On my way out of the room, my lady's maid steps up with a rasp-berry-colored, velvet cloak. I allow the servant to fix it on me, clasping it around my throat with a large brooch in the shape of a snowflake and glittering with blue adamas. The young slave arranges the ermine ruffed hood over my head so that my crown remains visi-ble. It won't do to have it hidden.

Then I lead the way down into the grand entrance of the palace and strike out across the blue and white lapis stone, my heels clicking. From the edges, servants stop to step back from their dusting and sweeping and lower themselves into curtsies or bows. I brush past them, preparing myself for the bite of the cold outside. When I am only a few feet away, the large front door swings open, inviting in a blast of frigid air. Even I suck in a breath, barely managing to suppress the choking cough which rises in my throat.

Outside, I make my way as slowly as I can down the icy steps, using the arm of my Captain Plaga as a railing. I use him all the way into my uncovered sleigh. Usually I would ride in a warmer, covered sleigh, but not today. As soon as I ascend the steps, my spell takes effect. The cold slips away, and by the time the horses reach the gates to the palace, I am almost sweating. Still, the people do not approve of magic, and for me to flaunt that their queen knows it so well and practices it so often would be foolish indeed. Superstitions like they have keep the growing houses from thriving. We cannot cast spells without the people's support—I cannot do them all myself. Not and keep them up. A warming spell of that strength must be refreshed every week.

I sigh and remind myself to sit tall in the sleigh as it glides along. The red and gold sleigh jingles with each step of the paired white horses, the driver staring straight ahead as he guides them through the gates. Ahead of us wait nearly the entire guard, soldiers dressed in charcoal-colored, wool uniforms, their hats lined with black furs. As they approach, my coachman stops the sleigh, and I perform the appropriate inspection and salute to the squadron leaders. When I arrive at the end of the line, I give the General of Merise's troops,

Lord Acutulus, mounted on his speckled gray stallion, a sharp salute, which he returns.

From there, he whirls his mount to face the troops and gives a command. As one, they urge their horses onto the path in front of my sleigh and fall into line, leading me through the main street of Merise.

If Winterberry were sitting in the sleigh with me, as she had been until she was seventeen for this farce, I would wave and smile.

My gaze lingers on a family of three. In her father's arms, a little girl with blond curls peeks from under her worn rabbit-fur hat, while her mother looks on with a slight frown. In the early years of my marriage to King Balint, the princess was excited to attend these birthday celebrations—even boasted of them. But once the spoiled girl realized I shared her father's love, Winterberry became sullen and rebellious. I had to lock her up, for the kingdom's own safety.

As we crest the hill to descend into the town center, I feel more than hear a whisper go through the guards surrounding the sleigh. I glance at them then around for a threat. I see nothing but people lining the streets. Except...in the distance, just before the city walls...

"What is that?" I demand, sitting forward. "Why is there smoke coming from the walls?"

A murmur goes through the waiting crowds as they see me and my men staring beyond them. Gazes follow, and cries break out as some point and shout, "Fire!"

The guards nearest me close in around the sleigh as my driver pulls the horses to a halt.

"What's happening?" I repeat.

"I don't know, Majesty." Captain Plaga appears at my side, urgency on his scarred features. "But we must return you to the palace. If it's an attack, you are in danger."

I spare only the briefest glance for my captain then instruct my driver to drive me toward the smoke.

"Majesty!" Another voice interrupts as Lord Monete, my advisor, comes bolting up to the carriage, his shoulder-length blond hair flying out behind him in his haste. "You must not return to the palace."

"What?" Captain Plaga snaps his attention back to the sleigh and me. "No, she must return—this could be a threat on her life."

"Or a distraction to do exactly what they want," Lord Monete retorts, glaring at the captain, his thin lips pressed together in distaste.

"What do you mean?" Captain Plaga fixes his gaze on the advisor. "What do they want?"

"To distract from the palace and the parade."

"Well?" Plaga demands. "What are we supposed to do, let them come to her? Hold a parade with the Queen in full view while the city burns?"

"No, but if you abandon this parade, the people will be furious. The princess has already backed out of her own celebration. There is too much unrest in the city for you to do the same."

"Even at risk of her personal safety?" Plaga scoffs. "You're mad. We're taking her up to the palace where she's safe. We can reschedule the parade for a later date." He jerks a hand through the air to indicate to his men to fall in tighter and for the driver to turn the sleigh around.

"And if she's not?" Lord Monete circles his horse around, keeping close to the sleigh. "If she's not safe in there?"

Plaga pauses, glaring at the advisor. "What do you know?"

"Only that there has already been one uprising, one rebellion in another city. What if their target is not whatever burns but the Queen?"

Twisting in my turned-around sleigh, I gaze at the billowing smoke only a few miles away, ignoring the bickering men riding on either side of me. They are both right. I can't run away from the parade, or the people would see my act as one of fear. I am not afraid. And they must know that.

The two men glare at each other above my sleigh as they move toward the palace, the driver not waiting for instructions.

I bite my lip. Then I call out, "Stop the sleigh."

Directing a fear-filled glance at me, the driver obeys.

I motion to my captain. "Find me a horse."

His overly large nostrils flared, Captain Plaga motions to one of his guards, and the guard spurs his horse off through the streets. I watch him go while Captain Plaga and Lord Monete glare each other down when not scanning the crowd for dangers.

It's not two minutes later when the guard returns with a saddled palfrey. I descend the sleigh on my own as the driver struggles to control the spooking horses. I brush away Lord Monete's offered hand and swing myself into the saddle. Without waiting for either man, for too much time has already been lost, I aim the horse toward the smoking walls of the city and kick it forward.

XIII

Animals

WINTERBERRY

O nce a day, the caravan stops, and we are let out of our jail two at a time to find a semi-private spot to relieve ourselves. None of us dare go far, crouching behind a mound of snow or merely using our capes to shield ourselves several yards away from the sleigh and reindeer. If we stray too far from the paths, who knows what might take us. We'll sacrifice our dignity before our lives, especially as slaves.

Upon our return, we are each given a hunk of bread and a cup of iced-over water then herded back into the wagon and locked inside. Some of us down the icy water and stuff the cup full of clean snow before we reenter the prison sleigh, our thirst more than the small cup will quench.

I have never felt more like an animal, and the farther we travel, the more contemplative the other men seem to become of Des and me. It is the animalistic leers the men cast that leashes Des to my side, even in her feverish state. Although we all wear various shades of fur from head to toe now, and the weather grows even worse the farther north we go, a few men stare at Des as though she is nothing but a whore for their pleasure.

CHAPTER XIII

I hand Des my bread. She must be starving; she is so thin and so young.

As we sit with Des eating the bread, the sleigh bouncing gently on the endless planes of snow, Des turns her round face up to mine. "Will you tell another story?"

The willow bark must have helped. I laugh softly. "Another story? I don't know how many other stories I know..."

She pouts. "Surely you know one more?"

I relent, for I know many tales. How else was I to spend my endless imprisonment in the palace except reading? "Anything in particular you'd like to hear?"

"Anything," Des murmurs.

I nod, and then I tell her a story of a sad queen who asked the gods for nothing but a baby. I leave out the part where she dies in the end. None of us needs to hear that. Not now.

XIV

Ino

RUS

Morning light breaks over Lord Tillmore's village, illuminating the snowy tops of the small houses and setting the ice and snow wall aglow with orange-pink light. With the clear skies, I spot a sprawling city only a few hours away while I stand at the front door of Tillmore's manor. In the darkness, it was a twinkle of lights across the snow, but in the morning, it is blanketed in snow and ice, awash with the pink glow of a rising sun.

I glance at the sky above Umbra's saddle, but it doesn't keep my attention. Instead, I turn to Swallow, whose pack is now spread throughout all three of the animals at the increase in his load. Worry drags me down, overwhelming me with eagerness to leave this village behind. For all its picturesque location and pretty snow and icicles, it is treacherous and polluted.

"It's rather beautiful, isn't it?" Cito murmurs.

Astra, the bird-like girl from the night before, overhears and snorts as she assists in readying the three animals for departure. She doesn't speak, for her master stands on the stairs above, surveying the group before him, and she plays her part well. Lord Tillmore's gaze lingers on her, contemplative, the humor from the evening before long gone.

A shiver runs down my spine. Our deal is far from confirmed. If we fail with our purchase, then we'll likely forfeit our lives. Tillmore won't be a business partner we can fool for long.

Tugging the final strap tight, I give Umbra a pat on the shoulder and step up to Tillmore.

"How long again, until you think you'll be able to make it back?" the lord asks.

"This time, I'd say give us two to four months."

"Four *months*?" He blinks as if in sudden regret of agreeing to our business venture together.

I grimace apologetically at him. "We have several places to go before Ostium. Our pace will be slow by then. We might return much sooner. But, just in case things don't work like we anticipate," I add, trying to soothe away Tillmore's surprise. "Just in case the border crossing doesn't go so smoothly."

"Right." Tillmore smirks, as if he's glad he won't be responsible for that part.

"I imagine each successive journey should be faster," I assure him. I wonder if he can see through my lies? At this point, I almost believe them myself.

"Good luck," Lord Tillmore says, offering a hand. "You have the list of items I gave you?"

"Yes." I pat my pocket. The cloud of my breath half hides us from each other in the early morning. "I'll return with those in tow."

"Excellent." Tillmore adjusts his cloak and dismisses us with a nod. "Good luck. Safe travels."

I face the group, a touch sad to leave this man's village behind. After an evening dining upon freshly picked produce and freshly slaughtered meat that wouldn't have been out of place upon a Heian table in the palace, I wouldn't be surprised if his slaves turned out to have magical powers or something.

Umbra jigs sideways when I mount, either excited to get away or rejuvenated after a night spent in a warm stable with all the food he could eat. In our weeks on the road, he's noticeably dropped weight, and he hadn't been a heavy horse to begin with. I almost regret not being able to stay here in the village longer. For Umbra and...

I glance back at Lord Tillmore, my gaze sliding to the slave standing silently beside him. "You haven't changed your mind?"

Tillmore gives a gravelly laugh and shakes his head. "No. You got the one you'll get." Still smiling, he tilts his head to the side and adds, "Perhaps if this one goes off successfully."

I offer him a smile, although my heart clenches in my chest. "Then we will see you upon our return."

Lord Tillmore nods his chin at the slave waiting beside Swallow. "Don't forget your purchase."

Swallowing thickly, I face the willowy blond girl and indicate that she should mount.

With large eyes, the teen slave girl dressed in white puts her foot in the stirrup and throws herself gracefully into the saddle. Relief is evident in her features, even though it mingles with concern.

I nudge Umbra forward and offer a lifted hand in a wave to Lord Tillmore.

We wind through the small village, people peering out the frosted windows at our small convoy.

The thin figure riding Swallow is only vaguely familiar to me as one of Elaina's gossipy lady's maids.

At fifteen, Ino, with her blond hair and dark eyes, could almost pass for a Canensian. And she was the only new one Tillmore would sell. Thank the Creator she was the one we wanted.

Astra was "not for sale," according to her master. I couldn't determine exactly why, but Tillmore had not even entertained the idea of selling the young thief who'd answered the door. It wasn't through any apparent affection but rather a sense of possession. Something about that girl—something personal—makes her worth owning to him. And without revealing a private interest of my own, I couldn't press it. I managed to talk to her alone before we left, just for a few seconds, in a conversation that now breaks my heart.

"I promise, we'll come back for you or send someone for you," I murmured as we brought food out to the horses in the barn together. "I won't leave you here under a cruel master."

Her face was dark and unforgiving. "I won't stop trying to escape. I got my momma back in Merise—I have to take care of her." The words were filled with anguish and anger.

A chill deeper than the weather slipped into my bones. "I thought you said you weren't sure if she lived."

"I hope she does."

"Can we—can we help somehow? Check on them perhaps? Send you a message?"

She shook her head. "You want to help? Get me out."

"Can you slip free? Meet us on the road?"

She glanced back toward the house. "No. I doubt he'll take his eyes off me today."

I bit my lip. If only I had a connection in Merise that could take her in. Or something to do to help her get free. I'm powerless here.

"You can't get me free, then you help my family."

Her eyes were bright with fury and despair. A fury and despair that I recognized as burning within myself. There was only one answer to give. "Where do I find them?"

Now, the cold, dirty-white road to Merise stretches out in front of us. Ino rides between us, Cito leads the way, and I bring up the rear while scanning the empty horizon for wolves and watching the snow berms for movement.

How do I tell Cito we now have a family to provide for? My stomach turns at the idea of having purchased another human being, even with it being Ino. How can Canens engage in this? How do they not see these people as people with their own rights? Not just animals to buy and trade?

Ino's been mostly quiet so far, acting stunned as we completed her purchase and she was told to mount up. I don't know whether

Tillmore gave her any warning, but there she was when we were ready, wrapped in a white, wool cloak with white fur on the edges of the hood.

Tillmore had given us four of his newest slaves to choose from; Astra was not one of them, or I would have taken her too. But Ino, the oldest of Elaina's maids, was pointed out to us in the growing house amidst a handful of other workers being trained to pollinate flowers, a critical task given the lack of insects in this frozen land.

A sharp, cold breeze slaps me back from the warmth of the growing house, making me wish I could illuminate the warming orb without risking its safety.

"How did you find me?"

Ino's quiet voice takes me out of my memories. I smile at her before remembering my scarf covers my face up to my lower lashes. "I tracked you."

"Me?"

"Elaina, you, the men who took you."

"What happened to them?"

I glance away, scan the horizon for the wolves. "I killed the gypsies."

"Good." Her voice is harsh, cold as the vacant hills before us.

"I spared the children."

"That's too bad."

My frozen eyelashes crunch in my surprise. "Why?"

"They'll become men and women." Her words burn with the heat of hatred. "They'll steal young girls and sell them. Like they did me and Elaina. And Vesta. And Daphne."

"I offered them sanctuary in Heia." I dip my head toward my shoulder. "If they take it."

Her gaze dissects me. "You are more merciful than I thought."

"Should I not have been?" My stomach squirms with unease. Anger begins to resurface, anger I thought I had eliminated when I killed the gypsies. All but their offspring.

Ino blows out a slow breath. "The children were responsible for watching us. Making sure we didn't escape. They beat us with sticks. Kept us weak from hunger. They ate their food before us. They threatened us." Her gaze grows more and more vacant as she speaks, as if the memories dance before her eyes. "I wish you had killed the lot of them. They killed Daphne."

My breath catches behind my wool scarf. "I'm sorry."

With fury clouding her eyes, she shakes her head and stares down at her mittened hands.

Disturbed by her hatred and my own growing regret, I shift in my saddle; Umbra's ears flick nervously. Fingering the hilt of my sword with my gloved hand, I give the horizon another scan, only there is nothing. Nothing...but a swirling, dark cloud hanging over what must be Merise.

XV

Conversations

WINTERBERRY

After I finish my story, Des drops off to sleep with her head on my shoulder, and the sleigh glides along in near silence. The sun rises high enough into the sky to illuminate our path and evaporate the morning fog, but the chill remains, and today it grows so much colder that even the guards speak of it. Our breaths shiver in front of us, our cheeks and noses barely poke out from beneath our blankets, and frost coats the blankets around our mouths.

Around us, a high howl sounds, breaking the stillness of the air.

Several of the men flinch. One of the younger ones nearly slides off the bench. "Was that a wolf?" he whispers, his voice breaking in terror.

My gaze turns to the guards; I'll take my cues from them. I have to assume they're prepared to handle not only a lone wolf but also a pack. We're a group of over a dozen, all men except for Des and me. The guards glance around, staring into the mists. Horses and reindeer give low snorts of unease.

Scenarios run through my mind. Wolves attacking, killing the guards. Would they be able to get us in the iron cage? I sweep my gaze around me. Not far past the cage, the mist swirls, thick as silk. There could be a dozen wolves out there, and we wouldn't know. But if they attack and kill the guards...all of us slaves will be trapped in the cage.

Then...we can escape. Maybe.

For hours, the wolf howls follow us. It sounds like a small pack, only two or maybe three wolves, and even though I pray for them to attack and kill the guards, freeing us from our slavery, I know it is useless. They don't. And I know they won't.

Yet as long as the wolves follow, we don't stop. We shiver in the back, the guards hunch over in their seats, and we press on until the wolves' howls are far behind us.

"I can't feel my mouth," I finally say. "Are we ever going to stop?"

"Not soon enough," the tall blond mutters from the other side of Des.

Across from us, Caleb shifts, lifting his chin from under his blanket. "Tonight? I don't know."

Des huddles closer to me under our blanket. I'm so cold that I can hardly feel her move. We need to stop and get her more medicine.

I shake my head. "And how long until we get to our new...home?"

"Another couple of nights, I think." Fully covered with his blanket, Caleb leans forward, tugging the blanket from his front to drape it over his shoulders and pull it tight around him.

I glance through the wooden partition in the front of the sleigh again and inspect the guards. They're relaxed again and yawning. The remaining guards, as well as Magister Marcus, ride their horses both in front and behind their goods—us. I grit my teeth, straining to try and find the Magister in the midst of all this mist.

Some time later, when it's been quiet for the last several miles, Caleb speaks.

"Today is the princess's birthday," he says as if starting a conversation.

I start. It is? It is. How had I forgotten my own birthday? My own coming-of-age birthday. I nearly laugh at the irony, then tears prick my eyes and my smile fades.

The tall, blond man next to Des snorts. "She's as dazed as a newborn lamb. With no hope of regaining herself."

A couple of the other men laugh.

My cheeks heat, and I tuck my chin under the scarf as I seek out Caleb's face.

"Yes, well, there are many who mourned the little Princess Winterberry when she fell from her favorite horse," Caleb says carefully. It's clear he sees my confusion and speaks for my benefit, but he doesn't acknowledge me other than that.

I can think of nothing to say anyway, for there was no fall, no accident. Not even a favorite horse. The Queen never let me ride after Father died.

"Now we'll see who dares to offer themselves as husband to her." The blond man snorts another laugh.

"Last I heard, the princess would never be of sound mind to rule," another slave says. "You think Queen Blanche will let her choose her own husband?"

The blond rolls his eyes but glances up front toward the guards. "Not if she wants to keep her talons on the throne."

A murmur goes through the slaves at the blond man's irreverent words.

"No man of Canens wants a mad wife, even if she is a princess," the blond continues.

I sit back, stunned at this twist in my own life.

"Perhaps a strong man beside her would give her strength," another man suggests with quiet laughter in his words.

The blond grins wickedly. "Or just give him a throne."

There's an unwilling titter of laughter from the others.

"I 'ave heard," continues the blond over the quiet laughter, "that the Queen wants a man for herself instead of marrying off the princess, and that every man who dares come for the princess will be offered the Queen instead." He grins and lowers his voice to a dark whisper. "But the Queen has never accepted any man, instead has them sent into the forest."

"For the huntsman," I breathe, and the words caress me with a chill.

"What makes you think the princess—or the Queen—wants a husband?" Caleb says calmly.

The blond pauses then shrugs. "Dunno. But I don't think either will ever find one—one's too simple, and the other is too smart."

The men laugh again, but the conversation drops off, buffeted away by a strong gust of wind that has us each clutching our blankets around us.

Des makes a sound, a low groan in her sleep, and shifts against me. Her forehead brushes my cheek, and it's burning hot. She coughs, and this time, there's a rattle in her throat that scares me.

We fall silent again, and shortly after, we stop to make camp. As soon as we are settled, I brew a tea with the remainder of the willow bark and press it on Des, forcing her to drink every last drop.

Tonight, few sleep. The wolves return, howling in the woods around us, a call to hunt or perhaps a warning about the hunters in their midst. I do my best to ignore them and to pretend that there is some in-between land in which I exist, somewhere that I am neither hunter nor prey.

XVI

Fire

BLANCHE

Wen I reach the fire, a crowd has already gathered before it. Smoke pours out of the top of a storage house, while flames leap out of the growing house two buildings away.

My stomach clenches. Merise residents pass buckets of snow down a line of people and throw the snow on the burning building.

Growing numb, I watch for several minutes before I realize several things. First, the fire burns despite the lack of fuel. Most of the growing house is glass, and yet it burns as though it's made of dry wood. Second, too many men stand around watching without attempting to help put out the flames. Third, the flames are far too efficient to be normal fire.

My stomach drops. It's a magical fire. A sorcerer has created these flames.

I scan the crowd. Who started it? Where is he?

Forcing away my racing thoughts, ignoring my churning stomach, I step forward. The rebellion has come to Merise.

I whirl on Lord Monete. "I thought the rebels were eliminated."

His eyes are round with fear. "There has been much unrest—I—I thought they were—"

Fury builds in me, bubbling up my throat and into my eyes. "It's impossible," I say, even though I know it's not. I stare at the crowd, searching for rebels as if they wear a brand upon their foreheads.

A man darts forward from the line, dumping snow upon the edge of the fire. At the assault, the flames hiss. For a second, it seems the fire has slowed, tamed by the act, then it erupts into a ball, jumping at the attacker. His shriek pierces the clamor. He drops the bucket, batting his hands at the flames on his wool tunic, screaming as the fire climbs his arms toward his face.

"Help me!" he pleads, but his flailing strikes away any helper.

Someone tackles him with a blanket, and the flames sputter. I can almost hear a chuckle from the flames as they die on the man.

"More snow! Water if you have it!" Cries for snow and water go up around the city as the crowd continues to grow and people jump in to help fight the growing fire.

A sharp breeze rustles through the crowd, and I hear the chuckle again. Alarm bolts through me, pinning my spine straight as a rod and hard as adamas.

It's enchanted fire. The snow won't work. Water won't work.

Enchanted fire means...no one but I can fight it.

Or let it devour the city. Let it devour not only the growing houses and storage houses, but the homes and my home.

Screams erupt from the crowd, and the chuckle rises to a shriek of laughter as the flames leap from the growing house before me to the one next to it. As one, the citizens reel back at the new inferno bursting into life. My horse gives a low rear, and I wheel the mare around, riding her in a tight circle but keeping her in control— barely.

I scan the extent of the fire. It will only be minutes before it stretches halfway to the palace. Minutes to act. Seconds...this is targeted at me. I aim my palfrey around the crowd, searching for the sorcerer controlling the flames. If I can find him, kill him...the fire might die naturally.

"The water isn't helping," cries someone.

"What else can we do?" comes an answer, the words full of despair.

"It's enchanted fire!" a gravelly voice calls out.

A murmur of fear goes through the crowd. I turn to the speaker who identified the fire and give him a hard glare, which he returns with equal force as if to ask, "What are you going to do about it?"

My breath catches. The people have long suspected me of being a sorceress. Those that do have treated me with a mixture of fear and hatred. They are the princess' staunchest supporters.

Temptation gnaws at me. It would serve them right to have them suffer.

One spell, a powerful one, will stop the fire in its tracks and save the city. But it will reveal my powers to everyone present—and everyone who is not here will hear about it for years to come. The magic will be obvious. I will no longer be able to pretend I am not a sorceress; I will not be able to hide.

I am <u>not</u> hiding, I tell myself. The people fear magic. And they won't trust me if—well, they'll trust me even less—if I confess to them just how powerful I am with a display such as this.

I growl deep in my throat. I can't do either.

Lord Monete draws his mount near mine. My palfrey snorts and dances in place.

"Majesty, you cannot take any action," he warns, as if he has been listening to the battle inside me.

I glare at him from under the heavy crown still resting on my head. "So I am to let the city burn?"

"We'll find a way." His blue eyes go blank. "Is there another—" He breaks off and looks around. "Is there someone else who might—"

"Look at it, Monete," I hiss. "By the time we find someone else, it will burn the city to the ground."

"If you do this, Your Majesty, there is no going back." His voice is forceful—the most forceful he has ever been with me, and it's clear that he disapproves of the idea of fighting magic with magic.

I narrow my eyes at him. "Don't you think I know that?"

"Not half of these people will be pleased. They would rather die."

"Are you certain about that? Certain enough to risk your life on it?"

He hesitates. "Majesty, although you might succeed today, if you display your powers, the rebels will not be quieted but will thrive. You fan the flames—you will give them the fuel they need to ignite the rest of the people against you."

I take another look at the flames before us. An entire growing house—and the crops within—is gone. Two more growing houses burn, while three of the five storehouses are in flames. "Then let them. I cannot lose any more."

The wind howls, the laughter rising to a shriek as I close my eyes and draw upon my magical stores. I haven't cast a spell like this in ages, not since— I push the thoughts aside and focus. The crackling heat of the flames burns against my exposed skin, bringing sweat to my covered skin. I draw upon the strength of the Canens crown upon me, using the magical powers of the adamas jewels. Each color works with magic in some way, with red enhancing the wearer's ability to perform magic. Thankfully, I put on the Rubini crown today, the one with the largest red gem ever found in the Canens mines. Now, I half close my eyes, forcing out the sound of the maniacal laughter and raising my hands.

My palfrey jigs sideways at the dropped reins.

I summon the power within me, feeling the burn of the magic as it travels throughout my blood, gathering in my fingertips with an ache like frostbite. The sky around us darkens, just like it had at the Witch's cottage. I knew one useful thing would come out of my visit to her; I've learned a new trick.

The crowd falls silent. Then power emanates from me with a roar that overtakes the laughter.

I open my eyes to a cloud-darkened sky. The air rumbles. My fingers burn. The air sinks in upon itself, biting cold. People in the crowd begin to look at me. Murmurs begin. Buckets fall to the packed snow with dull thumps. Mothers grab for their children, pulling them away. They stand and watch with horror written on their faces, gazes darting between their queen and the sky.

Face burning with the effort, I lift my stare to the blackened clouds. With a murmur from me, they shudder and rumble. A flash of golden light breaks through the darkness. Screams pierce the air. With another rumble, water begins to pour out of the clouds.

The water freezes halfway to the fire.

"There," comes Lord Monete's voice from beside me.

My eyes dart to the end of his finger, then follow it to a man standing behind the crowd, at the edge of the road behind them. He trembles, his eyes half closed as mine had been as he battles the magic I've summoned.

Why won't he just let me put out the fires? He's already revealed me—and destroyed half our food. I put aside my questions for the moment and whirl my palfrey toward him, spurring the mare on.

The man's eyes fly open at the sound of approaching hoofbeats. I ride through palpable fear as I approach, both his and the Merise citizens'. They scatter before me, and abandoning his task, the man wheels and flees. With surprising speed, he darts across the street toward the other four growing houses in Merise, along with one finished and partially filled storehouse and one half-completed storehouse.

A surge of anger fills me. I urge my mare on after him. I cannot allow him to destroy them all—it would cripple all of Canens. Exactly as he wants. But at the edge of the growing house, he stops and turns, sending me a taunting grin. Fury overtakes me. I pull my mare to a halt, glaring at the man.

"What do you want?" I call to him.

His grin widens, and he lifts a hand filled with flames.

My mouth parts.

He half turns to glance over his shoulder at the remaining four growing houses.

If he starts them on fire—

He draws back his hand, ready to throw the flames.

Why is he taunting me like this? Why risk his life to taunt me now? Why expose himself and turn the country against him and his magic? Is he trying to make the rebellion into a sorcerer's battle? I shake my head, forcing away the thoughts that stay my judgments. I can't kill him—I need answers first.

His eyebrow rises. "Step closer, and I let this fly."

I soften my tone. "What do you want? Let us talk."

Confusion darts into his expression. "Surely you can't be that removed from your people?"

"You are destroying the very lifeblood of Merise. Of Canens." Behind me, the flames burn on, casting a long shadow of me astride my horse toward the man, while the flames sizzle under continued rainfall.

"No." His voice is hard, the flame quivering in his hand. "You destroy it. Destroy us."

"How?" I ask, keeping my gaze locked with his, willing him to keep talking. A sharp needle jabs into the side of my head, a warning that my magical stores grow low. Keeping the clouds storming costs more energy than I expected; I can't do this much longer. I draw on the strength of the red gem again, and the clenching eases.

"You hide behind that crown, as if you deserve it. And yet you do nothing for those of us like you."

"Like me?"

His eyes flash with fire, red amidst the paleness of his gaze. "You know what I am. And you know there are more. We won't be put down any longer."

"I don't—"

With my half denial, he lifts his hand, and the flame jumps from his palm to the air. His eyes burn red with the reflection of flames.

High in the air, the fireball splits into four, each one surely destined for a growing or storage house.

Summoning my strength and calling to the storm, I react. Before he can speak or move again, lightning splits the sky. His red gaze shifts to the bolt and widens.

I keep my gaze on the balls of fire, and as the lightning strikes the sorcerer, I react to quench the fireballs. I send out a burst of energy, manipulating the air so that the fireballs struggle against a gust of wind. The wind holds them there, fighting as I draw on the strength of my crown to do what I must. It takes all my powers and the added power of the Rubini crown to drag the rain from the storm clouds down upon this new fire.

The fireballs sputter and hiss in anger at the intrusion. Then they fizzle out and disappear.

Gasps go through the crowd as I release the magic around them and allow the storm cloud to return to its spot over the blazing fire.

They open above the flames, and this time, the flames begin to sizzle and die.

I turn to the spot where the sorcerer stood calling forth his evil flames. Only instead of a scorched body or pile of ashes where his body should be, there is a puddle upon the snow where the lightning melted the spot at which he stood.

Faint headed, I ride my palfrey to the puddle and look down only to see my own pale reflection staring back, slightly wobbly as the surface ripples slower and slower.

Fury rises in the pit of my stomach. I will see him again. Of this, I am sure.

XVII

Merise

RUS

Halfway to the capital, I realize the cloud above Merise isn't dissipating but thickening, churning with a wind I can't feel. I nudge Umbra past Ino and Swallow, up beside Cito.

"What is that, do you think?" Cito juts his chin at the cloud.

"I don't know," I mutter. "But it can't be good." I glance back. "Ino, we need to hurry."

We urge our horses into a jog, risking their legs on the slippery road, and we reach the walls of Merise in less than an hour.

As we pass under the gate and through the stone walls, a gasp escapes Ino's mouth.

Umbra slows of his own accord as I gape at the charred remains of several buildings. "What happened?" I ask a peasant standing at the edge of the ruins.

The man evaluates me with a sharp look. "A fire," he says. "Magic fire."

"Where have you been?" a second man, this one short and weedy, pipes up.

"Not here." Calmly, I dismount and hand Umbra's reins to Cito, then walk toward the charred remains. "A fire?" I peer at the piles of ashes. "What buildings burned?"

The first man's gaze turns confused. "Storage houses. Three of 'em. Ain't it obvious?"

"And two growing houses," the second man adds, anger evident in his voice. "Half the year's product, gone, just like that." He snaps bare fingers in the air.

Around the ashes of the building, the snow has melted down to the ground. It's startling black against the white backdrop of snow; I cannot stop staring at the ground, dark as it is against the snow.

"And then, have you heard?" the first man says.

I tear my gaze from the dirt. "No. What?"

"The *Queen*." He pauses, scans the area around us, then motions me closer.

Following his gaze around and seeing no one paying any attention to us, I step closer. "What about the Queen?"

"She's got magic!" he exclaims.

"And?" I prod.

The man blinks as if I'm crazy. "And? She's got magic, you fool!"

"But, I mean—what did she do with it? Did she start the fires?"

The man leans back and frowns. "Well, no, someone else did that. She put 'em out."

"Did she hurt someone?"

Cito clears his throat behind me. Glancing at him, I absorb the "Let's not have everyone in Merise realize we're not Canensians right now" look with an amused twitch of my lips.

"But how did the fires get extinguished?" I ask the man.

"The Queen," the man says with a displeased grunt. "She used her magic."

"She—" I frown, becoming more confused. Perhaps my experience with the magic orb has already changed my outlook regarding magic, but then I never believed it was all bad. Heians usually act as though the mere mention of magic is magic itself—and therefore evil, although the taint of magic is far removed from our country after Edormisco's sleep.

"So...she saved Merise?" I ask.

"She let the storage houses and growing houses burn!" the man exclaims.

"Yes, but she didn't start the fire, did she?" I remind him.

"Maybe she did," the second man pipes up.

The first gives a cold chuckle. "I wouldn't be surprised if she did!"

"Why would she do that?" I tug off my right mitten and crouch at the edge of the ruins.

"She sat there and watched the houses burn—if she has magic, why didn't she stop it sooner?"

"Maybe she couldn't."

"I bet she started the fire herself—just so she could put it out and save the day," the other man suggests darkly.

I prod the burned pile. It's a mixture of wood, ashes, and glass. Why would they build with glass here? Even for a growing house, it would be ridiculous—and impossible—to keep heated.

"Could she?" I ask mildly.

"She coulda. Of course she coulda, with magic." The first man glowers as if the Queen having magic is a personal affront.

The man's words answer my internal questions. She could heat this building with magic. Or reinforce it with magic, perhaps. Interesting. What an ingenious way to feed the people of Canens without interference from other countries.

I glance around at the remaining growing houses. Three of the four have burned, two completely, and the one half burned has greenery peeking out of a shell of a building with burned supports and blasted-out glass windows.

Dozens of Merise residents pick through the ashes and glass, poking at the black piles with long sticks, uncovering red embers and, occasionally, a shriveled plant. A group of slaves picks through the half-burned building, carefully extracting plants that are charred and wilted, working quickly to move them from the ruined house to the remaining one. A myriad of emotions plays on their faces, sorrow, grief, panic, fear, and anger.

"Let's get out of here," I mutter to Cito.

"Where?" Cito asks.

I don't answer but lead us far away from the charred remains left by the fire. After finding an inn, I pay the stable boy for our horses to be tended to in the stable, and we claim a dusty table in a corner of the pub beneath the rooms. I glance around, making a note to enquire about vacancies. We'll need a room—or two—to stay in while we try to track Elaina through Merise.

The barkeep takes our orders, three ales and three specials, and we talk while we wait.

"Ino, what have you found out about how the slavery system works here?"

Her brow furrows. "Are you going into the slave trade as you told Tillmore?"

I laugh darkly. "Not unless we have to."

Cito pulls his hat from his head, his pale hair enough to blend in with the Canensians around us. "Well," she says slowly as the maid delivers our ales.

"It'll be a few minutes for the food," she says before disappearing with a sway of her hips and a wink that are certainly not for Ino's benefit.

"What were you going to say?" I ask.

"There's a way to figure out where slaves go after they're purchased. I overheard someone talking about it, and I asked because I was thinking maybe, if I ever escaped..." She sniffs, and Cito passes her a handkerchief he's produced from somewhere while I wait on the brim of my chair.

"There are slave records," Ino says.

"Records?"

She nods and tentatively glances around the half-empty inn, then pushes back her hood and hair, turning until the skin behind her right ear is exposed. There is a stamp, a tattoo, in blue against her pale skin. A list of several numbers and a symbol that I don't quite catch before she lets her hair fall back to cover it. "Each slave is branded or tattooed, sir. Those brands are recorded in a logbook, and we are given names that associate with the brand, if our new master likes. Temporary slaves bear a burn. Masters sometimes choose not to record the sales and trades of those, even if it is illegal to trade without a record. Permanent slaves receive a tattooed number that goes into the book and must be reported on every six months, whether we are sold or remain with the same owner."

I frown, my gaze turning back to Ino's neck. Ignoring the obvious that Ino has been branded a permanent slave, I say, "But the other girl, Astra, told us that you couldn't escape slavery?"

"You can't—not for what she's enslaved for."

"Which is what?" I ask.

Ino shrugs, a flush brightening her cheeks. "Murder."

I collapse back in my seat. "Murder? Whose?"

Ino shakes her head sadly. "I don't know, sir. But...I have heard rumors that it was a marketplace brawl."

"A brawl?" Cito speaks up, skepticism in his voice.

"Her father saved her life by taking her in as a slave."

"Her father?" I blink, stunned enough to fall over. "Who is her father?" I don't need to hear Ino's answer, but the words escape me.

Ino lifts her gaze from her ale with a frown. "Lord Tillmore. You didn't know?"

Anger quickly replacing my shock, I grind my teeth. "She didn't tell us that, did she, Cito?"

"No," Cito says in a grim voice. "She most certainly did not."

Ino shrugs. "It doesn't matter much—her father hates her."

"Clearly not, if he rescued her."

"It's not much of a rescue," Ino says.

"Regardless..."

The barmaid chooses that moment to appear again with scalding reindeer and vegetable soup. Only after our soup bowls are empty and our drinks half gone do I pick up the conversation again. "You mentioned brands and tattoos, Ino. What else do you know about that? Where are these records kept? And how thorough are they?"

Ino shrugs. "I've seen them just that once. I was there for almost two weeks." She sniffs but clenches the handkerchief in her fist as if determined not to cry.

"It's all right," Cito says softly, patting her hand.

She gives him a watery smile. "I thought I was going to die." She shakes her head and smashes her fist down on the table, rattling our crudely designed silverware. "They list the slaves' numbers, if we're tattooed, a physical description, name, age, and all those things. Where we say we come from—but that's hard to prove, which is why they tattoo us. But I think the official records are kept in a room at the palace. The Ministry of Labor has an office there. If you're looking for an escaped slave, you're supposed to go there first."

Cito's eyebrows rise. "That's an idea."

I shake my head almost before he's done speaking. "And get Elaina killed? If she's reported escaped—"

"No, no. Of course." Cito presses a sigh out his nose and reaches for his second beer. "That's a stupid idea."

Ino shrugs. "I don't know how it works. But I know any slave who attempts escape is supposed to be branded and punished— severely. Sometimes killed. Do you think Elaina would have done that?"

"You would know her better than I." I give her a pointed look.

Ino hangs her head. "Believe me, I've called myself a fool many times over this last month. We never thought..."

She trails off, but I have nothing to say to her. She helped Elaina into this situation. She should suffer for it too. She has, a little voice whispers in my ear. *She is suffering still. Always will. With a brand to remember it.*

Annoyed at the voice of reason in my head, I shift my gaze to the Canensians eating at tables around us. A few are soot-stained, clearly coming from cleaning up the fire remains; a family of four sits in the corner with that slightly lost look of travelers; and another table holds a group of men that keeps growing every time the door opens, letting in a gust of cold air every time. Dozens of cloaks hang from hooks behind the door, a fire burns across the room from our table, and a small window peeks out to the front lane, where the occasional horse is ridden past, guards walk by on patrol, and pairs or small groups of Merise citizens hurry by.

"Yes," Ino finally says with strength in her voice. "I think she would escape, if she had the chance. But they don't give a lot of chances here." She lifts her shoulder in a shrug. "And even if you try, there's not much chance to get very far."

I inspect Ino. She appears even younger than her sixteen years without her hat and cloak covering her head. Her blond hair, although unwashed, is golden and fine, with faint curls that wisp around her face where her braided hair has escaped its tie. If it weren't for the tattoo that peeks out along her neck, she would look just like a Canens noble.

"Ino, where do you want to go?"

"I'm sorry?" she asks, her face blank.

"We—we go almost surely to death," Cito says when I take too long to explain.

"But, I—" She bites her lip, and the firelight catches a sparkle of tears in her eyes. "I thought I might... I could be helpful."

Instead of answering her plea, I close my eyes, resisting the urge to rake my hands through my hair in frustration. How do I explain to her that we can't keep her? She'll slow us down, and my first priority is Elaina. Elaina, the princess, my sister. Elaina... Tears burn the backs of my eyes and close my throat.

"Ino, would you go and refill our drinks, please?" Cito murmurs.

The expression she turns on him is hurt, eyes full of sorrow, but she sees something that makes her suck in a breath, and a touch of hope returns to her eyes. She nods, gathers up the three mostly empty glasses, and disappears through the throng toward the bar.

"Sir, it might be helpful to have her along with us."

"But what do we do with her, Cito? Two men traveling with a

girl? A branded girl-woman? How could we be more obvious?" I clench my fist, tempted to slam it on the table.

Cito nods. "I think we're obvious enough as it is—without her. With your red hair? Our differently shaped faces and eyes?"

"I keep it hidden," I snap, motioning to the cap I haven't removed.

"Right, but I don't think traveling with a 'slave' will make a difference."

"We'd have to treat her like a slave to keep that illusion up. And it's another mouth to feed and a woman on top of that."

"I don't think anyone will care if we have a young woman with us. We could call her my sister, if we must."

"I care. We'd have to get her another room—it complicates things, Cito! You know that." I reach a hand out for my glass, only to find the spot empty, and this time, I do slam my fist down, hitting the spot where my glass sat a minute before. "Women always complicate things."

"Sir, please. She has nowhere to go. What is our other option?"

I remain quiet, watching Ino's blond head amidst many other blond heads at the bar. "If we take her—and I'm not saying we should or will—she'll have to be on her own. I won't risk my life for hers. Not with Elaina—" I break off, holding my breath in my ribs until it feels like they might explode.

"I know, sir." Cito scratches at his neck. "But she has nowhere to go. We must help her."

I tap my fingers in place. "I have an idea. One that you'll hate. And so will she." I lean forward, ready to go through with it. "But it's the best idea we have."

XVIII

Death

WINTERBERRY

We travel for two more days in a blur of rocking motion and just enough chatting to keep our lips from freezing. Sometimes one of the slaves will get up and dance around in the limited space we have, when their bodies are rebelling against them and their extremities getting frostnipped. It's not unusual for two of the men to be holding each other's hands or putting warm hands over the cheeks of another. Each has formed a bond with another slave—all except Caleb and the blond man, whose name I have learned is Laius.

Caleb speaks only when spoken to, and Laius grows angrier with every mile we travel. He won't last long like this, not if we are expected to be subservient slaves.

On the fourth night, we don't stop to make camp like we have the others, so we must be close to our destination.

The fog grows thicker as night falls, and the lantern casts an ominous glow over our features. Something uneasy settles over us in the cage. The reindeer pull faster, and the usually chatty driver isn't speaking.

I wrap my arm around Des and pull her immobile form tight

against me, nestling her sleeping form against my side. I hope the Manor has medicine, for her cheeks have bloodred circles on them again, and a deep cough shakes her body and mine whenever an attack comes.

Caleb sits across from us again, peering at Des through narrowed eyes. Last night, he caught me trying to escape my chains and took away the metal piece I'd found. He values his life more than his freedom; I would sacrifice my life for the freedom I have never tasted.

Now, he focuses on Des with an unnerving expression. To hide her from his searching gaze, I pull up the blanket, covering her entirely from view.

The air grows colder, and despite the blankets and Des's slight warmth, I am shivering so hard that my limbs shake. It's becoming hard to stay awake. Harder to keep my eyes open. I let them drift closed. I spent the night last night trying to pick the lock on my chains, and exhaustion seeps into my bones as deeply as the chill. I tighten my arms around Des.

The sleigh jolts. I start awake; I must have nodded off, for the men around me have shifted along the benches, the blanket has slipped from Des, and Caleb is sitting next to me, leaning over Des.

"Get away!" My voice comes out in a gasp more of horror than imperial command.

"Hush," he murmurs, reaching for Des.

I have nowhere to go, but I try to sweep her into the corner anyway; he just slides along the bench with me, hands outstretched.

"Stop—don't touch her—"

"Hush," he repeats more firmly, and his hands land gently on Des's neck.

"What are you—" I break off, staring now not at him but at Des's unmoving form. She is stiff with cold in my arms, unmoving and unable to be moved. Her cheeks are pale, icy. "Des?" My voice cracks.

Caleb's hands fall from her neck, and he lifts his gaze to mine. All he does is shake his head.

"Wha—? No." I blink and push her away from me, trying to look her in the eye, to wake her, to get her to move or something. To breathe.

The sleigh shakes around us, and the reindeer halt with a snort.

"She's gone," he says from beside me, not without compassion.

"No. She can't be. I was talking with her..." Sobs rise in my throat. I brush the little girl's hair back, peer into her youthful face. She is so pretty. Blond hair, pale skin, classic northern looks, but unusual soft brown eyes. Canens is a fair-colored country; dark features are often thought of as a polluted Canens bloodline. Is that why she's a slave? For nothing but her eyes? I didn't ask. Why didn't I ask about her?

On her, these soft doe eyes are gentle and exquisite. She will be beautiful when she grows up. She will be admired.

She won't grow up.

The cage rattles, and men are waking. The man formerly beside Des looks over his shoulder at us but otherwise doesn't move.

"Get out," a voice growls. I can't tell if it's the Magister or one of the guards, my thoughts are so scattered and my heart so broken. "Get out, or it's the whip for you."

Caleb glances at me and rises. "The little girl is dead."

"What did you do?" the voice snaps. "Get out here."

Caleb moves away, slipping out the door past the Magister, leaving me looking up at the man who bought a child whore and killed her. He motions to a weedy guard and instructs him into the wagon, as if climbing up inside is far beneath the snow he walks on.

The guard steps forward, past the Magister, and up the two steps into my prison. At the moment, I wish I had some plan to lock all the guards inside and escape.

The thin man swears as he looks down at Des, seeing without touching what I could touch and not see.

"Leave her there," he growls at me. "And get outside."

I hold up my wrist, which still, after all these days, connects me to her.

With another muttered curse, he sweeps aside his short cloak and pulls a key from his waistband with gloved hands in order to unlock my chains.

"What are you going to do with her?" I demand as he bends over my wrist.

"Dispose of the body, what else? Maybe we'll toss her over the walls for the wolves." He laughs, a surprisingly hacking, coughing laugh as though he has spent too many years smoking tobacco. "The worthless whore. Didn't even—"

"You will not talk about her like that!" My voice cuts through the fog, louder than I ever imagined speaking, with authority that startles even me. A shudder seems to go through the space around us, vibrating the very air I breathe. Something pulses in the sky, whether a storm or parting clouds, I cannot tell.

The thin guard before me freezes, his body going stiff, while another, rough-looking guard standing a outside the sleigh jail doesn't seem to notice. The outside guard fixes me with such a derisive look that my resolve flickers.

"Oh dear," the gruff guard taunts, "it seems someone has forgotten her status in the world."

"Would seem the girl needs a lesson." The thin one chuckles, his eyes gleaming, while the gruff one outside leers his approval.

I grit my teeth. Status is the furthest thing from my mind. And even if it weren't, there are more things that matter than status and safety. I glare at him as rudely as I can.

The thin guard steps forward in our jail, bending his bony form over me. "Allow me to remind you."

I do not shrink back from the hand that rises, not even when I see a collection of metal rings embracing his knuckles. It swoops through the air, crashing against my cheekbone with pain that sends me reeling against the bars and gasping.

Blows come one after the other, loud in the fog, closing over me as I clutch Des to my chest, refusing to let her fall as if she might be hurt, as if I am still her protector. Her body glimmers in my mind, protected from whatever blows land, all hitting me instead of her.

She is so light, hardly more than fifty pounds, maybe half my weight. How could I have missed her being so frail? Here I was thinking of ways to get us out of slavery, and instead she found her own route, the only one that I could not follow.

I stand tall before my owner's minion, taking my beating for my cheek and listening to the thuds of his fists, each of which are followed by flashes of pain in my head and light behind my eyes. I fix my eyes on him and do not fall, and I watch as his eyes grow mad with fury.

Finally, someone yells something, and through the fog, I see a large form move toward the guard. I weave on my toes, my arms never having left Des's body. My face throbs from the dozens of hits it absorbed.

A guard catches his hand midair, and the one who beats me halts.

He pauses to sneer then spits at me. I blink as spittle splashes across my cheeks, eyes, lips, and on Des's perfectly sloped nose.

Even though I totter on my feet and blackness closes in around me, I vow then and there to one day eke out justice against Magister Marcus. I will never forget his face nor his name.

XIX

The Merisian Palace

RUS

"Are you certain this will work?" Cito mutters as I aim us toward the Canens palace along with the crowd of onlookers and guests.

I glance up at the palace of the northern kingdom. Its dark spires reach into the mist above us, with mouths of gargoyles snarling down at us. It's nothing like the Heian palace with its pale stone and cheery appearance. I miss it. Am I homesick? How ridiculous. And yet, I'd love to be home in front of a fire with Elaina or enjoying a dinner of pheasant and fresh, young carrots from the palace gardens. I sigh. I am homesick. Immensely. Creator, please, give us something. This is our last hope. Let us find something. Let us find her.

"Sir?" Cito prods as we ascend the steps. "Are you—?"

"Yes, I'm certain," I assure him, though I'm not certain at all. "We'll find something here. Someone who knows something." I cast him a sidelong glance. "Remember our story?"

"Our—? Yes."

"What is it?"

"We are to say nothing if possible, but if pressed, to say we are traders from the borders of Ostium, looking into possible trade routes between Canens and Ostium. We are most interested in slaves as we know the plague in Ostium obliterated their working class, and they need people to work the fields."

I nod. All reasonable—mostly true. We don't want to be outsiders—the Canensians don't seem receptive to them at all. Our interaction with Astra showed us that, and now we're even farther from the Ostium-Canens border, which would make us even more conspicuous. Thank the Creator we managed to trade our crude, ill-fitting clothing for something authentically Canensian.

"And we are to work out as much about how the slave trade works as possible."

"And?"

"Keep an eye out for Elaina, of course," Cito adds, glancing around as if he's already neglecting his job. He's dressed formally, as am I, in a luxurious silk tunic and wool leggings of such softness that I doubted it to be wool until the shopkeeper showed us a sheep's pelt. This country never ceases to amaze—in good and bad. They are not the barbarians I imagined.

It was lucky that the palace was throwing a ball tonight and that my skills of charming a stranger was enough to make up for Cito's haphazard street skills of clumsily picking pockets in order to get us an invitation for the ball. Now I hold the two invitations in my pocket, grateful that there were no names on them. We look similar enough to those around us that we should be able to blend in without much of an issue.

Except for my hair. Curse this red hair.

Five minutes ago, I dashed into a shop and bought some black leather polish, streaking it through my hair and beard so that my hair is brown at least—less memorable perhaps. I don't wish to be remembered should things not go my way. But the polish does have a slight stench to it that constantly makes me want to wrinkle my nose in distaste.

Hopefully, no one else will get close enough to me to smell it.

We slip into the foyer amidst the guests. A dozen slaves are dressed in silk robes of white with gold embroidery on them in tendrils of snowflakes.

"Your cloak, sir?" one asks me.

"Of course," I say, slipping out from under its warmth. The heat of the palace greets me, not even a breeze of wind from the open front doors slipping inside. Magic? I marvel at it, wanting to step back into the doorway and reenter just to check. If this is magic, it is bold. What other spells has the Queen cast? And how have none recognized it for what it is before her public display in Merise?

Cito hands his cloak to the same slave, and we are each given half of a numbered, torn ticket with a matching number on the side the slave keeps. The man disappears with our cloaks while I say a quick prayer requesting that we don't have to leave without them. Not that I like that particular cloak, but it is rather cold outside.

We follow the crowd down a wide hallway as my eyes rove around us, unable to settle on anything. Strains of dark minerals line the rock composing the castle, but tapestries with silver and gold and other bright colors draw my attention, tapestries which are interspersed with royal portraits. All of the Queen. And her former husband...the late King Balint of Canens.

The King wears a golden crown laden with adamas, the gemstone that Canens once shared so readily with the rest of the Seven Kingdoms but now hoards. The King said he had shut down the mines, that continuing to dig for the gems was too dangerous for his people, but my father never believed that story. He thought instead that Canens grew greedy. Staring at the kind eyes of the King, I'm not sure what to believe, and I shift my gaze to the Queen standing beside him instead. It is not the princess' mother, Queen Helena, but the current Queen of Canens, Queen Blanche. She gazes out from the picture with a small smile upon her lips, standing behind her husband with a hand resting upon his shoulder. She, too, wears a crown, but a much smaller one, more of a coronet than a crown, almost too simple for her status as queen.

"Sir?" Cito prompts. "Shall we go inside?"

"What?" I turn and find that guests are parting around us, giving us strange looks as I admire the painting. "Oh. Yes." Giving the painting one last glance, I follow the crowd into a cavernous ballroom.

The ceiling towers several stories above, and more paintings and tapestries line the walls here. The spots of the walls that have no artwork are pieces of art themselves, with intricately carved marble in shapes I can't decipher. Some are plants or vines, while others have animals and faces in a curious symbolism I don't understand. Each seems to tell a story, perhaps about the origin of Canens, but it has been so long since we shared any pleasantries with this country that I don't know which myths they represent.

Passing by the art, I spare a quick glance up to find the ceiling painted with smears of color. Those must be the dancing lights I've heard about, the ones that color the sky. It's been so cloudy that we haven't been able to see much of the sky at all since we crossed the border, but I hear that the farther north we travel, the greater the chance we'll get of seeing them.

Someone bumps into me, jostling my attention away from the art surrounding us and refocusing it upon the people. I mentally shake myself. We're not here to admire the palace. We're here for Elaina. How could I let myself be so distracted?

Grimacing, I begin inspecting every single female face within sight. Cito follows suit, and we fall into silence.

"Let's split up," I say. "I think we'll be able to see more if we work through the room separately."

"Of course."

"You talk to people, I'm going to pretend to be looking for someone and wander around."

"Yes, sir." Cito snags two drinks from a passing slave's tray. "Here, sir. You look like you need this."

I murmur a thank you and take it, then move off into the crowd of gently swirling colors. No one gives me a second glance, even when I stare too long at a face. I must fit in at least. My hair doesn't stand out now, nor my clothing. Can it really be that simple to pass as a Canensian?

An hour later, I've finished my second drink and inspected the faces of hundreds of guests at this ball. In many ways, it's no different than a ball we might have in Heia. But in others, it's far different indeed. There is hardly a dish of food I recognize, and the people are dressed warmly, with little exposed flesh. In Heia, the women will often use balls as a chance to dress alluringly, but here women's faces and hair are intricately painted and adorned, and while their dresses are also intricately embroidered, they are, like mine, made from a mixture of thick silks and practical wool—and rarely lowcut. Although some of the bolder women have low necklines that they cover with scarves. A few don't cover their flesh at all, and every male's eyes alight upon them, some with less than savory expressions.

The slaves are almost easy to spot, simply for the colors they wear. It seems a rule that the slaves must be properly identified through both clear display of their tattoos and burn scars or through the color of their gowns or tunics. Only through my careful observation have I noted the five shades which mark a slave: white, red, black, purple, and green. Their gowns or tunics are always one shade of the color, with perhaps some white or black embroidery.

After inspecting the faces of a hundred young females, I begin to lose hope. Then passing under an archway into a smaller room where the musicians sit, I spot her. Her hair is no longer than when I last saw her, the day before she ran away. There's a slight wave to it, and it's half pulled back with a netting of tiny flowers containing it. When she turns, I see her profile, the sloped nose, the long lashes, the delicate cheekbones flushed from the heat of the room. She follows a man dressed in a finely embroidered tunic lined with furs and with a pale blue sash hung across it. His hair touches down upon his shoulders, blond and thick with manly waves, but not thick enough to hide his generous beard from my view before he slips out the door.

"Elaina!" Her name slips from my lips before I can stop it, but no one hears. The room is loud with the proximity of the music, and she moves after the man before her, out the open doors into the hallway. The crowd closes after them and chatters loudly amongst themselves, making it all but impossible to squeeze through. I resort to pushing, shoving when people don't move. Breaking free from the crowd, I finally burst out into the hallway but find it empty except for a half dozen guards.

"Elaina!" This time, her name is a whisper on my lips. "Where are you?"

The hall stretches out, empty in either direction. Right or left? Rapidly inspecting both directions, I choose right, back toward the palace entrance. Perhaps she's leaving early, that's it.

By the time I reach the front doors, I have convinced myself that I am correct. I race through the doors and gasp in shock at the cold air. Inside, it was easy to forget the chill beyond its walls, but now a shiver races itself down my spine and out through my naked fingertips.

"Sir! Your cloak?" a slave calls from the doorway as I pause at the top of the stairs and scan the waiting sleighs. "Sir, may I retrieve your cloak for you?"

How did they disappear so quickly? How—? They could not have left this quickly. They must still be inside, somewhere.

Ignoring the slave, I race back into the palace and take the hallway in the opposite direction. As I pass the doors to the ballroom, the music swells along with laughter and chatter, growing louder as the drink loosens tongues.

I dash down the hallway and slide to a halt at the end, my heart sinking. Two guards stand before a pair of frosted glass doors, reminding me of Lord Tillmore's growing houses. I stride toward them. Perhaps she entered—

"I'm sorry, sir, but you'll have to return the way you came."

"But I think my—someone I know just went in there," I say in my most charming voice.

"Sorry, sir," the second guard says. "No one entered here."

I narrow my eyes at him. "No one?"

"No, sir." The second guard adjusts his grip on his somewhat ceremonial spear.

"What's behind those doors then? Why can't I enter?"

"Nothing for you to see," the first chimes in, facing me fully with an eager expression in his pale gray eyes. "Either return to the ball or we shall have you escorted out of the palace."

"Out of the palace," I echo.

"Out of the palace," he repeats grimly.

I set my jaw at him, but I recognize the firmness in loyal guards. Peering through the frosted glass, I think I spy a spiral staircase just beyond them. "Fine. Thank you."

Lifting my chin, I turn on my heel like a soldier might and stride off down the hall. There must be another way upstairs, one that won't get me arrested.

When I round the turn in the hallway, I waste little time in opening doors before the other guards see me. Luckily, behind the second door is a narrow staircase. Without thinking, I dart in and up the stone stairs. Breath coming in pants, I reach the first landing and pause before slowly opening the narrow door. It opens silently into a well-lit but empty room. I almost close the door before my gaze catches on the wall. The portrait gallery.

Something draws me out of the stairway, and I step into the large room. Unlike any portrait gallery I've ever seen, the opposite wall hardly contains pictures at all. Those that remain are all of Queen Blanche. She's in a dozen different dresses, each with a large crown. The coronet from the entry down below is absent. Here is her true image. Why would she leave that picture up downstairs when she has so many pictures that are more flattering to her?

Of course. The people want to see their king. He was much beloved... But why would she want them to see him when she has all but obliterated memories of him and his daughter? Does she gain their love by displaying his portrait? Seems an odd thing for her to do, leave an unflattering portrait visible to all when she has so many others.

I walk farther into the room, entranced by the dozen images of the Queen. I should be searching for Elaina, but the palace is far too large for me to track her down. I've already lost her. If I find her now, it will be by pure chance.

Trailing along the wall where the door to the stairs resides, I pause at each picture, simultaneously disturbed and enchanted by yet another version of Queen Blanche. I come to the end and cross the narrow room to the odd empty wall space between pictures.

Stepping up to it, I gasp. It's a window. I scuff my boots forward and look out—and down. Below is the ballroom. Guests swirl upon the marble floor, skirts and long tunics flying out behind them as they dance to music I cannot hear.

As I turn away, I catch sight of a painting hidden behind a tapestry. Frowning, I approach it. With a glance around to make sure no one has entered silently, I reach out and push the tapestry aside. It moves along a metal bar just below the ceiling. Dragging the tapestry aside, I step back and peer at the portrait.

A floor-to-ceiling portrait of a younger Queen Blanche and the king greets me. Between them is a young girl, perhaps six years old, with such a cherubic face under her unusually dark hair that I all but ignore the king and queen. An expression of great sorrow on the young princess' face speaks to me with such power that I am moved to grief the longer I stare.

The artist has captured her ice-blue eyes so well that I feel as if she stands before me weeping. There is a glimmer of unshed tears in them, a misery that I can only imagine. Did this artist suffer for delivering a painting like this one? I shift my gaze to the Queen. Her eyes, by contrast, glint with victory. It's as if she's announcing to all, "I've won my prize."

The King is the only one who has a calm, unmoved expression, almost as though he is bored, perhaps a touch proud.

"You!"

Startled by the harsh voice, I nearly jump out of my boots.

"What are you doing in here?" A guard clomps across the

wooden floor and, before I can react, grabs me. "That's it for you, let's go. You don't belong here."

I don't bother to argue. I've wasted too much time here indulging myself; I've lost Elaina. And now, try as I might, I cannot get the haunted eyes of that little girl out of my mind.

XX

The Sorcerer

BLANCHE

I walk down to the dungeons through halls bathed in shadows. The empty halls echo with my footsteps, disturbing no one but a few slaves who pause their midnight cleaning and melt into the shadows as I pass, my simple silk gown rippling as I move.

The guard beyond the dungeon door opens his mouth when I stride in then closes it and falls to his knees. "Majesty. I was told to expect you, but I did not expect you this late."

"The new prisoner," I answer with, "where is he?"

"I will take you, Majesty." He rises but does not lift his head.

Before I can address him, a second guard emerges from the narrow, damp hallway of the dungeon.

"Wha—?" he begins. Eyes going wide, he falls to his knees in a late echo of the first guard. "Majesty."

"You, stay here at the door while I take Her Majesty to visit a prisoner," the first guard barks at the second.

"Yes, Majesty. Yes, sir." The man does not move from his kneeled position as we pass him.

I follow the first guard in his dark, gray-blue guard uniform that nearly makes him invisible in the shadows. The portly man clearly doesn't get much exercise in his job as a prison guard, and his skin is pale as if he's spent far too much time in the dark.

I follow him past small cells with thick doors ajar. This level of the prison is mostly empty, reserved for prisoners with short stays. Instead of stopping, we descend the sloping walk toward a closed door up ahead to the right. Only then does the guard slow.

"He is here, Majesty," the guard says quietly over his shoulder. Not quite meeting my eyes, he withdraws his keys from his belt, where they have been jingling every other step he takes.

He is not portly at all, I realize, but rather a large man of thick muscle. Well fed, but also well muscled. I smile inwardly to think that it is my garden and my growing houses that have kept him so well fed. And perhaps some snitching from the prisoners' plates? I can't begrudge him that for putting up with these people.

"You would like me to open the door, yes, Majesty?"

"Yes." I focus on the thick, wooden door reinforced with metal which separates me from answers.

The door sets me ill at ease. The nearer I come, the more drained I feel. It's not until I stand before it with the guard fumbling for the key that I realize why.

Anti-magical stone. He needs a magically reinforced cell to prevent him from casting magic. I fight back my own shudder.

"Will you go in, or shall I remove him?" the guard asks.

I consider, inspecting the stone that surrounds us. It won't protect against potions, but it will keep him from casting a spell against me.

"I will go in." Even magically powerless, I am hardly defenseless for I carry a knife in my skirt pocket. "I will enter, and you will lock me inside. I will knock—" I hold up one hand with five fingers spread, "—times when I am finished with the prisoner."

"Yes, Majesty."

"Has he been cooperative?"

"Mostly, Majesty. He was...confused as to why he is here and fought the guards. He woke up as we were puttin' him in the cell and nearly rung one of us a new one."

"I see."

"You sure you'll be all right? Majesty?"

"Yes."

The guard opens the window into the cell, peering inside and pausing a moment as if the interior takes some getting used to. Then he barks through the opening, "Back against the wall. Stay there."

He slips the key into the gaping mechanism and turns it. The tumblers rumble and the door loosens in the frame before he drags it open, the hinges squealing their protest. The guard puts himself between me and my prisoner until he can confirm that the prisoner has obeyed. "Don't move," he adds for good measure.

Peering over the guard's shoulder, I observe the prisoner's expression of deep loathing and aloofness. My lips thin. He is not the fire wielder. And he may be difficult to convince to help my cause. But Captain Plaga has given me additional information that will, I believe, prove most useful.

The guard steps aside, and the prisoner stares at me with misgiving.

"I'll be right outside, Majesty," the guard says before setting a torch in the niche of stone near the doorway and closing the door behind me.

Inside the cell, the stones close in on me, suppressing me and the sorcerer alike. Hearing the key turn in the lock sends a shudder down my spine, but I force myself to hide it. Of the two of us, I know my escape is certain. For the sorcerer, much depends upon his information and identity.

"Don't expect me to bow," the sorcerer says, drawing a cold smile from my lips. "Not after this sort of treatment."

"I wouldn't. Although it might help your future to show some respect to your queen."

He snorts. He wears what he was arrested in: a thigh-length tunic lined with white rabbit fur underneath his heavy jacket and pants that are probably lined inside as well, either with furs or additional fabric, all accompanied by an expression of defiance I doubt has left his face since his arrest. He has not removed his rabbit-fur hat, but his gloves stick out of his jacket pockets, and his fingers twitch, betraying his nerves—or his readiness to respond with a spell he can't cast. I smirk.

"What is your name?"

"Shouldn't you know that? Since you had me arrested?" He crosses his arms, his eyes glinting in the torchlight.

"Perhaps I don't. Perhaps all I know is that you are a powerful sorcerer."

He shifts, glancing over her shoulder at the door. "And what does that matter to you?"

"You're right; it's never mattered before, has it? Not to me at least," I muse aloud, half to myself. In all honesty, there has never been anyone to bother with. Magic wielding in Canens is unusual enough now that people don't trust it and hardly recognize it when they see it. According to legend, after the Curse, all but the strongest magicians and sorcerers disappeared, and even the strongest had their powers curiously drained. Where it once took hours for me to regain my strength after casting a spell, now I had to wait days if not weeks, depending on the power of the spell.

I turn my mind back to the man standing before me now, for that is all he is within these rock walls. No one to bother with. But if he knows of someone I should bother with, then I will be more than intrigued. "Perhaps you should tell me whom I should be worried about, instead of you."

His chin juts out. "You shouldn't be worried about me. Or anyone but yourself. I didn't set the growing houses on fire. And I don't know who did—if that's why I'm here."

"Indeed." Slowly, I pace the cell. Three steps to the left and I hit the wall, then six steps to the right and I reach the other. It is a generously sized cell, and it makes me feel less than generous. I return to the center and halts. "I doubt that's true."

He blinks, the only indication that I might have called his bluff. "Whether you believe me or not, it is."

I consider shrugging but decide it's beneath me. Instead, I fix him with a scrutinizing look. "If you do not give me what I want, we will take this to the other room."

His eyebrows lift, a glimmer of amusement flitting through his pale eyes.

"And there, it will not only be questions I give you."

"Do what you will to me. I answer nothing." He turns his head away as if he thinks about turning his back to me then thinks better of it.

Now I smile. "Then I will have to arrest your wife instead. She is seven months with child, is she not?"

He goes still. The muscle in his jaw flexes, his face pale.

I allow myself an inner smile. Plaga was right about his leverage.

"You will not find her. She knows to go into hiding if I should not return home one night."

My smile widens. "My powers have not been well represented to you then. I can find anyone, anywhere in this world. Until I do, I will question you. And when I find her, you will very much wish that you had told me what I wanted to hear when I first asked."

He licks his lips. "What—what is it you want to hear?"

I take my time in answering him, letting him sweat as I consider whether I should just turn away, find his wife, and come back when he is convinced I will carry through on my threats. There are many empty cells nearby—ones which he could hear her screaming from.

"Who did you steal your magic from?" I finally ask.

"Steal?" The sorcerer is indignant. "I have stolen nothing. My magic is learned."

I tuck my hands into the folds of my skirt, reassured by the solidness of the knife there. "From what?"

"From my master. From books, from the ancients, take your pick. I have stolen nothing, not even a parchment to write upon." Each word is vehement, honest.

"And who is your master?"

At this question, he seals his mouth. I tilt my head.

"Whom do you love more? Your master or your wife?" I can see the words echoing in his head as I voice his thoughts. In the suffocating stone of the cell, my body feels tight, condensed into itself, and I grow eager to leave it. "Whom do you fear more?"

"I learned from Sagax." His voice breaks on the name.

"Is he better than you?" I've heard the name of the renowned sorcerer but have never met him.

"No," the man says reluctantly. "I eventually learned more than him."

"But he is skilled?"

"Yes."

"Does he have an uncanny ability with wizard's fire?"

The man juts out his chin again, the expression on his face answering my question.

"I see. And whom did he learn from?"

The sorcerer frowns. "I do not know."

"If I were to desire magical knowledge, outside the book-learning kind, where might I look?"

A deep V creases the sorcerer's forehead as he tries to follow my questioning and perhaps anticipate the next question. "I do not know. I suppose I would try the Fae."

"The Fae. The Fae?" I murmur the words, but they fill the air of the dank cell. Why have I not considered them myself?

Because the legends say they don't leave Edormisco, that's why, a voice answers in my head.

I shake my head. "Surely they would not be willing to help a mere mortal?"

The sorcerer lifts a shoulder. "I do not know. I have never spoken to one." He pauses, tilts his head to one side. "But if I were desperate, and needed great magic, I would ask them. I've heard some are willing to deal their magic—for a great price. Although I've also heard they deal in their own time and for their own purposes."

I fix my gaze upon his. "Which Fae?"

He licks his lips nervously, swallowing so visibly that his throat bobs even through the stubble on it. "I've heard the Blue Faery is willing. Perhaps for you, she might be eager."

I raise a brow.

"I mean, for whomever you seek magic for. She prefers to deal with a person who has much to offer her."

"I see." I consider him. "You may be right. Perhaps she will deal with me." I shift, itching to leave this prison and its oppressive stone. "You have been most helpful." I turn to leave and have my hand raised to knock upon the door when he speaks again.

"Majesty, you will let me go, right? Back to my wife, my family?"

I let my hand fall five times upon the door then, while the guard scrambles to answer my summons, face the man. "I will consider it."

Understanding and fear war upon his face. He lowers his head in a bow that is half acceptance and half submission.

Without another word, I turn and leave the oppression of the stone cell. I walk slowly enough so that the guard can lock the door and catch up quickly. But only halfway down the hallway do I stop, face him, and say, "Keep him there. Do not allow him to have visitors, speak to anyone, or send messages to anyone."

"Yes, Majesty," the guard answers, bowing at the waist.

"Tell no one of his presence here."

The guard bows once more, his head nearly to his waist now.

Without acknowledging him further, I stride away, shaking off the presence of the stone prison and reveling in the return of my powers the farther I go from the prison. The sorcerer gave me something, at least—two somethings, if I am completely honest.

Now I only have to find Sagax and the Blue Faery. I have a feeling that one might prove much more elusive than the other.

Part 3

LOST AND FOUND

I

Hated

WINTERBERRY

I t is not hard for me to become the one whom Magister Marcus hates. He blames me for Des's death.

I suppose it's only fair, as I blame him.

A square room with one of the other female slaves becomes my newest prison. Here my roommate is a large, no-nonsense woman three times my age and almost three times my width who is supposed to teach me my duties—until Magister Marcus the slave master sells me again.

My nights are restless, my days monotonous as Certa assigns me small tasks, testing my skills. I dread sleep almost as much as the waking hours. I crave the exhaustion brought on by the hard work, for it keeps the nightmares at bay. Nightmares of regret. Des dying. Her body stolen by the guards. Failed escape attempts. Slave sales. All of it haunts my dreams at night and wakes me with damp chills of terror.

"We'll train you in the simple things now and then step up to the more difficult tasks. You've clearly had a soft life before," Certa tells me as she thrusts a bucket of sudsy water and a bobbing brush inside it into my hands.

Bending under the weight, I don't have the breath to snort at her definition of my life while grappling with the bucket. Soft, no. A life of being served, perhaps.

She eyes me sidelong, like she might eye a horse or a reindeer for purchase. "I'm not surprised he bought you. He buys up all the reject slaves at the market," she tells me with a sniff of her nose, as her eyes travel to my bald, chapped head. She points to the floor in the slave quarters that we're supposed to be cleaning. Until my face is sufficiently healed, Certa and I have been instructed not to leave the slave quarters, but today is the last day, and to celebrate, Certa has instructed me to scrub the floors.

"Clearly he'll wait until you look decent again and then sell you to the highest bidder," she continues. "You'd best hope you don't get the red robes."

As I crouch to the floor, my heart stutters in my chest, and I look up at her. "Can he do that?"

She shoots me an "are-you-stupid?" look.

Of course he can. My life is his—he owns me. My blood congeals in my veins, turning me sluggish.

"Stop," Certa demands, grabbing at my arm when I nearly put the wet brush in a clod of dirt. "Do you want to dirty your water? Use the dustbin on that first."

I wince at the touch but nod and return my wet brush to the bucket. When I first woke from my beating, Certa was there, pressing her foul liniment to my wounds, allowing me to sleep until the headache left me. Still, I rose too early and vomited all over her fine silk serving robes. She took this in stride, however, holding me up by the arms as I sagged against her in tears of apology and embarrassment.

"You'd best get over this soon, or Magister will have you put in the dungeons." Her voice dropped nearly to a whisper, hollowness flickering in her eyes. "It's best to avoid his detection—unless it's for doing your job better than everyone else. And even then..." She paused in a rare display of emotion. She straightened. "It's best just to stay invisible."

I squinted at her as she eased me back onto the low, straw bed with its thick, wooden frame. "I won't let him forget what he did to Des."

She frowned. "Des?"

"The girl he killed."

"She died of the cold, girl, it's best you remember that," Certa said harshly, all indication of her earlier fear gone. "And it's best you forget her and keep yourself alive." Her eyes flickered over my features, lingering on the cheek which felt three times its normal size. "Perhaps you'll be able to be a serving woman if your injuries don't leave you scarred." Her frown deepened. "I'm surprised..."

Trailing off, she shook her head and turned away, bustling over to the small box at the foot of her bed. She rummaged in it, pulling out a small jar.

"Surprised at what?" I asked, feeling that I somehow needed to know what could surprise her about her master.

She turned back, her withered lip caught between her teeth. She exhaled loudly through her bent nose. Everything about her suggested a hard life—one unimaginable perhaps—but one that I might have before much longer. Bent back, skin that was red and chapped from constant cleaning and washing...red, rosy cheeks, porous skin, and cut and burn scars that lined both the face, arms, and hands...it would soon be me. The Queen would laugh to see me then.

Certa didn't have to cross the room back to me, for turning around brought her right back to my bedside. Indeed, as I sat on my bed facing hers, my knees nearly touched the mattress of her bed. One of Certa's eyebrows looked as though it had been permanently singed, with hairs barely half the length of the other. I wondered how many of these scars were from the attentions of the master and how many from working accidents.

"What is so surprising?" I prompted.

She uncapped the jar, and the sweet scent of cloves, along with something wretched, assaulted my nose. She paused with her fingers wrapped around the jar and the lid. When she spoke, she aimed her words at her hands. "I am surprised that he attacked your face." She lifted her gaze. "Even though it was a guard, and I hear he's been reprimanded, still it means your value had already gone down. Were you combative with them on the journey?" She leaned toward me then, urgency in all her gestures. The lid skipped out of her hand and under my bed, but she didn't bend to retrieve it.

"No, I swear—"

"You must be very, very careful from now on. Do your duty and nothing more. Get him to forget you exist."

Her words sent shivers down my spine that echo in my bones even now. Now that my face is finally healing from the guard's hands, my body has been bruised, battered, and abused from endless work since I woke up after his beating.

All traces of Certa's sympathy are gone now, a month later, replaced with harsh words and endless instruction on improvement. However, I have learned that this means she cares for me, for those she hates—and she hates many—she ignores.

I still find my cheekbone to be sore in a couple spots, and Certa to be even more quick to heap chores upon me. Under her tutelage, we have scoured the slave quarters so they shine. I think I know every way to clean I could possibly know now, and it's clear how Certa became such a respected slave, for her work is immaculate; she accepts nothing less.

Every day, I fall into my little straw bed, exhausted, and barely have the energy to treat my face as Certa insists. She never lets me fall asleep without putting the foul-smelling liniment over my cheeks, nose, forehead, and chin—every square centimeter. The stench of the concoction follows me throughout the day, and everyone wrinkles their nose as I approach. The other slaves mock me, but I bend over my work, thankful to have busy hands.

The next morning, I take careful stock of what is collectively called "the Manor," as I begin my work outside the slave quarters with a tour of the compound, followed by lighter work than most of the servants endure. I suppose it's Certa's way of protecting me, if she's capable of that. So far, I have only worked alone on small tasks or with her on larger ones.

Even now, I am not allowed outside the Manor grounds, but there is plenty within to keep me occupied. My previous explorations have shown me stables, where mostly slave men work to break horses, which the Magister buys, sells, and trains as a side business. And today shows me over a hundred rooms in the Manor, not including the slave quarters. While the slave quarters are barely more than a cave, with cold, bare walls and rooms that don't even have windows, in the Manor, there are tapestries and riches that rival the palace and heirlooms like I have never seen before from countries I have only read of. Every room is filled with furs and even stuffed animals that must be carefully dusted.

It is all so overwhelming and requires so much attention that I begin to ignore the artifacts I find. I could be dusting a sixth-century Heian vase and not realize it.

"Assume everything is worth more than you," Certa tells me.

I open my mouth to respond, but her hard gaze informs me she's not joking; everything in here has cost more than the Magister spent on me.

Since I lost a few days recovering from my beating, by the time I start assisting Certa with her duties, the other slaves I arrived with have already disappeared to their training posts. Certa has told me that Caleb, or "the giant man" as the other slaves call him, works at the stables, and Laius is somewhere else still, but I don't have the time or energy to find out where. It doesn't matter, I suppose, except that those are the only two others that I know, now that Des is gone.

Every thought of her brings a pang to my chest. How did I not realize she was dying that day? There could have been something I could have done to keep her alive. Something else. Given her my blanket. My mittens, my hat...

My thoughts taunt me as I scrub and clean hallways and tapestries. How could I have missed her dying in my own arms?

Bitterness creates a gaping hole in me that nothing will fill.

I slam the wet brush to the floor of the entry in the dark morning hours, sniffing back the moisture from my nose. It's better that she's dead. And not locked up in the Red wing, learning to do what they do. Hurting her. Breaking her. Gods, why did she have to die?

I pause in my mad scrubbing, hunched over the floor with my body aching from weeks of labor and my heart crushed from grief. She went peacefully at least. Not like Father. Tears prick my eyes. It's better this way. Death is better than being a Red.

Lifting my chin, I continue scrubbing, this time harder and faster.

The darkest section of this Manor is the place to which I hope never to be assigned. Certa has told me of it only in passing, telling me how she cleaned there for a few months before working her way out of the training brothels. What she saw she will not say. It must have been awful.

Because Magister Marcus doesn't just buy and sell any of his slaves. He buys them and trains them, including the Reds.

My heart twists in my chest, sinking to become an iron weight in my stomach every time I think of how Des would have ended up there. And I still could. There, where a Madame trains the girls that come to her. All young, all beautiful, all maidens. It's enough to make me want to heat a metal poker in one of the many fireplaces I clean on a daily basis and destroy myself with it, just to avoid ending up in one of those rooms—in one of those beds.

If he picks the pretty ones for the Reds...why hasn't he picked me? Perhaps I'm not so pretty after all—not as pretty as Father always said. At least before he married Blanche. Or perhaps Blanche managed to take all the beauty I had left when she threw me in prison and cut off my hair—

"Aren't you done yet?" a high voice interrupts my thoughts. "The slaves are waking up soon, and if you're not done by the time the Magister wakes, you'll be done for."

Looking up, I glare at the teenage girl with shaggy, curly blond hair and bright blue eyes, but before I can speak, she continues.

"Do you have a spare brush? I'll help."

I shut my mouth and, after a moment's hesitation, nod at the bucket near the wall. "Thanks," I mutter.

She's quick to grab it and set to work. "So you that girl that came in with the dead Red?"

My entire body seizes, and my hand stills its scrubbing. "Yes," I finally say.

"Thought so. They said you was bald."

I wince and resume my scrubbing, head down and wishing I had hair to cover my face.

"Now they're a Red short, and everyone's terrified they'll be the next assigned, what with the Red shortage and all." She glances my way at my squeak and shrugs. "He done it before."

"How long have you been here?" I keep my hands moving as I speak, realizing that I have almost half the entry still to scrub in the next half hour.

"Dunno. A year or so." She grins down at the floor. "Magister determined I ain't fit to be sold, so I stay. Somethin' 'bout not appearin' genteel enough."

"Ever think about..." I hesitate, glance at her, then say, "about escaping?"

"No one escapes from the Magister." She laughs darkly. "Besides, this is a better life than the one I had back home." Her glance this time is almost sly. "My pa sold me to the Magister."

I suck in a breath. "He—why?"

She shrugs and swipes at the floor, moving on to her next section, leaving the bit behind cleaner in less time than it'd take me. "Debts to the Magister."

"What kind?"

"Food. Board."

I dip my brush into the bucket of soapy water. "Food and board for what?"

"Our house, dummy. We lived in the village. Well, my pa and ma still do."

"Because they sold you."

"Yeah." She shrugs. "It was better me than my baby brother."

A shudder runs through me. "Would they do that?"

She shrugs again, and a lock of her mane falls forward to block her face from view. "Eh, maybe. If they get in trouble again, maybe. But the Magister don't care for young kids. He wants workers, not babies."

"So he's safe?"

She snorts then wipes the back of her arm across her nose. "He ain't any more safe than the rest of us, you gotta know that. Anyone with the money would buy a baby in a heartbeat." She shudders. "But he ain't no baby now. No one would want 'im. Where are you from?" she asks without a pause in breath.

"Merise," I murmur.

"Always wanna go there. Pro'ly never will." She shifts to a fresh spot again. "Pro'ly die here."

"Surely the Magister will release you before long?"

She casts me a wry grin. "I'm working for my family's lodging after I work off their debts."

I chew on my lip but can think of nothing to say. She's trapped in slavery with no foreseeable exit unless she betrays her family and throws them on the icy streets. "So...do people just accept slavery then? They don't try to fight it?"

She shoots me a stunned look. "Fight it? How could they?"

"I— Refuse to work as slaves, rise up against the nobles, or—"

"You talkin' treason, girl, and we don't do that here." She glances around, to both sides and then over her shoulders. "You don't talk like that if you want anyone to talk to you here. Or if you wanna live."

"What's your name?"

She casts me a suspicious look. "Pia."

"I'm Helena," I offer, not pausing in my work. "And I'm curious about this whole slavery thing. I never...never had much experience with it before."

She bends over her brush in silence.

"What do you think of the Queen? Of the princess?"

Pia glances at me then over her shoulders again and bends back over her brush.

I don't ask again, but a minute later, as I move toward her to a new spot, she speaks.

"I think the Queen is wrong. She doesn't help us...she says she does, but she hurts us instead. The princess...she's supposed to be dumb."

"Supposed to be?"

"Yeah, well, that's what some say. Others say she don't care, and others that she's dead."

"And what do you think?"

"I think she's alive. I think she cares. And she's not dumb."

My heart swells at the idea then deflates even quicker. Even if she believes in me, what do I do now? I'm a slave. I can't walk around telling people who I am; they'd never believe me.

The girl chatters on as we work, telling me that she's thirteen, she has four siblings, all younger than her, with the youngest, that she knows of, being two.

Although my heart breaks for her, and for her lifetime of impending slavery, she distracts me from Des. And I can't decide which is better: having had a lifetime of horror ahead of you and dying before you come to it, or else having a lifetime of service ahead of you and living to endure it.

I cannot help but be afraid at either future. Because I finally understand the power he has over me: power to end my life and leave no one to mourn me. He has finished the job my stepmother began. And it has only taken him weeks.

II

Duties

WINTERBERRY

"We work in the library today." Certa tosses my head covering at me as I roll out from beneath my covers long before the sun will rise over the mountains north of Monticola, the Magister's expansive village. "Hurry. The Magister likes to use it by midmorning."

Yawning, I drag a hand over the stubble on my head then rub away the sleep from my eyes. In minutes, I've pulled on my light, white wool robes and stockings, slipped my feet into the thick, leather slippers, and covered my head with a white rag. If I never wear white again, I'll live a happy life.

"Come on then," Certa says impatiently from the door. She shoves it open and doesn't wait for me.

I tie my rag around my head as I walk; if she leaves me behind, I'll never make it to the right place on time in this maze. Silently, I follow Certa down the tunnel from our slave quarters to the kitchen and storerooms, where we grab a cart that she pushes, and I grab a short, wooden step stool.

An older female slave dressed in white with purple on her sleeves strides into the kitchen as I emerge from the storeroom with a stool. "You'll be one short today," she's announcing to Certa. "Pia's gone."

"Pia? Gone?" Certa blinks at the woman, then half glances at me and shifts so that I can't see her face.

"Yes," the other slave says imperiously, not inviting questions.

Certa's head nods and she turns as the older woman strides back out the kitchen without another word. Seeing me watching, she presses her lips into a frown. "Let's get on with it then; we don't have the help we were supposed to."

Pia's gone? With a million questions on my tongue, I instead follow Certa across the Manor to the wing containing the Magister's living quarters. Smoothing the covering over my scalp, I enter behind Certa and halt, wide-eyed. Glasses, napkins, papers, and clothing litter the floor, couch, desks, bookcases.

"What the—" I gape at the room even as Certa bustles around, pushing her cart before her and whisking items onto it with startling efficiency. Another pair of hands would certainly help with this mess. "Why wasn't it cleaned last night?"

"There was a meeting here into this morning." She scowls at me. "And probably a sale, too. Get to work."

Dropping the step stool beside the door, I nod, her mantra playing through my head: servants are to be diligent, prompt, and invisible. Trailing along behind Certa, I find my fingers slower at picking up items than hers.

"Why wasn't the room cleaned afterward?" A particularly soiled garment has me wrinkling my nose and holding it between two fingers before Certa steps up, snatches it out of my hand, and shakes it in my face.

"Because even slaves like to sleep sometimes, princess," she growls.

My pulse races until she stomps back to her cart with the soiled garment in hand, sweeping up empty bottles as she goes.

She didn't mean it like that. She doesn't know. Slowly releasing my breath, I start to tidy the bar, putting stoppers on bottles and gathering the half empty and dirty glasses. She can't know. Who would have told her? I look nothing like the official portraits anymore. Especially with my hair shorn as it is. I snort. I look more like an adolescent boy than any sort of princess.

"Do we often get sold so...unexpectedly?"

"No."

Certa slams a towel down onto her cart, and the dishware stacked there rattle in protest. She ignores me as I slip the glasses in my hands onto her cart. I breathe a sigh of relief at her continued ignorance and scan the room before setting to work on the dirtiest areas.

"Certa," I say slowly as we work. "What do you think of the Queen and the princess?"

In a rare moment, her hands pause in their work. "About the what?"

"The Queen and princess."

"Why do you ask?"

I shrug. "I just...I'm from Merise, and I don't know what people here think about them, and I want to make sure that I don't...misstep." Perhaps someone overheard my conversation with Pia? Or she said something? I shake my head. That's ridiculous. Why would anyone care what one slave thinks about the Queen? And why wouldn't I be punished for it instead of Pia?

Certa resumes her work with extra vigor. "You won't find a lot of Queen Blanche supporters here. Not unless they're utterly loyal to the Magister."

"So he's on her side?"

"Side? The only sides are the Queen and treason."

"Well, of course, but—"

"That's it. It's with the Queen or be arrested for treason. I dunno about you, but I don't want to live out my last days in a prison cell."

She punctuates her words with such a glare that I don't bother asking anything else. It's probably best not to press the issue. It seems that the slaves don't particularly care for Queen Blanche, but they're too afraid to fight her. But if they're not happy with Blanche, perhaps gaining their support won't be as much work as I once thought. I sigh and shake my head. How can I get anyone's support if they don't know who I am? And me being a slave, what possible power do I have?

I huff and force my attention back to my cleaning.

Underneath the filth of the party are glass display cases containing artifacts and priceless tables from other kingdoms: an ornate side table made from the distinct black wood from Edormisco, Heian vases, what looks like a Heian book crafted out of vellum on display, a ceremonial mask from Ostium, a small rosary from Abbatia, and a beautifully crafted antique bridle from Ardor.

As I clean, I search for artifacts from the other kingdoms: Tepor and Avium, the lost kingdom. Few artifacts have been discovered from the lost kingdom, and those that still exist have been passed down throughout families for generations and are worth a fortune. The Magister's library, even in its filth, is a treasure trove of wealth.

Certa and I work in the silence of clinking glass and rustling fabric until the last of the tableware and rubbish is heaped atop the cart. Then we sweep around, tidying up pillows, removing stains as best we can from the couches and rugs, wiping up spilled liquids from the leather chairs and wooden tabletops, scrambling to finish the chore before the Magister arrives to catch us.

Invisible, invisible, chants through my head like a song as I work. How does a princess act invisible? I almost smile as I rub a damp rag over a glass case containing a book.

Peering closer, I squint at the title and read the words with surprise. Heian? I bend closer, wishing I could open the case and inspect it, but not with Certa there. There is something about this modest little book that has me curious. But for now, I make a note to come back to it one day.

Shortly after, I find myself humming, sweeping a rag of alcohol over the window, which somehow ended up with half a face printed on it in oil. Unable to reach the top, even with my step stool, I drag an armchair over to the glass and step up.

Certa glances at me and snorts. "It's a good thing there isn't anyone to see you here. You'd be in a fair amount of trouble using the Magister's chair like that."

I offer her a wry grin and thump my way to the ground to rewet my rag.

She frowns. "Those slippers are to keep you as quiet as a mouse." She rearranges the glasses on the cart to fit another pair in. "No one likes a noisy servant."

Wiggling my toes in my slippers, I dump alcohol over my rag then, without commenting, step back up onto the armchair I'm not supposed to stand on, and continue my work.

After I finish with the windows and return the chair to its location, I linger at the glass case holding the Heian book, absently swiping my rag over it again to look busy. For some reason, it calls to me, although I cannot recognize the title. I've studied Heian, know it well enough, but the only word I can pick out here is "history."

"I'm going to bring this down to the kitchen," Certa says when the cart cannot hold another object. "Now finish up quickly—make sure and tidy the shelves—then come downstairs and find me. We have lots to do today; there's a showing tonight."

"A showing?"

She doesn't look at me when she answers curtly, "A sale. For buyers."

"Buyers? They come to the Manor to buy?" My attention diverted, I turn from the glass case.

"Of course. Do you think he makes his living selling at auctions? He's above that."

Before I can reply, Certa is gone, leaving me alone to finish the library.

Shaking away my unease at this news, I tilt my head back to inspect my job on the windows and scowl. There's a smudge high up. A thump from a room nearby echoes through the library, and I start. Footsteps echo in the corridor, but no one enters. Uneasy at being alone here, I pull out the armchair again and hurry to finish cleaning the window. On my tiptoes, I swipe the rag against the smudge. Finally, I push the chair back into place, removing any evidence of my having used it.

It's as I'm stepping back from the chair that I look up and find a tall, blond man gazing at me with something akin to amusement on his features.

Biting back my gasp with a bite to my lips, I feel as though I got caught stealing instead of cleaning. Invisible, Certa's voice floats through my mind. I should drop my gaze, not meet his eyes. Instead, I meet his gaze with a glare of my own.

But at my boldness, he grins.

Disgust rolls over me, tightening my lips with disdain that I fight to keep from my features.

"And who are you?" The tall man walks toward me, his hands hooked upon his belt, a blade's hilt tucked into a sheath under one hand. He is the epitome of Canens features: sharp, bent nose; high, pronounced cheekbones; alert and interested eyes; and height which makes him formidable.

I straighten my spine under his gaze. "Helena. Sir," I add as an afterthought; even though I don't know who he is, he is clearly no slave or employee. He walks with a swagger that emphasizes his status, reminding me of the Queen and her retinue.

"Helena? Beautiful. And you a mere housemaid?" His pale eyebrows arch. Halfway across the room to me, he pauses and picks up my dirty window rag that I forgot when I was putting the chair away.

Fighting the flush that rises to my cheeks at his words—and more from his attention—I dip my chin in a nod, finally dropping my gaze, even though it galls me to do so. "Yes."

"Why have I not seen you before then?" Curiosity laces both his voice and features, which somehow softens his eyes and even his nose. It is as though he is the flame and I the moth. He terrifies me, despite his soft voice and easy words.

"I don't know," I answer, even though I know very well why: my injuries kept me from view, and slaves are to be invisible.

"Hmm. I make it a point to know every pretty girl the Magister brings in."

There is a pause between us. I won't acknowledge him thinking of me as a pretty girl, because to do so pushes me from the balance between the housekeepers and whores.

"I must be going. Unless there is anything you need?"

He motions to the rag he dropped on the desk, his unspoken intent clear. He will not pick it up and hand it to me, but neither does he step back from his position to allow me access to it.

Hesitating slightly, I step forward, crossing the room to him with a heart that seems to have gone silent. Only when I nudge myself up to him and reach out a hand across from him to pick up the rag does my heartbeat return, thumping so loudly in my ears that I cannot hear his breath.

Every second, I expect his touch, and I force myself to act with poise and take the rag normally, as though nothing is different. It's as I lift the rag and start pulling it back that he steps in, trapping me with his body against the desk, while his arm blocks any path I might find out.

My heart jumps into my throat, and I freeze, staring into his well-formed chest. He leans down, his breath wrapping around my cheek and neck. He comes closer, inhales, and then coughs, drawing back with a twist to his lips. "What is that gods-awful smell?"

Seeing my opportunity, I slip out from him and am halfway across the room before he can react further. Dropping the dirty rag, I exit the room on fast, silent feet, thanking the gods for Certa's evil ointment and vowing to wear it every day.

III

Sagax

BLANCHE

With a tug at the uncomfortable, wool cloak around my neck, I tie my palfrey at the hitching post of a building a dozen away from the one I seek. It has taken weeks to track him down, even with that sorcerer's help.

Sagax is not a man who wants to be found. But find him I have, and now it is time to pay him a visit. My breath forms a thick cloud between me and my horse as I stand before the mare.

I close my eyes and draw forth my magical stores, evaluating them and how much I have to work with. It comes at my beckoning, from the tips of my fingers and toes, even my ears and nose, gathering in my chest to be measured. I frown. I've refrained from doing much magic in the past few weeks, avoiding anything that might require me to use from my stores. Perhaps then I'll be prepared for this meeting with Sagax, yet it seems my magic has not replenished like it usually does.

With a short breath out my nose, I open my eyes and meet the palfrey's calm eyes framed with frozen lashes. The unusual cold spell must be sapping my magical strength. I have long noticed a correlation between the weather and my magical stores. When Canens has warmer weather, I have much more magical power, but when it is cold, it is as if my magic is sluggish, slow to react and respond to my desires. Did all Canensian sorcerers experience this? Glancing down the road to Sagax's unremarkable house, I hope so.

The palfrey huffs and shifts her weight, drawing my attention back. There is one thing I can do, although it would pain me slightly and I'd have to walk home. Perhaps if I don't complete the act, I'll still have a horse to ride.

Regardless, I cannot go into this battle without as much strength as I can muster. It's not something I like doing, but to protect my country, I must do it.

I pull off my glove and bury my hand in the soft region between the mare's jaw. The mare lifts her nose and smells my face, but I close my eyes and concentrate. I pull the living magic out of the animal, into my own fingertips and up my arm to join the magic stirring in my chest. The mare's head jerks up at first in the slightest panic at the experience then just as quickly begins to droop. Soon the mare is standing on trembling legs, her head swaying from side to side and her jaw resting on the hitching post as she pants feebly.

I take my hand away and study the mare with sorrow. "It must be done," I murmur to the mare's floppy ears. "Your life serves mine, as does theirs." But I pause before replacing my hand to finish the job. If I stop now, the mare might recover, might live. It will take days or weeks for her to return to full strength, and she will never be normal again, but horses are valuable here, and breeding and raising them has too many difficulties of its own to so discard her.

I sigh and touch the mare's nostrils, injecting just the tiniest amount of life back into the animal, a small amount of what is now coiled inside of me.

The mare inhales sharply, and her eyes widen for the barest of moments then sink closed again. Leaving her there, I travel on foot down the road to the sorcerer's house. I review the plan in my mind, hoping it works. If he talks, I'll let him live. If he doesn't...it will be best for him if he's a better sorcerer than me. I smirk.

I approach the building, taking in the cracked, frosted-over windows, the rickety wood that is easily a century old, and the roof laden with too much snow. My lips twitch. Looks are deceiving when a sorcerer lives inside.

Not bothering to knock, I push my way inside and find a drastically different sight.

Inside is a table spread with hot poultry and cooked vegetables, a half-full plate sitting before a man dressed in a tunic and trousers, his boots sitting by the door. A fire burns merrily in the fireplace across the room, and the room is sweltering after my time outside.

The man leaps up from the table, light ready upon his fingertips. With one command to my magic, I reach out and grab him with an invisible grip, simultaneously casting a suppressing spell to keep him from fighting back.

He chokes, his hand going to his throat as the light filters from his hands.

There is strength in him, a great deal. The sacrifice of the mare's anima will not be wasted here.

He coughs, grasping at his throat against the invisible hands.

"Sagax, I presume?"

His eyes widen then narrow. He opens his mouth to speak and coughs instead.

I loosen my spell on his throat so he can speak.

"I've been expecting you," he says in a hoarse voice.

"Have you? Decided to stay and face me instead of fleeing this time?"

"My mistake." He raises his palms to the ceiling. "I didn't expect you quite this soon."

I lift my chin. "Then that is your undoing."

"What do you want?"

"Why did you start the fires?"

His lips curve into wry amusement. "Haven't figured that out?"

I eye his table, heavy with fresh, hot food. "You eat well for destroying the growing houses. Why would you harm the city so?"

"You don't care about the city," he snarls. "You only care about yourself and your own glory."

"If you knew how much I sacrificed for the people of Canens!"

"I do know. You up in your palace, in front of a fire with more food than you can eat—you sacrifice nothing." His upper lip lifts in a sneer. "It's the people that suffer. And you make them suffer."

"Enough of this," I snap, tightening the magical spell. His magic scrabbles at the edges of my awareness as he tries to call a spell forward and fight me with it. I smirk. "You're powerless."

His face drains of color as his magic fails to find purchase against mine. "You kill me and you have no answers."

I lift my chin and raise my hand. "And that is your downfall. I don't need answers. I just need to kill you."

"I'm not the one who leads the rebels," he wheezes as I tighten my grip. His eyes begin to bulge.

"I—" I pause and tilt my head. "Who does?"

"Spare my life."

"Impossible. Your life is forfeit for the food you've taken out of people's mouths. You have signed your own death warrant. I should make an example of you."

"Please, spare me."

I narrow my eyes. "I should make an example of you."

With a quick decision, I cast my spell, and suddenly he sits on the floor, bound by legs and wrists in magician's metal.

He pants heavily at the release of my grip around his neck.

"In fact, you're right. I will make an example of you. By public execution."

His face pales.

I smile and cast one more spell, this one around the dwelling, one that will keep him from using his magic to escape. Then I turn and, ignoring his pleas, leave him there. I'll send my men back to gather

him. Along with some of that potion that will render him unconscious and utterly useless. Just like the sorcerer in my prison. Perhaps
they will be executed together...one final reunion for pupil and
teacher.

With a grin, I walk back to the palfrey and untie her. Leading the
exhausted mare, I make my slow way up to the palace.

IV

An Illicit Drink

WINTERBERRY

B y the time dinner arrives that night, I am exhausted with
trying to be invisible on my first full day of servanthood. I
have scrubbed and washed so much that my hands are dry,
red, and cracked, and no amount of Certa's salve is going to fix them
in time to start all over again tomorrow. How can I endure this every
day of my life? I shudder, thinking it.

Earlier in the day, I entered the kitchens to find the head cook
giving her scullery maid, Layela, a dressing-down with a short hand
whip. She apparently hadn't finished washing the stack of dishes
from the morning, and the cook screamed at her, punctuating her
shouts of Layela's incompetence with slashes across the girl's back. A
boy about her age stood in the room clenching his fists, shifting his
shoulders as if he felt the blows himself. I realized then that he'd been
at the receiving end of her whip recently. Her wrath abated, the cook
gave another half-hearted swipe then stashed the whip in the
cupboard beside the sink and went back to work without another
word.

Reentering the kitchen now at dinner, I can't help but give the cupboard a darting look then find Layela, hovering over the dishes and scrubbing, her head down.

I duck my head too and head toward the long table spanning the next room over. It's underneath the Magister's dining hall, and it's packed tight with three long tables and benches.

"Helena."

Bending to slide onto a bench, I look up to find Certa already seated a table over.

"Sir Gaiwen needs fresh towels," she tells me. "Go bring them to him."

"Now?" My stomach punctuates my question with a growl.

"Don't question me. Yes, girl. Go now while everyone is at the showings. Take some towels from the supply room—make sure they're decent quality towels, mind you, not the slaves' towels."

Nodding, I grit my teeth and cast the dishes before me a longing look, but I dare not argue. I'll just have to eat with the cooks and servers if I can't make it back in time. We housekeepers usually eat now instead of waiting for the rest of the Manor to finish eating—which could be midnight for all I know.

"Where is Sir..." I trail off, having forgotten who I was supposed to bring them to in the first place.

"Gaiwen," Certa says firmly, her eyes narrowing. "He's in the northeast wing. The Magister's wing," she adds at my blank look.

"Right. Sir Gaiwen. Northeast wing." I nod and set off, first to find the supply closet and then to find the northeast wing.

"And Helena!"

At the door, I pause and turn back, waiting for her to continue. She stands and crosses to me, putting out a hand to draw me in close. "Do not speak to anyone. Unless you see Sir Gaiwen. Or the Magister."

Frowning, I duck a nod.

On the trip up the stairs to the room, I consider her words. Did I do something wrong? Talk to the wrong person before? Or was she simply warning me to be invisible? No, her warning was more specific than that.

My stomach twists with unease as I drag myself up the stairs. Half my attention is on my meal, warm and waiting for me. It must be why I forget the room number Certa told me—or had she told me?—and I halt in the middle of the empty hallway, heart sinking.

It's late, and the hallway's stone walls are lit only by a few candles, leaving patches of dimness between them. Gripping the towels tight in my hands, I hurry through the shadows to Sir Gaiwen's room. When I knock, there is a gentle bustle behind the door, and then a young woman's round face peers around it at me with polite confusion above her white robes.

"Sir Gaiwen asked for fresh towels?" I ask her.

Her forehead creases in a frown. "I don't understand," she says in an odd accent.

I offer her the towels. "For Sir Gaiwen?" I say.

"Sir Gaiwen? Who is...Sir Gaiwen? No Sir Gaiwen here."

"I must have the wrong room." I frown at her. "Where are you from?" She stares blankly at me.

I try Ostiite. "Where are you from?"

She brightens. "Oh, I'm Heian. But don't tell anyone else that. How do you know Ostiite?"

"Heian?" My frown deepens, but I say in rough Heian, "What are you doing here?"

Her face brightens even further. "You speak it? Oh, I haven't been able to speak in my language in ages it seems. Ever since I left home. No one here understands me. How do you understand me?"

She talks so rapidly that it takes me several seconds longer than normal to process her words. "I had to study all the languages of the Seven Kingdoms as a child... Even Edormiscan."

"Really? Me too!" Her eyes light up with childish excitement.

She's unlike any slave I've met yet. I shift in the hallway, the towels growing hot in my hands. "What is your name?"

"Elaina. But Baron Tueor—my owner—insists on calling me Anna. Like it's the same name or something."

"How do you spell it?" I ask.

She spells out her name for me, and his name change makes sense. "Ah, well, in Canensian, we would pronounce your name as El-ah-na, not E-lay-na."

"Ooooh." Her eyes round in understanding, then she scowls. "Still, it's not my name at all. What's your name?"

"Helena."

"Well, Helena, it's so good to speak with another slave."

"Where is Baron Tueor?"

"Oh, he's at the preview downstairs. Said it would be all night, but he didn't want me down there." She rolls her eyes. "I don't know why, but he said there would be plenty of slaves to help him." She snorts. "Gave me a 'night off,' he said."

I glance behind me at the empty hallway. "So you're alone here?"

"Yes, want to come in?"

I chuckle. "You don't understand slavery, do you?"

She grins a bit wickedly. "Let's just say that I've never understood playing by the rules."

A reluctant smile lifts my lips. This is the sort of girl I need to befriend—one who is bold. My smile falters. But is she too bold? What if she confides in the wrong person? "You ought to be careful," I tell her, even as I contemplate how I might do the same thing as her. She invigorates me already, making me want to disobey the slave rules and stand up for myself.

"You want to come in?" she repeats with a widening grin.

The temptation to befriend her, this innocent-seeming young girl with beaming green-brown eyes, overwhelms me. "Sure. Just for a few minutes though. I've got to take these towels to Sir Gaiwen."

She waves a hand at the hallway and then grabs me, pulling me inside and shutting the door behind. "I'm so glad to have someone to talk to. You'll have to give me lessons in Canensian. I learned a long time ago, but I never paid attention. I swore I'd never visit this country. And now..." She rolls her eyes and strides into the center of the room, then holds out her hands and twirls back toward me. "Look at this. Here I am. Not only in Canens, but a slave." She grins as if it's a grand adventure.

I frown at her. She's the oddest slave I've ever met. "So you're really Heian?"

She nods, smiling broadly.

Her smile sets me at odds. It's as if she hasn't been affected by slavery at all—or she just refuses to let it affect her? I blink the thoughts away. "May I ask...what do you think of Canens?"

"It's freezing!" She laughs and hugs her arms around herself. "I don't think I've been properly warm yet."

I grin. "No, I can understand that."

Her expression turns contemplative. "Really, it's not what I expected."

"No? What did you expect?"

"Heathens."

"What?"

"We were taught that Canens was full of heathens. After the curse, we were told that those who were left alive were as cold and unfeeling as the land. But that's not true at all. I mean, my owner, Baron Tueor, he's not a particularly kind man. He's a bit crude and —" She shudders. "But most everyone else I've met...they're completely normal. They don't seem to be different from me or my people, or..." She shrugs and a pained look creases her face. "You're just people."

A surprised laugh works its way out of me. "Is that what others think of us? That we're barbarians?"

"Well...yes." She motions to me. "After all, the only people that have come out of the country in recent years have been covered in furs and looking...barbaric." She shrugs and continues. "But that's not true. I've learned that. You're just as normal as I am." She grins. "Which may not be that normal."

Another laugh escapes me. "How do you keep this spirit, Elaina?"

Her smile dims slightly but only for a moment. Then she forces it larger, brighter. "I refuse to let anything destroy me. Even though my friends are gone, and...and I don't know when I'll see them again," she says with the barest tremble to her lips, "I am alive. And I am well. And I am sure that my brother searches for me." She narrows her eyes at me. "What's your story?"

I lift one shoulder. "My stepmother didn't love me enough."

She tilts her head to the side, studies me for a long minute, then nods. "Yes. That seems to happen a lot here, doesn't it?"

"What...what have you learned since you've been here?" I ask.

"Learned?" She laughs loud and long. "Oh boy. You'll have to sit down for that one."

"I mean, about the people of Canens," I clarify. "About us."

"Oh." Her forehead creases. "Well, that they don't really like their queen. But they love their princess—if they think she's still alive."

My heart warms. "Really?"

"Yes. I think most want to believe she still exists and that she's still reasonably sane, or else they have no hope. And with the fire in Merise..." She tuts.

"What fire?"

"You haven't heard?"

I shake my head.

"Two growing houses burned to the ground, and a couple store-houses too. It's awful. The city isn't going to have enough food."

"How do you know all this?"

She shrugs and reaches for a couple of glasses. She pours some amber liquid from a glass into both and offers me one.

"Oh, I—I shouldn't."

She grins. "Neither should I. So quick, drink the evidence before it gets us in trouble." She holds out the glass with a mischievous look.

I glance over my shoulder at the door then take the glass and sip from it. "Whoa."

She giggles. "Like it?"

"It's...strong." I peer into the glass. "What is it?"

"Ostiite whiskey, I think?" She shrugs and sips again. "Good stuff."

I peer at her a little unsurely then shrug and take another drink. "It grows on you, I suppose."

She grins. "Thatta girl."

As I lift my glass to my lips, a sound in the hallway makes me start. I nearly drop the glass and look over at the pile of towels I left beside the door. Behind me, Elaina flies into action. She puts the decanter away and downs the rest of her drink as the footsteps near. She grabs the glass from my hand and downs it as well, grimacing and shaking her head. Then she runs a cloth over them and sets them beside the decanter by the time the footsteps stop outside our door.

I rush toward the door and to the towels, so when the door opens to Baron Tueor's face, I'm holding a pile of towels in my hands.

His eyes widen in surprise. "Why, it's the little chit from the library. To what do I owe this pleasure?" His words are slightly slurred, as though he's had a great deal of drink already tonight.

"I—"

"She had towels, sir," Elaina provides in her broken Canensian.

"I didn't order towels. We have plenty."

Elaina frowns, trying to understand. "I—yes, towels."

He shoots Elaina a glare then rolls his eyes. "She knocked on the wrong door?"

"Yes." Elaina bobs her head. "Yes."

"Sorry, my lord," I interject, "I was looking for Sir Gaiwen's room."

"Yes, Sir Gaiwen's room!" Elaina says in excitement, whether feigned or true, I'm not even sure.

His eyes narrow at his slave. "You let her in?"

Elaina's soft doe eyes narrow as she tries to understand his words. "Yes, yes of course." She motions to my hands. "She had towels."

"For Sir Gaiwen, you idiot," he snaps. Then he drags a hand over his forehead. "Forget it. It's like talking to a carrot."

My mouth falls. "I—"

"Get out of here, you worthless girl," he mutters. "Just get lost. Sir Gaiwen is across the hall. Go give your towels to him before I decide to be far less kind."

Before he acts on what he bluffs, and before I can determine if Elaina is simply playing dumb or truly that foolish, I rush from the room on my towel delivery.

V

In Merise

RUS

A modest spread of cooling porridge, salmon jerky, round beans, and tea covers the table in the inn's pub. I've spent far too much of our remaining gold on a large room for our stay in Merise. Thank the Creator we got Ino situated with Astra's mother after a day in Merise, or else I'd be paying for a second room.

City living. I flick a crumb of bread off the edge of the table and allow my thoughts to wander. The room isn't even worth it. This inn caters to merchants and traders, not foreigners who want creature comforts. What I wouldn't give for my feather bed once again. I flick another crumb and, this time, hit Cito where he sits across the table from me.

He frowns down at himself and brushes off his tunic.

I grimace my apology.

With a slam of the inn door, Ino barges inside, her face alight with excitement after weeks of drudgery. She doesn't have to look around to find us at our usual booth and quickly slides in next to Cito. She leans over the table and says in a low voice trembling with excitement, "I found a lead."

"What?" I lean toward her, my heart thumping in its guarded thrill. We've been chasing dead-end leads in Merise for weeks now. We've tracked down nearly every slave sold at the prior public auction, and we are no closer to locating Elaina than we were upon entering Canens.

"There is a caravan to the Magister's Manor," Ino says.

"A caravan?" Cito runs a hand over his face. He's aged since we entered this frozen land, with deeper wrinkles on his forehead and skin that's been frostnipped too many times already. He looks more like a hardened Canensian every day. I swear even his features grow paler every day.

"Yes, this caravan goes out every two weeks from someplace in Merise." She accepts a bowl of porridge from the barmaid. "Thank you." She ladles a heaping spoonful into her mouth and winces, waving a hand at her mouth to cool off the hot porridge before swallowing.

Cito glances at me. I shrug in answer. Whether or not we find someone to travel with, the only lead we've found in two weeks is Magister Marcus Tueor, who buys up slaves at the auctions for cheap, transports them, and trains them at his manor in the city of Monticola.

"Might as well check into the price," I say to Cito. "See if we can afford it or have to do a heist."

He frowns his disapproval at my jest but nods and sets down his mug of dark tea, already reaching for the hat with his mittens tucked inside.

She fixes me with a hopeful look. "For three?"

Halfway out of the booth, Cito pauses, eyes on me.

At the two pairs of hopeful gazes, I grunt and shake my head. "I told you where you'd be staying. Why do you think you've been staying with Astra's family the past week?"

Not waiting for any rebuttal, Cito nods and, doffing his hat and mittens, heads for the exit to check on the caravan.

"Are you sure?" Ino grips the spoon with a fist, her cheek flexing as she waits for my answer—the same answer I've given every day for the past several weeks.

"I'm sure. You won't go with us. What if the Magister sees you and decides he wants you there? You've been branded, Ino. How do we stand up against him if he decides something? Or what if you slow us down so that when we do find Elaina and have to run, we can't?"

She casts me a mutinous look. "I'm not a burden. You forget that I made it quite far with your sister."

I roll my eyes but refrain from pointing out that she also got kidnapped along with my sister. "You're not a help, either—not in this case. Two can travel faster than three, no matter how you look at it. Cito is the better partner for me."

She glares into her porridge, knowing I speak the truth. "I can help," she mutters. Despite the set of her jaw, a tear beads on her lashes and falls into her bowl. She swipes at it.

"You will be helping," I tell her. "We promised Astra we'd help her family. This way, we follow through on that promise and help her family, while also keeping you safe."

"What if you don't come back?" Ino dips the spoon into the porridge and raises it. A mound falls back toward the rest with a depressing plop.

I toss back the remainder of my hot tea. The custom of a hot beverage for breakfast is the one thing I've grown accustomed to over the past few weeks. It fights the constant chill of this land and steels me against the waiting ice outside.

"We'll come back," I promise. "Trust me. We'll find Elaina, and we'll come back for you."

"And Vesta? The other maid? My friend?"

I nod. "We'll do our best. But that's something you need to help us with. We don't know where she is or what direction she's gone. We can only track one girl at a time, and—"

"You must find the princess, of course."

Although her voice is low, I still glance around to see if it's possible we've been overheard. "Yes, we must. You know that. And you knew the risks when you accompanied her on her journey."

Ino's lips twist into an expression of loathing and regret, one I know to be aimed at herself, not me. She takes her duties seriously, so seriously that I wouldn't be surprised if she did some investigations of her own while we tracked down Elaina.

"And if Elaina's not at the Manor, you'll come back for me, right? I can help you?"

"We'll send a message to you either way," I assure her. "But it means you must stay at Miss Amasia's house. You must remain there."

She gnaws on her lip. "You know Astra is Tillmore's daughter. Her mother was once his mistress..."

"Yes." I wait for her to continue.

"What if he shows up at Miss Amasia's home?"

"Have you asked her that?"

"Yes." A trace amount of sullenness darkens her tone as she shoves her spoon into her porridge again.

We fall silent for a few minutes as both of us continue our breakfasts.

"And what did Astra's mother say?" I've already talked to the woman about her ex-lover, Lord Tillmore, and gleaned all the information I could out of the crippled woman. I know that Tillmore has no more use for her. But Ino must come to that conclusion herself.

"She said Tillmore hates her now. Thinks she's repulsive." Ino briefly lifts her gaze to mine and then shifts it aside. "I know she's right. He doesn't like anything that's not perfect and worth something. But still..."

"It's natural to be afraid, Ino." I lean across the table, consider reaching out a hand toward her, then think again. Although Ino's never given any indication of liking me, I don't want to mislead her or encourage her at this time, if anything, I must be distant, even cruel. "You must be brave. For Elaina."

Ino looks unconvinced but no longer mutinous.

"What would Elaina have you do, anyway?" I ask, half out of curiosity, half hoping that Elaina would—for once—agree with me.

She considers my words over a bite of her breakfast. "She'd have me stay where I was needed most."

I lift my brow. "And where do you think that might be right now?"

She sighs. "With Miss Amasia."

Inwardly, I smirk, although it takes all my courtly training for me to keep my lips stationary. "Then that's where you must stay. And we will return for you. Do you think Elaina would let us do otherwise?"

Finally, Ino's sullenness breaks, and she flashes me an impish grin. "She'd flay you alive if you didn't."

At that, I laugh. "You're absolutely right. And so I shudder in terror."

The door to the inn flings open, and with a burst of cold air that rattles the frames, Cito hurries in, shoulders hunched and looking miserable.

"What is it?" I ask.

He shakes snow from his shoulders and removes his hat, tapping it over the floor to loosen the clinging flakes before tossing it on the table and sliding in next to me. "A storm moving in. Bad. I've secured us spots on the caravan, but they won't be leaving until this storm passes. He said at least a week."

I grit my teeth. Another week gone. Another week where Elaina is a slave.

A small, warm hand over mine makes me look up.

"We'll find her," Ino says, all humor gone from her face. "I promise you."

Pressing my lips together, I allow her to attempt to comfort me, but nothing brings me comfort when I think of Elaina enslaved.

VI

A Summoning

BLANCHE

Burning sconces along the wall brighten my potion chamber with an eerie light. It's enough to see my potion work by but makes the words in the leather-bound book atop the worktable difficult to read. The small scrawl is laborious to decipher under the light of day, but now it's nearly impossible.

I sigh and pull from my store of magic within to brighten the room and illuminate the pages. The act is nearly effortless, a slight withdrawal upon my magical stores, but I detest burning it without good cause. Thankfully, I siphoned a great deal of magic off Sagax the sorcerer before his recent execution. It had been necessary to prevent his escape as well as to keep his magic from going to waste. I'd decided that a single execution would be most effective at this time, for perhaps the sorcerer in my dungeons will be encouraged to divulge more information after witnessing his teacher's death. Only time will tell.

The additional light eases the stress upon my eyes, though it fails to relieve my irritation as I read the nonsense scrawled upon a parchment. "Cursed Edormiscans..."

My rudimentary skills in their language is hardly sufficient to translate this book on magic, as most dictionaries don't list the words and tutors don't teach the words used in spell books, as if just the words themselves are evil. I snort. Foolish scholars, the lot of them. Where better to search for answers to magical questions than from the most magical of the Seven Kingdoms? I am lucky that I found this book in the Witch's cottage.

I flip the pages of the book over and begins to decipher a spell with the help of a thin Edormiscan dictionary I borrowed from Nosco, my scholar, upon my last visit. He had not fared so well, although I had spared him, since he'd given me just enough new information on christenings to convince me that he was avidly researching the topic. He had gone so far that he'd tracked down two books in Edormiscan concerning Fae legends and shared with me all information he thought pertinent. Of course, it did nothing to explain the prophecy, but it was something at least. Enough for me to spare him. Instead I executed Sagax, and Nosco had shuddered in terror.

I allow myself a small smile as I bend over the Witch's Edormiscan book, the untidy scrawl so difficult to read that I almost give up. Then I turn the page, and the first two words upon it jump out: Fae summoning.

My heart leaps. This. This is what I need. Just as the sorcerer said —the Fae. And of course, a summoning spell is exactly what I need. I won't have to go find them—they will come to me!

I scan the spell and again find myself slowed by the language barrier. Frustrated, I push the book away.

"Cursed Edormiscans." I huff out a breath, more heavily this time, and pull the book back into the light. "Why must they have their own language anyway? It's as dead as they are now." I growl before smiling. The Edormiscans, as much as the Fae had blessed them, also suffered greatly at the same hands. Their magic ostracized them from the six other kingdoms, resulting in a kingdom that was cut off from its neighbors and dependent on the whims of the Fae. It eventually killed them all. And destroyed their land.

I too slowly extract the meanings of the words and find myself with a list of ingredients. The only thing I don't have are...phoenix feathers.

Standing in front of my cabinets, I am forced to acknowledge that the phoenix feather jar is depressingly empty. I curse under my breath. I will find one. But where? The last phoenix I'd heard of fled south to Tepor, into the desert lands. I could search for years and not find it. It could be dead by now. Phoenix are elusive creatures.

Returning to the book, I scan the ingredients again and pause at the phoenix feather ingredient. I frown and reach for Nosco's dictionary. It is not phoenix but *phoenicia* feather.

With a jolt of triumph, I return to my cabinet and withdraw a jar nestled beside the empty phoenix feather one.

"Perfect." I remove a feather from the less magical and less well-known *phoenicia* bird and return with it to the book.

I collect the rest of the ingredients—faery dust, glacier water, snake eyes, and sapphire powder—and grind it together in a pestle of marble. I read the spell a dozen times, even double-checking my translations to confirm I'm not wasting the precious ingredients I have on hand. It will only work if followed exactly as stated.

When the ingredients are ground into a fine powder and my wrist aches from the effort, I read the final instruction.

Draw the Rune of the Fae upon the entrance you wish the Fae to use.

"Rune of the Fae?" I ask the empty room. Panic jabs me in the chest. "What in the goddess's name is the Rune of the Fae?"

Desperately, I flip through the entire book, but I see nothing to suggest what the Rune of the Fae might be. How am I to know this?

Furious, I slam the book shut and shove it from the table. I'm lifting the pestle when my gaze fixes on the book, now lying face-down on the stone floor at my feet.

On the leather cover is a symbol. I had assumed it was a symbol of magic, of the Edormiscans perhaps. But could it be the Rune of the Fae? After all, the myths suggest that all magic originally came from the Great Fae themselves.

I pick up the book and stare at the cover.

What do I have to lose? With a quick glance around my potions chamber, I collect the pestle full of dust and walk it to the window. Copying the image from the leather-bound book, I draw it in dust upon the pane of glass. I flip the book open to the spell and reread the instructions. There is no incantation to say, simply mixing the ingredients and then drawing the rune.

Closing the book, I step back and wait.

And wait.

VII

Caleb

WINTERBERRY

D ays pass in horrible monotony. But my discussion with Elaina has given me two somethings to focus on: my return to Merise and inspiring the slaves around me. I find the escape planning much easier than inciting the slaves. No one notices a little bread or butter disappearing on the way to a guest's room. No one notices a strip of jerky missing from the storeroom. Pretty soon, I'll have enough for a week's journey, and I need at least that. But trying to find ways to inspire the slaves is harder. Furthermore, any slave I talk to—truly talk to—I never see again. It's happened too often now to be in my mind. Every slave I've spoken to about Queen Blanche or about the unhappy state of Canens, I never see again. What's worse is that the other slaves have noticed it now. They won't even talk to me. And it becomes clear: I am being isolated from all but Certa.

So I focus on the escape. Instead of being relieved at the ease of this preparation, I feel uneasy, as though I am waiting for the lynx to pounce. I go through my days trying to remain invisible, while knowing that I am anything but. The Magister's eye falls on me with consideration whenever I am near him. Rare as it is, it unnerves me.

It is as though he, too, bides his time, waiting for something that I cannot fathom. Sometimes I look up from the corner of the dining room to find his contemplative gaze upon me.

Every day, I see more of the abuse such as the cook gave Layela. Those slaves who wield power over others extend physical punishment. But even those slaves are not exempted from the abuse of the lords and ladies or from Tueor or the Magister. We all bear the burden of many masters. No moment of our lives is our own. We stay up late to help with previews then wake early to clean up after them. Sometimes slaves are assigned to a particular guest at the Manor and must be ready for their requests at any time of the day or night. Many slaves exist on so few hours of sleep that they have accidents like tripping down the stairs or cutting off a finger.

So far, I have yet to reach the status of receiving one of these personal assignments, but the life of a slave closes in on me nonetheless. Desperate for something more, I begin to sneak out to visit Caleb and the horses. Although I have plenty of duties that could pass all of my time at the Manor, I find reasons to get out of doors. It brings a flush to my cheeks, a lightness to my step, to see the gangly yearlings and the rambunctious colts and fillies as they undergo training, even if just for five minutes instead of eating lunch in the uncomfortable atmosphere of the kitchen. When the chance presents itself, I watch the training of the young horses from the shadows. After a week of this, when I have watched three or four times, a voice speaks from the shadow next to me.

"Do you ride, Your Highness?"

My flesh jumps, leaving my heart pounding even though I know the low voice. I glance around, afraid to get Caleb in trouble or sold, but there is no one; we appear safe amongst the shadows for now. "Once upon a time."

"How long has it been?"

"Many years now." I think back upon the time of carefree rides through the snow with Father and shrug. "Since Father died. But it feels like many more."

"You sound older than your years, princess."

I cast a sad smile at the shadow beside me, considering all that I have learned in the past few years: from the time my stepmother took my crown, imprisoned me, then sold me as a slave to the highest bidder, to the death of Des, to the beating my defense of her earned, to the cook and her beatings, to all the little abuses in between, before and after, and my smile slips. How could I be anything but older than my years? Have I ever equaled my years? Or have I always outpaced them?

A pale yearling dances before us in the ring, nostrils flaring, ears flicking.

"What do years matter?" I ask. "It's experiences that matter, not years."

"Yes. Certainly my seventy have, combined, taught me less than this last year I have lived."

My jaw goes slack. I must have heard him wrong. "Seventy?"

There is laughter in his voice when he answers. "Indeed. Seven decades, and I still don't feel as though I have existed beyond this year."

"What are you that you look so young and yet have lived so long? What magic is at work?" I should fear him, I think, fear this entire conversation, but it is wonder coloring my words. He is the kindest soul I've met, and yet I know magic to corrupt, to turn even the kindest soul evil.

"Magic?" he answers, oblivious to my thoughts. "The magic of the mines."

I give him a sidelong examination. "The mines? You worked there?"

"Oh, aye. Many a year."

"I thought my father had closed them."

Caleb gives me a slanted look that asks how I could ever believe a thing like that. "They are too valuable."

"But—they are dangerous."

"Oh, indeed."

"What are they like?" The answer suddenly interests me more than anything else before me, more than the colt who fights his trainer or the quiet filly who trots in circles with a young man on her back, already surrendered to his control.

Staring at the horses, Caleb does not answer, and I imagine that he is staring not at the scene before him but at one behind him. Pity wells within me, for how can I help him escape this life except by offering him death? This life of slavery that has been more instructive than any seven decades of his own lived before?

Tears brim on my lashes, blurring my vision as a colt in the ring before us rears high, striking out against his would-be masters. He has spirit. Too much spirit. He has not given up, like I have. I have not fought since Father died. I haven't fought her.

But is it worth the fight? I want to ask the colt that, or maybe even Caleb. But looking at Caleb, I think he has surrendered to his position as well. Are we all like this? All us slaves, seeing no way out from our capture? No improvement over our lives? Will we all, like this colt, eventually be broken and reshaped into something unrecognizable? Something with no light in our eyes? I cannot stay here and let it happen to me. Not when my acceptance means acceptance on behalf of all enslaved Canensians. I have a responsibility greater than myself, and that is something I never understood in my prison; that was nothing compared to the struggles of normal life in Canens. I never understood it until now. I will not accept this life. I do not accept being a slave, especially at the Magister's hands. I will escape it —and escape him. And if they won't change their own lives, I'll change this life for them, every last one of them, so that they can speak freely, not sell their children, and live a life of comfort if they but try.

Caleb finally speaks. "The mines are difficult to survive for any but the strongest of men, but the *adamas* and its magical-enhancing qualities are real. Not that my long-lived brothers and I need it."

With stinging eyes, I blink away my tears, jerked back to the present as I am by his words.

He turns his face to me and murmurs, "What are those dangerous thoughts in your mind, Your Highness?"

I give him a watery smile. "I don't think I should confide in you, Caleb. You wouldn't agree with them."

A ghost of a smile lifts up the corners of his mouth.

"But you said you and your brothers don't need magic? Do you..." I hesitate, all the warnings of magic I've ever received and read about warring in my mind.

"What is it?"

"Do you have magic already?"

"Of course. Us giants are a rare race, but one with a magical lineage."

I twine my hands together before me, warming my bare fingers instead of pulling on my mittens. "And it doesn't corrupt you? You're the kindest person I've ever met, Caleb, but doesn't magic corrupt one's soul?" I rush through the questions as if it will make them easier to hear. "I'm sorry," I add. "I just—the only sorcerer I know is my stepmother. And she's..." I trail off as a shudder takes over my body that has nothing to do with the cold.

He chuckles lightly. "All magic is not evil. In fact, magic itself is not evil. It corrupts no more than power does, which is to say, it can corrupt quite easily."

I tilt my head to the side. "But can you ever trust it?"

"No more than you can trust power." He raises a brow at me. "Both can intoxicate and lead one down a dangerous path. But there are some who wield one or both without becoming corrupt."

I set my jaw and watch as the colt before us dances at the end of his lead.

"Why don't you come out tomorrow after your chores are completed? I will train you on them." He jerks his chin toward the horses before us.

"Truly?" I am unable to explain the leap of excitement my heart gives, the desire to have something worth looking forward to at the end of the day and a way to orchestrate my escape. If I have a horse that trusts me, escape will come easier.

"You're more than welcome," he answers.

"I would love to. And I..." I cast my gaze around the room, and it falls on a pitchfork. "I'll help you clean stalls in return, I—"

"You need not do that, Your Highness."

"Shh," I say this time at his use of the title.

He dips his head in apology and acknowledgment. "I ask no payment, for I serve only you, Yo—Helena."

I can't help but smile at his honest humility. Even though he tries to talk me out of my plans, and I know he will continue to try and do so, I trust him, and I know he is my ally. My only real ally. Anyone else would sell me out to avoid a beating—and I cannot blame them.

"I must go now. But thank you, Caleb. I will come back tomorrow, eager to be trained."

His head tilts at my words, but I don't wait to see how he understands them. If Caleb, with seventy years of experience in the mines and knowledge of magic, can teach me anything, I will learn it.

VIII

Lady Angelo

WINTERBERRY

"Helena, you're assigned to Lady Angelo's rooms today," says Certa as I enter the kitchens for breakfast early the next day.

I aim a shocked look her way. I'm hardly trained to wait on a lady yet.

"I know," she answers my unasked question. "But we're short of trained slaves and we have the big preview coming up. Just do your best."

Shutting my mouth against any retort, I nod and begin to ready the breakfast tray. I'll just have to try and remember what it was like to have breakfast brought to me in bed. I pick up the napkin and quickly craft it into the shape of a swan, then replace it on the plate. I'd had one servant—slave?—when Blanche imprisoned me. The woman had been four times my age, if not more. Or, I think, glancing at Certa, who is directing a half dozen other servants to their places today, maybe she'd just appeared that old because of how difficult this life is. But she taught me a few things in her spare moments, like crafting swans out of napkins and towels, and would even sneak books in to me, something to pass the days.

From the pantry, I snag some extra fruit and a dried strip of venison, feigning that it's for Lady Angelo, then sneak it into my deep apron pockets. I have to be careful though; it's too early in the day to start stuffing them full. A bit here or there might not be noticeable, but too much and someone is bound to notice unless I can get to my room and deposit the food in the canvas bag I stashed there after stealing it from the supply closet earlier in the week.

Determined to be "diligent, prompt, and invisible" today, I leave a sleeping Lady Angelo her breakfast tray, and until lunchtime, I manage to remain all but unnoticed by all but Certa. She assigns me tasks near Lady Angelo's room or the kitchens, where I might be found if the lady calls.

At lunch, I am summoned to Lady Angelo's room with a private meal for her. "Why isn't she coming down for luncheon?" I frown at the elaborate tray of fresh fruits and vegetables and local game waiting to go upstairs.

The cook purses her lips at me. "Just take it up to her room."

Hiding my grimace, I take the tray and disappear before the cook can grab her handy whip.

Stomach growling and heating with anger at the thought of this woman being served by slaves for no reason other than her status and birthright, I glare at the tray as I climb the servants' stairs.

At the top, I exit into the hallway and turn left toward the wing where Lady Angelo sleeps along with a dozen other honored guests.

I glance down at Lady Angelo's tray. A fresh apple. Just like the Queen would grow in her growing house. For some reason, one of Pia's stories returns to me then. Blanche and the nobles eat well while the rest of us eat scraps from the table or nothing at all.

With a glance around, I slip the apple from the tray and into my apron. Then I rearrange the tray so that it looks balanced again. Nothing else there will last in my bag, or else I would take more. But this might make me a friend in the stables and keep them quiet while I execute my plan.

Steeling myself, I shift the tray to one hand and knock on the door.

"Come in," answers the frilly voice of Lady Angelo.

I push my way inside and find her still in bed, dressed in a silky mauve robe with rabbit fur lining the wrists and neck. Repulsion rises in me. Why does she deserve this treatment? Why does any person deserve someone to wait on them in such a way? If I ever become queen, I will do away with slavery in all forms—even for myself. No person should be so humbled. If they wish to serve their queen, or to serve another, then they may, but they will be paid for it. They will not be enslaved to it.

"Ah, I see you're still walking freely. Unpunished," Lady Angelo says with a cold shard of ice in her voice.

Unpunished for what? I straighten my spine, trying to keep my face impassive. "Yes, my lady," I answer, knowing it will annoy her.

She crooks an eyebrow at me. "Set that down over there and rearrange my pillows for me. This bed is horribly awkward, and I'm feeling so ill today, I don't think I can manage to get out of bed."

This time, I have to turn my back to her in order to hide my frown, so I set down the tray and pretend to smooth a tablecloth. Ill? She's probably just unable to sleep outside of her own bed. This bed is probably better than what she has at home—it's better than what I had in the palace after Father married Blanche.

I inhale quietly for patience then turn and walk to her. She watches me with her cold eyes and barely leans forward for me to fluff her pillows. I fight the urge to assault her—either with my words or hands. Instead, I put my anger at this entitled woman into her pillows, punching them fluffy and shoving them down behind her back as she instructs, all the while trying to avoid touching this woman who disgusts me so much.

She leans back when I am done then shakes her head. "No, that's too hard." She directs me to move the pillows around for what seems like another ten minutes before she is finally satisfied. All the while, I fume but force my hands to be at least a little gentle in order to hide my anger. I fear that I fail, for she is smirking when she finally announces herself too hungry to continue this and demands I bring her tray over to her.

She narrows her eyes at me as I position it over her lap. "That's all. You may leave."

Holding my head high, my jaw clenched, I turn to leave.

"Oh, wait," she calls out. When I turn, my face carefully neutral, she motions to the fire. "Tend my fire first."

With a half glance at the crackling fire in the fireplace, I grind my teeth but bob a nod. It's another ten minutes before she's satisfied with the size of the fire, placement of logs, and position of the fireplace tools, and she finally allows me to leave—after demanding I return in no more than twenty minutes to retrieve her luncheon tray.

Carefully, I close the door behind me, the sound no louder than a bird's chirp in the hallway. I maintain control until I dart into the servant's stairs, then let the door close and pound my fists against the wall with a muffled shout. I can't endure this life much longer; I can't serve people like Lady Angelo or my stepmother or the Magister with all their entitlement and derision for the commoner—not if I want to keep my life much longer.

When I've released the worst of my anger, I descend the stairs and return to the kitchen, where I eye a loaf of bread cooling on the countertop. Perhaps I could sneak away with something like that? Lady Angelo did say to return in twenty minutes. Perhaps I can pretend that she wanted something else.

"Is this loaf for anyone in particular?" I ask one of the other kitchen slaves.

The young woman shakes her head and busies herself in her task, shifting her body so that I can't see her face.

I watch the slave shape a few bread loaves with deft fingers. She doesn't dare to look at me, as if just that act is treacherous. "Is it an extra?" I probe.

Sparing me the quickest glance possible, the woman gives me a motion that is half nod and half shrug.

"Can I take it to Lady Angelo then?"

She nods once.

"Thank you." I grab a tray for the bread. It would ruin the image if I were to bring a lady bread clenched in my hands. I arrange it nicely and add a fresh cup, another pot of hot water and citrus, and a fresh napkin. The other slave disappears with a tray of shaped bread loaves, and I feel a pang of disappointment at her reception. But...I can't blame her.

When I make it out into the hallway, I slip the bread from the tray and rearrange the items again. In her room, I find that Lady Angelo has fallen into a light doze—thank the gods—so I sneak in and retrieve her tray, slipping out again with relief. It's only an hour later that I am called back, and I realize my escape has not been so smooth as I imagined. And so I spend the rest of the day waiting on Lady Angelo as well as sneaking food from the kitchens under the guise of bringing it to her. In so doing, I manage to fill out my pack with dried fruits, meat, bread, and even a skein of wine. I have to grin. Now if only I knew when I could escape, and where to go, then I would have a great deal more confidence in my attempt.

When I go to bed that night, I feel Certa's gaze lingering on me, but I don't have to feign exhaustion to crawl into bed and turn away. I cannot confide in her. For all her gruffness, there is tenderness under her exterior. She cares for me, for all of us. And she tries to protect me from the cook and her beatings. She keeps me busy to keep me out of trouble, probably sent me to Lady Angelo to keep me from trouble. I squeeze my eyes shut as a tear pushes through. Please, please, don't let harm come to her because of me.

With that prayer on my lips, I fall asleep, and for the first time since arriving, I sleep soundly.

IX

Monticola

WINTERBERRY

When I wake the next morning, it is to the feeling that something is wrong. After several minutes of lying in bed, I realize it is too quiet. Turning, I find Certa's bed empty.

I bolt upright. She has never left the room before without waking me. I don't wait to find out where she's gone; instead I pull my night clothing off and my white work gown and stockings on. I'm beginning to hate white. And purple and black and, especially, red. If I ever get out of here, I will never wear them again. I'm so sick of seeing all of us branded by these colors and our pasts. I raise my hand to my neck, where the captain marked me before sale. It's healed now, simply raised numbers in black against my white skin. Unlike most slaves, my hair doesn't cover it, and I wear my shame for all to see. Even if I stole clothing, exposing my neck would expose me.

My blood fumes at the reminder, and I wrench my hand away from the tattoo as if it burns. I finish dressing in a hurry and wind my way through the maze of hallways to the kitchens, where I overhear my name before I even enter.

"Where's Helena? Lady Angelo has already rung this morning," a female's voice says.

Wincing, I stop, ready to wheel around until they find someone else, but Certa has already caught sight of me. A flash of something like regret darkens her eyes.

"Helena." She motions me forward.

I'm not sure if I imagine the reluctance in her tone or not, but I approach with decided reluctance of my own.

"Lady Angelo has specifically requested for you to be her lady's maid today," Certa says gravely. "She has plans to visit the shops in town and will need assistance."

"Oh. Yes, ma'am." I bob a curtsy then pause. "But I have nothing to wear to town. No hat or boots or—"

"There are the necessary items in the slaves' closet. See the master of the garments for supplies before you attend to Lady Angelo."

"Yes, ma'am." When I hesitate too long, she shoos me away, shielding me from the cook's evil glare.

As I slip out the wide door of the kitchen, I hear the cook say, "What does that little pip of a girl have that everyone wants?"

I pause just outside the door, thinking they might reveal more or at least distract me for another minute or two before my dreaded day with Lady Angelo begins.

"Hush," Certa answers, but her scolding is mild. "You shan't talk about her like that."

"Why not?" the cook mutters defiantly, but her tone is muted, as if she concedes to Certa.

Defeated, I trudge off to find the master of the garments. Perhaps this day with the lady will come in useful; now I'll have clothes to escape in. With a mischievous smile lifting my shoulders, I hurry off to scour the closets and gain as much advantage for my escape as possible.

With a few smiles and pathetic motions to my bald scalp and frostnipped fingers, I convince the master of garments to give me a luxurious white cape, along with light gray wolf mittens and matching hat, fur-lined leather boots only one size too big, and thick wool stockings that fill the extra space in my boots. By the time I march myself up to Lady Angelo's room, I'm ready for whatever she might throw at me—as long as she only throws me in a snowbank.

Another maid has been helping ready her for the excursion but bobs the lady a curtsy and hastens out of the room when I appear. I watch her with envy. Surprisingly, Lady Angelo is waiting for me in her warm fur cloak; she sneers at me.

"You take longer to ready yourself than a queen. For all that, you'd think you'd look better." She smirks and brushes by me, then stops at the door, shooting me an expectant glare.

Gritting my teeth together, I open the door for her and step aside.

She pauses in the doorway, gaze lingering on me. "You really are resentful at heart, aren't you?" She gives a tinkling little laugh. "We'll fix that. At the Magister's, no one stays like you for long. I've helped him break many a young woman just like you."

Lip clenched between my teeth, I refuse to give her the satisfaction of my anger. Instead, I dip my head and wait for her to move on. When she does, I follow. And seethe.

A sleigh with two dappled gray horses awaits us outside the Manor when we exit. It's the first time I've left the Manor since my arrival, except for traveling to the stables, and the first time I've ever left via the front entrance. I trail several feet behind Lady Angelo, carrying a blanket to drape over her legs for the ride in the sleigh.

A male slave helps Lady Angelo into the sleigh and then assists me as well while a manservant climbs up front with the sleigh driver. My gaze lingers on him, not on his flushed cheeks, or his youthful face, but on the hopelessness in his expression. She does mean to break me. So does the Magister. We're all broken here. One way or another. I simply won't allow her to.

Despite my determination, Lady Angelo's constant insults on the journey into town alternates between making me furious and causing me pain. From my looks to my performance, I can do nothing right for her. Still, I refuse to let her words into my heart, and I refuse to stop feeling. Instead, I sit across from her in the sleigh, a smaller blanket over my lap, and stare out from the covered sleigh.

All too soon, we are in the midst of the town square and the driver halts the sleigh. I jump out, slipping across the snow in my eagerness.

Lady Angelo crooks a brow at me as she descends with poise, her heeled boots emitting a soft squeak upon the hard-packed snow. She shakes out her cloak and surveys me. "Now, I'll need your assistance carrying my purchases. So stay close."

The manservant from the front of the sleigh falls into step ahead of us, pushing his way through any crowd and creating a path for Lady Angelo to follow.

I fall into a dull plod behind them and quickly have my arms fill up with parcels filled with Lady Angelo's purchases. When my arms are full, she instructs me back to the sleigh. As I wind through the streets, a familiar-looking face bobs through the crowds, trailing behind a nobleman and his retinue. I only see a flash of the features, but the girl's expressive eyes and youthful curls are too familiar to ignore.

"Pia!" I call out before I can stop myself, suddenly too desperate to ask her why she has gone so quickly from the Manor before the preview could be held.

She hesitates, half turning, and scans the crowd. Her gaze jumps over me and then flicks back. Her face pales. Ignoring me, she hurries after her master.

She darts around a corner and when I reach it, she's gone. Huffing out a breath, I let her go. Perhaps I'll just get her in trouble with her new master if I chase her now.

Instead, with the excitement I had felt at seeing her quickly ebbing away, I finish my journey to the sleigh and deposit the parcels.

"Is she almost finished?" the driver asks as he adds the last parcel to the back.

I shrug. "Doubt it."

He seems to bite back a chuckle, and I spare him a grin before heading back to find Lady Angelo and her manservant. As I'm returning down the now-empty street where Pia disappeared, I pause. A strange chill runs down my neck. I glance behind me. There's no one there, but the odd feeling doesn't go away.

It doesn't go away all day. A feeling like I'm being watched or someone is right behind me lingers over my skin like an unclean touch. On the way back up the road to the Manor, I pay close attention to the city this time, searching not only for someone following me and for Pia or any other slave I might recognize, but examining the city itself.

The road to and from Monticola is wide and winding, giving me an excellent view of the city walls. Tall and dark gray, they encircle us, keeping us safe—whatever safe is these days. It's only safe from the predators without, not those within.

I peer at the stables as the sleigh twists up the path back toward my prison, and when we wind around, my eyes follow the wall a quarter mile beyond to a gate half covered in icicles.

Narrowing my gaze, I lean forward, frowning at the gate before a shift in Lady Angelo out of the corner of my vision draws my attention. I straighten and fold my hands in my lap, belatedly forcing myself to act unaffected.

She tilts her head but says nothing.

I keep my gaze down, but inside, I fume.

X

Flight

WINTERBERRY

Under the cover of darkness, when the Manor sleeps, I slip from my bed, careful not to wake Certa. As I grab the sack I've hidden beneath my bed, she grunts and turns over.

Freezing, crouching beside the bed, I count her breaths. One, two, three...all the way to ten. I inch up to my feet and carefully lift my cloak from the end of my bed. Exiting the room, I grip the stolen cloak and thick boots I never returned to the slaves' supply closet in one hand, my bag in the other.

Heart jumping in my chest, I tiptoe from the room barefoot. Outside in the slave quarters, I sink down and slip my feet into the thick socks and boots, then rise. My feet are uncomfortably heavy in their overlarge boots. Even the thick socks don't keep them from slipping around. My first steps are startling loud in the silence, and I flinch before quieting them.

When I reach the hallway that leads to the only exit from the slave quarters, I relax only a little. Inhaling slowly, I try to calm the trembling in my limbs. I can't grow weak now. Even though my plan is only half formed, if it works, it will get me out of here and back to

Merise, where I can... I don't know. Infiltrate the palace? Kill my step-mother? A shudder runs through me at the thought. I am not a killer.

I force my thoughts back to the task at hand and staying quiet. My intentions will be obvious if I am caught out of my room at this time of night with a sack of food and dressed in a heavy dress, furred cloak, mittens, and more layers than indoor slaves are given.

I inch open the exterior door to the slave quarters. The stab of cold air assails me in warning. I glance behind me. All is quiet. Post-poning will only cool off the slave quarters.

Taking a fortifying breath, I pull the hood of my cloak over me, tuck my bag further under my cloak, and squeeze out the door before I give myself a chance to think of whether there are wolves of the animal or human kind outside.

The door clicks closed behind me. Turning, I grip the handle, sudden panic making me think I've made a mistake. But the door is locked. No direction but forward now.

Ducking my head and glancing around, I dart onto the packed snow path toward the stables. Every footfall upon the snow crunches and raises an echo into the empty sky. It is a clear, cold night, the coldest I've felt in ages. Stars blink above me, joined by a crescent moon giving little light and half hidden by a wisp of clouds. The faint brush of the goddess's hand lights the distant northern sky with green streaks too pale to illuminate anything. I should have brought a torch—but perhaps my light will help me out if I can't see. I snort at the strange optimism. Whatever this light is, it's probably magic of some kind, and I don't—can't—trust it. Not that I've seen it again since my attempted escape—and I haven't heard that little voice again either. Tonight the voice feels even farther away.

I hurry along the path toward the stables, finding the way eerily empty.

My feet hesitate, but I force them onward. The door locked behind me; I can't return. To turn back would require going all the way around the Manor and entering the main doors. At this hour of night, I would either see no one or see exactly the ones I would not wish to see and be severely punished.

The walk to the stables feels longer than usual in the cold solitude. Finally, out of the shadows, I see the building. As I hurry toward it, a twig snaps to my right.

I stop, my mouth going dry. Guard or stray wolf? I hold my breath so it doesn't create a cloud in front of me, obscuring my vision. Turning my head toward the sound, I search the landscape of skinny trees and white snowdrifts. No movement.

The cloud shifts out from before the moon, revealing a sliver more of light, which shines down upon the clump of trees that separate the stables from the town walls. This has to be the stupidest plan…I'm leaving the safety of Monticola's walls. Inside these walls there might be one, lone wolf. Outside, there are packs that I have no chance surviving against.

I should have stolen a weapon. But slaves could get killed for that sort of thing, and I don't have time now. We're not allowed to have weapons, not unless we're being trained as soldiers. Even my small knife could have gotten me killed for a rebellious act, had I not lost it in the palace dungeons.

I push open the door to the stable to an empty aisle and animals heavy eyed with sleep. Light from the moon outside glints through windows in the ceiling, cleared of snow, which create tunnels of light that fall upon the center aisle and a few select stalls.

Distracted by the sight, I let the door fall shut behind me. A dull thump echoes through the stable.

I flinch; my heart thumps. The grooms all sleep at this end of the stable in order to prevent people like me from stealing the Magister's horses. I hide in the shadows for several minutes, but there is no sound of a door opening or anything that isn't the gentle rustle of slumbering horses. Slowly, I release my breath and ease my muscles.

Thank the gods for the shadows in this stable. And that the floor is soft. As long as the horse doesn't neigh, we can escape without waking anyone.

CHAPTER X

At the first stall, I pause and peer over the door. I am half tempted to visit the stallions' barn and steal the Magister's well-trained mount. Although sorely tempted, I doubt he would yield himself to me. Attempting to steal him would be a death sentence. Best save that sort of revenge for when I become queen. I allow myself a small smirk.

There are three stable buildings, one specifically for stallions, where the Magister's favorite animal resides, one for pregnant mares and nursing foals, and this one—the largest—for all riding horses and horses in training.

Continuing down the aisle in my search, my feet halt at the stall of a snow-white colt. His eyes are ice blue and have a wild touch to them. But I have seen him in the ring, and although he is still half trained, he is quick and eager to please. I have been making friends with him in my visits, and he snuffles sleepily when I wake him.

"Hi, boy. Care for a midnight ride?" I whisper to him as he swishes his long tail against his fetlocks.

Ears twitching forward, he comes curiously to the front of his stall. I hold out the apple I sneaked from Lady Angelo's tray, and he makes it disappear faster than my stepmother could magic it away.

"What do you think?" I whisper as I move his long forelock from his eyes. "Fancy freedom?"

He huffs air out his nostrils, nosing me and my hidden bag for another apple.

"No more, not yet," I whisper, reaching for the rope beside his stall. I have to find him a saddle. I could ride without one if I must, but—

The colt's ears twitch again, and he lifts his head to stare over my shoulder. I feel the gaze before I see the watcher.

Heart sinking to my toes, I make sure my pack is concealed before turning around.

From the shadows two stalls away, a very tall man lurks, his arms folded across his formidable girth. Caleb.

I grimace. Would that I had found a different stable hand tonight, for they might be more willing to allow me to escape.

Shoulders sinking, I expel my breath in his direction and wait for him to move. "Will you turn me in?" I ask when he doesn't approach.

Three heartbeats later, he steps out of the shadows with a saddle held in his arms before him. "This way," is all he says, then he walks toward me.

In every line of his face, I note a deep sorrow as he passes me. He finally looks his seventy years. Trailing my hand along the white colt's face, I say a mute goodbye then follow Caleb.

He walks half the length of the stable and stops outside a quiet stall I have never visited before. He is tall enough to peer inside without difficulty, but the door on this box is higher than the others, and I must stand on tiptoe to peek inside.

Something lunges at me, and before I can react, Caleb has moved me from harm's way. Hardly before I realize what has happened, Caleb has already released me, and I gape up at him. "What is that?" I demand.

His lips twitch, and he reaches an arm over the stall door, grasping something. His murmur is too quiet to understand, not meant for my ears, and a few moments later, he motions me forward with a flick of one finger. "Calmly," he murmurs, though I am not certain if he means that for me or the beast within.

This time, I don't peer over the stall door but through the bars on the side. I can't stop my gasp.

Inside is a horse made out of spun silver glinting in the moonlight filtering through the stable's roof window. His eyes are alert and intelligent, his muscles well formed and taut.

Caleb makes a soft sound in the colt's ear, and the animal bends it toward Caleb, seeming to relax slightly. My eyes, however, are round with unabated disbelief. *This* is the horse he expects me to ride out of here? I won't make it five feet before being thrown.

"What is this beast?" I whisper.

"A specimen of Ardor's Gelu Rigens."

My brow furrows. "I thought their uniqueness was legend."

"Truth," he answers simply.

The stories of such animals are legendary. It is said that the Ardorites post guards around their prized horses—guards who carry long-range weapons. When I was young, guard's children used to play that they were guarding Gelu Rigens, and one child had to be the thief and steal the stuffed animal—or for older kids a live goat or sheep—without getting caught. Sometimes I had watched them from the windows in my rooms.

"But it's illegal to have one outside the borders of Ardor, isn't it?" I ask.

"We don't abide by Ardorian rules, do we?"

I pause. "No."

Our voices carry in the stable, and we have woken other horses, whose heads poke over their doors in their curious natures. I have backed so far from the silver horse's stall that I stand before his neighbor's.

"He won't hurt you," Caleb says. "But he is fast, and he will be strong-willed."

I take a few steps toward them, gaze flickering between the pair. "I can't have him challenge me while I escape."

Caleb cups his hand over the horse's face, running it from the corners of his eyes to cover his nose briefly. He whispers something, and the horse, although he cannot breathe with his nostrils covered, flicks his ears and blinks slowly. "He will take care of you. Get you far from here. He will take you to my brothers."

Something about Caleb's actions feels like more than wishful thinking, and shifting the sack digging into my shoulder, I nod. "All right. I trust you."

"Trust *him*." He does not smile, and his solemnity is more concerning than anything else he could have done. Instead he dips his head into a nod and enters the stall with the saddle and the blanket that attaches to it. Within minutes, each which feels too long in my state of nervous excitement, the colt is saddled, a white blanket covering his haunches to help keep him warm, and Caleb is walking him out into the aisle.

"Princess, because I risk my life by helping you, I have one thing to ask of you."

"Of course. Anything." As soon as I say it, there is a twinge of regret in my ribs like a knife slipping in, but the words are out and I do not regret them.

"Get as far away from here as you can. Leave the country. Cross the frozen lake into Ardor. Hide there. Build an army. Come back and defeat the Queen. For the sake of my brothers. And, if it means anything to you, for my sake."

His final words weigh me down more than any of the others. His brothers I couldn't save. Some of them escaped, but others, like Caleb, were sold. He will probably never see them again. Not unless I return as queen. "I do think that's more than one thing, my friend."

A smile warms his eyes. "'Tis one. Merely a suggestion on how to accomplish the one."

In a flash, he has pressed his cold lips to my forehead and thrown me into the saddle. He throws open the back door to the stable, and I know he means for me to take the back gate out of the city.

"Ride fast, my liege. Ride far," he says.

And that's one command I intend to obey.

XI

Found

WINTERBERRY

I ride fast and hard. Faster and harder than I have ever ridden before.

I fear that I will kill my colt with what I ask of him, but I cannot hold back.

And so we ride.

Hoping to keep us safe, I keep most of our miles to the roads, except for me cutting over from the north gate we left through and down toward the main gate. It's the only exit I know that might lead to civilization instead of the wild. But I cannot go through Merise; it would take too long, and I am sure to be recaptured in the capital. Instead I continue pointing the colt toward what I think is south, although I cannot see much to determine it.

I'm guessing. The acknowledgment, even silent, only intensifies my worries, and I push the thought aside.

At first my colt stretches out his neck with relief, as though being confined to a stall has been a miserable life for him. Then after many miles, his pace begins to slow, his head begins to droop. And at the foggy sunrise, when light glints through the darkness of the sky, I let him pick his own pace.

Under my layers of furs, I shiver violently, but I don't dare dismount and walk, even to stay warm. Instead, I keep the colt near the road, listening for the crunch of travelers' sleighs and for the yips or howls of wolves. I don't even have a weapon to protect myself.

As I think it, something dark gray emerges from the fog before us. I bite back my gasp, straightening in the saddle and unconsciously leaning back. Uncertain, the colt stops with a quiet huff, his ears arched toward the shape.

A wolf. Oh, gods, it's a wolf.

From the fog, a wolf-like shape emerges, ears pricked toward us, beady eyes staring. My heart begins to hammer in my ribcage. I haven't even made it a day, and I'm going to die from a wolf attack. Gods, what was I thinking? I'm so unprepared.

I slowly tear my eyes from the wolf ahead and scan the silvery fog around us. It's too thick to see anything; the wolves have the advantage. Surely there's more than one. Probably surrounding us right now. And what can we do?

As I'm questioning myself, the colt lowers his head and begins to move forward. I pull at the reins without thinking, too terrified to let the horse move me.

He snorts and pulls back. When I don't loosen the reins, he turns his head to look back at me. *Trust me,* I think I read in his eyes.

Trust him, Caleb's words echo in my head.

With foreboding in my stomach, I loosen the reins.

He turns ahead and slowly steps forward, nose outstretched until I barely hold the reins.

I hold my breath as the wolf doesn't move. Is it dead? Wounded? Playing dead?

The colt continues his approach, not stopping until we stand right before it.

I squint through the fog, confused. Why isn't it moving?

Then the fog shifts, and I gasp. It *is* dead.

I swing down from the saddle, careful to keep a tight hold of the reins in case the horse spooks. I'd never find him in this fog, and I'd be dead for certain then. Slowly, looking carefully into the face before me, I tiptoe forward. But within another step, it's clear the wolf is dead. And for a long time. And the man wearing it, for who knows how long. He had kept the head to his wolf pelt, crafting the face into a hood that he'd drawn up as protection against the cold. But in his frozen hands, the man holds what could be my salvation: a sword.

Putting aside my distaste for touching a dead man—and stealing —I reach out and give the sword a tug. It doesn't move. Grunting, I try harder. The man tilts toward me. In horror, I let go, reeling backward. He settles back into place, and the colt gives a snort behind me.

"Don't you dare laugh at me," I mutter to the laughing horse. I hook the reins on my arm and use both hands to pry at the man's fingers. Thank the gods his eyes are closed; I couldn't do this with him looking at me too. He probably fell asleep and never woke up. Like Des. Like I might.

I shove the thought aside as I shove aside my cloak. It takes me another minute to pry his fingers free from the hilt. I fall backward at the sudden release.

The colt snorts in an amused way as my rump hits the ground.

Letting out a breath, I pause to shoot the horse a glare before dragging myself to my feet. "Watch it, or I'll leave you out here to survive the wolves on your own."

The colt blows his answer out his nose, as if to say he would be more adept without me.

"I have no doubt of that." I fiddle with the strap of the sword's sheath and manage to attach it to the horn of the saddle. Then, glancing around, I drag myself up into the saddle itself. "Good thing you're not a tall horse," I tell him.

In answer, he starts moving before I give him any command.

I grin, but my grin slides off my face as we pass the frozen man under his wolf cape. The wolf's false eyes stare at us as we pass in some sort of warning: get off the road? Or don't linger? Regardless of what the warning is, it all amounts to the same: it is not safe here.

Unnerved, I nudge the colt into a trot.

Not an hour later, a snowstorm rolls in. At first, I try to keep us moving, but after a time, it's impossible. The snow is so thick I wouldn't see if we were going to run into a tree—or a sleigh. I concede defeat, and the colt and I huddle together and watch the snow gather around our legs. At least fresh snow will make it harder to track me. And harder to travel.

Finally, when the snow abates, it has fallen halfway to my knees. Without wasting time, I remount and look around us. Light is breaking above, a little bit of sun through the clouds, but far down on the horizon. It's almost evening. We wasted hours sitting there while it snowed. And now... I look around. Which direction is south?

Every direction is white and unremarkable. No trees or mountains, not with the clouds hanging around. If I had the time, I would camp overnight and wait for them to dissipate, hope for a clear morning.

"Well," I say aloud to the twitching ears of my mount. "I don't suppose you know the way to your homeland, do you?"

The horse's ears twitch back at me, and then he aims his head to our left.

I tilt my head in consideration. *Trust him*, says Caleb's voice in my ear again. "Okay, then. I'll trust you again. Ice. Are you all right if I call you 'Ice'? You need a name."

He snorts and throws his head without giving me any clear answer. When I nudge him forward, he shakes himself free of the shin-deep snow with eager steps.

We travel the entire night, under the stars, the waning moon, and the moving paints of the goddess. Her presence reassures me, reminds me of a time when I believed she was there to protect me, that she loved this country. Back when the country loved her, perhaps. Has she cursed us?

I jolt in the saddle, nearly banging my nose on Ice's neck when he stops short and refuses to move.

With heavy, ice-laden lashes, I blink at our surroundings.

We are traveling along a line of scrawny, far-spaced trees, but I don't know if I travel south or east or west or even north. If I travel north, it is to certain death. Traveling anywhere but south will not give me escape. A wind stirs up the snow around us. I glance back. Not a dozen feet away, our tracks are already washing away. Beyond that, it is all white; I see no one in pursuit. Perhaps they have left us to die. I face forward, where the endless white continues. Perhaps that is the worse of the fates, to die here.

When Ice refuses to move on, we sleep. He burrows into the snow so that he nearly disappears. I tuck myself in next to him, resting my head against his shoulder and pulling my cloak and his blanket over us both. Our breathings even out and match each other for a few breaths, then his slows further. Then I am aware of nothing until I wake to the sun beating down upon us.

Stiff, I wince and push myself off the colt. His head is up, and he blinks down at me, as if he waited for me to wake before moving. My heart swells at his thoughtfulness and at Caleb picking him out for me. I climb out of the snow that surrounds us. During the morning, as we slept, the wind blew a drift around us, covering our legs and part of the colt's back. Now I push my way out, and he follows. I stumble to my knees, barely catching myself with my hands before I receive a face full of snow. The colt lunges to his feet behind me, and in a moment, his nose is gentle against my back, checking on me.

I laugh a little, because there is nothing else to do. I can't scan the horizon looking for anyone following us, as the low white clouds turn the horizon into a hidden place. But I search the snow around us for the saddle I took off the colt when we stopped and dig it out from under a foot of snow. He shakes his body all over, like a dog ridding himself of water, and lets out a low snort as I toss the saddle back on him.

"I know, I know. You had a good life," I tell him. "I know you probably want to go back to your safe, warm stable, where there are oats and hay for you. There are other horses to chat with, and you don't have to worry about anything but what you face in the next training session." I sigh. "I'm sorry. But I need you more than they do."

I feed him a few of the oats that Caleb packed in the saddlebags. "Not too much. They have to last until Ardor, you know," I tell him as he lips them from my hands eagerly.

Ardor. By then, the snow might be melting, we might come out of this curse, and maybe, just maybe, we can make it across the border into a new land, with a fresh start, free from the pursuing monsters.

Within an hour, the wind is so strong that it pushes against us, and we can do nothing but walk. Our frantic, desperate, furious escape has turned into a crawl. I pray that we at least go in the right direction. I don't think I could bear it if we were wrong. North brings death to me—and to all of Canens.

Later that day, the ground under us begins to tilt. And by nightfall, it becomes clear that we have gone north after all. The skies have cleared, and although dusk settles in its familiar cloak around us, the moon illuminates the mountain range under us and the smooth forest and fields behind us.

Despair rises in me, clawing at my chest. How could I be so stupid?

Ice plods along with his head down, determined, even as I pull at his reins. He snorts and yanks his head from my control, bit between his teeth.

Giving up, I allow him to lead me. Perhaps farther astray, perhaps toward something only he knows. But what I do know is that he is determined and he is willing. And I am too shattered to think or react.

He walks until the sun is long gone and the sliver of a moon rises in its place. He winds around the mountain, and the air grows thin around us. I begin to think of the first tale I told Des and about the dragons that live in the mountain caves. It is a good thing I don't believe in dragons. But perhaps there is a cave somewhere nearby...

Almost as soon as I think it, Ice turns into the mountain. A rush of air comes up from underneath us, and the snow thins. Ice's hooves hit rock with a clang instead of thumping against unpacked snow. He halts. I reach out a hand.

I slide from his back, trailing a hand along his neck. "Good boy. You found us a place to sleep, didn't you?"

With a tired snort, he cranes his neck around and looks at the saddle as if to ask me to remove it.

Immediately, I do so, and I pull some grain out of the bag for him as well. By the time I am ready to give it to him, he has lowered himself to the ground and gotten comfortable. I hold the oats under his nose, and he digs in. Then as he drifts to sleep, I pull out the bread and some dried meats for myself.

It is nearly silent in the cave, except for the sounds of Ice and me and a faint whistle as the wind whips by the cave's entrance. I curl against Ice's back again, my cloak pulled over us as before, but this time, I am too worried to sleep, perhaps too exhausted.

Instead, I lay out our supplies before me. One small loaf of bread, a few strips of meat, some frozen fruits, and enough oats to get Ice through another two or three days at most. Dispirited, I slowly repack the supplies.

My original plan won't work. We won't make it to Ardor with only this. I wasted an entire day's travel going the wrong way. But Merise is even farther—I have no choice but to keep the mountains straight at our backs and keep going.

I wipe a hand over my face. I can't give up. My life is not mine to give up. I must survive. For the sake of all of Canens. Des, Certa. Layela, Pia. Caleb. Every slave I've met that needs freedom.

Sitting up, I hug the bag to my chest, determined. The wind whistles outside, but I ignore it and begin planning my next move.

Although riding during the day exposes us more, I need the light to make sure I keep the mountain behind me. Today was wasted travel because I could not see the mountains. I have to change our plans.

I yawn and lean back against Ice, pulling my cloak up to my chin. Waiting for the daylight, I fall asleep.

Sometime later, I am woken by Ice's snort and his shaking body. Moving away from him so he can stand, I rub at my eyes, aware of light shining into the cave, bright and almost obnoxious, except for a long shadow that cuts the sunbeam in half. As Ice rocks to his feet, I stare directly into cold gray eyes.

My instincts scream at me: *run, surrender, fight!* But I do none of it. Ice stands a few paces away from me, unsaddled and unconcerned. Were I to run with him now, even if we could get out of the cave, I wouldn't have time to take our supplies or even saddle him. Within a day, we'd be dead. If we escaped that long—again.

"Well, I wasn't expecting to find you so easily, I admit that." His wolf-like lips twitch into something more like a grimace than a smile. "I suppose I overestimated you."

At the surge of anger in my blood, I snap my teeth together. The Queen always told me that. And I hated it. "Overestimated?" I demand in a voice as cold as my numb jaw.

Silent, he stands in the cave's entrance, a considering squint narrowing his eyes. "I've wasted two days tracking you down."

I glare. "So I guess you underestimated me, then."

"I wouldn't say that..." He trails off.

I dart a glance at the saddle and supplies six feet from me. What was I thinking last night? How was I so complacent? If I can just distract him and draw the sword...maybe there's still a chance.

"I certainly wasn't expecting you to be such a fool and head north," he says. "And then trap yourself in a cave." His chuckle is low and long, echoing in the enclosure. "Thank you for making my search easier." With another smirk, he motions to someone outside the cave.

His attention diverted, I lunge for the sword. Ice skitters backward at my motion, and I scramble for the hilt with numb fingers. My fingers finally close around the hilt only to find the blade stuck.

A pair of feet appear in my vision.

The fight goes out of me.

Without a word, the Magister stoops and picks up the sword. He weighs it in his hand, his lips turned down into his beard. "This is a nice weapon."

I close my eyes, defeat tasting bitter.

XII

The Fae

BLANCHE

I throw the glass of wine into the fire and clench my hand as it erupts. When the Fae do not wish to be found, they will not be. It has been weeks since I cast the Fae summoning spell, and there is nothing to show for it. Nothing.

I curse at the fire in my potion chamber, searching my mind for spells and potions I have forgotten or ones I might stretch to my purposes. I grip my hair with both fists and give a sharp tug, frustrated even more when my hands just tangle in the silky strands. I tug my hands out and grip the fireplace mantle instead, staring at the flickering fingers of the fire.

If I cannot break the Canens Curse, Canens will be forever doomed. I won't trade with Ostium. And especially not Heia or Ardor. I refuse to buy food for my people from another country.

But...if I don't, and if the growing houses don't thrive, then I must raise the army and march on the other countries. But in their weakened state, without enough food for all, how are we expected to win? I cannot carry an entire army on magic. We must first win another country, take control of their food stores. But one country won't be enough to feed all of Canens... Just the army... And them just until they win another country and then another after that. If I control them all, then I can feed all of the Seven Kingdoms with ease. There is food for us all...

My hope crashes at my next thought. How can I even win one country with a starving army?

Anger growing, I let out a growl. In response, the bottle of wine and everything else on the table beside me flies off the surface to crash into the stone wall across the room. Irritated at my lack of control, I give a muffled scream, and more of my possessions leap from the next table as if I have picked them up and hurled them at the ground.

I clench my teeth and shut my eyes, attempting to calm myself. It's not like these things will help me if I can't even summon a Fae or I cannot break this damned curse of Canens.

A tsking sound comes from behind me.

I whirl, magic ready to fell whoever has seen me in distress. But the spot beside the door is empty. I continue turning, searching the room, until I find the one who made the sound: a woman beside the window who holds up a finger in a mocking gesture.

"I wouldn't, if I were you."

A flare of anger begins its climb to my cheeks. "Who are you? How did you get in here?"

The woman, a plump woman of indiscriminate age, looks decidedly foreign. Her hair is wavy and dark, unlike most of the Canens people, her skin several shades darker than any Canens resident. Her eyes are slightly slanted and lips straight and thick.

"Well?" I growl. "Who are you?"

The woman gives a little scoff. "I am whom you have summoned."

The anger stumbles in its rise to my cheeks; I step back in shock. "The Fae?" My mouth drops open before I can catch it. "Well, it took you long enough."

The faery tilts her head to one side. "I had to see if you were worthy or not."

"I *am* worthy." I take a step in the Fae's direction as my cheeks heat.

"I see." The faery doesn't appear impressed or dismayed by the claim. Instead, she simply watches me, as though she can gain the measure of me by this simple act.

"What made you come now?" I demand.

"Your persistence," she finally says.

"I am persistent." A faint smile taints my lips, and I force my body to calm.

"Yes." There is no emotion in the Fae's voice when she speaks. "What do you think I can do for you?"

"I am in need of answers, faery—what do I call you?"

"Faery is fine. For now."

My suspicion of the Fae growing, I nod. Keep her happy. Tell her what she wants to hear. She's no different from any lord or duke in court. "As you wish. Then what I need—desire—from you are answers. Answers to questions of magic and curses."

"Ah. Magic and curses. I thought you'd had enough of those two things in your life." The faery raises one dark brow.

I turn away, my gaze skipping over the mess of books, bottles, broken glass, and parchments scattered around my potion chamber in front of the cheery fire. "I'm looking for ways to counteract those curses," I say finally, turning back to face the faery.

The faery's eyes widen, and a slow smile dawns on her lips. "Counteract the Canens Curse?" Her smile transforms her face from beautiful and poised to one full of mischievousness and intrigue. "I can't say anyone hasn't asked me that before, but...it is exactly what I want to hear." She tilts her head. "And to have someone with so much power in her...someone whom I can actually help."

I straighten. "Then let us discuss."

The Fae nods. "First, do you mind if I clean up this mess? I cannot stand a cluttered room."

"By all means."

The faery pulls a thin stick out of her skirts and swipes it at the mess before the fire. In a blink, the mess has disappeared, broken glass becomes whole, and contents return to their containers. The items fly back to their spots and even the rest of the tables appear tidier.

I give an appreciative quirk of my brow.

The faery moves to a nearby table, where she peers down into my small cauldron and scans the potion recipe next to it.

"This looks promising," she remarks without a glance over.

I shake my head. "It's satisfactory."

"No?" The faery peers into the cauldron again. "I think adding a pinch of mint would counteract the negative effects quite nicely."

I pause. "Mint? That would have a nice effect upon the stomach, wouldn't it?" I go to my shelves and draw down the jar of fresh mint, picked from my own mint plants in the growing house.

"Just a pinch, dear," the faery says, reaching in and taking two small leaves out. She crushes them in her fingers over the cauldron and tears them into tiny pieces before adding them to the simmering liquid. The murky brown liquid bubbles at the addition and hisses, but then turns a pale green and gives a little sigh.

I watch it in fascination. This beauty potion I have been concocting and drinking for years has always made me sick for the entire next day, but with mint added, perhaps it will save me a most uncomfortable day every week.

"That ought to do it. A beauty potion, no?"

"Yes. How did you—?"

The faery smiles knowingly. "A faery knows her magic, m'dear." She stretches out her hand and gives a little shake of her finger. A jar materializes out of thin air, and the potion lifts from the cauldron and siphons itself into the jar, where a stopper plugs it safely inside.

"I need to learn that," I say without thinking. I give myself a little shake at the faery's modest laugh. It sounds like snow falling, soft and pleasant.

"Yes, it is a useful trick." The faery tilts her head and passes her the bottle. "You could do it, you know. If you harnessed your magic right."

"What do you mean? Harnessed my magic right?"

The faery frowns, curiosity in her eyes. "Dear, do you not realize what you have in you? Who taught you to use your magic?"

I shake my head. "I taught myself, mostly."

"Where did you attain your magic?"

I hesitate. "That is not what we are here to discuss."

"No, but it is important that you recognize it."

"Recognize what?"

"The sources of your magic." The faery raises a brow.

"What does that matter, faery?"

"Ceara."

The faery places the vial down on the table beside the cauldron and waves her wand over the cauldron, which cleans itself miraculously. I feel a pang of envy.

"It matters, dear," the faery says with clearly forced patience, "because the source of your magic determines what kind—and how strong—your magic is."

"My magic is plenty strong to reverse a spell—"

"You'll need more than the power to reverse a spell, dear. You're going to need a blood sacrifice and a strong counter spell in order to break the Canens Curse."

My heart leaps. I try to hide the eagerness from my face and hide my hands in the folds of my skirts. "You know how then? To reverse the Canens Curse?"

The faery shrugs. "The only way to reverse it is to convince the ancient dragon who cast it to forgive the curse and retract it."

I can't hide my shoulders slumping, but I rally myself, desperate for any information that might lead to breaking the curse. "Then it is a dragon that has cursed us? I've never seen proof of that, merely conjecture and rumors—"

"There's plenty of truth in conjecture and rumors," the faery

Ceara says wisely. She smooths down the folds of her blue skirts with both hands.

"Yes, of course there is," I say impatiently, "but in this case, I was hoping for something a little different. Maybe a spell that could be cast or a potion to..." I trail off, not knowing what a potion could do.

The faery raises a brow as if she has the same thought.

"...a potion that the spell caster might drink to increase her strength perhaps," I finish.

"Yes, well, we all hope for something easy, don't we? When situations become difficult, it's understandable to want an easy solution."

My nostrils flare. "What do you know about my situation? What does anyone truly know about what difficulties I have faced?"

"I know far more than you think, Blanche." The faery sniffs, lifting her narrow nose into the air. "I know what you've lost and what you're trying to gain. It goes far deeper than this country, Blanche. Far deeper than even you realize."

I grit my teeth. This faery doesn't want to help me, but only herself. Of course; what could she possibly want from me? "You seem to want even more than I."

"I only want what is mine." Ceara's liquid tone hardens. "I only want what has been taken from me by my sisters."

"And what does that have to do with me?"

"As little as your concern for the Canens Curse has to do with me," the faery retorts.

I narrow my eyes. "What are you proposing then?"

"A little bit of help for us both."

"And if I help you—do whatever it is you want—then you will help me break the Canens Curse and find..." I hesitate, fearing to voice my true desires.

"Find whatever you desire," the faery says knowingly.

"All right, what do you want then? What will I have to do?"

"Only what I ask." The faery shrugs. "It is nothing unusual, nothing you might not have done before."

I consider. "And how do we break the Canens Curse?"

"The same way we will break the *regina maledictum*."

The what? I almost frown, almost lets on that I don't understand. It doesn't matter. Whatever is necessary to break the Canens Curse must be done. I lift my chin. "It is the only way?"

Ceara tilts her head, her dark curls falling over one shoulder. "Yes."

"Then I accept."

"Excellent." The faery is suddenly beside me, my own knife glinting in her hand. She grasps my hand, and before I can object or raise a protective shield around myself, the faery has drawn the knife across the palm of my hand.

I gasp at my dripping hand and watch as the faery does the same to her palm and then, with a deft move, presses our palms together and murmurs a word I don't catch. As she does, a blue glow gleams where our palms meet.

"Now it is sealed," the faery says, her blue eyes glinting harshly in the light. "Now we must follow through."

A tingle shakes through my body, then the light fractures in our palms and snakes out from between our flesh to wrap around our joined hands. It tightens upon us, cementing our hands so that I cannot remove mine. It burns hot until I can bear it no longer, then as suddenly as it appeared, it fades, snaking its way back the way it came. When I steal my hand away, there upon the line of blood is a glimmer of bluish light, and another upon the faery's. As I watch, the light continues to fade until it disappears into my hand, drawing the cut closed behind it until only a thin, white scar remains.

"What did you do?" I demand. "What—"

"A blood-binding spell. Don't worry about it. It merely keeps us honest. But it does bring me to our first ingredient." The faery waves a hand in the air, but her palm is already healed of the wound she inflicted.

I check my own and find even the scar gone. I turn both hands over in wonder as the faery clears her throat and continues.

"We need the blood of the seven eldest princesses from the Seven

Kingdoms. And you shall help me get it." Her lips curve into a wicked smile. "And in return, we will make you Empress of the Seven Kingdoms."

A slow smile mirrors its way onto my lips. I lift my gaze to Ceara, who stands in front of one of my mirrors. In the mirror behind her, I catch sight of my own face, the shock in my blue eyes, the mussed hair where I gripped it with both fists in my earlier frustration, the day-old dress that I forgot to change, just as I forgot to eat dinner tonight. But locking eyes with my own reflection, I see a vision of myself.

A fog stirs in the mirror as I stare, and out of the mist a different image appears, one of a tall, regal queen—no, based on the sash she wears and the tall crown laden with gemstones and precious metals from all of the Seven Kingdoms, an empress.

"Empress." I don't know if I whisper it or the faery or the mirror or my future image does.

Empress. Yes. That will work nicely. It will answer all of my questions, solve all of my problems. Yes. Empress Blanche of the Seven Kingdoms has a wonderful ring to it.

XIII

Punished

WINTERBERRY

Whatever dungeon I was expecting to be thrown into when I returned, it wasn't this.

One guard takes Ice and walks him toward the stables. Another guard grabs me by the arm and holds tight, ignoring the small crowd of slaves that watch with expressions ranging from shame to fear to disgust.

It's as if I've embarrassed them by trying to escape. Has no one else attempted? Are they too afraid? I shake my head. I should have been more afraid. I've just been foolish. I glance at the guard we're waiting on, who speaks with the Magister a few feet away, their voices low.

Finally, the Magister nods. "Take her down. Secure her and leave two guards on her."

I'm going to prison. Again. My heart thumps dully in my chest. All that effort and I have nothing to show for it. It even looks like the other slaves don't agree with what I did. What is wrong with this place? This country?

"Get in," a guard behind me snaps and pushes me through a side door to the Manor.

I stumble on my cape and fall to my knees, barely getting still-numb hands out to catch myself from falling on my face. My cap tumbles off my head, leaving it bare and cold. I reach for it, clenching it in reluctant fingers, and when I look up, the guard in front stares at me with pity on his face.

He crouches down before me. I stand my ground, even though every part of me is screaming to shrink away before he can hit me or worse.

But he doesn't touch me. He doesn't need to. He leans close, his well-trimmed beard nearly brushing my nose, and says, "Today you will learn why no man, woman, or child dares escape from the Magister. Tomorrow, you will wish you had never attempted. And by the day after, you will never again dare to *think* the word 'escape.'"

His words send a chill over my body.

"Now get up. And take the punishment you deserve. Perhaps in ten years, you will outlive this shame." His matter-of-fact gaze moves from my head to my toes and back up. "But perhaps you will be one of the few that doesn't learn."

Turning his back on me, he steps to the right and unlocks a door.

A fist behind me clenches my cape, dragging me up into the air and throwing me down on my feet with a jarring thump that chatters my teeth.

We descend a short set of steps behind the locked door. A dank smell suggests we're underground, and the lack of even small windows does little to keep the chill out. I shiver and follow two guards, flanked by two more.

Hopelessness and fear washes over me. Even if I made a run for it now, how far would I get? Will I really become like the others? Not daring to think of escape? Grateful for the small security I have and escaping greater punishment every day? Scrubbing floors until I die? I bite my lip. I will never be satisfied with slavery. For myself or others. Never.

The thoughts straighten my spine and lift my chin. Then a little voice whispers in my ear as if a faery has perched on my shoulder. *Do not appear proud.*

I jolt as the voice continues.

The guards will want you to be cowed. The longer you hang on to pride, the harsher your punishment. Appear cowed, appear humbled, and the punishment will be lighter.

Holding my breath from the first whisper of this entity's words, I force myself to listen to the words in them and lower my chin, hooding my eyes in the hopes of keeping the determination I feel from my face. The voice has been gone for so long, and yet now it's returned. I don't know how to feel about that, so I try not to think at all. And definitely not about escape. Or, like before, failed escape.

We walk what feels like a mile down the hall before the guard opens a small door and steps aside. When I pause, the guard behind me shoves me again, and I stumble over the threshold.

For a moment, I think the guards will close me inside, lock me in a cell. Then the one with the torch enters, illuminating the darkness.

As the guard lights the lamps with his torch, I stand in the center of a room that is far from an empty prison cell. An oil lamp sits on a desk near me, a table stretches up to the ceiling against one wall with strange pulleys attached, and closed cabinets line the wall. I shudder, and something bumps my shoulder. Flinching away, I look at it to find a length of rope hanging from the ceiling behind me.

The blood drains from my head, pooling in my toes and heels and leaving me dizzy.

The guards don't speak. The one in charge motions for two of the four to leave, and they salute him. Then without a word, he builds a fire in the cold fireplace, and the one who kept shoving me from behind positions himself beside the only exit to the room.

The guard finishes with the fire, leaving a set of strange-looking tongs in the flames, and takes his post on the other side of the door without a word to me or the other guard.

Left in silence, I am free to investigate my surroundings. Instead,

I move toward the fire, warming myself. I can't drag my eyes from those tongs; fear stirs in my gut.

It's some time later, when the tongs burn red-hot, that the door finally opens.

Relief and fear mingle in me at the sight of the Magister. He has not changed clothes but still wears his white, fur-lined tunic and trousers that I first saw him in when waking in the cave. In his hand, he carries a large, cream-colored cup that looks as though it's made out of some type of antler.

He brought a drink to my torture session? Great. Let's just get this over with. Whatever you're going to do to me, do it. Belatedly, I remember to cast my eyes downward as I silently challenge him.

He steps inside and, with a nod of his chin, dismisses the two guards. Both salute him and exit, closing the door with a snap.

Positioning myself near the fire, I gaze at him with what I hope is a picture of repentance. At least I don't have to feign my fear.

He walks farther into the room and pauses at the table. Setting down his drink, he pulls out the chair and sinks down into it, sighing in apparent exhaustion.

Perhaps he is. I hope he is. The only problem is that he can rest, torturing me for however long he wants. I am at his mercy. A person should never be in my position. Never. Even those guilty of treason should be executed quickly and humanely. Isn't that what my father did?

I frown. I don't actually know. All I know is that one traitor who died before me, alone, in the dungeon, as an example. An example of what, I'm not sure anymore. But I know who it was for.

"You think you're here for torture," he begins. "But that's not how I work. I don't gain loyalty by torturing my slaves, even when they misbehave." He sits back in the chair, his gray eyes surprisingly gentle and looking almost regretful. "But when a slave of mine disobeys, like a father, I cannot sit by and allow her to go unpunished."

I lift my chin, steeling myself for what will come.

He tilts his head at me, considering. "You think you're special, don't you? You think you are exempt from the laws that govern this country?"

Hesitating, I say in a carefully controlled voice, "No, sir."

"Don't lie to me."

I bite my lip.

"What is your name again?"

"Helena." Revealing my mother's name to him feels like a betrayal, like I have given more than myself up to him. For a second, my gaze drops to the floor, before I can demand obedience of my body.

A smile parts his lips. "Helena. Of course. How could I forget? After the late queen?" He phrases it like a statement, but it's somehow a question. One I refuse to answer.

He sighs. "I can see that you won't bend easily. But don't worry. By the time you are sold, you will be utterly devoted to me."

I can't help but snort my disbelief.

He smiles. "Yes, I've had many slaves give me the same reaction. Until they realize how kind I truly am. I wish to help you, Helena."

"Then let me go. Release me."

He motions to my neck. "You are a branded slave. How far do you think you would get?"

I grit my teeth.

"I know you don't believe me—about anything—but I speak truth." He stands and walks to a cabinet darkened by a shadow against the wall.

He is too calm to be delivering a punishment. In this moment, he reminds me of my father. My shoulders loosen a notch then tighten as he drags out a clanking metal object.

"Do you know what these are?" He turns around and places them on the table between us.

I shrug one shoulder. "Shoes."

"Metal shoes," he agrees.

A small shiver works its way down my spine. They are smooth, silvery metal slippers, except for one part in the heels, where something sharp sticks out, and a shackle like a strap that encircles the ankle.

He catches my glance, and his eyes darken. "I am sorry to have to do this to you. But I will not be considered weak—by you or others. You must receive your punishment."

I clench my hands into fists to halt their trembling.

"Take off your shoes."

"What?" I ask.

He repeats his instructions.

Wear a pair of shoes? That can't be my punishment.

But as soon as my foot goes in, a gasp escapes me. The barb cuts into my heel. I stare at my foot and then at the other shoe. There is a half-inch spike in the heel.

He leans close to me, his mead-sweet breath buffeting my cheek. "My slaves always remember their punishments. You are no different from the lowest slave I own."

He motions down to my feet, and I swallow.

I don't want to put the other shoe on.

To put on the other shoe, I have to balance in the metal shoe. As soon as I do, the spike pierces my skin, diving into the flesh of my heel. I wish I hadn't thawed myself out at the fire as much as I did before the Magister arrived.

"A little big, but they'll have to do," he says mockingly.

My glare is cut short by a stab of pain traveling from my heel up my leg. Shifting my weight, I gasp as the shoe on the other foot stabs me.

Wincing, I attempt to keep my body's weight on the ball of my foot in the inflexible metal shoes. But the barbs bite into my heels, no matter how I stand. Tears prick my eyes.

The Magister picks up his cup and drains his drink, ignoring me.

Then he turns to the cabinet where he found the shoes and points.

"Do you see that contraption?"

Turning, I see a strange-looking thing made of metal and spikes. I nod, silent.

"I will give you one instruction, and if I find out it has been disobeyed, you will be wearing that."

I glance at the item again, but I can't tell what it'll do—or even where it would go on my body.

"Keep your mouth shut." His gaze is hard, his stance relaxed. He will follow through on his threat.

"Sir?" I ask.

"Speak no word of what transpired in here or why you wear those shoes. Or even what you did to deserve them."

I swallow.

"Some will put it together, undoubtedly. But others will not understand." He strokes his beard with his free hand. "Do nothing to illuminate them. Understand?"

I am to utter no word, no explanation, nothing, for the metal shoes I wear. I am, for all his intents and purposes, mute. Until he decides further. That should be no problem, as I don't speak to anyone except Certa anyway.

At his expectantly waiting expression, I say, "Yes."

He turns to leave.

"How long?" The question bursts out of me.

Halfway to the door, he turns and considers me. "Until you prove yourself compliant."

My stomach squirms and drops.

XIV

Shown

WINTERBERRY

O nly hours before the next night of previews, after nearly three days, stuck in the spiked shoes with no relief except the little given by Certa's salves, the Magister summons me to his chambers.

A silent, petite girl in white leads me from the foyer up the servants' staircase to a part of the Manor I have never visited.

I drag myself up the stairs with the help of the railing. At the top, the slave girl waits for me but still doesn't speak.

What a pair we are.

She leads me out a door into a hallway that doesn't look familiar. After a few turns, every step of which is excruciating, she stops outside a nondescript door and, checking that I follow, knocks.

"Enter," calls a voice, and the girl pushes open the door.

I trail inside behind her.

"Excellent. Thank you, Maria," says the Magister from his seat at a writing desk.

She bobs a curtsy and leaves the room, closing the door with a gentle click.

Waiting for his attention, I stand in silence, constantly shifting my weight forward off my heels as much as possible, and watch as the Magister finishes his task. After several long minutes, he sets down his quill and stretches luxuriously.

I grit my teeth. My calves ache, my back aches, my heels ache. Every part of me aches from this punishment, even my tongue.

Still ignoring my presence, he sips from his wineglass, folds his letter, and finally stands. He takes me in, his gaze going from my toes to the top of my head and back down. "Looks like the shoes have done their job."

Don't let him see the anger in your eyes. Don't let him see that all the shoes have done is fuel your desire to escape. I jump at the whisper in my ear, but I drop my gaze to the floor.

The voice. Anger stirs in my gut. Even it has been silent these past three days. It didn't help me before; it isn't helping now. What use is it?

"Yes, I think the shoes have worked well." The Magister pulls a chair over and motions me toward it. Hating myself, I sink into it with a grimace and sigh. Without speaking further, the Magister removes the shoes from my feet.

When the first one comes off, a cry escapes my lips. Blood has dried around the heels, and the spike drags reluctantly out of my flesh even though the Magister's hands are surprisingly gentle.

"I do apologize," he murmurs, grasping my naked ankle firmly and peering at it before lowering it to the ground. He repeats the process with the second foot, and a groan emerges from me this time.

"Yes, it is painful, isn't it?" He inspects my second foot a bit longer than he did the first. He squeezes the outer edges of my heel until I gasp. "I do apologize," he repeats as he takes a small bottle from the table next to us and unscrews the lid. He dabs a bit on his fingertip and presses it to my heels. The salve cools the pain almost instantly, and by the time he's wrapped a clean bandage around the heel and repeated the process with the second foot, I'm gaping at the relief.

If I didn't hate him so much, I would almost forgive him.

Finished, he sets my foot on the ground as gently as he did the first. "You may go."

Wanting nothing more than to escape him and his touch, I nearly bolt to my feet, grateful to at least be able to completely walk on my toes now.

"You may speak now," he tells me. "But do not mention your punishment or your escape."

Lip between my teeth, I nod.

"Go on then."

I don't wait to be told again.

Only hours later, I am dressed up in my white, silk robes. Throughout the night, I stand on a low stage in the dining room next to a pretty young girl I've seen in the kitchens. Her long blond hair has been curled, while mine is released from its typical rag and stands up on edge despite Certa's attempt to tame it. The girl's cheeks are beautifully flushed with rouge, and her skin glows with good health. By contrast, mine are white with frostbite. Judging by the looks coming this way, one of us is drawing attention, and I have a feeling that it is her. With my frostbitten hands, my lame feet, my boyish haircut, my too-skinny frame, I am not a picture of a strong, healthy servant.

The Magister laughs at something one of his guests says, and I turn to him. For several minutes, he does not acknowledge me. Then his gaze slides to mine, and a look of shock passes over his face so quickly that I think I imagine it. He smiles at his guest and talks another minute before I watch him step over to another slave. I vaguely recognize him by his purple robes with gold embroidered on the sleeves. Certa pointe him out to me in my early days and told me to stay away from him. He is the main slave overseer, who manages the male slaves.

The overseer glances my way once and bows his head to the Magister a moment later. I frown, but the Magister turns away and so does the slave.

Dinner begins, and I quickly grow bored. None of the slaves in line are given tasks, but we all stand with military precision along the wall.

As dinner winds to a close, the serving staff clears the dishes and brings out the port and dessert liqueurs, along with an array of cheese and fruits to accompany them.

It's only now that the guests begin to turn their attention to the slaves. Two dozen guests, each looking for something "special," something worth coming all the way out to the Manor for.

"Time to go," a voice murmurs in my ear, and a finger pokes me in the side.

Jumping, I straighten and follow the other slaves in the first row. The half a dozen slaves, including me, walk around the dining room to the other side then stop to stand before the table. We each step forward when we are instructed by a woman slave, a step below the overseer, dressed in robes of white with purple embroidery on the sleeves.

Introducing each slave, she tells the table what we are trained for and our potential but never mentions our names. Some she talks about with barely concealed dislike, and it's clear that to stay on her good side, if you wish to escape here—without being tracked down and dragged back—is the only way out.

When it's my turn, I take a step forward as every other slave has and almost gasp in pain. The woman scowls and commands me back into line. What? She's not going to talk about me at all? Anxiety turns to despair as she motions Layela forward. I'm never going to leave this place alive.

"Moldable," the woman is saying about Layela when I get over my shock of being dismissed. "Still young enough to be trained if her training here isn't exactly what you're looking for. She won't stay here long, she's so pleasing to watch."

Some staring faces change expressions at her additional words, heads tilting to the side in new consideration, lips pursing out under creased foreheads.

I want to scoff, to laugh at the absurdity of it. But it's not absurd;

it's frightening. They're buying people. My country is in the business of selling people. People who, like me, might have done nothing wrong. Nothing to deserve this. And who knows who we have enslaved? I'm a princess—the heir princess of Canens—and they are trying to sell me...

But I'm a princess. And this system is built to obscure our identities. So that anyone might be sold. I'm a princess, and no one knows.

For the first time since my return to the Manor, I feel a little flash of hope. What would the Magister do if he knew the truth about me? Would he try to sell me back to my stepmother, convinced that I was sold by mistake? Would he release me if I promised to make him wealthy—wealthier—when I became queen? I have this leverage, and I never realized it before.

Slowly, I turn and find him staring at me. His jaw is set, although his lips smile as Lady Angelo leans over from beside him to speak. Her attentions draw his away from me, and my presence is absorbed like snow melting on wool.

There is nothing he wants from me that he doesn't already have access to by owning me now. And I become certain that he knows I am no mere peasant, even though he paid an orphan's price for me on the blocks.

XV
The Manor

RUS

Checking my image in the oval mirror hanging above the sink basin in the Magister's Manor, I squint at the short eyelashes, each lash well-abused by the frigid, week-long caravan trip from Merise. I dip my fingertips into the basin of hot water on the table under the mirror and run my damp fingers through my wavy red hair, leaving it slicked back where it had been sticking out and improperly crimped thanks to the beaver hat I've been wearing for the past week. Due to the late start from Merise and the weather on the way here, we've already missed the first day of the slave sales. We arrived this morning, weaving through Monticola, catching glimpses of snow-laden houses and freezing residents in the Magister's duchy.

Thankfully, Ino stayed with Astra's family, although she put up a fuss until the very end, and the promises I made to return to her weigh heavily on my mind. At least she's safe there under our instructions to stay out of trouble. We have to return to her after this, with or without Elaina.

I mentally shrug my thoughts away and use more water to slick back my hair above my plum-colored tunic with its white collar and my warm but thinner leggings and tall boots. Without enough time before dinner for a bath, I've already ordered one for after dinner—just to thaw out. I'd drag every bucket in myself and heat it at the fire myself in order for a bath at this point. Being at the Magister's does have its benefits.

The luxury of warmth still hasn't completely sunk in yet, and with just a glance to the window, the bitter cold taunts me. The storm rolled in shortly after we arrived in the Manor, and the sky is now black outside the window. Snow mounts on the windowsill, scratching its icy nails against the windowpanes.

I shiver. The snow and cold has a long reach that trails down my spine with its frozen fingers. Even though I've had enough cold to last a lifetime, the anger of the storm speaks to me, and I move to the window. Outside, it's a dull, muted black with white streaks blurring the air and hissing at the buffeting winds. Safely inside with a crackling fire heating the room, I breathe out a long breath of something like contentment.

A knock on the door jolts me not only from my thoughts but back to reality. I head toward the door, my final trace of good humor leaving me at the dark turn of my thoughts.

Behind the thick, carved wood is Cito, his hair freshly brushed and wearing a clean, high-necked tunic and trousers. He's not shaved, but then our Heian days of being clean-shaven are over as long as we stay in the cursed lands. He has trimmed his bushy beard and washed his face though, slicking his growing hair back behind his ears just like I have.

"Cleaned yourself up, I see," I remark, throwing the door open wide and motioning him inside.

"You as well, sir," he remarks, stepping in. He closes the door behind him while I collapse across the luxuriously wide bed. A moan escapes me. Why didn't I lie down earlier? This is what Paradise must feel like.

I throw one arm over my eyes, blocking out the light from the fire and the candles lining the room. Don't get comfortable, Rus. Elaina could be here. Enslaved, serving people like me. I shouldn't be enjoying this while she suffers. I clench my fists, closing one around the thick velvety fabric of the bedcovers. "Any sight of her?" I ask.

"Not yet. It's going to be a big job to find her here," Cito says, his voice muffled through my arm and the distance between us.

I take a breath and imprison it in my ribcage. "I know. We'll have to talk to the slaves in charge of others."

"They'll be less likely to talk," Cito remarks. "Of course, you might have luck with the women. Older women have always liked you."

I snort, but I'd pay any price to have Elaina back and Cito knows it. "How can they do this to their people, Cito?"

Footsteps creak across the wood floor, muffled by the skin rugs. "I don't know, sir. But I suppose we all do bad things to one another in the name of good."

I peer out from under my arm as the bed sinks under Cito's weight. "How can this be in the name of good? She was stolen, sold, probably abused...given no choice in her life here... One of her maids was killed, Cito. *Killed*."

Cito nods, his gaze fixed on the black window but far distant from anything within these walls. He gives himself a shake. "It's not about the good we can see but about the perceived good of others."

"There is no good in this, only evil." I sigh and aim my gaze upward at the ceiling, painted the same pale blue color as the hall outside. "I've gone over and over it again in my mind, Cito. I have nothing to show for dragging you across this country. I should have given up. It's been months of slavery for her now. Maybe we passed her and didn't recognize her. She could be somewhere that we've already been."

"Or she could be here," Cito says gently.

A dull ache reawakens in my chest, one that I've battled since the day after Elaina's departure. It took a day for the truth to settle in, for my immediate search to be denied, to find out that she was long gone with the gypsies. Pushing away the thoughts, I force myself up and rake my hand through my hair above my ear, gripping it behind my head for a count of five before letting go.

"What if she's not?" The words slip out of me without my permission, but I find the ache in my chest lessened with them. "What if we don't find her? Here or anywhere?"

Cito sighs, facing me with a gentle expression. "Then we go back home and grieve for her."

Folding my lips between my teeth, I nod. Renewed, I push myself off the bed. "Then let's find her. I don't fancy returning empty-handed."

An hour later, Cito and I hurry down the stairs into the majestic entrance, late for dinner. We'd spent the past hour wandering around and asking as many slaves as we found about possible Elainas.

"Do you think we'll see most of the slaves here tonight?" I ask. "They've said this is the biggest preview he's ever had, won't that mean our chances of finding..." I trail off and glance at Cito, but don't bother saying Elaina's name aloud. "It's better, right?"

Cito lifts one shoulder in a shrug. "I think so. As good as we could ask for, perhaps."

Not reassured, I chew on the inside of my cheek and trot down the last few stairs.

"Is the dinner this way?" Cito asks a lurking slave, who nods and points down a long hallway.

"The double doors," the man says.

"Thank you," Cito replies while I dart down the hall. "Are we late?" he calls back in afterthought. "Will we have missed anything?"

"Just the first drink, perhaps," the slave answers. "They have not been seated yet."

"Thank you again," Cito replies.

Curse it, we are late. We've lost valuable time we could have been searching for Elaina. Not that we weren't, but we only found a handful of slaves in the halls.

I speed up and, in a few moments, arrive before the double doors where two slaves stand in charcoal tunics that go high up their necks.

The men reach for the doors at the same time, pulling them open to permit us entry, staring straight ahead as soldiers in a palace might do.

This _is_ a palace, I remind myself as the doors swing open to reveal a glittering scene. The Magister is practically a god in this country. Second only to the Queen. Guests stand together in bright colors that seem to sparkle after our week of monotonous grays in the caravan.

Inside the door, another slave, this one a woman dressed in flawless white silk with blond hair down to her shoulders in gentle waves, extends a sheet of paper to us. "For your perusal," she says with a slight bow of her head.

"Thank you," I say without looking at the sheet, my gaze instead scanning the cavernous dining hall. People swarm all over like ants building a nest, at least a hundred guests with drinks in their hands, chatting and laughing as music plays gently in the background. This isn't a sales block, it's a party—where they trade, buy, and sell people. The thought revolts me. I turn back to the slave at the entrance. "Is the Magister here yet?"

"No, sir," she answers softly.

Choking back my disappointment, I thank her. "Oh, and what is this?" I lift the sheet of parchment.

"It's the list of slaves for sale tonight," she answers. "All the information you need to bid tonight is on there."

Forgetting to inhale, I gape at her.

"I see," Cito answers for us. "Thank you, miss." Taking my elbow in his fingers, he walks me toward a tall table set up with drinks. I hardly look up, instead devouring the pamphlet in my hands.

"There are no names, just a description, base price, and skills listed..." I turn the sheet over. "Fifty of them. And this is just tonight's. There are two more nights of this, right? A hundred and fifty slaves?" Despair washes over me. So many, how will we ever find Elaina?

The slave tending the table blinks with ill-concealed curiosity at my exasperation.

Cito pushes a drink into my hand. "Drink this," he commands, moving us away from the curious eyes and ears of the drink maker. "You need to calm down."

Right. We'll find Elaina. We will.

I toss back the drink, tilting my head back and catching sight of the high, painted ceiling. This one, like the foyer, depicts a mythic scene, here of a yellow dragon being chased by half a dozen warriors in dragon-scale armor.

"It's too pretty in here," I mutter.

Cito leans forward. "What?"

I point to the ceiling. "It's too pretty here. Reminds me of home."

Cito gives me a strange look but inspects the ceiling of the dining hall. Much like the palace in Merise, the room is at least two stories high and painted gloriously. Yellows, reds, golds, silvers, just as many colors as in the foyer, but this one is clearly intended to be a topic of conversation. Had the warriors from the ceiling dropped into our midst, they would be larger than life, dressed in their glittering dragon scales and carrying their sharp swords and large shields. Before Cito can speak, the music dies and a fanfare sounds a heart-beat later.

I scan the entrance, but the doors we entered through are closed with no signs of opening. Then the crowd begins to applaud at the other end of the room. I crane my head around but can see nothing. "Come on." I begin moving through the crowds to a position where I can see the Magister. Let's see if we can get close enough to speak with the man himself.

"Welcome, my guests, to the Manor," says a low voice with a hint of roughness to it, almost as if he's caught a cold that makes his lungs rattle.

"Excuse me," I murmur, curiosity pushing me through the guests to find a better viewpoint.

The crowd gives us a few affronted and curious stares at the pushes but parts easily enough. Soon, we stand off to the side of the man speaking. He's a tall, thin man that has the lanky look of a half-starved wolf. From my vantage point, I study the Magister as he welcomes the guests to his manor. His tunic and leggings are even finer than my best Heian clothing. Furs are ruffed around the Magister's wrists, and I have the sense that the Magister would smell finer than I do—or than I would had I been able to bathe tonight.

As the Magister speaks, the doors open and a long line of slaves enter. As one, all the guests turn and watch the line of men enter. The slaves keep their gazes down, no defiant looks here like with the slave at Lord Tillmore's. I clench my jaw. What would Astra do here? She'd be whipped into compliance, I imagine.

A slave drifts into my view carrying a tray of drinks. He has short dark hair and feminine features. I blink, my gaze stuttering on the slave, distracted by the face despite myself.

"Drink, sir?" he asks.

The he is a she, I realize with a jolt. And there is something strangely familiar about her. This slave with short dark hair is undoubtedly a female. I scan her then push her image aside, my eyes darting to the line of slaves still entering. No women yet. No girls. Just men. The words go through my head in an instant, leaving me free to stare at the unusual girl before me. She must be foreign. Yet those eyes...clear as a cold winter's sky, vaguely familiar—and like all other Canensians have. Her lips, wind chapped and red. But her skin, pale. She can't be Canensian, but she must be... She reminds me of someone. Wait, if I could have mistaken her for a man, could I mistake Elaina for one too? I call Elaina's face to my mind. A boy, perhaps. If she shaved her head and—

"A drink?" she prompts again.

With such confusing thoughts, I accept a drink from her tray, my gaze locked upon her. If she had more hair, she would resemble a painting or a statue. She really does remind me of someone. But I've never seen a woman's statue with so little hair. Not even a woman warrior. The thought brings a smirk to my lips.

"Anything else, sir?" she asks with something like cool, forced politeness.

Shaking my head, I watch her walk away, walking high on her

toes, her face stoic and...angry. She reminds me of Astra. She knows her worth. And she resents her presence here.

With her head high, she scans the crowd as she limps off, pausing frequently to offer drinks to others or simply, it seems, to rest her feet.

Reluctantly, I pull my attention back to the lines of slaves entering the room. Ignore her. She is not Elaina, she is not impor— she is not whom I am here for. Still, my gaze continues to find her in the crowd, wondering what her story is.

XVI

Not for Sale

WINTERBERRY

A s I did the night before, I stand in the dining hall. But this time, I am a server. I've been taken off the preview's sales list, and I don't know whether to rejoice in that or not. Wandering through the crowds before the bidding begins, I realize that I missed half the preview the night before. Worse, this activity makes my heels ache like never before. They're—if possible—sorer than the night before, and I pause every few steps in order to rest them, whether or not I'm refreshing someone's drink.

The lines of slaves stand at attention all through dinner as the serving staff, myself included, walk to the table and back to the kitchen in order to change courses and offer new dishes.

Most of my time, however, is spent standing in silence in a line of other servers, just like the slaves on display, only we hold trays as still as we can and try to avoid attention.

My gaze slides across the faces of the slaves for sale. Some are three times my age, others half of it. It's the old and young ones that break my heart equally. A couple of men are stooped with age, standing as straight as they can but in a pose that sinks forward over the evening. Then there's a boy that looks no more than eight, standing at the end of the line, his chin lifted high but wobbly at times, as though he's trying to keep back tears. And there's one who's had an injury that's left his face marred and his left arm mangled and hanging useless at his side.

I pity those ones—the cheapest ones, the ones deemed useless. Certa tells me that the older ones are usually exiled to a spot where they are all but forgotten, such as cleaning up the animal waste or the slaughterhouse. They are the ones that are bought by the cheapest guests, the guests who don't eat among the masters but who arrive under cover of the twilight to exchange money for a human that is barely breathing. They are the slaves rarely given a showing at all.

So why are they here? Why not sell them without a showing? I'll have to ask Certa. Not that it matters much. They'll be sold. Given a new master. One that will probably be as cruel as or crueler than the Magister. Hopelessness threatens to overtake me. It doesn't matter. I'm going to be stuck here, because he for some reason won't sell me, and they go on to suffer.

At the next change in courses, I slip down to the kitchen, taking a precious minute to breathe. I slick my two-inch hair back with wet hands before picking up my tray of rolls near a pitcher of wine. I'm not allowed to serve wine yet; it's a hefty responsibility, the ability to stain a highborn's clothes. One that makes me almost laugh.

Trudging up the steps and back to the dining hall, I turn over in my mind the images of the men I've seen tonight. All the men around the table are large and intimidating, except for two who appear more delicately featured. Almost so delicate that they look out of place amongst the rest. Surely the one's coloring sets him apart. One has unusual wavy red hair, the other has darker blond hair. Neither are bad looking, and the redhead is closest to my age, closer than any of the rest at least, although he has more feminine Canens features. I let my gaze slide past them, inspecting the others around the table one by one.

"Psst!" the slave girl beside me hisses in my direction. "He wants you."

"Wha—?"

She jerks her chin at the table, and I follow it.

Three or four of the noblemen are looking our way, one motioning to me with an impatient look, the redhead beside him leaning back, a calculated expression in his eye, while the blond beside him glances at the redhead. I hurry in their direction, the rolls tipping on my plate.

I bend over slightly to lower the tray beside the bored one, and he takes a roll, flipping it in his hand before taking a bite. As he does, his eyes land on mine, and I inwardly curse. *Be seen, but do not see. Hear, but do not be heard.* That was the guidance I received tonight.

"Wait," the redhead says in a slight accent I can't place. "Is this one for sale? She *could* be a pretty little thing."

His friend's eyes linger on my frostbitten fingers.

The redhead gives a brutal laugh. "With a bit of work."

Heat churns in my ribcage, but I keep my eyes down to hide my fury.

The russet-haired one leans toward me, and his nose wrinkles. "That stench though," he mutters loud enough for the entire table to hear. "If all women smelled as such, we'd die out."

My cheeks grow hotter.

The table laughs heartily, and I risk a glance at Marcus to see his cheeks flush under his trimmed beard. I'll probably receive a talking-to about hygiene after this meal now.

"Perhaps if you cared about humanity in any sense, you wouldn't care what a person smelled or looked like. Instead you'd treat her like a human."

The guest's mouth falls open in shock at my rebuff and twitches as if suppressing a smile.

"That's enough," the Magister says, his voice cold. "I'll see you punished for your impudence."

I raise my chin at him, defiant. "I'm certain you shall. I'll be on my toes waiting for your...discipline."

The Magister makes a motion with his hand to hurry me back to my spot against the wall, but the straw-haired man interrupts, reaching out for the tray, and slowly takes a roll.

"Thank you," he says, deliberately meeting my gaze.

Without speaking, I nod at him. They are not from Canens. I examine them both before I straighten and turn back to resume my place against the wall. Who are these men? And why are they here? I should watch them. Find out more about them. They could be allies. Or enemies. I study them from a dozen paces away.

"Sir, how many slaves do you think you have on the premises?" the redhead says.

The Magister dips a forkful of poultry into his melted butter. "I can tell you exactly, Mr. Solem."

"Exactly?"

"Down to the exact number," the Magister replies with a hint of pride.

"I admit, I'm impressed at this entire operation. My friend and I are considering a venture into the slave trade—not around here, of course—but your operation is flawless. Well, almost. But no one can ever fully control another, can they?" the redhead asks, a hint of amusement in his eyes.

To my trained eye, the Magister tenses, his shoulders tightening ever so slightly at the veiled insult. My heart thumps in my throat. Although my owner doesn't look my way, I know he won't let me escape punishment now.

The blond companion clears his throat. "Your operation is difficult—if not impossible—to improve upon, my lord."

"Thank you." A polite smile stretches the Magister's lips into something more like a wolfish snarl. "It's been decades in the making."

"And it shows." The redhead takes a bite from the roll I've delivered to him, and I wish that I'd poisoned it.

Enemies, I decide. They're certainly enemies.

XVII

Broken

WINTERBERRY

My heart thuds dully in my throat. This time, he has put me in a cell.

"For your own protection," the Magister's soldier said when he dumped me inside after the preview dinner ended.

That was hours ago.

This is worse than waiting for my stepmother to appear.

I knew—or thought I did—what she wanted from me. I do not know what the Magister wants—only that if he wants me dead, he would have killed me already. Perhaps after he dragged me back to the Manor.

There is a sadistic twist to him, something deep inside him I see in his eyes, one that I imagine only emerges in private. That is the one that terrifies me more than the Queen. And then there are the moments that I think he is like a father, feeling regret at his punishments.

Waiting, I rub at my fingers. I turn my hands over in front of my face. Are they like my mother's hands? Slender, long fingers? Graceful wrists? Thin, hairless arms? My arms are probably thicker than hers, for all the scrubbing and cleaning and work I've had to do lately.

I haven't thought of her in years, not really. They say she was beautiful, with icy pale skin like mine, along with blue eyes the color of a clear icicle on a bright winter day. They say her hair was the color of spun gold, that she was a woman over whom wars had been fought.

I don't know that I believe the legends about her, but the legends are plentiful.

The door to my cell opens.

"Well, my fair Helena," drawls the familiar voice of my master. "It appears you've finally landed in the place I found you."

"Here I thought you found me at the gallows," I retort.

"Gallows?" He tilts his head, considering. "No. Although you weren't far from that. To think you've come so far...your looks have quite improved."

Standing proud before him, I raise my chin. "Do what you will. But you won't break me."

"No?" His smile turns sinister before he turns and walks out of my cell. "Bring her along," he commands to someone in the hall.

A guard enters and drags me out, even though I don't resist. What use is there in resisting? Instead I scramble to get my feet under me as the guard pulls me down the hallway and into the same room he brought me to when he fitted me with those metal shoes.

Now, the large table squats in the middle of the room, the table with leather straps. My feet hesitate under me, but the guard yanks me inside.

Various instruments of torture surround us, sending a chill through me that has nothing to do with the temperature drop in this room.

I can handle whatever he dishes out. I must. I won't give him the satisfaction of letting him know how much he hurts me.

To my surprise, the Magister motions to the guard, and he brings me to a chain attached to the wall. He wraps a handcuff around my wrist and walks away, leaving me with four feet of chain. It's impossible not to feel vulnerable as the Magister stands beside the table with his implacable expression.

My heart thumps as I wait, staring into his coldly pensive eyes. Then he says the words that freeze my soul. "Bring her in."

"Her?" Breath coming in short gasps, I turn to the door the guard disappeared through. "Who—"

Then the world falls out from under me as Certa is brought in with tears streaming down her face.

"No," I whisper. "No, please." I rush toward them only to be pulled back by the chain around my wrist. I fight it, yanking at the wall with all my strength, stretching out my opposite fingers toward Certa and the table, barely feeling the bite of the metal into my flesh as I struggle to reach her, to free her. "Certa!"

"Helena," she whispers. Her eyes go huge, mouth forming an O before she drags at the guard. "Oh, please. Please don't do this! I have been loyal, I have."

The Magister smiles his calm, knowing smile at me, but there is a thin line of tension pinching the edges. That tension is my hope, and I cling to it.

"What are you going to do to her? Please don't hurt her—she didn't do anything to deserve it. Please." Tears are brimming over my lashes now, but I do not care. How did he know exactly where to hurt me?

Hanging onto the guard, who has a disgusted look on his face, Certa sobs uncontrollably, tears flowing down her cheeks. He wrestles her toward the table and, at the Magister's instruction, binds her wrists and ankles to the table using its attached straps.

"Please," I beg.

He ignores me, and so I do the only thing I can think of: I fight my chain, backing up and running with all my strength, allowing it to jerk me back in the hopes that I can loosen it from the wall. All it does is nearly yank my shoulder from its socket.

The Magister casts me a disdainful look, as if I have somehow slipped in his estimations. "Stop it, before I am forced to bind you further."

In answer, I run away from the wall again, only a soldier catches me this time and shoves me so hard that the back of my head slams into the wall behind me.

Groaning, I roll onto my non-wrenched shoulder. Feet pass by my face, and I ready myself for a kick that doesn't come.

Silence falls in the room, except for Certa's muffled sobs and the scratch of booted feet on the stone floor. Trying to blink away the haze in my head, I push myself up onto my elbows, the grit from the floor digging into my palms and under my fingernails.

Rolling onto my haunches, I slowly lift my head and find the Magister crouching before me, his gaze steady upon me. I refuse to give even an inch and glare at him defiantly.

"Do you think," he says softly, "that I chose you out of the rest of them by chance?"

"I—" I break off, my stomach clenching. "What do you mean?"

His smile turns smug, but he does not answer me. On the table behind him, Certa struggles but barely. It is almost as though she has given up on her escape, surrendered to her situation.

I can't blame her. We are both at the mercy of his whims now. But I have to help her—have to get her out... I turn to the Magister. What does he want to hear? How can I convince him to let us go without hurting us? He will hurt us. But perhaps I can keep him from killing us. Apologize. That's it. Apologize.

"I'm sorry," I say, my lips trying to stop my tongue from saying the words so that they come out clumsy. I wet my lips and try again. "I'm sorry for ruining your dinner."

The Magister stills, his back to me. "I'm afraid that's not enough now. You've undermined my entire business, you know, with your disrespect." He reaches for a table laden with blades and tools, readjusting one so that it sits straight alongside the next.

I try to catch Certa's eye, to apologize to her for getting her into this, but she stares at the ceiling, silent tears leaking from the corners of her eyes and down into her grizzled hair.

"I'm sorry," I whisper to her.

The Magister continues to rearrange his tools with gentle clinks, ignoring us.

My shoulder and head aching, I steel myself for whatever might come, while my mind races through possibilities. Could we escape? How? I have to get free from this chain first—and then we'd have to flee. Again. I'd have to steal horses, and I'm not ready—I have no food or supplies, or—

And I'd have to disable or kill the Magister, at least temporarily, else I couldn't free Certa. But if Certa refuses to go with me, I can't leave her here to die, for she would then.

Thoughts slowing, I wilt against the wall, knowing with one glance that she would not go, and if she did, recapture would be imminent. If I left without her—I'd never forgive myself.

"Winter."

My head snaps up at the voice.

He smiles. "You see," he says in a tone that reminds me of melted butter, hot and tempting, "you think you've escaped your past, but you've forgotten that pasts have a way of tagging along. And you..." He tuts at me. "You have quite a past."

My teeth grind together loud enough for me to hear them over his words and Certa's quieting sniffles. "Oh? And what is your past that has tagged along? I'm sure it's worse than mine, if <u>this</u> is your present." I motion my unchained hand at his torture chamber.

Something burns in his eyes, almost as strong as if a fire is reflected there. Then with a blink, he hides it. "Perhaps if you had bothered to learn your place, you would have learned mine as well." He steps nearer. "Past and present."

"I know your place," I spit. "It's a level down from here, and it's burning with sulfur."

His eyebrow lifts. "My, my, my, aren't we feisty this evening. And here I thought you might soften, given the bargaining chip I bring to the table."

My stomach twists as he turns to Certa. "No." The word slips from me without conscious thought, a word I cannot bring back once spoken.

"No?" he echoes innocently. "She is no bargaining chip? Or you will not soften?"

"Certa..." My mouth forms her name on a breath.

"Ah. So she is."

"Why did you buy me?" I demand, trying to keep him talking, keep him away from her.

He smiles like he has been waiting for the question. "A great commission. By a great queen who wished to teach her daughter her place."

I gasp then spit, "*Step*daughter," and bolt to my feet to glare at him with all the hatred I can muster. "And she is not great. She is evil." My gaze flickers behind him at Certa.

"Greatness and evilness are sometimes one and the same," he murmurs. At my glare, he continues. "You can be great while being evil. But you can be great without being evil and evil without being great."

"Well then, you two exemplify that contradiction quite well. For she is greatly evil, and you are purely evil."

His smile widens to reveal large, sharp teeth, and he spreads his hands as if displaying a feast before him, bowing slightly. "I learned from the best. I merely hunt in her shadow."

My jaw goes slack as his words sink in. "You—you what?"

He peers down at me over his long, blond beard. "You really never knew?"

"Knew...?" Even though I begin to understand, I hesitate.

He approaches, and although my body shudders, I stand my ground. "You are a special project for me. You will be my perfect little winter...*princess*." He trails a fingernail down my cheek. "You see, the

Queen has taught me that not all pain is physical. The hunt has never displayed that. No animal can feel like a human, after all.

"But you...you have shown me that physical pain will not change your insolent behavior." He raises a knife from his belt and runs a finger down its blade.

"The Quee..." I trail off again, knowing what I cannot accept to be true.

His smile widens. "Yes. I learned many arts at her feet." He brushes his silvery hair back and smooths his well-trimmed beard. "Yes, she has given me the charge of a lifetime. And after a lifetime of serving her, she has rewarded me with...you."

I stagger back from him until I thud into the wall. "You are the huntsman." This is the man who terrorized my dreams since my father died. The one whom I was threatened with, the one whom I feared above my stepmother. He is the enemy chosen for me, not her.

His teeth glint in the torchlight, and he wipes his mouth with the back of his hand. "I am the huntsman," he whispers, eyes burning with delight as he asserts his character.

Behind him, Certa lets out a wail, breaking my heart in two.

"So let us begin." He faces her with a flourish, knife in hand.

And then I begin to learn the art of torture. First by observation. Then by participation.

XVIII

Existing

WINTERBERRY

I hover at the brink of existence.
  I know I live, and yet I know I do not wish to.
  Beyond all, I know that Certa is dead.
And he let me live so that I must live with that knowledge.
Only revenge maintains me.

XIX

Forgotten

WINTERBERRY

Days must pass before I awaken. My eyes are caked with sleep or pus, something that seems to glue them together stronger than anything I've ever encountered. My lashes stick together, unable to be pried opened by my dry eyes. Lifting my hand to wipe at them, I find my arms reluctant to obey. I am too cold, my arms too heavy. Even my thoughts are sluggish.

I cannot remember anything. Nothing but... No. That I *will not* remember.

With no sight, I resort to my other senses, listening for anything around me—the breath of another living being, the scrape of shoes on stone or dirt—inhaling through my nose, and making a list of findings in my mind.

It is quiet, abnormally so. I must be alone, for there is no one breathing beside me, no guard shifting as they stand; there is no one to nurse me. My face is hot, while the rest of me is cold. Either it's infected, or else simply healing blood is at work in my bruises.

The air is dry, icy, and bitterly cold, but not windy. Furs cover me, keeping my body warm, only leaving my face exposed. Even my hands have mittens, and my toes are warm despite having lain so still for so long. When I try to move, everything aches, that deep ache I always get when I sleep too long and the day dawns cold and wet.

The ground under me is not as hard as stone, nor is it as soft as my bed. It is something like straw atop packed dirt. There is the slightest barn scent to the room, as though I could be in an old stable or a place that used to have animals but no longer houses them, or perhaps it is just the musky smell of straw. Yet it is the ice-cold embrace of steel around my wrists and ankles, the only coldness against my flesh, that recalls me to myself.

In the end, it seems it is nothing more than I have returned to prison. A sigh mingled with a sob rises up in me as Des's face and then Certa's ruined body flashes before my eyelids. I couldn't save them. And now I am imprisoned, unable to avenge them either. Why do I only make enemies? Why must all my friends die while my enemies live?

My fists clench; my eyes burn. Tears squeeze out at the corners of my lids, wetting my lashes and slowly freezing. I allow myself to cry, letting the tears work their blessed magic. Soon, my lids are loosened, and I pry them open to investigate my surroundings.

The sight wrenches my breath from my lungs.

I am in a prison.

Except that this one is made of a dirt floor and straw-covered, smooth, stone walls, and, two dozen feet high above me is the only exit: a circular mouth covered with an iron grate.

I am in an *oubliette*.

XX

A Dream

RUS

"Rus?" A timid voice speaks through my dreams. The gypsies taunt me, drawing their thin swords, dancing around like cats with claws. My head aches.

"You thought you'd be able to stop us? We have taken your girls for years, sending them to the frozen north for gems."

"Rus?" the voice speaks more urgently.

A gypsy slashes at me; another pushes my shoulder.

I wrest myself away from them. "You won't take her. Tell me where she is, or I'll kill you all."

"Rus! Wake up!"

My knife in hand, I bolt upright in the darkness; a muffled shriek fills the air. "Who's there?" I demand through my fuzzy thoughts.

A skittering sound is my only answer, something like a leaf trembling in the wind or the whisper of a harsh fabric against wood. My blood pulses in my ears.

"Who's there?" I toss back my bedcoverings and throw my legs over the side of the bed, knife held at the ready.

"Rus?" the quiet voice says again.

Distantly, through disbelief and shock, recognition knocks.

"Is it really you?" the voice asks.

"Elaina?" Her name, spoken so often, feels foreign on my lips, as if it cannot be her. But wariness almost immediately sets in. I've told dozens of people about her—dozens just here at the Manor. Any girl could come to me, wanting me to rescue her, pretending to be Elaina.

"Rus." She speaks through a sob this time, and a sudden object hurtles itself across the darkness into my arms.

I tense, reminding myself not to trust anything until I see it with my own eyes. Still holding my knife, I allow myself to wrap my arms around her, guarding my heart against the very hope I have begun to surrender since arriving at the Manor.

"Is it really you?" she cries into my nightshirt. "I thought you'd never find me. I thought—" She breaks off, her body shaking.

"Elaina?" I push her back from me, even though my heart insists that I pull her close. "I must light the fire. I must see you."

Sniffling and nodding, she still clings to me as I reach for the side table. My fire has fallen into embers; it must be early morning, but the sky is dark and cloudy outside the window. I didn't bother with letting the maid in to warm my bed or pull the drapes—how could I let a slave like my sister do such tasks?—but now I wish I'd at least let her tend the fire.

After fumbling around the fireplace, adding a log and a few pieces of kindling to the cooling embers, and continuously glancing back at the silent shadow sitting on my bed a few feet away, I give up on restarting the fire and reach for my lamp instead. I lift the glass covering and struggle to strike the flint with trembling hands. Finally, the lamp's wick catches, and I lower the glass around the flame, my gaze catching on the knife blade which tosses the flickering light back to me.

Almost reluctantly, I turn to the girl.

Dressed in a dark over robe, she bends half over, covering her face with her hands. Her long, dark blond hair falls before her face, shielding her features from my view. As I shift toward her, her bright red tunic peeks out from her opposite shoulder, and my stomach turns.

Cautiously, still too afraid to hope for what I see with my own eyes, I position myself in front of her and bend my knees.

"Uncover your face," I say, keeping my voice light and as gentle as I can muster. If this girl isn't Elaina, I will kill her.

Sniffling heavily, the girl drops her hands from her face and fixes dark, round eyes on me.

My heart clenches in my chest, and I throw my knife on the bed behind her, pulling her into my arms and crushing her against my chest. "Elaina. Oh, Elaina."

I fight back my own tears as she sobs until my arms cramp and I remember that we have no time for this reunion.

"Elaina, Elaina. We must make plans. We must— You must calm and tell me what has happened."

Sniffing, she pulls back and nods. "Yes, yes. I know."

"Start at the beginning. No, wait, don't. Tell me how you got here, who you are here with."

"I'm here with Baron Tueor."

"Are you?" A chill runs down my spine. Baron Tueor. I met him at the previews. Or saw him at least. But I didn't see her, and the final night of the sales was last night. Which was exactly why I drank too much. I touch a hand to my forehead as my head pounds.

"Yes." She sniffs again and takes the handkerchief I press at her. "He bought me in Merise, at the auctions. And I came here with him. He's the Magister's brother."

"The Magister's brother?"

"Yes. He's favored by the Queen. Well, they both are."

"That doesn't matter," I say to assure her and myself that we're going to defy the odds. "How did you get to my room?"

She shrugs. "I told him I needed rags and I had to go find some."

"Won't he be waiting for you?"

"He sleeps heavily. He drank more than you tonight. He has no idea where I am. You're across the Manor from him."

"Well, how did you find me?"

"I saw you at the preview."

"What? You were there?"

"Yes. I was next to the Baron."

"Wha— How? I searched the face of every slave in that room, you weren't there."

"I was," she says quietly. "He dresses me as a noblewoman in there."

"A noblewoman?" I almost growl. "You're only thirteen."

"Almost fourteen," she says, but instead of defensiveness, there's only resignation, as though the fact has changed her life in more than one way that she regrets.

"Yes, well..." I want to ask, but I don't.

Her eyes flick up to my face. "He treats me well enough. No beatings like the gypsies. He likes my body, so he won't hurt me."

I grit my teeth, clenching my fists as fury drives its way through me. "How can we get you out? Will he sell you?"

"No." Her answer is soft but quick. "He won't sell. You'll have to steal me. And he'll come after me, if he can."

"Will he? Will he be able to, I mean?"

She lifts a shoulder in a shrug. "If no business comes up."

"What does he do? What might distract him from you?"

She shakes her head. "The Manor is big, I can avoid him for the day, so we need to leave in the morning. He'll notice if I'm gone at night."

I wince at her matter-of-fact words, but she's continuing as if they are nothing.

"He's got a full day out in the town planned the day after tomorrow—I mean, tomorrow now. So if we can leave by then, we should. I don't know when my next chance will be."

"Right. We'll do it then." I rise and begin to pace across the room as my mind turns.

If we leave before light tomorrow morning, we'll have the day to cobble together some food and supplies from town. We can't take things from here without revealing ourselves. We'll have to steal a horse, since I left Umbra behind with Ino. He was too thin and tired to make the trek north, and she felt the weight of my promise to return at the gesture.

But where will we go? Back to Merise? We have to get Ino yet must Elaina to safety first. We have cousins in Ardor, and the Ardor border is only twenty miles from here. We can cover that in a few days, if the weather holds out and no storms blow in. The frozen lake to the south is safe for travel across the border; I know Canensians have used it in the past to enter Ardor. But—

"Rus?" Elaina's quiet voice interrupts my onslaught of thoughts.

I turn, apology ready on my lips. "I'm sorry, darling. I'm just trying to think."

"I have to return to his rooms."

I stiffen at the thought of her returning to that man's bed. "I know. I know."

"But I can plan on leaving tomorrow?" There's such sorrow and such hope in her face that my heart breaks all over again, worse than ever before.

"Yes, darling. Yes, I will take you from here tomorrow, even if the gods of Canens throw the worst storm in history our way."

A small twitch of her lips is the only answering smile I get, but I'll take it.

XXI
Rumors

BLANCHE

"My Queen." Shock on his face, the Huntsman bows before me, his wolfish face properly deferential as he stands in his own chambers, a fire merrily crackling behind him. He motions me inside and closes the door with a snap behind him. "I did not expect you so quickly."

"I have methods of quick travel. Though they be exhausting."

He motions me to a comfortable leather chair. "Then please, sit."

I all but fall into the chair, exhaustion pulling at my limbs. "Tell me what has happened." I take the offered glass of wine from him. Even in my state, I feel his heartbeat increase in pace. Interesting. For a hunter.

"Well, Majesty, as I said in my note to you..."

"Tell me everything. Again." I sip from my wine, not even bothering to look into his face.

"She has been...rebellious here, Majesty. To say the least. Even on the journey here, she was a challenge. All saw that she had fire in her eyes. She wouldn't take an order simply because it was given. But she clung to a little Red on the journey, and that seemed to calm her. Unfortunately, the Red died upon arrival at the Manor." He pours himself a glass of wine and sips from it, staring into the fire before shaking his head and continuing. "After that, she seemed to calm a little. She at first seemed to fit in relatively well, taking orders from her training slave, one whom I trusted greatly. It grieves me..." He trails off. "Well, her troubles started after she began to get friendly with other slaves. She began to resist her chores, speak back to the nobles, and commit other such impertinent acts. She was seen once or twice sneaking food from the kitchen."

I lift an eyebrow.

"She made an escape attempt." He shrugs. "I allowed it, because failure is the most effective teacher." His lips twitch into a smirk. "But she was a fool to think she could escape so easily."

"And now?"

His lips fall, and his face shadows. "I was a fool to punish her so lightly the first time, my Queen. I am forever in your debt."

"What happened?" My voice is deathly quiet this time. His heart is a frantic race of a rabbit's pulse, despite his calm outward appearance.

"I used the shoes the first time. Your aunt's shoes. They were...effective. But then... She challenged me in front of them all. At a preview. She made a mockery of this manor, of slavery, of Canens."

"Of you."

His jaw clenches. "Yes. Of me."

"And then what happened? Why did you send a raven to me?"

"I had to punish her. I had to break her."

"How?"

He lifts an inscrutable face to me. "I made her kill another slave."

I pause as shock rushes over me in its gentle embrace. Then my lips curve into a glorious smile. "Excellent. And?"

"She broke," he says simply.

Perhaps I won't have to kill her after all then.

"How?" I lean forward, my exhaustion forgotten.

"Her mind. She...she is not there any longer. At the sight of the blood, she...she screamed, screamed for her mother and father. She refused. She would not do it, and so I made her. Together, we sliced her teacher's throat, and I forced her to watch the life bleed from her."

"Marcus!" The door slams open with a loud bang, making both of us flinch in our seats. When I turn, I find Baron Tueor striding in, fury on his face. "Marcus, I—" He stops with an open mouth then falls into a kneeling bow before me. "Your Majesty. I—I had no idea."

"Close the door," I instruct the Magister.

He nods and crosses to the door. There, he frowns at something in the hallway, then speaks low and casts his brother a glance.

"Something wrong?" I ask.

The Magister shakes his head. "No. Just a slave."

I turn to Tueor and say in a false tone of discipline, "What do you mean bursting into your brother's rooms?"

"I—I apologize, Majesty. I was unaware he had company."

"And what was so urgent that you needed his presence?" Amusement bleeds into my words. "I do not wish to interrupt your conversation."

"Well, I—" He breaks off and looks to his brother with pale eyes.

I shake my head. "Rise, take a drink. Do you have a spare glass?"

"Of course," Marcus murmurs, his gaze flashing between us both. He pours his brother a generous drink and hands it to him.

"So what was it?" I ask. "Please, share."

Tueor glances at Marcus then moves toward the fire, staring at the flames before turning back and answering. "My needs are no concern, Majesty. If I had known you were here, I would never have dared enter."

"Of course, but now you're here. It must be important."

"I apologize. I had some information for my brother regarding something we'd overheard last night." He gives the Magister a significant look, which his brother returns with an innocent expression of his own.

"I see." I sit back in my chair, draining the last of my wine. "Then let us resume our conversation, Marcus."

"Of course, Majesty."

"So now where is she?"

With a half glance at his brother, the Magister reclaims his seat. "She's in the <u>oubliette</u>. Waiting."

"Perfect." I smother a yawn. "She will be easy enough to find in the morning then."

"Yes, Majesty. Very easy." He gives another deferential tilt of his head.

"I will take to my rooms then." I set down my empty wineglass and glance between the brothers, catching their loaded expressions. "Unless there is something else you wish to confide in me?"

The Magister's heartbeat increases.

Tueor clears his throat. "Majesty, I—"

"There are rumors in town," Marcus interrupts.

Tueor's brow darkens, his fist clenching above the mantle.

"In your town?" I arch my brow.

He shrugs. "In mine, in others."

I glance between the brothers. Tueor resembles nothing of his brother; his pale hair and strong, wide face contrast sharply with Marcus's narrow, wolfish face. "Rumors of what?" I finally ask.

"Rumors of rebellion." Tueor tugs at his tunic.

"Rebellion?" I push my glass toward Marcus, exhaustion forgotten. "I think I might need another glass for this discussion."

He refills my glass and waits for me to take a deep drink.

"And what rebellion is discussed?"

"Some of my loyal slaves tell me that there is grave displeasure after your extinguishing of the growing house fires."

"Oh that." I scoff. "I've heard as much from Lord Monete."

"The rumors have spread all the way to Monticola." He seems impressed by this, the lines on his face deepening with concern. "There is rebellion talked about."

"You know very well what to do with those who are speaking of rebellion," I scoff. "You take care of them."

"I always eliminate any whisper against the throne," he says quietly. "These are different."

"How so?"

"They won't be silenced so easily. They come from the nobles."

A chill runs down my spine. "The nobles? Such as whom?"

"Unfortunately, I don't know."

I narrow my eyes as anger flares inside. "Then why tell me now?"

"To put you on your guard." He remains calm, his heartbeat even slowing, his breath steady in the face of my anger.

With another drink from my glass, I control myself. "Put me on my guard?"

"Against your own."

I half close my eyes, calming myself with a deep breath. "Who would dare to speak against me?"

"My brother and I were unable to discover who it might be. But they were a guest here at the previews this past week. They might still be here."

I take a sip of my drink. "What was said?"

"Some are very angry that you used magic. Even to protect Merise. They think magic should be separate from the throne; they are afraid. I've heard that from more than one noble."

"Well, their fear is good. It keeps them in their place."

"Except it also brews discontent, in this situation," Tueor says boldly. "Many I have spoken with express the need to fight the Canens Curse with magic. And now that they know you have magic..." He trails off significantly.

"Of course. They want me to fix things." I sigh heavily and wipe a weary hand over my eyes. "If only it were that simple."

"Majesty, I think I might be able to help you with that," Baron Tueor says.

I pry open an eye to narrowly glare at him. "And what might you do?"

His shoulders lift and straighten in determination. "I think the nobles grow too bold for their own good. It might be time to make them fear something more than their queen."

"And what might that be?"

"An army ready to defend their queen."

A slow smile parts my lips but falls off just as slowly. "Yes, well, there are a few things to handle first. But perhaps you, Baron, can help with raising that army."

Eyes glinting, he falls to his knee, one fisted hand clapped over his heart. "I would be honored, Your Majesty."

"Excellent. In the meantime, I must rest and consider before dealing with my other problem." As I stand, Marcus dips his head in a bow. With a half-amused glance at the two men, one kneeling, one's head inclined, I turn and stride away, my steps weary but my mind whirring with plans.

XXII
Memories
WINTERBERRY

The minutes become hours, which then become days. I am, as I fear, being forgotten.

There is no food, and at first, my stomach growls insistently. Then it quiets, as if it has given up, surrendered to our circumstances.

I begin to lose track of myself. My lips are dry, cracked. The cold seeps through my furs and into my bones. I think I see a blue orb hanging in the sky. Has the sun gone blue? But as I reach out my hand for it, it murmurs, the wind buffets it away, and it is gone.

I am hallucinating.

My mother visits me, with her clear blue eyes and swelling stomach. She runs her hands over her belly, smiling a hopeful smile, as though she doesn't know the future she's condemning her daughter to.

I close my eyes and sleep. And I dream of the mother I never met.

XXIII

Rescued

RUS

"We can't do it! This was not in the plan," I insist as Cito bends over the unconscious girl wrapped in furs. Glancing back in the direction of the Manor, I find it dark with no hint of movement from the few lights burning in the village, but our enemies aren't just in the Manor. The city walls tower a quarter mile in front of us, the gates closed but not locked. Above, the lights burn and dance in ribbons of purple and green from behind a thin smudge of clouds.

Cito ignores me and my concerns and peers closer into her face. "I think she's coming around."

"She needs treatment," Elaina says. "Were we supposed to leave her there to die?"

I glare at her. "This is about getting you out—not about saving anyone else. We already decided what we're doing, and saving another slave was not planned for." I turn to Cito. "We stick to the plan. Send her back to Monticola, let her take her chances there."

"No!" Elaina says, horror on her face. "You can't do that to her—he'll kill her!"

"She's probably dead if she comes with us anyway," I say reasonably, nodding down at her. "She's barely alive right now."

Elaina narrows her eyes at me, her heavy breaths clouding the air between us and softening her glare. Placing her hands on her hips, she takes a step toward me. "If you send her back, I'm not coming with you. I'll go back to him."

My jaw drops in disbelief at the little thirteen-year-old challenging me. "I'll tie you up and take you by force then!"

"I'd like to see you try," she retorts, eyes flashing. "We're taking her with us, or we aren't going at all. Don't you know who she is?"

Exasperated, I spread my hands. "No, Elaina, no, I don't know who she is—" When she opens her mouth to respond, I hurriedly add, "—and I don't care. She's the woman who's going to get you killed is who she is!"

With a disdainful look that only a thirteen-year-old girl can give, Elaina clamps her mouth shut and turns on her heel, striding to Cito to kneel beside the prone girl. Turning away from them, I throw my hands up in the air and let one come down atop my hat, smashing it onto my head as I let out a growl. Annoyed, I take a few strides away from them, hoping to catch hold of my temper and do something useful, like watching for wolves.

The winter chill is thick tonight, with no clouds for warmth. The moon is a semicircle hiding behind the Manor's highest turret, making it difficult to see anything but the darkest shadows. She's going to get us all killed. Because she insists on saving a slave girl that can't even walk. A slave girl the Magister clearly wants dead.

A shadow moves across the wall, jerking my attention to it. I follow the shadow up to the sky, where a black smudge moves across it with practiced ease. A bird? At night? I shake my head. Who knows what kind of evil creatures truly live in this land. As it passes over the wall into the town, another shadow moves beneath. I narrow my eyes at the gate less than a quarter mile away. A gust of wind roars against it, and it squeaks on its hinges, creaking halfway open before falling back against itself with a frozen crash.

I watch it a minute longer, but nothing emerges and no further shadows whisper from the clear night.

Convinced the darkness holds nothing but shadows and unseen predators, I turn back and find Cito and Elaina still bending over the girl. Might as well snap things up. We can't stay here forever or else the wolves will find us.

Pressing out a sigh, I step up to them. "If we're taking her, let's get her up on a horse. Elaina, you'll ride with me. We'll throw her over the packhorse and—"

"You won't throw her over anything!" Elaina returns hotly.

"Elaina Kara, do not test me right now," I growl at her. "I do not have the patience for this. If you want me to take her, I will take her how I see fit. She is not fit to ride upright—I cannot hold her, it is not worth the health of our animals. You are the smallest and lightest, and though I despise the idea of bringing her at all, I will do it for your sake."

She opens her mouth then snaps it shut. "Fine. Thank you." She turns to Cito with all the air of the princess she is, all trace of her tears the prior night gone. "Let's get her on the horse. We'll have to tend to her health when we're farther from the Manor."

Cito glances at me. "What about the—"

I silence him with a glare. "Let's get her mounted. We must start moving."

"Try the orb," Cito says. "The old man says it has healing properties. It's going to be better to travel with four healthy people than—"

"What orb?" Elaina's eyes round as she stares between us.

I grit my teeth. "Hades, Cito. We don't have time for this! We don't even know if it'll work."

"It did before." Cito is quiet but certain.

I groan inwardly. I've not had the chance to even look at the orb since our race to Lord Tillmore's, and I have no desire to bring it back out now as we make our escape. "Cito, I won't ride with it again. It will reveal us to everyone!"

"Then take it out now and take a few minutes to let it work. At least enough to revitalize her."

"What orb?" Elaina asks. "What are you two talking about?"

"An old man in Ostium gave us a magical orb when we were following you into Canens. It saved our lives—kept the wolves away from us as we traveled to Merise and even healed a cut on your brother's hand."

"It could reveal us. It's a light, Cito."

He glances around and pulls off his cape. "We'll hide it under this."

"Fine!" Rolling my eyes at his answer for everything, I throw up my hands again and go to my pack. "Fine. I can see I'm outnumbered." Jaw clenched, I locate and pull out the small box. I move back beside the girl sprawled atop the white expanse of snow and kneel. Before I can open the delicate clasp on the box, I have to pull off my mittens. Elaina bends over my shoulder, trying to see the glass orb. I take a deep breath as I remove it and set it on the stand next to the slave girl's head.

"Here." Cito takes his cape and angles it over the light and the girl's face so that any light will be hidden from a distance.

I mutter the words to illuminate the orb. We all lean back at the immediate brightness, shielding our eyes and squinting until they adjust. How long will they insist we sit here and wait for something to happen?

"Amazing," Elaina murmurs. "The old man just gave this to you?"

"Shh," I mutter, not wishing to continue any discussion. "Hold this." I hand her the edge of the cape and position her hands low over the light, then move to the girl's face, nudging down the scarf to reveal the blotchy red spots on her cheeks. She's very ill. Infection, most likely. "Do you know this girl, Elaina?"

"I told you I did," she says with a short, smug tone.

Feeling slightly as if I've seen her somewhere before, I stare into the gentle face of the girl with short hair. How had I first mistaken her for a man? Even in sleep, she looks like an angel. But something more than that bothers me about her. Eyes still on the girl, I say to Elaina, "Who is she?"

"Are you sure you want to know?" Elaina's voice has lost its smugness, replaced with something like concern.

At the change in her tone, I look over to find her worried gaze upon me.

"Now I think I need to," I remark. The magical orb seems to be working, taking away the chill from the air and even making me calmer.

The snow crunches beneath her knees as Elaina shifts her weight back and forth. "Well...she... Well, I think... She looks so much like a painting I saw in the palace at Merise..."

A painting... I narrow my eyes at Elaina. No. It's not possible. I turn back to the girl.

"Miss, you'd best tell us what you know," Cito says, his voice the calm but stern tone of a schoolmaster.

Elaina puffs out a breath. "I think she's the princess of Canens."

A shocked silence greets her words, then Cito barks out a shocking laugh too loud for the quiet, cold night. "What are you talking about? Why would the heir to the Canens throne be a slave?"

"The same reason a Heian princess might!" Elaina snaps.

"All right, all right," I concede simply to make peace between them.

"But you're an enemy to Canens."

"I wasn't an enemy to the gypsies who sold me," she retorts.

"Fine, but—" I begin.

"Just listen, Rus. I overheard Baron Tueor and the Magister talking to a woman, I think it was the Queen."

"The Queen?" Cito asks. "How do you know?"

"Well, I wasn't able to see her, so I'm not completely sure, but I recognized the voice, I think. She sounded different, tired perhaps. But I'm almost certain it was her. And she was talking about a girl, a slave, that she was interested in, and the girl was in the *oubliette*."

I wait for her to go on, but she stops, staring at the slave girl.

"That's it? She might be interested in this girl for a dozen other reasons," Cito says.

I glance at him, feeling as though we've switched roles.

Elaina gives him an icy glare. "Such as what? What slave would possibly warrant the Queen of Canens' attention?"

"Well..." Cito starts then falls silent.

He looks to me; I lift a shoulder. "She's right. There's no reason for a queen to care about the fate of a slave unless the slave is someone important. And if this were the princess...that would matter."

"But, sir, I think it highly unlikely that we have two princesses enslaved in Canens..." Cito protests.

Turning back to the girl illuminated by the orb's light, I scratch my chin absently. "I saw a painting in the palace at Merise, Cito." I point the finger I used to scratch myself at the girl. "It was an old painting, but I recognize her. She is the princess, unlikely as it might be."

Cito blows out a heavy breath. "Then what's our next step? Do we save her or kill her?"

Elaina gasps. "Kill—? She's as innocent as I am!"

Cito snorts. "She's Canensian."

Both my companions have furious expressions on their faces, so outraged at the other's opinion that I almost laugh aloud. "In this situation, Cito, Elaina, I think we err on the side of caution. Let's bring her with us. Perhaps she'll prove herself useful." I turn back to the prone girl, the possible princess, to find her eyelids fluttering. "And I think she's waking. But let's not tell her who we are." I aim a warning look at Cito and Elaina. "Not yet."

Cito nods firmly, but Elaina's agreement is reluctant.

XXIV
The Wolf
BLANCHE

I pause, my paws a whisper against the hard snow trail I walk. I smell them, just up ahead. Three horses, two men, Winter-berry, and someone feminine...someone less familiar. But with a lingering scent I recognize. It takes me another half dozen steps before I place the scent. The Baron. But not him. Someone who has spent much time with him...

My nostrils flare with a human emotion. Jealousy? If I could chuckle in my wolf form, I would. But instead, I open my mouth in a gaping grin. I will kill his little Red and eat her up.

I quicken my pace, my tail twitching with anticipation. The shadows move along with me, barely a hint of them in this dark night with its faint brushes from the goddess, but I see more clearly than ever before. I will take care of the Red because he touched her, and then her...her brother? Oh, interesting. Very interesting. There is another...a man. Yes, he's fearful. He will be simple to dispose of. Perhaps he will even flee. And my darling stepdaughter...oh, she is ill. Very ill.

My large paws carry me closer in near silence, tracking along the same divots in the snow the humans made. I am nearly upon them now. They haven't moved, but there is an odd glow ahead that lights my way.

"It's working," the girl says, awe in her voice. "Look at her face—the cuts are disappearing."

The men bend over the princess, distracted.

Now is my chance.

Gathering my power, I propel myself forward.

Just before I reach them, one of the men looks up.

"Wolf!" His shout breaks the silence of the air.

The three scatter, leaving the princess on the ground. The younger man, the one who doesn't reek of fear, dives aside, pushing the standing girl with him—his sister, yes, his sister. The other man reels backward, his fear stinking the air between them. The light underneath the cape goes out, snuffed out by the snow.

My paws land on the coward's shoulders and push him down, into the snow. But before I can lower my jaws to attack, something thumps into me from the side.

Yelping, I leap off the man and roll over to find a horse near me. I have frightened them. I dart away as the stallion lunges at me with his teeth, ears flattened.

Loyal beast.

Snapping at him, I dart around and come at him from behind, swirling out of the way of his sharp hooves with the agility of a dancer. I snap once more at him, delighted when my fangs tear into his flesh. Screaming in pain and fear, he kicks out and lunges aside. His back hooves fall upon the fearful man, who was trying to crawl away, as I roll with the kick and come up in a crouch, licking my bloody fangs.

I raise my nose in the air, scenting the others. The faint stench of magic mingles amidst the fear. I glance to the coward. The light he had been holding is buried within the snow now, its magical pulse gone, but he digs for it as though it is a weapon to fight with. Curse this wolf form...it's too hard to sense magic, and I don't know what that item is.

I dash around the frightened horse and find the other girl scrambling for something on the horse's saddle. Mouth open in a grin, I attack. The girl shrieks and falls; the taste of her blood is hot in my mouth.

A sharp prick attacks my hindquarters. I yelp and reel in fury.

The second man stands, a crossbow aimed at me, reloading.

With a snarl, I lunge. He drops the bow into the snow and reaches for his sword, but I don't give him time to draw it. Although his hands come up to protect himself, he's too late. My fangs dig into his neck, ripping at the flesh. His last breath escapes, not from his mouth but from his throat.

Fur dripping with blood, I stand over him a moment. The snow quivers with silence. Above me, the goddess's lights dance. The horses have scattered, only the one I hamstrung standing near, hip deep in snow with terror in his eyes.

With gentle steps, each one more painful than the last as the arrow in my thigh burns, I pad over to the prone girl and lean over her.

The girl opens her pale eyes, reflecting the lights above within them.

"You..." she murmurs. "How did you find me?"

I open my mouth and, already tasting victory, clench down upon the princess' throat.

The girl struggles, pulling at my white fur, yanking out tuffs. When the girl stops, I release her, wanting to see the light leave her eyes. Ragged gasps escape the girl's chest. Mouth gaping in a grin, I press my paws down upon the throat and watch as the eyes bulge then begin to dim.

Don't kill her. Curse upon you if you do, I remind myself, letting up on the girl's neck before life leaves her body.

Wincing, I sit upon my haunches and survey the scene; I hear only my own breath. Only the goddess' light illuminates them now. I lift my nose and sniff the air. Two of the horses have bolted at least a half mile away now. I smell death upon the one standing before me. Only the coward and the girl still gasp...

I close my eyes. My skin ripples. I growl, and the rippling stops. I begin to pant. I am weakening. I must return to the Manor, and quickly. Get the blood. I open my eyes and glance around. With my teeth, I tug at the edge of the white cloak abandoned by the girl. It has the coward's scent all over it. Must have been what he was shielding the light with. I snort and, holding it with my front paws, rip off a mouthful of fabric.

At the princess' side, I drop the cloth and lower my teeth. Blood. Just a little bit of blood, and I will have all I need from her. Then I can rid myself of this headache forever. Soon. Very soon. If only I could kill her now.

Already tasting victory, I sink my teeth into the girl's flesh. Hot blood courses over my tongue, full of life and death at once. My animal nature rears its head, and I am tempted to tear, but I spit out the flesh and press the torn fabric to the neck. Then when it has turned from white to red, I lift it in my mouth.

As I stand, there is a movement a dozen feet away, and I see a man lifting a crossbow. The coward lives.

"*Incende*," he says in a broken voice.

A light bursts out of the snow, brighter than the full moon on a clear night.

Reeling backward, I nearly drop the bloody rag in shock.

The coward raises his loaded crossbow and aims.

I jolt as an arrow grazes along my ear. Biting back my yelp of pain, I flee and race the dancing lights back to the Manor.

XXV

Winter

RUS

Every part of me roars.

Wind whistles by my ears, but the air feels warm.

"Sir?" A voice, familiar and yet hoarse, whispers in my ear. "Sir? Are you—?"

Slowly, things begin to come back to me. A wolf, white with wild blue eyes. Blue eyes. I scrunch my eyes shut as the images cascade over me. Blood, teeth, torn flesh...

I pry my eyes open, expecting a frozen battlefield.

"Sir," Cito's voice breaks with relief. His lashes are so coated in clumped frost, I'm surprised he can see anything at all. "I thought—"

He motions to my neck, and I raise an aching hand to it. My bare hand touches something rough and sticky. Dried blood. I sit up, the world tilting around me, fragmented images returning to my conscious mind. "Elaina, is she—?"

"I don't know." Cito gulps audibly and brushes a hand over his eyes as though wiping away tears before motioning to his right. "I think—"

"What happened?" Gaping, I push myself onto my elbows,

ignoring the pain and remembering the teeth, the surprise attack, the blood. So much blood.

Cito points to where two bodies stretch out. "The orb..."

Right. The orb. We were bent over the slave girl, watching her wounds knit together under the orb's magical powers, and then...a wolf attacked out of nowhere.

"I activated it just before the wolf left, I...thought maybe there was a chance—" Cito breaks off. "I don't know if it has enough magic to bring us all back. The light grows dim."

"What?" I scramble onto my knees, and my arm falls into the soft, deep snow. Cito tugs me free and back onto the packed snow. I blink down at my hands, pale against the circle of darkness underneath. I look up. The sliver of moon has moved, and now it is on the opposite side of the sky. Faint tendrils of red snake through the dark sky above. How long were we unconscious? How long did the orb's magic take to work?

I follow the light of the orb, dim as it might be, and find Elaina upon the snow, her body prone just as the slave girl had been. Except she's covered in blood, much like I am.

Crawling toward her, I refuse to believe what I see. My heart leaps into my throat, strangling the sob that threatens to escape me.

"Sir, I don't know if the magic can save us all, but I think if we give it enough time... Perhaps it can save one of them."

I look at Cito, my heart hammering in my throat. "Time? How much time do we have?"

"I don't know," he answers, "but we must give the orb time to work. Already the light goes down."

"Do you think the magic has run out?" I ask. "And how can we decide whom the orb will save?" I blink at the two girls. Do we move one out of the orb's reach? Put the Canens girl farther away? We'd surely kill her then.

"I don't know. But I think it's dying regardless," Cito answers.

"Do you think when that light burns out, the magic is gone?

Perhaps it just needs to recharge or..." I trail off, hope scrabbling at me inside, grasping for a foothold.

Cito glances at the light, expression a mixture of hope and anguish.

"I think that's how it works," he says. "I think once the light dies, the magic is gone forever."

"Forever?" I stare at the two girls sprawled out on the snow, one a sleeping princess, the other a martyred child. "What happens if one of them doesn't wake?"

Forehead creased in worry, Cito lifts his shoulders in a shrug. "I don't know."

My stomach knots. Elaina's skin is bloodless except for where her own blood has been streaked across it. Like me, she has her throat ripped at, only, unlike mine, it has not knit together. It remains bloody, holes evident in the flesh. The slave girl...she could be asleep, she looks so peaceful.

The sound of my grinding teeth jars in my ears.

If she lives and Elaina dies... I cannot even complete the thought. I traveled across the cursed country for Elaina, not for a little slave girl —not even should she be the princess of Canens.

With nothing else to do, Cito and I settle down and wait.

I hold the orb close to Elaina's face. After a sidelong glance at me, perhaps judging my placement of the orb, Cito kneels at the two girls' feet and murmurs a constant stream of prayers for their lives.

Forcing my eyes to stay shut only works for a minute. They fly open, and I check Elaina's wounds. Under my relentless gaze, her flesh begins to knit together by an invisible hand, so slowly that it's only when I blink that I see it.

Yet she remains immobile.

"She's moving," Cito says, elation in his voice.

I peer at Elaina closer. "She is?"

There's a heavy silence while I search Elaina's body.

"No." Cito's voice sobers. "The other girl."

A second later, the slave girl's pale eyes open. Something like terror crosses her face. She doesn't seem able to move except for her head, and her eyes dart back and forth between us before the panic subsides. She takes a deep breath, and her arms begin to move.

"You," she says in a hoarse, scratchy voice. "From the sales. Who are you?"

Cito turns to me, but there's no time for explanations.

Ignoring the girl, I turn and reach for Elaina, my fingers finding her throat, feeling the remnants of the wound. Under the blood covering her face and neck, there are dozens of little nicks and cuts that haven't gone away, remnants of where the wolf's teeth have torn her flesh. But there's also, so faint my fingers can't quite believe it, a pulse.

My breath whispers over my beard. "She's alive. Cito, she's alive!" I bend over her. "Elaina, please wake. Elaina." A sob breaks through my words, cutting me off.

A shadow falls over us. The girl has rolled over toward us, leaning over my sister's body. I fight the urge to push her away from the orb's healing powers.

Elaina, please...wake up!

The girl's face crinkles as she stares down at Elaina.

"Elaina?" she whispers my sister's name on a sob like she knows her, like something about my sister belongs to her.

I clench my fist at my side.

The girl raises a tentative hand, and as she does, her fingertips emit the strangest, softest glow. A reflection of the orb's light? She reaches for Elaina.

I lean forward, but a hand catches my shoulder, and I turn to Cito, who shakes his head slightly at me.

Her fingers touch my sister's cheek. The girl's eyes close, and the light presses out from her fingertips, into Elaina's flesh. A glow burgeons under her skin, building until she shines from the inside out brighter than the dimming orb. I stare at the slave girl. She must be acting as some sort of conduit, passing on the orb's power.

Then in the same instant the girl collapses over Elaina's body, the orb goes out, the sky bursts into dancing lights above, and Elaina's eyes fly open.

I reel back in shock then forward in disbelief as Elaina's eyes flutter shut again and the glow drains from her body, leaving us in startling darkness.

"Elaina! Elaina! Wake up. Wake up, please, Elaina." I beg her, pushing the girl off her chest and pulling my sister into my arms. "Wake up, sweetheart, please, wake up." Hope surges and drains in my chest as her breathing fades to the merest whisper.

We stay the remainder of the night like that, the lights dancing above in greens and purples and reds and me clutching at Elaina's body, praying for a miracle, while the girl lies beside her. Cito regathers the horses and then watches over the girl. Occasionally, my glance steals over to her, and disappointment pulls heavy upon me to find the girl moving while Elaina remains stubbornly still.

Finally, the girl has fully risen, although she's clearly weak. Her blue eyes are filled with sorrow that overflows into tears as she gazes at Elaina.

"I thought... I thought..." she murmurs.

But whatever she thought, she doesn't say, and I don't care.

"We must move," Cito finally says.

"I agree," the girl says, having regained enough strength to stand.

"We'll put the two girls on the most surefooted horse," he says, "and you and I will ride the others toward the lake. It's full day, we can make good time, for the horses have healed—even the one the wolf almost killed—and perhaps reach there before tomorrow night." He glances back the direction we've come. "They will come for us sooner or later, sir, you know that."

Although his words are correct, they weigh my very soul with despair.

Raising my head from the top of Elaina's takes almost as much of my strength as it takes for me to lift her in my arms and follow through with all of Cito's instructions. He is right, of course. But if she dies, I might as well let the Magister catch me, for I have failed.

But I won't let her die in this cursed country. Even if she dies, we will take her home, bury her where she belongs.

In my heart, I know it's impossible. If she dies, her body will never make the journey home. But at least we might bury her in Ardor, where our mother was born.

As I release Elaina into the girl's waiting arms atop a strong gelding stolen from the Magister's barn, the merest thread of hope pulls at my heart. For there, in the midst of my grief, Elaina's eyelids flutter open, and she casts me such a gentle smile that it could melt all of Canens. I raise my hand and cup her cheek. "Live, Elaina, you must live."

Her eyes flutter shut again, and she breathes a sigh onto the girl's chest.

The girl adjusts her load against her body and fixes me with a stronger gaze than I expected. "I won't let her die, Rus," she says in a voice that ripples with conviction.

The shining blueness of her eyes reminds me of the light that surged from her fingertips. It seemed to both frighten the girl and infuse her with strength. Now, she sits tall and straight on the gelding, her arms an iron circle around my sister. "See that you don't," I finally tell her.

Her gaze burns into mine, determined ice against burning fire. "As surely as I am Winter, your sister will live."

An odd sort of calm steals over me; I do not doubt her.

Epilogue

Epilogue

BLANCHE

M y eyes are reluctant to open. My body is strangely incapacitated, much more than if I had just expended my magical stores.

I blink at my surroundings. A pale blue canopy stretches above my head, and I follow it with my eyes to the edge where it falls into twisted fingers of fringes. This isn't my room. Where am I? The Manor. I must be at the Manor.

I turn my head, and a moan escapes my lips.

"Ah, the Queen awakes."

Instead of the comforting and steady voice of the Magister, or even the rumble of Baron Tueor's, a feminine voice, full of mocking and barely contained irritation, speaks.

I pry open my eyes again to find Ceara lounging in an armchair, her one leg crossed over the other in a manly posture undoubtedly intended to impress her lack of care for my well-being upon me when I woke.

"Where is the Magister?" I croak.

Ceara shrugs, peering at her nails. "Somewhere around here, more concerned by other things."

The events are coming back to me. I sit up, looking down at myself, half expecting to be covered in blood. Instead, my cleaned gown is hanging beside a nearby chair, and I am dressed in a golden gown of silk. My head pounds in protest at the quickness of my motions, and I put a hand to my head, moaning.

The Fae chuckles and leans forward. "Magical headache? I've heard about those."

I glare at her. "Haven't you ever gotten one?"

A disdainful look is her only answer.

"Right, Fae."

Ceara gives a mocking incline of her head. "I would say 'at your service,' but I'm not here for you."

"Then what are you here for?"

"Did you find her?"

I narrow my eyes. "Find whom?"

"Don't play coy with me. You must be here because you stashed the princess here."

Unimpressed, I blink slowly.

"Is she here?" Ceara leans close to my face and all but hisses the question. "We *need* her. *You* need her."

I glance around the room, my gaze skittering over the clean dress and darting around for the bloody object I did bring back. "The..."

Ceara grips her knees with both hands and waits for me to continue. "The what?"

"I retrieved her blood."

The faery's eyes round in disbelief. "What?"

"The princess' blood. I retrieved it."

"The princess' blood. You retrieved it? How? When?"

"Where is the Magister?" I ask instead.

"After he went hunting the four people you didn't kill?"

"I didn't—" I sit back against my pillow in shock. "But I did kill them. I ripped their throats out. Except for her."

"Apparently not. The Magister has just returned."

"Then he has killed them."

"I wouldn't count on that."

"What?" I throw back the sheets from my legs, the added pounding in my head adding to my fury. "What do you mean you *wouldn't count on that*? Where is my huntsman?"

At my words, the door to the room swings open, and the faery disappears with a faint pop, leaving me staring at a slave, wide-eyed with shock. "You are awake."

"Of course I'm awake!" I thunder, regretting it when my head pulses with every syllable. However, the pain doesn't stop me from snapping, "Bring the Magister to me, immediately!"

I stride across the room, ignoring the throbbing in my thigh with every step. A quick inspection while I await the Magister shows me that my wound has been treated and wrapped but festers. I ignore it; as soon as I have access to the right herbs and potions, I can heal myself.

My pacing, even slow as it is with my limp, keeps my blood hot, so when the Magister enters the room five minutes later, my blood is near boiling.

"What happened?" I growl at him. "Why are they not dead?"

He falls to his knees before me. "Majesty, I tracked your prey after you returned with your wounds, intending to confirm that they were dead."

"Wounds?"

His gaze flicks up, pausing slightly on my thigh and then flicking to my left ear before falling back to the ground. "Yes, Majesty."

I touch my ear to find a divot in it that was not there before. Curses. "Go on."

"I found the spot where you attacked, but there were no bodies."

"No bodies?" The anger has left my voice, replaced with shock. "How are there no bodies?"

"I do not know, Majesty."

"The light," I breath, putting a hand to my forehead. "That cursed light. I knew I should have crushed it." When he falls silent, undoubtedly confused, I glare at him. "Go on."

"I did not know if you intended their deaths or not. So after following their tracks for a little ways, I returned here. I believe they are weak, but all four of them live." His head lowers further.

How do they all live? I shove my disbelief aside and grind my teeth together. "You let them go?"

"I—" His gaze flicks up toward mine. "I did not know your intention."

I lift a brow, trying to summon my typically calm demeanor. "Why did you return?" I ask slowly and coldly.

He bows his head, exposing his neck to me. "I needed supplies, then I can follow their tracks and bring her back."

"So what are you waiting for? Go!"

"I shall. I would be gone but for your summons."

I glare at him, fury rising in me. Behind him, the faery reappears, her entire body glittering as if in some strong emotion. I don't concern myself with trying to determine what it is. Instead, I close my eyes and call forth my dwindling store of magic. I should have just enough for this. When I open my eyes, the Magister is still bent before me, unsuspecting.

"Marcus, my huntsman, serve me with your entire being. Forget your other duties, forget your life. Remember only that you serve Queen Blanche of Canens. Go after the princess. Do not stop until you find her. Do not quit your quest until her heart lies in your hands. Then return it to Canens, and put it in *my* hands."

He rises, an expression of calm upon his face. "Yes, Majesty. My heart and soul are yours. Her heart will be yours."

Bonus Material

Turn the page for a bonus fairy tale.

Winterberry's Birth Foretold

Queen Helena emerged from her sleigh behind the two mismatched horses. She had taken a less conspicuous sleigh, for anyone who saw her here would know her purpose.

An old woman dressed in red tartan rags with a black scarf enveloping her hair worked in the small garden before the dark cottage. The garden contrasted so sharply with its setting that Helena gasped. Winter had eternally set upon the country, and a gentle snowfall had begun on her journey. But this woman's garden seemed protected from such weather; her garden remained lush and green. Roses lined the fence, pushing through the fence and reaching into the sky.

The old woman didn't seem to notice her guest's arrival, for she worked tirelessly on a rosebush lush with black roses in full bloom, trimming back the wild parts with a sharp knife. While the other roses were picturesque, rising up the fence and spiraling around in careful, allotted positions, this rose invaded the ones beside it.

The woman growled at the greenery as she reached for another vine.

Helena thought this might be a good time to speak. "Excuse me?"

The woman showed no sign of hearing but pulled the bush toward her and sawed at the thick vine. The rosebush must have been many years old to be so thick and unyielding.

Thinking the woman simply had not heard her, Helena let herself through the small wooden gate. "Excuse me?" she called again as she walked across the garden. At a small misstep, Helena looked down, and she paused, uncertain.

Below her feet, the luscious green garden had turned to snow. Mouth parting, Helena lifted her gaze and gasped at the sight of the old woman standing before her. Her blue eyes bore into Helena's, nearly the same shade as hers but shockingly different set against the wrinkles that drew the old woman's eyes nearly to a close as she squinted at the Queen of Canens.

"Are you—?" Helena trailed off, not sure what to ask. The people called her the crone, the witch doctor, the spirit woman, the seer, the dreamer...anything but by her proper name. Helena didn't know what to call her.

The woman's mouth twitched as though she knew what Helena was thinking and nodded slowly. The humor left her face entirely though, and the two women stood staring at each other for seconds that turned to minutes.

"Hold out yer hand," the old woman said. Her voice was unexpectedly sweet, and Helena obeyed without much thought, almost as though thought had been stolen from her.

The crone seized her hand and pushed something into it, something that bit back.

Helena gasped and pulled away. Onto the snow fell a black rose from the crone's garden and, beside it, three drops of Helena's crimson blood. Anger burned through the Queen. This woman obviously had no idea of who Helena was, of how she could have this woman's house and everything around it destroyed, should she desire it.

The old woman turned away with slumped shoulders and a great weariness. "Come inside. I will tell ye what ye want to hear."

Mouth open, Helena debated. Then her gaze fell on the rose and the bed of snow beneath it. Magic was at work here. Magic that had not been seen since the ancient days. She didn't know whether she could trust it, but perhaps it would give her what she desired the most, where no one and nothing else had.

When Helena pushed through the small wooden door into the cottage, the crone motioned to a chair at a round table slightly offset from the middle of the room. "Sit. I shall make us tea."

Helena brushed the dirt off the chair before easing herself into it. The years were adding up on her lithe frame, and after her long journey here, she wanted nothing more than a warmed bed or a blanket and a chair by the fire. But the old woman's cottage had mere embers in the small fireplace. Boiling water for tea would take an hour; Helena hoped to be gone by then, but she had come for a purpose and must see it through.

To her surprise, a minute later the old woman pushed piping hot peppermint tea into her hands. "Drink. It warms ye," the woman commanded.

Hesitating only slightly under the woman's hovering form, Helena drank. She had to gain this woman's trust, didn't she? Swallowing, she lowered the cup, but the woman tapped the bottom of the cup before it could touch the table.

"Drink, drink. Finish it," she insisted.

Startled, Helena raised the mug again and gulped the scalding liquid down. Warmth flooded through her body, all the way to her toes. When she swallowed the last time, the crone put her hands on Helena's cheeks and turned her face toward hers. The old woman's eyes were unexpressive as they searched the Queen's, looking for something that could not be spoken.

"Hmm. Aye. Aye. I see."

"I—"

"Ye shall have a girl child," the old woman growled abruptly, all sweetness gone.

Queen Helena drew back, frightened at the command. All she wanted—had ever wanted—was a child to call her own. It was why she'd come. But how had the crone known this?

"And ye must name her Winter. For she shall live in perpetual winter." The old crone's voice hardened, as if she waited for Helena to reject her offer.

How could she resist holding her own child, her own daughter, in her arms? For this was the very thing she had prayed for years. "Of course I will," she murmured. Faithfulness was rewarded after all! "But when—?"

Before she could go on, the crone gasped and drew back, dropping Helena's hand. She stumbled backward, head shaking from side to side. "No. Ye must go. I mustn't be a part of the evil that shall follow. No. Go."

"What?" Queen Helena leaned toward her, confused. She shook her beautiful head, her blond curls trembling under the sudden change in atmosphere. "What evil? There is no evil—"

"No," the crone moaned, raising a hand to shield her startling blue eyes from Helena's. "No, she must not come here, she mustn't..." She collapsed against the wall, sagging under the weight of whatever vision she had seen.

"What? Who? The baby? My baby will not be evil," Helena murmured, more to herself than the crone, who couldn't see or hear anything but her vision.

The crone lowered her hand and came at Helena so quickly that she raised her hand in alarm. "Ye will die. Before ye hold yer babe in your arms, ye will be dead."

Ice inched into Helena's limbs, making its way through her veins, seeking the warmth of her rapidly beating heart.

"No—don't let it be," she begged. The ice invaded her, slowing her heart and making her fingers hard to bend. Her cheeks and ears burned at the cold as though a winter storm had rolled in without Helena's notice.

The crone had a distant look in her eye, as though she did not see Helena any longer, and when she spoke again, it was in a different voice, one masculine and harsh. "The babe will be dethroned by her stepmother, thrown out into the cold to serve the blackest of men, the kingdom will be in peril, under darkness and eternal winter. Yet she will persevere. She will falter, but not fall. She will bend, but not break." The crone blinked, and her gaze focused again, boring into Helena's frightened eyes. "Ye must have this child. For she shall save the kingdom."

"But—" Helena shook her head. She didn't want a child to be born to such a fate. More than her own desires, she did not wish to throw such a future upon an innocent child. "No. I've changed my mind." Her head shook like a puppet's wildly bobbing on a string. "No. I don't want—don't need—a child of my own. I won't."

The old woman's mouth twisted into a smile, revealing broken, blackened teeth. "It is too late. Ye already grow the babe of which I speak."

"What?" Helena gasped, a hand rushing to her stomach. While the rest of her felt numb from the cold, something in her stomach beat steadily, warmly. Was it someone? Another heart whose warmth could not be stolen by this strange magic at work?

By the time Helena returned home, she had decided that the crone was foolish and knew nothing. But as she was driven home, it began to snow, heavily.

Nearly nine months later, Helena was dead.

But Winter lived.

Would You Leave A Review?

Did you enjoy this book? Don't be shy about telling a friend!

Indie authors thrive *only* with reviews from readers like you. Reviews sell books. Retailers take into account how many reviews a book has received when determining where a book shows up in searches and what book to promote to their readers.

Other readers also read these reviews, and it can tell them what to expect. Rate it high or low, be honest, and help future readers pick their next book.

I promise, leaving a review is not scary and it doesn't have to take a long time. Just a rating and a few words to say what you liked (or didn't like) about this book will suffice. And I treasure each and every review written, whether it's three words or three hundred, whether it's flattering or disappointing.

And thank you, from the bottom of my heart, for reading and reviewing "Fog & Mist"!

Just scan the following QR code and find the "leave review" button on the purchase page.

Thank you for supporting indie authors!

- Kelsie

Review links:
Amazon
https://bit.ly/4nX61w5

Kobo
https://bit.ly/49ecRZD

Barnes & Noble
https://bit.ly/47gT6xR

Apple Books
https://bit.ly/4qskUZd

Goodreads
https://bit.ly/43jspHO

About the Author

Kelsie Engen grew up in North Pole, Alaska, where the long, snowy winters taught her to love reading and writing of all kinds. Today, she spends her days writing and editing (or as much of them as her family and pets allow), escaping the subzero temperatures by delving into magical, uncharted worlds.

She still lives in Alaska with her husband, children, cats, and dog —all of whom provide a million joyful distractions from getting her next book written. (But she wouldn't trade it for anything.)

To stay up to date on new releases, behind-the-scenes peeks, and other bookish shenanigans, sign up for her newsletter at www.Kelsie-EngenAuthor.com. You can also email her at **scriptor.librorum@gmail.com**.

Where to find her online:
• Instagram: @KelsieEngen
• Facebook: KelsieEngenAuthor
• Pinterest: KEngenAuthor
Website: www.KelsieEngenAuthor.com

Also by Kelsie Engen

Find all my books at my website:

www.kelsieengenauthor.com/buy-my-books

WORKS BY KELSIE ENGEN

- SERIES:
  - The Canens Chronicles
  - A Canens Chronicles Short Story
  - A Seven Kingdoms Faery Tale
- STANDALONES:
  - Spurn the Moon
  - Finding Home
  - Bernadette & the Stranger

Scan me

https://bit.ly/worksbykelsieengen.

Or scan the QR code for the link above and links to all stores.

Honorable Mention 2019 Writer's Digest e-book Fantasy Fiction

Finalist 2020 Young New Adult Fiction (17 years and up)